Paraíso

By B.D. Weddell

This is for Shirley, my best friend and the one person I always enjoy traveling with.

Love you always.

Table of Contents

Prologue

Kamatayan di kayang pigilan,
Ganun din ang kapanganakan,
Minsan binglang dumadating
nang di mo inaasahan
Minsan hinihintay,
Minsan sapilitan,
Katulad ng pagkakamatay

-Pagpanaw

500 kilometers south off the coast of Acapulco Mexico, a small pinpoint in a vast blue of the Pacific, lies the island of Bonidada. The commercial island was home to the Bonidada Resort, which was supposedly in competition for *the* best vacation resort behind Bora Bora and even Easter Island. White, sandy beaches, flourishing tropical plant life, and of course the resort itself, makes Isla Bonidada one of the best spots for a swim and then some for the young, romantic, and especially the rich.

The boat arrived on June 18th, two days before the arrival of the first group who would be on the island to participate in the Bonidada Vacation & Counseling, as was the island's primary business. The boat that came in was a fishing boat, weather-worn and leaking in multiple places. The lettering on the side was Baybayan, and therefore illegible to the crew at the dock. The overseer of the Bonidada port and five men who lived on the island six months out of the year (exchanged biyearly by other workers who primarily lived in Mexico or other parts of

Central America), sailed out to the boat which had crashed into a nearby coral reef.

The ship was deserted, devoid of life and any sign of what had happened to the crew. But in multiple rooms including the captain's quarters, there were saturated and brown stains of blood that the crew couldn't recognize, especially in some areas where the stains were blackened with age. There was no radio on the boat, and it was impossible to tell if there had been a struggle with the ship no doubt being rocked it's entire way here. When it was discovered to belong to the Philippines, the crew returned to the island and a broadcast was delivered to the Acapulco Coastguard to retrieve the vessel and find out who it belonged to or to simply dispose of it.

Mr. Crockett who was the primary owner of Isla Bonidada did not care what happened to the boat as long as it was off the island before the tourist group arrived. The men who ran the Bonidada Resort, fulfilled their man's wishes, and finished completing the necessary arrangements before the arrival of their latest customers. Ten couples, all from America except for one from Canada, who would be coming expecting three weeks of rest and relaxation away from the modern world and all their problems. That was Bonidada's promise. That was Crockett's most important promise to his clientele.

It was their promise that they had to keep, come Hell or high water.

1st Letter

I came into this country forty years ago. I was one of the few survivors and despite what the others had said I doubt that I was the sole reason we got off the island alive. I only brought what I could on a harrowing desire for revenge and that is all I can say about it.

My wife, God bless her soul, had suggested that I keep a diary and write down what I could never seem to be able to tell her, or anyone else for that matter. When you experience something truly horrible or gruesome your mind isn't the only thing that you block out, it's the rest of your very being. It's like a terrible secret you've sworn to keep on pain of death. In my old home, we called that unnecessary baggage. But maybe she's right. She's always been right, after all, marrying her had been the first smart thing I had done since coming to America, and I believe I'm man enough to admit that. After all, if I can't even tell her what had happened, I might as well face myself and tell it straight, no holds barred.

So, I guess I will write it.

The best place to start I guess is at home.

My mother was the healer of our village, the only person keeping many of us alive since we didn't have first-world medicine. With third-world medicine however comes third-world myths and legends, and looking back on it I should have really paid attention to them. I hear American children telling legends of giants and other strange cryptids, but they don't really believe it. Why should they? They think it's fun, a game, just like I had.

Anyways, my mother was the only one raising me and my older sister. She had been aware of the murders taking place along the river, and when she came back from the city there would be whispers of a shapeshifter murdering folk and leaving them facedown onto the ground usually with their throats torn out or their bellies ravaged. I've seen the first body when the murderer came to our village, our poor pastor who had been out at night saying his nightly prayers. In the end, he had said his last. They say the Holy are the true inheritors of heaven, that only those like Jesus can rise there and overcome the evil in the world. That may be the case spiritually, and I believe it still with every ounce of my being, but there is *physical* evil here in the world unaccounted for. Because God allows that evil to exist so that we can choose to be good and overcome.

But sometimes that isn't enough. Sometimes good doesn't always win. Life isn't a fairy tale, and I was seventeen when I was proven right. I was seventeen when I lost everything and everyone I loved.

I should have listened to my mother. I should have listened to God. But even then, would it have made a difference? I wonder that still, at times when I find myself awake late in the night. Always the same question in the end: Would it have made a difference?

I doubt that very much.

One

It was June 20th, 8:22AM. Amos Mulderich stood on the porch of his island hut drinking a cup of coffee he had brewed for himself and John Hopper, the overseer of the port and overall safety of the island. John hadn't come yet, he would be coming out of the Crockett Grotto by now, after checking and ensuring that the ziplines and swimming holes were still in prime condition. He would come soon, and have his coffee same as Amos, black, with a shot of Fireball whiskey.

He was watching the horizon, enjoying the eastern winds blowing against his tanned face and causing his black hair to ripple freely like molten ebony. The wind would be bringing in the guests faster, and they should arrive no later than 9:00, providing nothing had happened at the launching point back at the coast. Three weeks, then they would have only three days to prepare for the next group. Then the next, and the one after that, and the one after that. In and out, all throughout the year. They wouldn't be going home anytime soon because Isla Bonidada *was* their home.

Unlike many on the island, Amos, John, and the head chef Kyra Lewis, stayed year-round. They had no families to recall (whether they cared to or not) and were the perfect candidates to ensure James Crockett's island was the best and most profitable in the Pacific for American couples. Three natural leaders who found their own little island to rule over.

Three weeks...

Amos had been on the island for over eleven years now. He had lived a wonderful life here, working hard and bringing in fatter and fatter paychecks every month. All of which was directly deposited to a bank in Florida, where he planned to go at the end of this year to retire early and have his own spot on a beach in Malibu and never work again. John had plans of staying for another year, and Kyra had no plans of leaving anytime soon.

That was fine with Amos. He would keep in touch with them. The two of them had been all the family he needed since he left his home back in Colorado. Away from his own parents, away from college debt, and away from bullshit companies who didn't want you to start your own psychiatry business. Amos was a specialist for family counseling, and it had earned him all of his money this past year; the most he ever made while attending the Colorado College. He would retire at the age of 32, how many people could say that? Not many, that's for certain. Especially when it came to the people he catered to.

Three weeks. Then twenty-seven-ish weeks until the end of the fiscal year.

Since the weather was usually perfect year-round with the occasional hiccup here and there, Bonidada followed their schedule year by year, 365 days and beyond. But not this time for Amos Mulderich. It wouldn't be a repeat like the cycle of an old playlist this year. Less than a year left here in Bonidada, then he would be able to live the rest of his life beyond in Malibu. Amos couldn't be happier with the prospect. Unless by some miracle, his term actually ended *today*. A call from Crockett perhaps to say his services were no longer required, thank you for all your hard work, now kindly fuck off.

But that was very unlikely.

Just gotta get through this, he told himself not for the first time. He didn't feel ready to deal with another group. He never did.

But, duty calls.

Footsteps coming up the weathered walkway towards his hut, the squeaky seventeenth step making its own announcement the loudest. He looked down to see John coming up the weathered boards. He was a tall black man who originated from Jamaica, built like an ox, and as tempered as one. He grunted a hello to Amos, who offered him a cup of coffee. He then offered some of his whiskey, which John accepted, all the while topping his own cup off in the process.

"Ben called," John reported. "They're about forty-five minutes out."

Amos checked his watch. "Nine-thirty-ish then."

John grunted. "Nine-thirty-ish."

"How was the grotto?"

"Beautiful."

"The lines?"

"Secure and fine."

"Swimming hole?"

"Perfect level."

"Excellent."

"I need to make a trip up the peak though," John informed him. "Gotta make sure the lookout point is still stable."

"It was fine last week."

"We had strong winds last week."

Amos took John's word for it. The man knew his way around the island as well as the sea, knew how the winds and storms battered at civilization out here in the islands. If he wanted to make sure something was not going to collapse underneath the rich folk from the mainland, Amos believed him and allowed John to do his job as Overseer. That had been their silently agreed-upon method of doing things around here; Amos left the island and it's attractions to John, and John would leave the psycho-babble counseling, entertainment, and paperwork to Amos. The 'circus act' as the old fart would put it at times.

"Crockett called too this morning," John told him, scratching the back of his head which was covered with ashy hair.

Amos looked at him. "Oh?"

"Yeah. Last-minute check-in. Apparently he's in Paris now, making a stop."

"A *stop*?"

"A stop."

"In Paris?"

"Correct. Left Berlin yesterday. Apparently he and the wife are touring all of Europe. Plans to be in Greece after tomorrow."

"Berlin. Then a 'stop' in Paris, then a stop in Greece?"

"There he plans to stay for an extra day," John said with a shrug.

"Jesus," Amos said shaking his head with disbelief. "Must be nice."

John nodded. "Fuckin' rich folk. He had a message he wanted me to relay to you."

Amos grunted. "What's the message?"

"He said have a good day, stick to the schedule, and most importantly, and I quote: 'Quit screwing the guests.'"

Amos smiled wryly. "Okay John, but that Kelly girl came onto me."

"Her sixty-year-old husband doesn't think so. Apparently been calling for Crockett again and again, demanding you to be fired if crucifixion wasn't an option."

"Jesus..."

"He ain't in the wrong to think that, you know."

"Okay," Amos said with a laugh. "That guy was a creep. Marrying a woman forty years younger than him? He probably picked her up as a minor."

"He *was* a creep," John agreed with a slight smile. "Doesn't matter one way or another. Just keep it in your pants, end of story."

"Fine," Amos relented. "I'll be more professional this time."

"You better. Otherwise Crockett'll can you."

"He would be hurting no one but himself this early in the season," Amos said confidently.

"I wouldn't act so sure," John warned, his eyes shifting just slightly to look at his partner. "He's already talking to some people from Seattle."

"Good for him."

Amos wasn't worried. The sooner he was gone the better. Sure, he might be missing out on the rest of this year's pay, but he had enough saved to live off for at least twenty years, maybe even more if he picked up odd jobs here and there. Bartend out on the beach or maybe bag some groceries just to keep himself from getting bored and poorer. The more he thought about it, the less Amos was concerned with the future unlike most people in the world. As far as he was concerned, he was still *way* ahead of the game and very fortunate because of it."

"Anything else?" Amos asked.

"Yeah," John said downing the last of his coffee while checking his watch which sat on the conjoined fist. "Put some pants and a shirt on. We got guests coming."

Amos drained his own coffee, and took it inside with him to put away and change. "Aye-aye, Captain."

John grunted, amused. He didn't leave the balcony just yet even as Amos stepped inside. He was looking out at the horizon where the two shades of blue met where eternity seemed to go on and on forever out here. He loved his life on the island, and though he would never say it, he was going to miss Amos. He knew of Amos' plans and had made no attempt to dissuade him. He encouraged it, and promised to have a farewell drink with him when this was all over. That would be all Amos would give to the young man, but that was good enough at least for Amos himself.

But if there was one person on the island Amos would miss the most with the exception of Kyra should she ever catch him saying so, it was John.

For now, however, it was time to get to work.

Two

There were not ten, but eight couples on the *Santa Bonita* sailing towards Isla Bonidada. One couple had suffered from a robbery and were dealing with the property damages, and the other had cancelled due to their daughter's sudden surprise wedding, which was up for debate of course.

Fourteen people in total would be guests at the resort, ferried by Max Benson on his boat which sailed smoothly and swiftly to get to the docks in time. The island was just a haze across the shiny blue horizon, but it was there, and the passengers were awestruck at the sight.

There she was, in all her glory. A hump of bright green that stuck out of the sea like the peeking head of a magnificent floral beast. They could all see the stone peak sticking up like a jagged tooth at the very top, and the clear warm waters only enhanced the sheer beauty of the place.

Even Andy White had to relinquish his frustration for a moment to appreciate where he and his wife were going. At least this trip would not be a *complete* waste of time. Isla Bonidada was stunning, and he was now actually looking forward to his time spent here with Cynthia.

He and Cynthia had been married for six years now. He had just started his hotel management career when they first started dating and after saving up a good sum of money, started his first hotel in New York City. Whites had become very popular, and quickly became a steeple in the hotel business with the possibility of a second being opened in Las Vegas. At this point, he had become very rich, and Cynthia had stuck with him all throughout the ups, downs, and in-betweens. What had made her very special to Adam, was the fact that she had been with him *before* he really started making money, before he offered her to quit her job at a shoe store to work with him and eventually never have to work again after. If he were to try and date anyone now, it would be mostly for the sake of his money no doubt. If he was a shallow human being, and Adam didn't believe that he was, he would be just fine with that. New woman every night, pay her off, move on.

But he wasn't a shallow man. He wanted to still love and feel loved. He loved Cynthia, believed he did anyway, and when she had pitched this Couples Vacation idea to him, he was skeptical, and...

Let's not kid ourselves here, he reminded himself. He had been angry, embarrassed even at the prospect of counseling, let alone on some resort. But at this point he was willing to do whatever it took to rebuild the bridges that had been in dire need of repair between them. He wanted to love her as he had before, and the fact that Cynthia offered this trip at all meant she hoped for the same.

Christ, for $25,000 just for the three weeks here, it better be worth it.

He turned his gaze away from the approaching island to look at his wife. Tiny, not anorexic but still 105 pounds soaking wet. He always told her to eat some more, but that always led into an argument anyway and so he had given up trying to tell her so. Dyed black hair, icy blue eyes. His age, 34, and wearing a white blouse which underneath if he was lucky tonight, clung black lace. Her purse was between her feet which were sandaled, same as his daypack which he would not put on until they docked or made port, whatever it was called. The rest of their luggage was somewhere below deck, along with everyone else on the *Santa Bonita*. She was drinking a Bloody Mary, and he a Screwdriver. The other passengers had drinks too, except for one who opted for bottled water because of the fact that the woman was pregnant. Personally, Adam didn't think going on an exotic vacation while pregnant was the most genius of ideas, but, to each their own.

The Whites had gotten to know the others on the departure dock just before the boat came to pick them up from Acapulco. There had been many shaking of hands, most of them their age but a few were old and wrinkled. At the same time all were relatively healthy, strong, and firm, the signs of either someone who worked very hard for a good portion of their life, or had been able to keep their body from running into the ground from years of retirement. All came from all over the country and beyond, all decently wealthy and like Adam and Cynthia, here to rekindle romances with one another.

One couple that stood out to Adam the most in particular, was a young man and woman about his and Cynthia's age. Not that he minded any of the older people going on the trip with them, but it was just easier to speak to someone who had similar years of experience as well as relatable memories that didn't date back to the second World War.

Ethan and Shawlyn Duncan from Phoenix Arizona had introduced themselves just after Matt and Gabbie Winklemann (pronounced as the German 'w' as 'Vinklemann'), two spokespersons for an online search engine similar to Google or Bing. Ethan was a composer for music and tracks for indie games and movies, and Shawlyn a stay-at-home mother. They had one daughter at home, and another child presently on the way. This was the woman who had taken water instead of the other beverages offered on the boat. Shawlyn had allowed Cynthia to rub her slightly enlarged belly when Cynthia couldn't stop staring at it. Smooth, ebony skin contained a life inside which Cynthia was able to feel shift at the unknown presence beyond the protection of the womb. She was 20 weeks in, so she said, and Ethan who was finishing his latest soundtrack, planned to dedicate it to the child should his customer be all right with it. If it was a boy they would name him Roger, and if it was a girl, they would name her Kiya.

Adam smiled, despite feeling envious of the couple. Here they were, having a child of their own and had another on the way, something he knew he would never be able to have for his own. All the money in the world and even all the women in the world wouldn't make a difference. His family name would die when he finally perishes, and Cynthia would never bear a child unless she divorced him or cheated on him.

Cheated...

The couple looked happy enough, and Adam wondered why they were here at a

(c'mon, let's be honest here ladies and germs)

therapy getaway off the coast of Mexico. Yes, Isla Bonidada was a tropical wonder for the Pacific, and obviously a lot of the world's rich would come here. But in the end, the island was primarily for couples seeking counsel in a stress-free and easy-going environment. If Ethan and Shawlyn were here, it was for a good reason.

These next few weeks were dedicated to this group for the sake of romance rekindling, and that made those two no different than Adam and Cynthia, or anyone else for that matter. All were here for their own reasons, whether they displayed them on their sleeves or not.

In fact, Derian and Carla Anderson, another couple who had come in from Florida, seemed to loathe each other. Each having turned to their partners and badmouthing one another like two kids having a playground squabble. Adam was told Carla is a whore who likes making clothes capable of showing as much skin as possible, and Cynthia was told Derian was a pompous asshole who couldn't help but stare at every other woman besides his own wife. The two of them only nodded sympathetically but not really hearing the Anderson's opinions of one another, as did everyone else who would rather keep their affairs private.

At any given rate, Adam wished he and his wife the happiest vacation here. He hoped they all enjoyed their time here at Isla Bonidada. He only prayed that it would be worth it.

He noticed the Bateman couple watching as he and Cynthia conversed with the Duncans, and he got an uneasy feeling from Anton Bateman who was watching with pale gray eyes. He was an older man, possibly in his upper forties or lower fifties, but looking younger, with an *ancient* Jessica by his side. Jessica looked out of it, stoned by all the medication pumped in her veins. She was in a wheelchair, an oxygen mask close at hand in case she needed it. A bit old for traveling in Adam's opinion, as well as too old for this other guy; God knows what he must have to think about to get it up at night for her. Bateman had a clean haircut as dusty gray as a jackrabbit's hide. He looked strong too, probably a real body-builder back in his youth. Those strange gray eyes continued to watch Adam and his wife with barely any interest at all. He was merely observing the conversation sitting across from him, and that alone made Adam feel claustrophobic and uncomfortable.

He turned his gaze towards Cain and Winnifred Ashton, two independent business owners (IBOs as they called themselves) from Amway talking to Paul and Victoria Jackson who owned a string of retail stores across the US called respectfully, 'Jackson's.' Cain and Winnifred were both wearing their Sunday's best despite the heat and the sea spray. They had appeared happy and giddy throughout the wait for the boat, and Adam had and still thought the two were odd. As for the Jacksons, they listened with feint interest, Cain looking forty and his wife in her twenties. Her hair was blonde as fresh wheat, wearing a swimsuit under a pair of jeans and a black blouse. Adam didn't know how long the two had been married, but he couldn't help but feel a little disgusted. The Jacksons and Woldemontts both consisted of old men and young women, and most rich men took on young wives. At what age exactly was a question Adam didn't like popping into his head. Cynthia had the same opinion. It seemed that along with the Duncans, and the Andersons were the only couples who married close enough to their age. Not that Adam was ever going to say it out loud what he thought of huge age gaps. It would make no difference anyways; most opinions rarely do.

As for Brad and Leslie Woldemontt mentioned earlier, he was a musician and she just some girl he picked up while on tour. He had played guitar since he was a boy and throughout high school he played in bars, school plays, anything to get his name out there. In that time, he had become famous and started his own band by the age of eighteen. He had gone on twenty years running and still going. He had been divorced twice and then came along his 'number one fan' who probably flashed him at a concert and he got a spotter to bring her to the back in order to meet her.

Or have sex with her, Adam thought more likely.

Maybe that happened, maybe it didn't, one way or another the two apparently got hitched. Hook line and sinker. This assumption made Adam despise the man and he knew it wasn't fair to either Brad or Leslie. He didn't know their story anymore than they knew his and Cynthia's. In Adam's opinion, regardless of how this vacation/couples therapy went, he hoped it stayed that way.

All the while that he was talking to the Duncans with Cynthia and the boat continued to bounce across the mighty blue towards the island, Anton Bateman took them all in with eyes that seemed to absorb every single molecule within reach. He missed nothing, the way most of the men rubbed their knuckles or joints from arthritis, the way the younger women sat and hoped to catch the attention of the younger men, and the way the Ashtons carried themselves with a sense of giddy happiness and blessing. He didn't mind them being happy, why the hell shouldn't they be? They were on vacation. But it was the way they tried to rub off some of their glee onto others, specifically the Jacksons who they were talking to, that rubbed him off the wrong way.

Anton took a particular interest in Derian and Carla Anderson out of all of them. Not because of their childish squabble between one another, but because of their professions. Carla was a clothes designer, which she never failed to let others know, but Anton didn't care about that. He was more curious about the husband, who sat silently and as alert as he himself had been. Anton guessed military, maybe a general or a captain. Either way, Anton was sure that if there was a problem, Derian was the guy to go to. Not that there would be any problems after all. After this vacation, he and Jessica would stay in Mexico for a few years. Maybe go further south towards Brazil, or some other country. Australia, maybe there. He had always wanted to go there.

He watched the approaching island, ready to be off this boat before he vomited. He was terribly seasick, but he sat still and quiet, not giving a single hint that he was ill. No one on this boat was to see any weakness in him, especially Jessica who sat just as quietly in her wheelchair next to him. She had wanted to come here, and he had agreed. That didn't mean he had to like it.

Three

Max Benson drifted the boat closer to the docks where he had his boys hop on over with ropes and tie their sailor's knots to the posts. Once the boat was stabilized on the dock, a gangplank was stretched out for the passengers to walk out on. Benson shook each man's hand and what few women offered theirs on their way out and watched them walk across the weather-stained dock to the beach where the others were waiting.

Giving his orders to his boys concerning the boat, he followed close behind, a nod passed towards Amos and John along with a few other employees all dressed in white shorts and Hawaiian shirts. Amos was wearing the green one with the tigers on it- Christ that was ugly. The women wore white skirts and flower necklaces and they rushed past the arriving passengers to help Ben's boys with the luggage that would be sent to the beach houses while the tour was given.

The floor was Amos' now.

Amos gave his performance, stretching out his arms as if he were about to embrace the entire group that came up onto the sandy beaches down the stone pathway that cut through it like a river. The couple with the wheelchair were the last to arrive as Amos greeted them all.

"Friends! ¡Hola! Welcome to Isla Bonidada! Mr. Benson had already checked you all in, so we will cut right to the chase. My name is Amos Mulderich, and this is my friend and partner, John Hopper."

"What'd you say in Spanish for?" demanded the oldest of the group, Matt Winklemann, surprised and quite frankly appearing outraged. "I was under the impression that this was an *American* island."

Amos only smiled brighter, unwilling to give in to his sudden impatience for this man. He would have to keep an eye on Winklemann. Anyone who made demands or complaints right out of the gate were often trouble. His wife on the other hand was quite the looker, that Gabbie. Mexican herself maybe, long black hair, a hardbody. Just Amos' style.

Keep the pee-pee in the teepee, he reminded himself.

The opening speech continues.

"We are the heads of this blessed island, along with our head chef, Kyra Lewis who is sadly not here with us at the moment, as she is preparing a magnificent feast for all of you. My colleagues and I are here to serve you, and help you find your way back into the love that made you all meet in the first place. While your luggage is being taken to your respective huts, shall we embark on a tour of this magnificent island and all that you shall experience during your time with us?"

Why yes indeed. Everyone said that the tour *should* begin, which Amos was happy to oblige. This was after all his most favorite part of the entire job.

"Good! Then first things first we need to set the major ground rules while on Isla Bonidada. Yes, you are all here to relax and enjoy some time away from all the hubbub from wherever you are from, but it is also a place of healing both in your heart and your minds. You are all here because you decided to take a chance with your spouse and get through all the hardships that everyday life just doesn't give you the time to do so. So, while on this island, I must request upon three things."

"What are they?" Adam White asked appearing concerned, as they all were. This was the most difficult part of the job, but necessary in Bonidada's interest.

"First off, while the island is yours for the time you are here, you *must* be with someone from this resort if you plan to do any sightseeing off the trail which will be marked on a map we will give you during the tour. Any trespassing of any sort will result in you being sent back to Mexico with *zero* refund. Don't say we didn't warn you," he added with a wink.

Everyone mumbled agreements but no one appeared scorned or outraged of the possibility which was good.

"Secondly, with correspondence to the first, there will be a curfew where you must either be on the designated beach, or your hut until the following morning. There will be more on that later. Thirdly, all cellular devices are recommended to be used sparingly if not at all, and are absolutely *not* allowed during counsel or events, as Bonidada has a strict no photographing or recording policy when it comes to the resort. In fact, if you so wish to eliminate such distractions entirely as a vacation should be, you can hand it over to my friend John who will keep it in the basket that's at his feet."

Not surprisingly, this was met with protest as it always had. Everyone either looked at one another nervously or straight-out defied Amos' third rule. "I need to work!" "I need to be in contact with my boss!" "What about my children?" Etcetera, etcetera.

After a moment, Amos raised his hand and waited patiently for the clamor to die down. "Please understand that you are not going to be cut off from the rest of the world. There are phones here you can use if you must check in with family or friends or business, but I highly recommend to not use cellphones here. This place is meant to be secluded from the rest of the world, a little piece of heaven unreachable and unseen by everyone else. Here, there should be no stress from work, school, family, or whatever else causes you immense stress. This is to ensure that you receive the full experience of Bonidada Resort, and focus more on yourselves and your significant others which will result in better healing for you both."

He waited a few seconds for this passage which he recited so many times before sink into the guests. Only Derian Anderson spoke up in a final attempt to get what he wanted. "You really expect us to just not use our phones?"

Amos didn't even hesitate. "Our methods have always proved fruitful in the past. Trust me when I say, when the world is off your shoulders, you can keep your loved one in your sights and see what both of you have been missing. If you *really* want to keep your phones, then by all means. No one's gonna wrestle it out of you. Not that it matters though because there is no public WI-FI so it will be of no use to you anyway. But the moment I hear it during a counseling session or important event, it will be removed along with *you*, and you won't get to enjoy the rest of the trip and all we have to offer. Plus, you'll be missing out on important key details concerning your wife who is here with you, not your boss or whoever is not on the island."

Unable to find some sort of argument, Anderson relinquished his iPhone as well as a very few, these of which were placed in John's basket to be taken to the main resort building. Amos assured everyone that if they needed it for whatever reason then they needed to discuss it with him. He also reminded them about the public phones inside the main resort. He knew that they would forget all about their phones soon once the real fun began on the island, whether they relinquished them or not. Or so he hoped.

"All right," Amos said clapping his hands once to seize their attention again. "If you will follow me and John, our chariots await!"

They first stopped at the main building which was a short walk from the docks. On the northern side of the beach were the huts and to the south were a pair of buggies that they were to take the tour in. After introducing the guests to the elegantly-dressed staff as well as give them a chance to admire the indoor pool, spa, Bonidada Restaurant, and medical center, they all loaded into three buggies and drove down a paved pathway around the island and all it had to offer as well, all the while Amos giving them all the information via speakers through a radio in the front buggy where he rode shotgun with the driver.

They passed by the Bonidada Pit, where a firepit almost thirty feet in diameter sat in the middle of a set of concrete and wooden tables with a stage at the head. Here, bands would be brought in to play live music over a lavish dinner similar to that of a luau. Further down the path in a secluded area within the tree line, sat a couple of hot springs pocketed by the dormant volcano that made up Isla Bonidada. Within the center of the bubbling pools of mineral water, sat a gazebo of bamboo and palm leaves where couples could receive massages. The women of the group were absolutely thrilled with the idea. The men were mostly interested in the next destination, which was deeper in the line of trees where they passed underneath some ziplines coming down from the peak of the island heading towards the Western docks where Amos mentioned snorkeling.

"Once in a while," he mentioned. "We plan an expedition for diving with Great Whites with a partnered company."

"People pay money to dive with maneaters?" asked Anton to his wife, his first words to her since their arrival to Isla Bonidada. The Whites who were sitting behind the couple, were surprised he could even speak. They sat with them and the Duncans with one driver, while the others were in the other two buggies.

Up front, Paul Jackson asked Amos what other sharks or sea life were in the area, his wife Victoria just as eager to know.

"We get sea turtles who often lay eggs on the beach," Amos answered delighted for the question. "All of which are *not* to be disturbed, I would like to add. Starfish can be found in some of the surrounding reefs too. Whale sharks also inhabit these waters, although they tend to remain further from land than most other creatures. Occasionally, we will have schools of Hammerheads, and Acapulco Damselfish, or as the neighbors call them, *jaqueta acapulqueña*. Big-time fishermen often pass by searching for sailfish, tuna, and dorado, with an occasional roosterfish although I've never seen one. If any of you are big fishermen, I suggest checking out some of the big-game fishing in Acapulco when your time here is at an end. Any questions so far?"

Asking the driver for the radio, Winnifred Ashton brought the device to her lips and clicked it while asking, "Are there any wildlife on this island we need to be concerned with?" Her husband rolled his eyes as if she had just asked the dumbest question of the day.

Amos answered, "Good question. This island as you have discovered is relatively small. If any of you are movie buffs, I would say it is about as large as the island off of Castaway. The reason I say that is because the island is too small to house many animals predatory or not. The vegetation is not good for herbivores to live off of as there wouldn't be enough to sustain them. However, there are snakes on this island as well as the protected seabirds who nest here. Other than a few crabs as well, there isn't anything here that can harm a human being. The snakes are small and non-venomous as well; nothing to be concerned with."

Shawlyn Duncan shuddered audibly. To her it didn't matter if the snake was venomous or not; the only good snake was a dead one in her opinion.

Victoria Jackson was watching the tree line and taking pictures with her camera. She caught a glimpse of a Kiskadee bird perched on a nearby rock. When she showed her husband the photo on the screen, he was delighted. It annoyed Gabbie Winklemann though, who was bitter that she had not brought her own camera here. If she had known she would have to give up her phone, she would have brought her camera that her daughter had given her as a birthday present, wherever in the house it was now.

At this point the group had arrived at the cave entrance to the Bonidada Grotto, where individual dates would be set up for couples to swim, eat, and enjoy the peaceful world hidden from their eyes. When Derian Anderson asked if they could go see it now, Amos politely told him that once his and his wife's specific date came up, then they would see it.

"It's meant to be a *surprise*," Amos told them all. "And it will be worth it, I guarantee it. Our men are working on the finishing touches to the walkway, and you will be happy with what you see. When you are done, you will return to the main coastal line via the ziplines you saw us pass by earlier, if not transported by our professional drivers if it may suit you."

"Scary," Carla Anderson said. Her husband on the other hand looked thrilled. Derian might as well have heard that they would be going skydiving soon, one of his favorite pastimes. After all, who doesn't like jumping out of a plane that wasn't only *slightly* crazy?

Anton cocked his head as the buggies continued to bounce their way past the entrance. "You hear that?" he asked Adam without looking back.

"Hear what?"

"Sounds like a clicking sound..."

"Clicking?"

"Yeah, like something between a rattler and a chittering insect, I dunno..."

"A cicada?" Adam inquired remembering how irritatingly loud those bugs could get.

"No, not quite that..."

Anton asked the driver what that clicking sound was, and the driver who had also heard it shrugged. "Probably a woodpecker," he said in such a thick Jamaican accent. Anton practically thought the man would say, 'mon.'

"There are woodpeckers out here?" Ethan asked, now hearing the distinct clicking as well. Their wives heard it too, although Jessica didn't seem to care.

"I don't know…"

As they got further and further away from the grotto, the clicking became more distinct and progressively louder. A sound that to Adam sounded like a pair of hollow pipes clanging together.

Or chittering teeth, the idea suddenly plunged into his brain.

Louder and louder it became the further away the buggies passed the grotto. Everyone had noticed now, and listened intently as Amos tried to suggest what it could be. The men working on the grotto's boardwalk for example, but no one was buying it, not when it sounded like the sound was now coming from *inside* the buggies.

Tiktik-ka-tiktik-ka-tiktik. Tiktik-ka-tiktik-ka-

It stopped as suddenly as a slam on the breaks. The sound had risen almost so loudly that the whole island could have been hearing it, only to stop completely, as if someone had switched off a broken record player. Now only the buggies engines were audible, along with the crunching of soil, and the occasional squawk of a bird, although to Adam and everyone else the bird even sounded tense and hesitant.

Amos cleared his throat and spoke to them all. "Well, whatever it was, ain't nothing to worry about. Probably an animal or our men. Right, John?"

"Sure," the old man said who was driving the first buggy. But even he looked uneasy from the sound. He knew every creature who crawled on this rock, and knew every sound the island made. He had never heard anything like that before. "I'll call the boys in the grotto when we get back."

"That would be best," Amos said confidently, and without the radio.

Their final stop was a clearing breaking down to a slope towards the beach which was the Bonidada Cove. An enclosure of a reef held in a stagnant chunk of the sea against a perfectly white beach. Coming down from a cliffside of black rock and weed, came a waterfall from the grotto's main waterline, which emptied into the sea into a roaring beauty of mist and rainbows that took everyone's breath away. This was the cove where couples could swim with dolphins who are owned by Bonidada and live here in the cove. The trainers who were on the beach were tossing fish into the water where shiny sleek bodies of gray were snatching them up and then performing nautical maneuvers worthy of Flipper. The trainers waved to the guests and their mammal partners did the same, skittering across the wake and waving their flippers while whistling happily.

"Are those safe?" Matt Winklemann asked through the speaker, his eyes never leaving the dolphins.

"Safe as houses," Amos said. "There is still so much to show you all, but that will come when the time comes. In the meantime, we must return you all to the main beach and get you all settled in. I am delighted to have you here with us, and thank you for choosing Bonidada Resort as your place of marital healing and devotion."

Everyone applauded happily as the buggies made their way past the cove and back towards the main beach where they would get to see their huts. Everyone was delighted by what they saw, and those who were indeed having troubles with each other became hopeful, even Adam who took his wife's hand tenderly and gave it a squeeze.

She squeezed back.

They would figure it out together. They had to, or else they would leave this island no longer together.

Four

Inside the Crocket Grotto, surrounded by slick stalagmites and stalactites that encircled a hole in the ceiling that let in bright sunlight like a gaping mouth, two workers were placing the finishing touches on the bridge crossing the grotto's pool.

The water that bubbled up here from deep underground would eventually snake its way down the island and into the Cove where it would join the ocean as a never-ending source of clean freshwater only to be tainted and salted by the vastness of the Pacific. Birds chirped and sang among the vines and moss, and bright perennial lilies and peonies attracted many dragonflies and butterflies which gave the grotto an unearthly feeling that made everyone on the island feel like they stepped into some fantasy world of clean and unbridled beauty.

André Valesco and Tamia Gonzalez were accompanied by André's dog, Rosco. The terrier was resting at the base of the bridge while its master and her compadre worked on the railing just as the tour was taking place past them. While those in the buggies heard the strange clicking and wondering what it could be, they heard nothing but the birds and the gurgle of water between their screwdriver's whirl or their hammers strike. They were both lost in their work and the beauty of the grotto.

The two had been friends since childhood, both coming to work for Bonidada Resort from Matehuala. Tamia's boyfriend in fact, worked in the very kitchens Kyra Lewis was in charge of. The three of them had come here just shy of their eighteenth birthdays to raise money for college in the States. André, being the oldest of the three, treated Tamia and Roberto like siblings, and had helped the two elope from their homes and get them to the island for work. Once they made enough, they would go to the States and from there, a new life for them all could begin. Maybe André would find himself a man for himself, be it as those back home never appreciated his 'blasphemous' life choices. Dubbed as the 'devil's child' he hardly spoke to his family anymore. Tamia and Roberto were all the family he needed at the moment; at least they accepted him and didn't judge him for being gay.

That of course was the 'nice' way his family had put it. Never mind the fact that André had done well in school, stayed away from drugs and didn't get himself involved with the Cartel (unlike a particular brother of his), but because of what kind of people he liked he had been hounded as if all that awaited him in life was hardship and the gates of Hell. If Hell really was a place, it was at the Valesco family dinner table, where any conversation or good will from André went to perish and become buried.

"*Martillo*," André requested, to which Tamia tossed him the hammer so he could hammer a stabilizing beam into the railing of the bridge. He then followed this with asking for a "*Destornillador*." He felt like a doctor from television asking for specific tools or a swab while he performed brain surgery, which fixing a bridge was a far cry from, but it was just as tedious while at the same time relaxing as therapy. There was nowhere else in the world André would rather be other than America, than here doing what he loved. He loved to build, loved working with his hands. Tamia, having none of Roberto's cooking skills, had the same conclusion in mind, although her hobbies would include more of building little knick-knacks for houses. Birdhouses, crucifixes, glass memorials, that sort of stuff.

They were talking about Roberto as they worked, André occasionally breaking the conversation to ask for a specific tool or for Tamia to help him hold something down, with Tamia occasionally busying herself with Rosco who was enjoying the attention of being scratched between his ears. Despite this attention however, Rosco did not relax and felt tense. It was as if the mutt was hearing something it's masters could not here in the grotto.

"¿Cuando te quieres ir?"
"Pronto."
"¿Eso es lo que quiere?"
"Si. Quiero tener una bebé."
"Oh! ¿Vos si?"
Tamia shrugged. *"No sé. Pensando-"*
Suddenly, the dog jumped up and began to bark towards an overgrowth of tropical blues. Before the two workers could react, he then charged across the bridge and into the foliage, where he continued to bark and snarl despite its owners now standing erect and calling for him, whistling.

"¡Rosco!" shouted Tamia. *"¡Regresa aquí!"*
"Maldito perro..." André grumbled.
They had started for the direction Rosco had been headed and were just at the end of the bridge when a yelp made them stop in their tracks. Then there was silence. A shifting of the leaves caused them to grow uneasy. Rosco had found something in the brush, no doubt. The two had believed it to be some bird or lizard, but the dog's sudden

yelp of pain made them fear the unknown of what Rosco had discovered. His feet set in place, André removed a pocketknife from his front pocket. Tamia removed the hammer from her belt, clutching it so tight that her knuckles had gone white.

"*Rosco,*" she called nervously. "*Venir.*"

A whimper, and a shaking of leaves. Then the dog came back out, looking tired and worn out. The two relaxed, whatever it was the dog had given chase to, it had gotten away and left the old mutt literally dog-tired. As Tamia dropped to one knee to inspect it, she was glad to see that he was uninjured.

André stooped and stroked the dog's black flank. "*Estúpido.*"

The dog looked up at his master with intelligent dark eyes that took in André's reflection as if Rosco would absorb him. The dogs black fur looked darker, as if he had rolled into something. He would need a bath later down the road.

He paused as he looked into the dog's eyes. His reflection, visible in the light coming in from behind down the mouth of the grotto, was reflected in the dog's eyes as if he were hanging upside down. He tilted his head, and his head shifted in the opposite direction. Rosco then licked André's palm, and he forgot about the strange reflection as quickly as he had noticed as he loved on the animal, just grateful that nothing bad had happened.

Tamia suggested they finish the bridge and get back to the resort soon. "*Amos puede necesitarnos.*"

"*Seguro.*"

They got back to work and Rosco returned to his original spot, receiving the same attention as he had before. Although he was no longer panting or even moved to scratch or lick himself.

He only sat there, watching the two work. Watching, listening, absorbing.

42

Five

When they got back to the main beach everyone was dismissed and escorted to their respective huts that they would be staying in.

One employee for each couple went down the beach with a fresh drink in hand (bottled water for the Duncans due to Shawlyn's pregnancy) and approached the line of huts along the slope. Up the walkway they all went and the guests were given the keys to their huts before being reminded of dinner in the next hour or so. The sun was still in the sky just above the horizon, casting an orange and purple tint across the beautiful ocean that many of the couples couldn't help but stare at before entering their hut.

Every hut was built and decorated the same, and Adam and Cynthia couldn't be happier with their place of rest for the next few weeks. They had both been in elegant hotels before, the best by far being the Venetian in Las Vegas during their honeymoon, but this hut really took the cake; relishing the sensation of the tropics and making them both feel like they really were on a real vacation.

A beautiful dining room with a table of sandalwood sat in-between two wicker chairs decorated with seashells. Across the ceiling were vintage bulbs contained by brass lamps. Across the room was a bamboo door that was open, revealing a bedroom the color of coral and having a lush bed with white sheets and comforters. The windows were open, letting in the breeze from the sea in and bringing with it a clean, salty scent that took the White's breaths away. In the same room was a jacuzzi bathtub big enough for two, with rose pedals sprinkled over the edge of the shiny porcelain and around the marble steps leading to it. On the corner sat a serving platter with fresh tropical fruit like sliced pineapple, mangos, bundles of grapes, and more along with two bottles of wine, one red and one white, and finally a card that thanked them for choosing the Bonidada Resort in elegant, gold print.

On the bed were two paper cranes positioned to appear as if they were holding another note in their paper beaks. Upon taking the note, Adam read it aloud while Cynthia located their luggage stacked neatly on the floor beside the sliding glass door leading out to the balcony where to lounge chairs sat overlooking the beach and the sea beyond. Above the chairs, a bamboo windchime clinked and clonked in the light breeze, bringing a peaceful sound along with Adam's good reading voice as he read the note.

"Adam and Cynthia White, again, thank you for choosing Bonidada. I hope your stay is both relaxing and meaningful. This is a place of healing as you no doubt heard many times already, and I hope you both are willing to take that seriously. While here, I also hope you both find the passion and love that allowed you two to meet the first time and will carry it with you when you leave this beautiful island. The Bonidada Family is at your service, and I trust in Amos Mulderich to give you the first true vacation you both need for both body and soulmate.

"Your friend and neighbor, James Crockett."

"He the guy who the grotto is named after?" Cynthia asked.

"Seems like it. I wonder if he is the owner of the island."

"Probably. If he is, then he is running quite the crew here." She was taking off her sandals and propping herself up onto the bed and let out a long and relaxing sigh. "I *really* like this place."

"Do you?"

She smiled, closing her eyes in content as she laid there.

He couldn't help but admire her now. When she wasn't stressed, when she was finally able to cut loose and just relax, she looked very beautiful indeed. His eyes scanned her from feet to head, taking in everything he had fallen in love with when he first met her and how much he had grown to love her still despite their current differences. When was the last time he actually admired her with such love and devotion, if not even just lust or desire?

Her tiny feet, strong calves, smooth thighs under that blouse, too small of a tummy and smaller breasts, her soft neck and tiny hands and bony shoulders, and that black hair that always reminded him of the night. How long had it been since he looked upon her with no ambiguity? Had this been the Cynthia he had been with these past few months? It hadn't seemed like it during that time, but now as he looked at her...

How long has it been since we even had sex? he wondered.

Cynthia noticed his gazing and smiled seductively enough, kindly giving in to his admiration. "See something you like?"

"As a matter of fact, I do."

Cynthia reached over to the nightstand where her drink sat. She sipped from the straw which was curled and was joined by a pink umbrella sticking out of the coconut cream. As she drank, her lips puckered tightly over the straw, she was watching her husband.

When her lips at last departed from the straw she said coyly, "I see something I like too."

Adam returned the look with a grin. "That a fact?"

"Yes. Unfortunately, he's all dressed up, hiding all the best parts."

"That could be arranged."

A pause, and then a nod. She sat the glass down, and looked at him with a more serious expression. "Adam, are we gonna be okay?"

Adam frowned. Not because he was unhappy with the question, but because for the first time in a long while, he was not distracted by work to ignore her question. The two of them were far from home, far from work and family struggles. Here they would have to face their problems head-on, and no distractions were allowed. He would have to honestly answer, and give thought to the possible future ahead of them.

But Claire...

"I hope so," he finally answered truthfully. He sat on the edge of the bed and began caressing her leg. Not out of necessity to change the subject, but in order to feel her and somehow see if she was really present, and let her know that he was. "I really, honestly, hope so."

She nodded. "You think this is a good idea?"

"It was your idea at first. Don't you?"

She nodded again. "I think so."

"Then that makes two of us," he said giving her thigh a light pat. He was about to say something else, when a piercing growl filled the room, leaving the words dangling off his tongue and not reaching Cynthia at all.

Cynthia started to laugh. "Hungry, are we? I *told* you to eat something before we left for the docks."

Embarrassed, Adam tried to shrug it off. "Yeah, yeah, whatever."

"Have some of the fruit."

"I'll pass." He hated fruit. Too sweet for his taste. "Besides, I wanna wait until dinner."

"How long do we have?"

"Probably half an hour now..." He was looking up at a wall clock that was crafted with carved fish in place of roman numerals. They had been sitting here for that long already...

"I could sleep here right now if I wanted to," Cynthia said stretching her body out hands over her head and her legs splayed out. A series of sharp pops crackled through the air as her spine stretched.

"You feel relaxed?" asked Adam.

"*Definitely.*"

"Hopefully dinner puts us in a food coma then. Because I wanna sleep like the dead."

"Ditto."

Dinner was in the resort's ballroom which was used to host dinner parties by private individuals. The lavish room was decorated with bright blue curtains and fresh vines and flowers that made the room smell floral and clean. Small round tables with white cloths were scattered about, with a couple per table. All were dressed in their best suits and dresses, and Adam had changed into his own gray and silver suit with black shirt and shoes. Cynthia had changed into a black gown to match, and she looked absolutely stunning. She was wearing her diamond earrings and a black rose corsage that came with the dress. She was also wearing her wedding ring on her finger, which Adam was delighted to see. How long had it been since she wore that thing?

Kyra Lewis introduced herself after Amos and the entire crew made sure everyone was seated and had plenty of water, fresh-baked bread, and wine. Sipping on their Cabernet Sauvignon, the Whites took in the older woman who carried herself with both a sense of authority and at the same time tender motherhood.

She was tall, big-boned, and as black as the purest of coal with beautiful curly locks and fingers as thick but as delicate as a pianist's. She welcomed and greeted everyone formally, going to each and every table and hugging both men and women affectionately. By the time she returned to her spot between Amos and John, she clapped her hands and made her declaration. At the sound of her clapping, waitresses and busboys came out of the kitchen doors pushing carts that carried individual platters of food to each and every table, one cart per table, with all platters covered with a silver lid containing each portion of the elegant meal Kyra and her cooks had prepared throughout the day.

"Without further ado," said Bonidada's head chef. "Dinner, is served!"

The meal was extravagant and delectable in every way. A duck roasted with apples, onions, sage, and honeyed orange juice was grilled to perfection to the point where the fat melted in one's mouth, the leftover grease used to concoct the perfect addition to some roasted fingerling potatoes with herbs and spices. Each person got a leg or thigh and a breast, the breast being the most juicy and the leg piece tasting sweet and rich. Grilled asparagus that had been brined in a solution overnight and topped with melting parmesan joined the duck and potatoes, all the while more bread, salad, and wine were served throughout the entirety of the meal. The Duncans in particular, were conversing about the meal in a way that critics would in five-star restaurants, detailing everything they tasted from smell, texture, saltiness or how thoroughly everything had been cooked. Everyone enjoyed the meal in some way shape or form, except for Anton and Jessica, who would have been happy with cheese and crackers. Jessica had no taste in her buds anymore, having lost that sense years ago. Anton did not care for the taste of the food as he constantly watched everyone in the ballroom, looking too big for the tuxedo he had brought for the trip.

For dessert a flambéed pineapple crème brûlée was served with a small scoop of handmade vanilla ice cream which completed the meal and made everyone feeling full and satisfied. Everyone praised and thanked Kyra and her team for all their hard work, clapping and cheering at Amos' request. It was turning out to be a very successful first night, both in business as well as personal affairs between each and every couple who came to Isla Bonidada.

Adam who scooped up the last of his own crème brûlée, shoved it into his mouth and groaned contentedly. He patted his stomach when Cynthia looked his way, her own desert only halfway done.

"Stuffed," he said with a smile.

"Want to help with mine?" Cynthia asked him.

"You got this."

"I don't think I do," Cynthia said now laughing. "It's all so good and so much…"

"We're on vacation, indulge yourself."

Cynthia smiled and taking a scoop of the baked vanilla, she held it out towards him. It was a minor gesture, but it was one that Adam appreciated very much. It made him think of when he and Cynthia had been first dating, how they would give each other tastes of their food or feed one another. It was something the two of them had always shared back in the day, something they had not done together in a long, long time.

Adam, while full, accepted the bite gratefully, smiling at Cynthia as he chewed while his wife smiled back, her eyes full of love and adoration.

This is a good idea, Adam told himself again and yet despite this, he couldn't help but add, *I hope.*

2nd Letter

When Father Bacani was killed it had sent the entire village into disarray. Of course we had no idea about the situation happening in the city at the time, but it was just as we had feared and everyone avoided the church and the statues of Christ altogether in fear of what this could mean if the man could be killed inside the church's courtyard which should have been holy ground.

I remember how it was being a kid. The kids in my village were always so friendly to one another when they were in groups. When they were with their family or other friends, they would smile and talk with you and treat you like one of their own. The whole village was family; you couldn't walk more than five minutes without being stopped and asked about you and your kin's health.

That was before Father Bacani's death however. The pleasantries persisted, make no mistake, but it felt reserved somewhat, even as a kid I noticed this. Once people were by themselves however, they become suspicious and weary, simply because of the fear that had taken our village like a plague. After the Father died we were all haggard with both grief and worry. The rumors surrounding the man's death had been going on, but I wasn't buying it. I can't speak for anyone else who might have had their doubts, but I was too old to believe what was being whispered among everyone who would listen. What we had was just murder, plain and simple, or so I thought at the time, and to believe any superstitions of any sort to me in regards to the death was not only disrespectful, but stupid.

But I was still a kid then, I thought I knew better as we often do at the time. Because the superstitious rumors and the suspicious glances everyone was giving one another was just the beginning. That was when the literal witch hunt began.

Father Bacani was found literally hollowed out. He was face down in his garden, his stomach and chest ripped open and the entrails removed. I remember going with some others to see the body once the word got out, and I remember his torso, the ribs snapped and peeled back like a pair of bloody wings in the front, the inside of the man hollowed out completely into a dark and red hole. I remember my friend at the time vomiting, and the men assisting with the body telling us to run off but we have already seen it all. Even Bacani's head which rolled on his neck loose and limply, I saw had been cracked open like an egg, the space inside the confines of his smashed skull just as empty as his chest and belly.

He had been seeing a woman in the village, most of the talk had been, and without warning mere hours later, most of the villagers, primarily the responders to the murder, had immediately taken the woman in question seeing Bacani and strung her up by her feet by the church's entrance awning. They then placed some wood and started a fire, with a cauldron boiling water beneath her. I had thought they were going to boil her alive, but instead the elders used poles to spin the screaming woman around and around to the point where she vomited, most of the bile spraying everywhere with some landing in the bubbling cauldron. Everyone watched in sober nonchalance while the children laughed and pointed. I was with my mother and sister during this time, and I had asked my mother what in the world those men were doing to the woman.

I will never forget what my mother said to me.

"They are trying to get her to release the black chick, which is to be boiled in the cauldron."

I understood what the black chick meant, but I didn't know what the significance of such a torture was meant to prove. The old legends and the old traditions were only frightening everyone more than necessary. This was merely an excuse to punish someone due to the demise of Father Bacani. He wouldn't be the last victim of murder though, and everyone knew it when in the end, the woman didn't vomit up any black bird. Everyone had left while the elders let the poor woman down, who at this point had so much blood in her head her face looked purple. They had taken her inside the church for more questioning, and no doubt in order to attempt an exorcism.

My mother, on the way home, told my sister and I both, to "Come home as soon as we are done working on the docks. Do not straggle, and do not stay after dark. And whatever you do, if you see a strange pig or dog or any animal that is unfamiliar, flee and tell someone. You understand me?"

I understood, but I had no intention of being out late at night in the first place, and I didn't care much for the last bit of information she gave me. I didn't care if I didn't recognize someone else's livestock or pets or not.

I should have taken heed of her warning though. Not a day goes by when I don't think back and wish I had not been so stubborn. The first real sign of my foolishness was when coming home I noticed a large crow perched on the side of a building. I didn't think of it at the time, but I believe now that that bird had been watching me, and I my mother's words despite them ringing in my ears, I had silenced them. I should have paid attention though, I should have heeded my mother's warning. It would have saved the life of my sister, who would be the second victim on her way home that night.

When I had returned home, Mother had placed a needle into the door of our house, as well as filled a jar with coconut oil and placed it in the room next to our alter where a carved statue of Jesus Christ stood black amidst towers of burning candles and incense. She had a patient with her in the backroom, and she was also saying a prayer to the old woman who was suffering from blindness. She then placed a trumpet flower into the old woman's hair, and sent her on her merry way as fast as she could.

"Tao po," the woman told me on her way out. I remember feeling ill at the greeting, for I had not heard it before personally, but knew what it meant.

"Why the flower?" I had asked my mother.

"For protection," mother said simply. "Protection from the evil one."

Blessings were common in our village. Blessing for the sick, good fortune, and of course, well-being. The 'evil one' she was referring to was no doubt the killer. But despite what the old woman had said, it brought back the old superstitions I was forced to believe throughout my younger childhood. I was disgraced by the very idea of it, but I would have been a liar if I said it didn't plague my mind, especially when I would awake the next morning and find out my sister's fate.

"Tao po," was not a greeting or a blessing. It was a declaration. Something only humans were capable of saying. Don't ask me why because I do not remember the reasons. The saying specifically means, "I am human. I am not a monster."

This is difficult to write, so I'm going to quit while I am ahead. It's the last luxury I deserve, but I think I paid my dues and deserve at least a little peace before bed.

Six

André Valesco was washing dishes that night during the dinner and talking to Roberto. All the while Rosco sat outside the kitchens as usual, and was offered bones and scraps of meat from the other cooks.

When André was off for the night, he noticed that his dog had not touched any of the food which was a surprise to him. Rosco was a real glutton when it came to snacks, especially from Kyra's kitchens.

"*¿Sin hambre?*" he asked his dog.

Rosco merely looked at his master, and licked André's outstretched paw.

"Yo, André," one of the Jamaican cleaners said as she passed by. "Maybe your dog is just full. He looks like he's gotten bigger."

"No way," André laughed heartedly, but he took another look at his dog and considered it a moment. It wasn't a drastic change, but Rosco *did* seem a bit bigger. He didn't notice it at the grotto because he was more concerned with Rosco's safety when he came out of the brush.

His eyes too come to think of it...

At the end of the night, once the guests were returned to their cabins the workers were sent to their own quarters which was behind the resort in portables that had been purchased off of old sugar cane plantations. It was a tight fit, but André and his ten fellow inhabitants, Roberto included, were comfortable enough.

Bunks lined all three walls except for the front where the door was, where an oven and sink and a couple of containers were stacked for them all. One of the workers, a veteran named Ricardo was baking some brownies that had some marijuana in it to go with the celebratory beer that was being passed about for a successful first night. There was one other dog other than Rosco who lived with the men, a Pitbull named Princess. Usually the two dogs were friendly, but tonight Rosco didn't seem to care that the other dog existed, even when Princess had first started to growl at him.

André turned to Victor who owned the dog. "What the hell is wrong with your dog?"

"Fuck you, she's fine. Your boy just playing hard to get."

"Funny, ," André said laughing. It was all fun and games, but he was worried about Rosco. The way Princess was staring at him and growling but not looking willing to attack or do anything to harm him. The pit-bull was rigid, her haunches coiled like piano wire, and yet she did not attempt to approach Rosco, who appeared to not care whether she was there or not.

It surprised him more when Rosco quietly strolled over to the opened front door and stepped out into the night. It was only then when Princess had ceased her growling, and even Victor looked confused by this. He got up and stepped outside to call Rosco back in, but the dog had already disappeared into the night, his black fur camouflaging him in the midst of the darkness.

Estará bien, André decided. He wasn't going to worry about Rosco. If the dog wanted out, it was probably just to piss or take a shit. Either way, he'd be back. Rosco always came back.

He never did that night.

Seven

At some point Roberto had left the party early to meet up with Tamia.

Everyone knew they were going out but promised to keep it a secret. All workers were expected to be in their portables until 5am when it was time to get everything ready for the following day. But everyone liked to cut loose once in a while, and Roberto and Tamia had planned to meet tonight in order to get some well-needed alone time.

They met just outside the perimeter fence, and then taking the cool dusty path into the forest, they made their way in the direction of Crockett's Grotto with a basket of leftovers from the kitchen as well as a bottle of wine left unopened and would not be missed from the cellars. Should Kyra Lewis catch wind of missing inventory, there would be hell to pay, but neither Roberto nor Tamia were concerned.

It took longer to get to the grotto on foot, but it was still worth the trek. As they walked the salty air cooled their skin and the sounds of the nocturnal animals on the island sang their songs of greeting and desire. Inside the grotto once they arrived, silvery moonlight peered into the overhead opening, casting the waters below into a gleam of liquid silver. The plants smelled fragrant mixed with the tinge of sea salt, and the chirping of grasshoppers and bats sang through the air like a chorus of the beauty of night.

They spread out a blanket from their summer homes and placing the basket between them, they began to have their picnic. Roberto popped open the bottle of wine, and the two of them discussed over the wine and food about their future together. Where they would go to school, what sort of home they would have, when to finally be married, and at last, the possibility of a child. Bonidada Resort paid exponentially well, given how long they had to work over the course of a year and what said-work entailed. They would enter the United States richer than either of their parents combined. They were happy, happy with each other, and happy for the future. As the wine settled onto their mind like a heavy blanket, their love became too great a thing to contain, and Roberto moved in and began to help Tamia unbutton the front of her blouse.

"Roberto…"

"Mi amor…"

Neither of the two young adults noticed the black terrier entering the cave. They didn't notice it taking notice of them before crossing the bridge and returning to the brush of vines and bushes where the real Rosco laid dead, already felled upon by worms and flies. The black dog had been eviscerated, its entrails spilling out of its slit belly like escaping worms. Beside it, untouched by the flies and maggots, rested a headless body.

The fake Rosco began to shift, and once it became what it had been before, the missing head returned to the headless body, the section of the neck where it parted sealing as if the flesh were made of putty and was being fused together by an invisible toddler. The body began to stir and twitch.

It opened its eyes, and inhaled every smell in the area. The moss, the bugs, the flowers concealed in their pedals, the passion of love from two young adults who were oblivious to the danger they were in. Easy prey.

It opened its maw of rows of shark teeth and began to chitter. As it did so, the rest of the grotto fell completely into silence, as if the animals and insects understood immediately what was prowling their home now, and did not wish to meet it.

The hut closest to the grotto was that of Matt and Gabbie Winklemann's. The two were looking over the scheduled time list that had been given to them after dinner. They had made their appointment for breakfast to be delivered (they intended to sleep in tonight) and would be free to do whatever they pleased on the island until 1:00, where they would have their couple's spa session, before the rest of the day commenced.

"Wish we had our phones," Matt said turning on the alarm on the clock by the bedside. His wife was already in bed, naked and covered in the comfy sheets of the bed. She was waiting patiently for him, hoping that he would make love to her. It had been so long, and they were on vacation, they were to focus on one another and nothing else.

Unless, she thought to herself bitterly which only made her feel insecure and wanting to put some clothes back on. *He's thinking of* her.

When he was done Matt got undressed and stood naked in front of the mirror. At 49 going on 50, he was in decent enough shape for the owner of a chain of retail stores. He was still admiring himself, his abs his arms and thick legs, when Gabbie asked if he was ready for bed.

He smiled dashingly at her. "I think you and I should take a bath first. Get the sand out of us first."

She smiled, pleased by the offer but internally worried if she had brought some sand with her under the covers.

Oh well. "Sounds wonderful. Should-"

That was when they heard the ticking. It was loud, as if the sound was coming from just outside their window.

Tiktik-ka-tiktik-ka-tiktik.

"You hear that?" Matt asked nervously. He glanced at his duffle bag. His gun was in there, but did he want to take it out now? Gabbie might be upset if she sees it. But if that was the case...

Tiktik-ka-tiktik-ka-tiktik! Tiktik-ka-tiktik-ka-tiktik. Tiktik-ka-tiktik-ka-tiktik!

It was the same pattern repeated again and again. At this point Gabbie was clutching the sheet tightly around her body, as if trying to conceal herself within it. She told Matt to take a look outside, and he groaned inwardly. Still, he was the man, he had to make sure.

(That's right, Matthew. So don't be a pussy. Be a man!)

How long had it been since he had heard *that* one?

He decided not to get his gun, and slowly and quietly, walked for the sliding glass door leading to the balcony of their hut. He stood there with his hand on the door for the longest time, wondering what would happen should he open it.

Tiktik-ka-tiktik-ka-tiktik. Tiktik-ka-tiktik-ka-tiktik.
That sound...
Tiktik-ka-tiktik-ka
What the hell is that?
Tiktik-ka-tiktik-ka-tiktik.

He gripped the latch tighter, and with a gasp he threw the door open and jumped outside. His bare feet were cold against the boards of the balcony, and the chilling wind coming in from the north made his skin erupt in gooseflesh and licked the sweat off his brow. As soon as he stepped outside, the sound had stopped. The clicking was no longer there.

He stood there for ten seconds. Fifteen. Twenty. Then he walked around the balcony and tried to peer around. There was nothing. The sound had stopped as suddenly as it had begun.

"What is it?" Gabbie asked from the bedroom.

"Nothing, must have been a bug."

Or someone is fucking with us. This thought made Matt angry, and he thought of yelling outside for whoever it was to come up and do it to his face. But he quelled his anger, thinking that he shouldn't let that bother him if it was the case. It wasn't like it would matter soon anyway. Whoever the fucking comedians were, they wouldn't be laughing for long.

He returned to his wife, to his bath, to his vacation. For now, he only had to relax.

At the same time, Roberto and Tamia were in a tangle on their blanket. The moon shone over their shiny bodies as they made love. They touched, they kissed, they caressed, licked, and loved. When they were done, they laid back with their faces up to the stars. Stars that shone through the roof of the grotto like a diamond vein from an ancient mine. They were happy. They were satisfied.

And just as quickly, they were dead.

It had crept around and had come up from behind them. Neither had heard it coming until it was too late.

Tamia was the first to get attacked. In a blur of black leather, she was attacked from above as if Spiderman had become a monster ready to devour rather than kiss. Her eyes widened as a maw full of sharp shark-like teeth blotted her vision of the overhead sky, and then it was biting into her face. It bit through the bone and ripped the front of her skull clean off. Roberto screamed. She screamed, the sound coming out like a moan rather than anything a human being was capable of, and then the creature hooked its claws into her shoulders and like a child tossing a doll, threw her over the nearby bank and into the grotto's pool, only to splash about blindly as she slowly bled to death. She was screaming, her mouthless face incapable of forming words and expressing horrible gurgled sounds like a howler.

She could hear Roberto screaming and amidst the horrible cries of her lover, she could hear the horrible crunching sound which she knew was her frontal lobe and faceplate of her skull being chewed and swallowed by the monster who at the same time had turned on Roberto.

It came in fast as he was sitting up and starting to stand. With a brutal slash of long claws, his belly was slit open and his entrails spilled over his thighs and knees like wet eels. He remained sitting, trying to hold his guts back in as if they could be pushed back, but then the creature was upon him now, it's tongue wriggling out and forcing its way into his mouth and ramming deep down his throat like a rapist. He collapsed to the ground beneath the creature's weight, his airway clogged as the tongue continued to wriggle deeper down his throat until he could feel it in his chest. It tickled and ached, and he tried to fight back but the thing held his wrists down as it began to feed.

He felt excruciating pain as the monster slowly devoured his internal organs. The heart, lungs, intestines, liver, gallbladder, everything. The entrails that had spilled out were immediately sucked back into his gut like retreating feelers. It took no time at all and Roberto was dead staring into the face of the monster, those evil eyes of red that were intelligent, and just as deadly.

Tamia meanwhile had struggled in the water long enough. She tried to keep her head above water, despite not knowing where to or what to do. All she knew was pain, every nerve ending in her face and head screaming in agony in her head. She couldn't close her mouth for she had none, she couldn't breathe in properly because she didn't have a nose. She couldn't see, only hear Roberto's cries and struggles as the thing that attacked them began to feed. She tried to swim towards the edge, but the grotto's pool was deep with the edges too steep and slick to climb out of, and with nothing to grab ahold to, Tamia struggled, struggled, and then began to drown from the loss of blood and from her brain shutting down as the major part of it's being was missing, joining Roberto's entrails in the process. She died never knowing just what it was that attacked her, nor did she know if Roberto was okay or not.

The thing then took flight on large wings and scooped the woman out of the water that had turned crimson with her blood. Bits of gray matter from her brain had spilled out, but it let them float about in the water like old sponges. Let the vermin take care of that as well as the blood. It carried the body of Tamia towards its place of refuge and then went back and retrieved the now hollow body of Roberto.

It had to be smart this time, it had to make sure it covered it's tracks.

As for the dead dog, it took it out towards sea, and then released it into the water. Let the fish and sharks make a meal out of that mongrel that dared to attack it.

Hungry still after so long a fast, it returned to where it had stashed Tamia and Roberto's body and after ripping Tamia's midsection open for easier gain, it began to feed on her insides. It would take care of their little picnic later.

For now, it was hungry, and it had to eat. Only then would it make its plan as to what to do next.

Eight

Derian and his wife Carla were out on the beach after a good breakfast of French toast made with Rumchata, with an oversized platter of bacon to go with. The coffee had been rich, the orange juice freshly squeezed.

They were lounged out, taking in the morning sunshine as the morning tide came in. They weren't talking to one another, but they weren't fighting either, as their servant noted to John who reported to Amos who was in the main office of the resort watching everyone from the cameras while catching up on some paperwork.

Isla Bonita had roughly forty hidden cameras around the resort and beach area where they have light posts and walkways. He could see the Andersons on the beach. There was also a camera in front of every hut. All the other couples were inside except for Paul Jackson who was out on the balcony naked and in blissful ignorance that he was unable to be seen as he took in the rays of the morning sun like some pacific island god.

Amos also saw that Kyra and her crew were in the kitchen cleaning up after breakfast and prepping for the lunch that would be passed around just before the guests were designated to their scheduled spots for either a spa day, an adventure at the cove, or a counseling session with him. John was with him, reporting everything that was going on for the morning routine; Ensuring everything was in place and no one was slacking or called in sick. Ever since Covid, there was very little wiggle room when dealing with sick days on the island; especially since they only had a few trained nurses on duty in case of an emergency.

"Apparently Roberto isn't in," John then told Amos near the end of his report, a cigarette sitting unlit between his lips. He subtly added, "Again."

"Well, where the hell is he?" Amos demanded. "Tamia is supposed to be with the cove crew preparing for my session with the Whites as well. I swear those two…"

John smiled. "I checked in with some crew members who reported them going out last night. Look up camera t-nine between twelve and two. They are seen heading up to the grotto, but they haven't come back. We already sent some people up there for final prep concerning today's couple, but the crew didn't find anything."

"Nothing at all?"

"Nope. Just that terrier the couple owns."

"We *really* gotta put fucking cameras up there."

John couldn't help but smile. "Then we'd be able to see what every couple does going up there."

"Not like we don't already."

"Good luck getting Crockett to agree to that."

Amos frowned. John was right. On more than one occasion when guests were taken up there, they would ask for some privacy and the guide in question would allow it. The guests would return with dripping hair and soaked clothes. They would either be swimming or skinny-dipping, which was *technically* encouraged, but it didn't make Amos like the water. He liked Crockett's Grotto, but he didn't care much for the water that resided there, even if it eventually emptied out into the cove. And still Crockett intended to keep it that way.

"That doesn't matter," said Amos. "Maybe we should be more strict; Stop letting everyone fuck around up there."

John took a jab. "Maybe *someone* should stop fucking around down *here*."

Amos looked at him. Smiled, and then returned his attention to the couple on the beach.

A young couple who resented each other, and yet spent their morning together. That was good. Derian laid back in black swim shorts and looked like a track runner with firm and well-defined muscle. His wife, tall with strong legs and a good, plump ass to go with them, laid on her stomach with the back of her bikini undone in order to get some sun on her back and shoulders.

Amos leaned back and crossed his arms. He was thinking about their relationship, what he would discover and what he would have to do in order for them to patch up. Most couples who never challenged one another and instead talked bad behind each other's backs had some unresolved issues that they refused to bring up and instead let them get eaten up by their own thoughts. Whether this was the case for Andersons or not, he would have to find out eventually.

John was still talking about Roberto Carlos. When he was finished, Amos nodded without really having heard what the old man had said.

He said absently, "We'll keep looking. They have to be around here somewhere."

"Should we send the footage to the mainland?" asked John. "Have someone come in and check in?"

"Nah, it'll be fine. How many guys and gals don't show up back at the portables because they are passed out from drinking or smoking?"

John shrugged. "At least once or twice a week."

"And they *always* come back," Amos assured him. "Roberto probably got drunk and passed out. Tamia just ended up in the same cups as he. Or maybe she left and didn't come back the same way, who knows."

"The two of them were as tight as coils, Amos."

"Then I dunno, we'll check in every so often and if those two aren't back by tonight, we'll do a full search of the island while the guests are asleep. If nothing by then, we'll have someone come out here to help."

"Fine." John had thought about bringing up that they were on an island, and sometimes couples went out to sea for a night swim. Shark attacks were not a thing here on Bonidada, but wildlife never followed routine 100% of the time.

In the end, he let the matter drop as Amos was fully engrossed in his spying.

At this point, another couple were coming down the wooden steps of their hut and heading towards the beach in the direction of the Andersons. It was Matt and Gabbie Winklemann. Amos watched as the couple converged on the other, and began to talk.

Another day, another dollar.

Derian opened his eyes, having heard the crunching of sand beneath two pairs of rubber flipflops. He sat up and turned to see Matt and Gabbie Winklemann coming towards them, their eyes on another set of chairs about ten yards away. They said good morning, and then made themselves comfortable. Matt had a six-pack, and Gabbie a screwdriver. She sat down into the lounge chair and after removing her shawl, laid back in her black bathing suit. She wore a wide-brimmed hat and sunglasses, and hadn't acknowledged the Andersons.

"Want one?" Matt offered one of the beers to Derian. Busch Light, Derian's most despised brand of beer; it might as well have been just flavored water as far as he was concerned.

Derian noticed that Matt was checking out his wife, staring with her outstretched legs and thighs and across her rear and up her exposed back past him. Derian sat up more, blocking Carla from his view.

"I'm good, thanks," Derian said staring directly at Matt.

Matt took the hint, and sat back while cracking open one of his beers. He took a long drink, and propped the can against his belly. He was not a big man, but he had developed a beer gut. How long would it be before Derian himself got one? Probably soon, it wasn't like he worked out anymore. There was no need.

Derian, after a moment longer of studying Mr. Winklemann, sat back in his chair and closed his eyes. He listened to the waves rolling across the sand, the distant call of a seagull. It was peaceful here, and he needed some peace and quiet in order to rethink about his life a little bit.

Derian Anderson, twenty-years serving in the military with four tours of Afghanistan under his belt. A navy seal who had experience in extracting important persons as well as taking out dangerous leaders in the middle east. He once had his own team, Seal Team 60, which consisted of five men. Only one was still alive today, that being Derian himself. He had lost his men in a bombing incident at the US Embassy in Tanzania. He had seen people shot, he's seen people die. but watching his fellow men being blown into bits made him rethink his career a bit. When he was finished, he moved to New York where he met Carla, and after three months, they married. By then Derian had found another career. One of which he felt was no different than being a Seal, although the pay was considerably better.

The pay was good, and it helped to invest a lot into Carla's line of designer clothes. A pitiful brand in Derian's opinion, but not entirely pointless as her stretch had clearly pointed out. They were richer, and her name was almost on every cover of magazines over the world. She had asked only once what he did for a living, and he had told her he worked as a contractor fixing hot tubs and jacuzzies. That was a lie, but Carla had believed it and still did so today. Although when he had started taking more and more contracts which took him away from home more, she suspected that there was another woman. The stress on her was unfair, but the truth would just be dreadful for her to understand.

He knew he wasn't making it easier by venting his anger and frustration in the same matter as she had been: bad-mouthing him to everyone and anyone when he wasn't around. He had done the same out of spite, but it did nothing more than push her away. He still loved her, and believed she loved him as well. After all, his first three contacts paid for the funding she needed to get a foot into the door and start her own line of clothes. He protected her, cared for her, and wanted nothing more than her happiness. This trip was for two reasons for Derian Anderson. One of course was to patch up the strained relationship between him and Carla, and the other was to celebrate him officially retiring from his job. Carla believed it to be the end of his time as a contractor, when in reality it was so much more.

And if that nasty creep Matthew didn't stop staring at his wife he would be the first to find out soon enough.

He glared at Matt, who smiled sheepishly and returned his gaze to the ocean while rubbing his wife's thigh. Disgusting. Guy probably watched porn too when the wifey wasn't around. Or worse, maybe he had an old Playboy which he kept at the nightstand to stare at when he did it with her. He looked the type.

Derian looked at his wife and suggested they go and check out the bar together.

"I'm fine here," came her reply without looking at him.

"I'd like you to come with me."

She turned her head to look at him. Those icy blue eyes staring at him, as if trying to read him. She never could though, even when she believed she could. At last she sighed and asked him to help tie her bikini. At least she had *some* common sense, especially with Matt right beside them.

When they were out of earshot and walking towards the resort, that was when the accusing jabs started. Whenever some guy looked at Carla uncomfortably long and Derian said something, she always had to make it a bigger deal than it already was. While most women would tend to just get out of there and leave it at that, Carla decided to use it to her advantage in order to attack Derian. But who no matter how she thought of it, no matter what she said, he was still only looking out for her own wellbeing, which is what he is doing now and why can't Carla see that? Married or not, creeps had eyes for anyone with a pair of tits, even when said-tits belonged to someone else.

But that wouldn't matter. Just more fodder for the cannon known as Carla Jean Anderson.

"Oh! Didn't like the way the guy was looking at me?" she demanded.

"Obviously not," Derian said trying to keep his voice level. Any frustration or anger audible in his voice would only amplify the heat, and cause the cannon to go off sooner, maybe even louder if he was unlucky enough.

"I wonder if what I think of him is the same way other women think of you when you stare for too long."

"Jesus, Carla, come on. Not here."

"Why? Because it's true? Now that you are on vacation being waited on by half-naked women, I bet you are *relishing* it here, aren't you?"

Derian had to bite his cheek to keep from saying anything. His anger would only result in hurting her and he didn't want that no matter how irrational she was being now. The only way to win was to not give in to her goading. This would undoubtedly piss her off, but it was better than giving her more fuel for the already-raging inferno.

"You're just gonna ignore me now?"

"What are you having?" They were approaching the Tiki Bar now, a bamboo shack with a fat Mexican wiping the plastic counter down with a washcloth.

Carla frowned, the fire still in her eyes Derian could tell despite his wife wearing sunglasses. "Mojito," she grumbled.

He ordered her drink as well as a J&B on the rocks and they sat at one of the tables that stood close to the shack near the line of palm trees. As they drank, they watched as a hermit crab scuttled across the sand towards the ocean which brought with it the salty air and soothing sound of it's rolling tide.

Feeling relaxed now, Derian decided to try his luck. He sat his drink down, and then turned to face Carla completely, who was sitting across the table from him.

"Carla," he said. "Do you really think I look at other women?"

"Obviously."

"I don't. But you don't believe me."

"Obviously."

He nodded. "Look, I chose this place so you and I could talk. *Really* talk without you busying yourself with work." He looked at her bikini and said, "I noticed you are wearing one of your brands."

A long pause, and then she asked sheepishly in a way that Derian always thought was cute, "Is it hideous?"

"No. It's lovely." It was always good to compliment her clothing, regardless of whether or not it really was 'lovely.' But Derian wasn't lying this time.

Carla's face softened, her small lips pursed around her straw. Half of the drink was gone now. "Well, thank you."

Derian nodded. "But yes, I wanted to make sure we had the time to talk. With me being retired, I will be at home more often now."

"Will you?"

He nodded again. "To be honest, I think I might take up painting or something."

That made Carla smiled. "You paint terribly though."

Derian smiled back. It was true. He was atrocious at painting. "Doesn't mean I don't enjoy it."

Carla nodded, either out of sympathy or kindness. "What would you paint first?"

"Dunno yet. Maybe I'll paint you."

That made her bark out a laugh. "You gonna paint me like one of your French ladies, Jack?"

"Maybe, if you are lucky." Derian couldn't help but keep smiling.

This was good. The coals were dying, the fighting momentarily but graciously over for now. He was happy. He was actually enjoying talking to Carla again. When was the last time they could talk like this? God but it had been a long time.

Carla looked down into her drink, as if trying to find something in the flute glass. "If you are going to be home more often, you might get lonely."

"I'll have Dante to keep me company," he said.

Dante was their Sphynx cat, who was currently being taken care of by one of Carla's friends while they were away. When they had first gotten the cat (it had been a birthday present to Carla), Derian had been repulsed by it, calling it a 'nutsack' cat. As time went on though, he had gotten attached to Dante, who always curled up on his lap when he would return home and watch television. Those were the days he would try to keep his mind occupied, and not let the earlier days get to him. That was when the trouble between him and Carla started.

Now he had to make up for both lost time, and her concerned self-esteem.

"You could work from home too," he said. "You do that anyway."

"Not everyday though."

"As often as you could then. I'd like that, anyway."

She studied him. "Would you?"

"Yes."

Carla stared a moment longer, then nodded. She took a sip of her drink and then muttered, "Sorry I was such a bitch earlier."

Derian hated it when she did that. Another one of her tactics was to say she was sorry but at the same time make it clear that she was still unhappy. As if *he* were the one actually calling her the bitch, which he never called her such a word in his life. It was her way of saying, 'I'm sorry, but not quite sorry.' He hated it when she did that, trying to sneakily put words into his mouth.

He let it go though, and decided on the safest approach. "I'm sorry too. Sorry it's been so long since we could actually sit and talk like adults."

"Well..." She reached over and took his hand. Her hands were small, with long spider-like fingers that circled around his rough knuckles. He loved her hands. He loved the softness they had, the scent of vanilla from the lotion she used, the shine of her black fingernails.

"Well," she said again. "It's a good thing we are here, isn't it?"

"It is. I think though, we should be a hundred percent honest when we actually get to talk to Mr.

Mulderich. No holds barred; let's get everything out of our system and sleep on it after. Deal?"

Carla considered this, and then gave his hand a squeeze. "Deal."

Derian was glad, and he finished his drink.

3rd Letter

Araw-araw kitang nami-miss, ate.

My sister had been six months pregnant. Her husband used to be a fisherman, until he had died from influenza. She was living with my mother and I, as she was unable to care for the child by herself. I remember seeing her go to work the night of her demise. I remember feeling really bad and didn't understand why. The next I saw her, she was dead.

She was missing three days since the night of her disappearance. Everyone searched throughout the village as well as into the jungle. When someone finally *did* find her, a wild boar had taken her body and was eating away at her flesh. The boar had been black, and everyone went into hysteria. People stabbed the pig in the back, whipped it with the tail of a stingray, and some even went as far as to throw holy water upon it even as it screamed and snapped it's dangerous tusks. When we finally got to see what had happened to my sister, we were mortified. The pig had eaten huge chunks of her leg, most of the meat missing and exposing bone. But the most terrible sight of all, was her torso. She had been ripped open from between her bosom all the way down to her naval. Everything inside her was gone, including my unborn niece. She was buried, and my mother told me we were to go to Capiz for more herbs and to enlist the help of a true Babaylan. When I inquired what good such a person would be, she looked me in the eye and questioned my faith.

I've *always* questioned my faith. All the superstitions I had been taught to believe and fear my whole childhood was a lie. I had come to this conclusion myself, when there was never any circumstantial evidence to prove it. I was after all, a 'rational and yet naïve child' as my mother often called me. My sister had always been the dependable one, the one that kept the traditions as a woman. As a man, I would need to ensure that my family followed the holy laws of God, and kept the peace with the spirits of evil. But now I saw evil as nothing more than what mankind has made. My sister had been killed by a dangerous serial killer from the very city that my mother wanted to reach out for to gain help. To me, that was like sticking your hand into a hornet's nest to enlist their help after being bitten by a snake.

There is a saying that I know now, that I wish I knew back then. That too much reliance on religion made you ignorant. However, too much reliance on science and logic would make you arrogant. There has to be a middle ground in order for one to live a rational life. You had to have faith, but you must also have the capability to ask questions and make a hypothesis. Because both can easily be changed at a moment's notice. Pluto might become a planet again. A secret passage of some bible or holy book might be dug out of some archeological digging site.

But I was young back then. I was too arrogant to believe my mother and trust in my village who had killed every black chicken, dog, any animal with a black coat that they came across. They would spread salt or ashes on window sills and make sure they had jars of special coconut oil nearby, as well as bolos at their bedside or a whip made of a stingray's tail. My mother had one, and nowadays she always kept it at her side, coiled and reminding me as I think about it today like a Filipino Indiana Jones. Wrappings and knots from Father Bacani's old robes had been hung on doorsills, and the church's holy water had been distributed to all.

We were to leave the following day, my mother and I. During work, I was surprised to see a crowd on the shore while I was fishing that day. There was a man being whipped and beaten by the general public, hands forcing his face to look up at the sun as if they expected him to burn. I knew him. He was someone from Capiz who had moved out here to get out of the city which he too believed was cursed. Because of this, he had been shunned and ignored for the time he had been in our village. Today however, he was to take all the blame for the two dead who turned up in our village. He was exorcized by one of the other priests of the church, had holy water splashed onto the wounds inflicted by the stingray whips. My mother was there, watching, rubbing spices into the wounds to see if a reaction would come. Hissing sounds with pain, but nothing like what she was expected.

"Malinis siya," I heard her say, and only then did the people leave him alone. Left him on the shore, bleeding and sobbing.

I had gone to him then, and helped him to his feet. He had thanked me feebly, and hobbled to his hut. He didn't want anything to do with me or the village any longer. He suffered from XDP, dystonia as I had learned upon further research here in the States. Back home, they called it the curse of Turning, and being a former resident of Capiz only solidified that belief among my people. His body was always stiff and rigid, his limbs twisting as his muscles remained contracted. As far as I or anyone else knew, he was only able to relax while asleep. This did not make it easy, for many believed he was in the process of turning into a monster. Now that I know the actual word for the disease he carried, it only makes me pity him more. Because even if I were to go back and inform everyone back home of what he and many other men on the island had, no one would believe me. They would call me arrogant still, for believing that it was merely a sickness, rather than a curse of being touched by a demon.

Then again, maybe we have all been touched in some way shape or form. Some of us are just better at hiding the curse than others, hiding our sin and evil intentions. Like the serial killer who stalked my home and killed my sister was walking among us. I believed it then, and I believe that I was right thinking back on it.

How can you find a killer walking among you, who walked and talked like you?

Nine

While Derian and Carla were having their drinks, Adam and Cynthia had gone out onto their balcony and Adam laid back completely naked, only sunscreen covering his body as he lounged out and allowed the sun to bake him like a gingerbread man. Beside him, Cynthia was likewise tanning, reading a paperback while on her stomach. They remained that way for half an hour, flipping in-between before returning inside to shower and get ready for the day ahead.

At the same time, Anton was helping Jessica out of the shower and drying her off with a fluffy towel. He then dressed her, and when she expressed that she was tired he lifted her out of her chair and gently got her in bed. He tells her that he's going to go out and get a drink. He was walking towards the resort and had passed Derian and Carla as he entered the resort.

Cain and Winnifred were at the bottom of their stairwell, talking to their neighbors who happened to be the Woldemontts. They were talking about their night's stay, about Brad's music, and the conversation was directed towards the beach where they lounged out with Matt and Gabbie, Matt now watching the two women who were talking while their husbands took a dip into the warm waters.

Finally emerging from their huts were Ethan and Shawlyn, Ethan walking slowly beside his pregnant wife as they made their way down. They spotted Adam and Cynthia having just finished getting ready, and waved them over, asking if they would like to do lunch together. They said that was a great idea.

Matt watched them too from a distance, his body smothered in lotion and him wishing he was smothered somewhere else.

He had an erection. The little guy had bulged in his swimming shorts and he made sure it wasn't completely visible. It was there not because of the women, and age didn't particularly matter to him. It is because of the *possibilities*. No, it wasn't because there were many women here, young, old, mostly Mexican or black, the whites being mostly the other guests. It wasn't necessarily about *them* that made him so horny. It was what he was *planning* to do which got him excited. Gabbie, who had noticed him readjust his shorts, lowered the paperback she had been working on and glowered at him.

"Matthew."

He turned to look at her, not annoyed but also not happy. He was just there, a blank slate, those empty eyes seeming to absorb her now. That was good. She was supposed to be *all* those eyes were absorbing.

"Seriously? You're doing it here?" she demanded bitterly.

"Doing what?" he asked, sounding exasperated.

"You know damn well 'what,'" she practically hissed. She slammed her book shut, frustrated now. "Am I not enough or something? We are here for *counseling*, aren't we? Might as well throw down our cards now."

Yes, dear. As a matter of fact, you aren't enough at all. You never were. You think the girl at the club was the only one? You are delirious if you really think that. You won't ever have to see her *again, but that won't stop me because quite frankly, you are* not *enough. I have needs, and you don't satisfy me. No one does.*

"You *are* enough," he said instead. He was not sorry that his wife had caught him flirting with the girl, a pretty little blonde named Alex Higgins who was twenty-two years old and had a rocking ass. No, he was sorry that he got *caught*. Because now it only complicated things, and he needed her to be ignorant regarding the real reason he had booked this trip almost a year ago. Not in celebration of another successful year for the new search engine, at least in their particular branch (in fact this year was the absolute worst year, and Matt was counting on over a hundred lawsuits and stations closing down due to thousands upon millions of accumulated debt; not that Gabbie knew about that either), but because what used to satisfy him was nothing anymore. It was like pornography, you watch it too much and you either grow out of it or simply become numb; nothing looks or sound good and you end up deeper down the rabbit hole where bestiality, dominance, violence, things like that helped you to burp the snake. He had planned this trip as a farce to celebrate an unsuccessful year. Returning to the States was not an option, at least not with Gabbie anymore. Should she find out what had happened to their firm, well, that would only make things *more* complicated.

No, Isla Bonidada was to be Matthew's last little going away party. He had booked this trip with Gabbie not out of a desire to rekindle something that wasn't even there. He had booked it so he could do the one thing that has been on his mind for the past eight months. One last thing that would make what had happened to Alex Higgens look like a misdemeanor.

Gabbie finding out that he was a flirt (for the time being) only complicated things. There had been a long conversation both in the car and at the house. Gabbie wouldn't leave him though. She was Catholic, and did not want to be shunned by her family because of divorce. But ever since then they had not slept in the same bed together until last night, when Gabbie apparently felt safe and secure enough that she had Matt's complete and undivided attention.

Well, Gabbie, you couldn't think anything further from the truth.

"Then why don't you *prove* it?" Gabbie demanded, likewise drawing Matt back from his thoughts. "Be a man and *prove* it!"

"Not so loud, you'll draw attention."

"You're *already* drawing attention, looking at them all and panting like a hungry dog!"

"Keep your voice down," Matt said standing up, disregarding his boner and saying he is going to go and shower before lunch is served at the resort. But Gabbie wasn't done yet. She followed him still calling him out on his bullshit and calling him names. With each step up the wooden boardwalk, Matt lost more and more of his patience and was suddenly glad that he was alone with Gabbie now. He shut the door behind them and locked it, and turned to face Gabbie who was now pointing at him with her closed paperback, her face a mask of red fury.

"You are a *pig*, Matt Winklemann. I should *never* have married you! All these secrets, you going out behind my back, no wonder it takes forever just for you to cum!"

"Keep your voice down, Gab," Matt warned her, now thinking about the gun in his duffle bag. He considered it, but thought it too loud.

"I will not!" she snarled. "You hear me, I will not!"

Making a decision, Matt brushed past her and entered the kitchen. He proceeded to grab a glass from the cabinet and fill it with water from the refrigerator. All this listening to shouting was making him thirsty. All the while Gabbie continued her little rant as he drank watching her through the bottom of the glass. The distorted whirls of the glass made her look monstrous, not at all like the woman he had married.

Think about that, Gabbie. You have no idea how lucky you have been. You could have been like any of the others. But I chose to marry you. You have no idea how lucky you were that you got to marry me. Because if you didn't...

"You know what?" Gabbie said throwing her paperback at his chest. It bounced off of him and landed to the floor with a slapping sound. He didn't even flinch. "Fuck this. Fuck this vacation, and fuck *you*! I hate you, Matt. I cannot do this anymore, as soon as we can get off this island, I want a divorce. You hear me?"

Matt had finished his drink. She was close, a yard maybe five feet away. "I hear you," he said.

She placed her fists on her hips, her lips pressed hard together. "Then say *something*. Don't just stand there."

"You *really* want me to say something?"

"Yes!"

"Okay."

In one quick motion, Matt lashed out and clocked Gabbie across the head with the glass. It shattered, spilling glass everywhere as Gabbie cried out in shock and pain as glass dug into her temple. He was still holding the bottom of the glass, which now looked like what a bottle does smashed in order to stab and gore. With it, he seized a fistful of Gabbie's hair and pulled her in close. He drove the glass into her throat, blood immediately spilling into the cup as her eyes bulged. Matt felt his erection returning, as he looked into those eyes and forced Gabbie to the floor, driving the glass deeper into it to where he thought he could hear the glass grinding against bone.

She gurgled and choked, her arms and legs swinging feebly about in an attempt to get him off but he was too strong. Blood pooled beneath her head, and Matt punched her in the nose, crushing it and causing her head to bounce off the floor. All at once he felt so much better; as if the cure all along was to just go with the flow. He never liked complications, and now this…

He held her tight as she bled, relishing in the sight of her, feeling the rage come and letting it ride its wave.

Taking her bikini top, he ripped it right off to reveal her perky breasts and he squeezed one of them hard, his thumb and index finger crushing the nipple in a pinch that would have felt like a clamp had seized it. His hands were covered with her blood, and he reached into his pants and using her blood as a lubricant, began to jerk himself off.

"Oh, you're satisfying me *now*, Gab. How does it feel?"

More choking, more gurgling, more blood spilling. The disbelieving eyes staring back at him frightened, hurt, and begging the question, Why?

This was what truly excited him. It was a dull excitement, due to it being done too many times before, but since it was his wife, it had that special tinge to it. It would be nothing compared to what he planned to do here on Isla Bonidada. He was just getting started.

He jerked himself off as Gabbie died, slowly, painfully, watching his face twist and spasm in his sick, deranged excitement. This complication was finally done with, and he could treasure her still until the time came.

Meanwhile, it smelled the blood upon passing but it had eaten well the night before. It did not need to gorge itself. So it kept walking past the boardwalk leading to the Winklemann hut back towards the resort, where lunch was to be served before the day officially began. It strutted about feeling good in its new skin as it took everything in with sharp and intelligent eyes of crimson.

Ten

Lunch was served on a back patio near the rear of the resort. It was a high-fenced area with palm trees reaching over it like giant hands.

There was a bocce ball and badminton court out in the planted grass, and the picnic tables were stationed on a fifty-by-fifty platform of concrete and wood carved with tribal markings. Large umbrellas stood tall over the guests who drank glass upon glass of iced tea and margaritas, and the workers waited on them hand and foot while Amos stopped by each table one by one to discuss any questions or concerns about the schedule for this week including where to go if say a couple had the whole day to themselves; including what was available and what wasn't.

The general rule he liked to follow and thought it always worked out in years past, was that only one couple would have a different 'experience' per day, each one unique even if it happens at the same spot like the grotto or the cove. There were more places he hinted on the island that the guests didn't know about, and wouldn't know about until the day they got to see it.

His first official counseling session was with the Whites which would take place *inside* the waterfall emptying into the cove. The Duncans would be hiking and ziplining from the peak of Crockett's Grotto. Anton and Jessica Bateman had the first free day to do whatever they wanted on the beach, resort, or in their own hut. The Ashtons and Jacksons would have a double-date beyond the cove where they would be partaking in diving along the coral reefs, as well as take a boat trip around the drop-off. The Woldemontts would be learning how to windsurf, and the Andersons would be wine tasting and would have the rest of the day to themselves thereafter. Finally, the Winklemanns would have their own spa day back at the Gazebo, which Amos was worried about since Matt had come to lunch alone, saying his wife was sick.

"Maybe food poisoning," he had said. "No need to be concerned, I'm sure she is fine. She just needs to rest and not be disturbed."

"I'm sorry to hear that," Amos said sympathetically. Kyra expressed her own sympathy by giving the man a second slice of chocolate cake after a wonderful chicken and rice lunch with some tropical fruit.

Matt thanked them for their hospitality, and dug into his dessert once they had left him alone. What did it matter if his wife wasn't around to join him for a spa? What did it matter that they weren't going to at least try to enjoy their last days together? He sure as hell enjoyed the latest morning they had together and would no doubt enjoy being with her until the end finally arrived. Getting all the stress rubbed out of him would only make his last night on earth all the more relaxing. He'd more than likely be getting rubbed out by some sexy hardbody masseur who he could probably grope and bribe with a couple hundred. Maybe a little more than grope if he was lucky enough. He would at the very least like to have one last good fuck that wasn't going to be his wife's corpse.

As for the others, they all enjoyed their meal and were excited for the day ahead. The day was hot, but the wind coming south was refreshing and smelled of salt and seaweed. They thanked every worker and tipped with what money they brought along with them, all except for Anton and Jessica who barely said a word the entire time.

Ethan Duncan in particular was watching him, thinking what a creepy character he could be for a story.

When they had finished eating, they had joined the Whites and began discussing about how they should meet up later in the evening and share a couple of drinks on the beach (with the exception of Shawlyn). Now that lunch was finished everyone was free to roam about until they were to meet with their specific guide out front, and while most stayed on the patio to talk or go play a round of bocce ball, Matthew Winklemann stood up from his spot and decided to walk around the resort.

He passed through the front entrance, talked to the desk clerks and then went about the vast hallway and observed the many rooms and stations past the ballroom where they had been last night. He mentally counted how many paces he was walking as he did so.

There was a stairwell to the left and right after the ballroom before the hall continued on. It no doubt went to the maintenance or hotel rooms upstairs. When there was not enough room for the patrons, this resort was no doubt used in order for those unwilling to pay the price for the huts so that they too could enjoy the marvels of Isla Bonidada. The stairwells were blocked off with a thick barricade rope and a sign that read 'authorized personnel only.' Matt knew that the workers didn't live in the building, they lived in some portables or complexes out beyond the back patio. He had heard some of the workers discuss it in Spanish. He wondered if that Amos guy and his 'partner' John lived here though.

He doubted it. He also doubted that there was any reason for them to keep a lot of things up there if they weren't expecting guests. He moved on, deciding to stick to the ground floor for now. If he can risk going up there later though, he probably would.

Sure enough, there was an indoor pool and spa, a workout room with dumbbells and motor equipment in case anyone wanted to work out, and a side entrance to the kitchens which was located in the back of the ballroom. Further down was a sort of game room, with foosball, air hockey, a miniature bowling alley, dart boards, a lot everything you could expect to find in a bar or some guy's mancave. There was even a miniature movie theater with leather seating wrapped around a flatscreen almost a hundred and twenty inches corner to corner. Matt could imagine the sound quality by looking at the surround speakers. He wondered how his favorite movie would have looked on a television such as this.

A couple of bathrooms, a supply closet for the housekeeping crews, a conference room with a large oak table with red velvet seating, and an indoor tennis course soon followed. There were other rooms as well, but the doors were locked and Matt couldn't look through for there were no windows.

He passed by many workers and made sure not to attempt any door without first making sure he was alone. One of the doors looked locked with just a key, but two of them had a keypad. None of the other doors throughout the resort had keypads, which meant these were important. He noted how many steps each door was located at, fifty-two, sixty, and seventy. The last door was the rear emergency exit at ninety-two paces. There was one more door which upon checking, saw that it was the year electrical and plumbing room. Thick pipes passing hot and cold water stood out the most, an emergency crank beside it. In a plexiglass box, stood the power supply which no doubt went to a power station somewhere on the island. If he could find the station (probably by following some ground wires) he would have access to the main power system.

"Excuse me."

Matt turned, looking the part of an embarrassed tourist who was lost. The girl standing before him was small, Mexican, and very pretty. In her hotel gown, he could see a small pair of breasts but wide hips. Just his type. The name badge on the gown's lapel dubbed the girl 'Tamia.' Interesting name.

"I'm sorry, I guess I got lost. I'm looking for the bathroom?"

"You passed it sir, down that way." She threw a thumb back in the direction she came without taking her eyes off of him. He would have to play it cool now. She didn't look suspicious, but that didn't necessarily mean anything.

He apologized again. "I'll head back right now."

He walked by her, her eyes staring straight into his own. He was always the one to study a person by their eyes, and this girl was no different. But something about the brown spheres that stared back at him made him uneasy. For one, there wasn't the slightest bit of uneasiness or discomfort from the girl. She wasn't afraid, annoyed, or even suspicious. Her eyes looked dead, as if she didn't care what he did just as long as it wasn't her having to tell him no.

Also, they were close enough for Matt to see his reflection in her eyes. His face inside them was upside down. That didn't seem natural to Matt but by then he had already passed the woman and was making the ninety-two paces back towards the main lobby of the resort, not the forty-nine paces it would take to go to the restrooms/locker rooms.

He dared a glance back. The woman hadn't moved. She wasn't following him to make sure he was leaving in the right direction. She had gone into the maintenance room, he could tell by the opened door. A few seconds later, she stepped back out. She paused, watching him go and still not following. Matt didn't like that. It wasn't normal. He had the feeling that the girl was still watching him even as he entered the bathroom and stood alone before a urinal with his cock out. Might as well pee a little. It was difficult though, for he still felt watched even though he was way out of that girl's sight. It felt as if she was looking at him through the walls.

That's stupid, he thought, scorning himself for being an idiot and getting scared like a stupid little kid. But that didn't stop his hairs from standing on end, his arms now riddled with gooseflesh.

Just a girl. Nothing else.

Still…

He zipped up his fly and stepped out of the bathroom without washing his hands. He turned the corner and leaned against the wall, now watching the entrance to the main hall. He waited there for five minutes, saying hello to every person walking by and politely declining any help or refreshments from them. The girl hadn't come back yet. He dared to look down the hall again to see if she was still there.

Of course she wasn't. She was a worker, she could have gone anywhere just like everyone else down that hall. More workers shuffled along, one of which had a black dog walking alongside them. A security dog? No, a terrier is not a good guard dog, Matt thought. He had nothing to fear though, he wasn't concerned with the girl. None of the workers around would have noticed him or her passing by, the conversation had taken place between them and them alone.

She might tell someone though...

Who cares, I'll just say I got lost.

Besides, he wanted to take some time to walk around the island after his spa and see if he couldn't find a power station of some sort, something that no doubt *wouldn't* be so crowded with workers. For now, he just had to enjoy his time here while he could.

Tamia though...

He'd fuck her. For sure. Creepy as it had been the way she handled the situation with him, he'd fuck her all right. More than that, actually.

Maybe he would.

Eleven

There she goes again...

Paul Jackson was at the bar getting an Apple Jim Bean on the rocks, the waitress, a pretty Mexican with dyed blonde hair having topped his drink with a green apple slice on the rim. He tipped the woman and then turned around to spot his wife conversing with that hotel manager, Adam and his wife. The conversation looked innocent enough, Cynthia laughing at something Victoria had said and Adam smiling politely. His wife was probably either telling them a story or complimenting Victoria on her dress. She herself was in a white dress that covered her bathing suit, all set to go for the diving trip with the Ashtons. A nice conversation between a woman in her forties and a young couple who were starting off strong and rich, unlike her who married into a business that had a rough start but eventually became a retail powerhouse; not a Walmart or Target mind you but still very profitable. She married into the *business*, but not Paul Jackson.

She had married him before he got rich, yes. But even still back in California, he was better off than most in his neighborhood. He lived in a barren desert area away from most of the cities, in a town of less than a thousand people, Victoria Parkison being one of them. Jacksons was one of two markets in town, and it had grown only more popular as more people got off the highway. Unlike his one and only competitor at the time, Mary and Max's, he had access to a lot of resources thanks to his father's partnerships the factories many of the men in town worked at. As a result, he had better product, more of it, and was able to afford low and yet sustainable prices. This made the market for a second store on the horizon, and by then Victoria had eyes for Paul and the business, and Paul like any man would, fell in love. They would marry once they opened his third store in Redmond Oregon.

By the time he opened his sixth store in Texas, with the others in Washington, Arizona, Utah, and New Mexico, Paul and his new wife had married and moved to Colorado where they would open the first central store which would lead to more being opened on the other side of the U.S. It was here when his business would boom to the third and second degrees. It was also unfortunately when his marriage went *down* a degree or two, with the discovery of his wife with another man in his bed.

He had just gotten the news of another branch in Colorado and had rushed immediately home, leaving his current store in the hands of his most trusted manager. He had purchased flowers and champagne, his usual routine for bringing good news. He had hurried home as quick as he could meaning to surprise Victoria and celebrate. By the time he got there, he already knew something was wrong. He didn't see or hear anything, but thinking back on it there *had* been a feeling, brief and minor, but it had been there all the same. He would sometimes beat himself up at night for not understanding the sensation sooner, but it only left him feeling miserable considering that there was no way anyone could have predicted what he saw.

He had pounded up the stairs two at a time and shoved open his bedroom door hard enough to make it crash into the wall just as he caught sight of a man trying to sneak out the bedroom window, his wife trying to get dressed while still in bed. There had been a fight, the bottle of champagne thrown at the man and causing him to topple over and fall onto the driveway. The distance between their bedroom window and driveway was not great but definitely damage-inducing, and the man had suffered from a terrible concussion and the kind of gashes and scrapes often associated with driveway accidents. Despite his injuries, Adrian Milton did not press charges given the circumstances. That had been a good thing but at the time during his outrage, Paul had wished the motherfucker had broken his neck.

He had turned his attention from the presently-unconscious adulterer to his wife, and a greater fight ensued. It started with the usual 'how could you's' and the 'why's' and gradually became a screamfest, both him and Victoria bellowing at the top of their lungs and pushing Paul to the point where he thought of not just slapping her but also punching her teeth in. This was something else that he often wondered in the dead of night, whether or not he *should* have. He never did though, and the two put their little 'issue' on pause in order to take Adrian Milton to the hospital.

Once everything was taken care of and both Paul and Victoria were home, the two talked. Despite how angry he was, how hurt he was, Paul wasn't going to leave Victoria. He didn't believe in divorce since God hated such a thing as much as sin itself. Victoria decided she wasn't going to leave him either, but it was for more selfish reasons rather than religion. She promised that this had been the only time, that she had been stuck in some limbo and didn't know how to get out of it. None of this made sense to Paul, but Victoria had asked him to give her a chance and to forgive her, and he had promised he would try.

Trying turned out to be a bigger mistake on Paul's part. It wasn't just the betrayal that made him feel so miserable, but it was the humiliation more than anything. The feeling of being a cuckold because that was what he was and called himself whenever he looked at himself in the mirror, watched as his marriage went from bad to worse. It got to the point where he and Victoria hardly said a word to one another, and there was no passion for love anymore when they went to bed. What was worse, was that after a period of time, she never stopped. She was careful though, getting good hotels so that she never cheated on her husband in their own bed again, but by then the damage was already done; the bonfire had raged into an inferno and when Paul was finally told the truth after he confronted her about the statements saying he spent a few nights at one of the best hotels in Colorado, he finally snapped. He didn't scream or hurt Victoria or anything some men may find appropriate to do once they found out that they were cucked again. Fool me once, shame on you. Fool me twice…

At any rate, Paul Jackson gave up on Victoria completely, and had gone completely numb.

They got two separate beds, and now that they were rich and had a bigger house back in Colorado, they practically slept in separate rooms. In the news and on the paper, they represented the perfect couple working together for a brighter future, bringing Jackson's to the United States which would never go the route of Walmart which would run smaller businesses out. They wanted to represent a community of family and kindship, and they had become very good at it. Behind closed doors, there was steeping hatred and adultery. Two completely separate people living separate lives until it was time to smile for the camera. Paul and Victoria Jackson were no better than two strangers forced in the same studio apartment regardless of the reason behind it. He had his own bed, his own bathroom, study, everything. Hell, he could get another woman for himself if he wanted to.

His lawyer had ensured him that everything that was his remained his in the event of a divorce, and Victoria would receive legal repercussions should she act against him via his property. The same was provided to her and all her personal belongings. As for things they shared, from food to their wedding albums and gifts, they agreed to disagree and shared it still, and would deal with the splitting should the day ever come that they finally break their vows. Evidently, she had spoken to some attorneys of her own, consequently shackling him to the rabid dog that was his marriage.

Shackled was too good a word for it. Imprisoned wasn't much better. What's worse was that even if Paul could consider himself a sonofabitch and just say fuck it, leave Victoria and start anew business or not, he couldn't bring himself to do it. He was too afraid to let Victoria go despite her unwillingness to even be near him. He couldn't even bring himself to find another woman for his life, he just didn't have it in him. And while no one knew what was really going on behind closed doors, he felt less and less of a man with every passing year Victoria remained in his home, as his 'wife.' He was successful, yes, but a failure when it comes to marriage, he never felt more less of a man than he did presently. It was this indecision that really made him feel like a failure. Left him staying awake at night, thinking about that first day, and how the events after had led to this pathetic excuse of a marriage.

All because of you, he would say. *You pathetic cuck.*

This trip to Isla Bonidada was meant to help rekindle what they had seen in each other before, before both of them became no more than relics and Jackson's was willed off to his right-hand man back in the States.

At first, Victoria had been hesitant about the trip. Expressing that what they had was working just fine and that maybe it was too little too late. Sure, they were still legally married, but there was no romance left in them, and perhaps it was the fact that they had no children between them that made this lifestyle much easier. In the end, she agreed to go with Paul, if he really wanted to see if there was anything left between them. Paul had been delighted, thinking maybe this was their chance not only to rekindle, but to gain some closure on what their life together had been and what it could be now.

But the way Victoria was looking at that manager now, proved that nothing had changed, and nothing could be 'rekindled.' Victoria was a whore, and he had married into her willingly, and had chosen to stay with her. Like Hosea who was told by God to marry the harlot, Gomer. There was a point to it, and Hosea believed it just as Paul believed there was a reason why he and Victoria had wedded in the first place.

But let's be real with ourself, cuck. You're not Hosea, and God sure as hell didn't tell you to stay with her. You chose it. You chose it, and you're too much of a fucking loser to end it.

Loser. Just as bad as pathetic, almost as bad as a cuck.

In the end, Victoria didn't give a rat's ass about marriage. She didn't give an inch about Paul, and little by little, Paul had been losing his own faith in his belief in this marriage. Now that he was alone at the bar watching his wife flirt openly with the hotel manager, he had no faith left to give. Now he didn't care if anything was rekindled. Now he only hoped that she would burn. Have a heart attack or get raped or something, something that would hurt her.

But again, how many times had he told himself that?

Paul started when he felt something cold and wet touch his fingertips. He looked down to see a black terrier looking up at him with large black eyes. Smiling at the dog, he stooped and began scratching the mutt's ears. After a moment, it began to wag it's tail appreciatively, still looking up at Paul with at least some hint of pity.

At least someone wants my attention… he thought.

While Paul was struggling with himself, John was looking at the cameras puzzled and a little disturbed. He had watched the Winklemann man walking alone down the hall, not receiving any attention from the workers passing through when they should have inquired where he was in the first place. Then he stopped near one of the pump rooms, which was a big problem. He was relieved when someone finally decided to ask what was going on, but he was immediately disturbed to see who it was.

He had watched Tamia watch the Winklemann guy return to the main lobby, only to disappear into the pump room herself. There was no camera inside the room, and John cursed that fact for the fifth time this year.

A moment later, and then the dog came out. John sat there, rewatching the footage puzzled and going back several hours finding no trace of the dog ever going *into* the pump room.

How the hell did that mutt get in there?

He rewound the footage again, saw Tamia come out of the women's restroom, and a moment later, saw the dog walking into the bathroom along with a group of women earlier. Earlier footage revealed nothing of Tamia having gone in there.

"What the hell?" he demanded, now watching the dog who was with Paul Jackson, receiving attention near the bar. He radioed someone to go and check on the pump room, and he waited anxiously while watching the dog still. He watched as Mr. Jackson loved on the dog and gave Rosco the attention he clearly wanted. John was thinking how big the dog had gotten, and if he had rolled in something back at the grotto for his coat seemed a shade darker, almost pitch-black like soot. At the same time, he occasionally glanced back at the camera pointing at the end of the hall near the pump room, hoping Tamia would step out of there.

Victor, the man John had called, was coming down the hall and he had disappeared into the pump room. John felt his heartbeat flutter, his muscles tensing as he awaited his man's report. After a brief moment of silence, Victor asked John to go back to channel four and he did so.

"Talk to me," he told Victor through the receiver.

Be-boop, went the walkie. "No one's in here," Victor confirmed. "Place is dead quiet."

"Got it. Thanks for checking, Victor. Lock the door on your way out please."

"You got it."

John returned to channel one and slumped into his security chair. He felt sick to his stomach and didn't understand, nor did he appreciate it. Tamia Gonzalez had not reported in, and she and her boyfriend were M.I.A. He had to have been mistaken, that couldn't have been her.

Then who was it, and where did she go? And where did the dog come from?

John returned his gaze to the main lobby. Paul Jackson had met with his wife and the Whites, and Rosco was padding alongside another worker who played with him generously while making sure to keep in pace of her current destination. He didn't like that dog. He never had to begin with, now seeing it and that girl

(*again, who the hell is she?*)

had perform some sort of magic act (if one could call it that), he had an unsettling feeling in the pit of his gut. He would have to keep a close eye on the dog, and that woman should she ever come up again.

Right, what am I gonna tell the others? 'Hey, everyone. There is someone around the resort who looks like Tamia but I don't think that is her. Can you give me a holler if you see her or someone that looks like her? Much appreciated. While you're at it, keep an eye on that dog. If it is in one room and ends up in another without explanation, let me know immediately.

Dumb. It was dumb to even try to explain it to himself and John was dumb to try and word it as well as he had anyway.

Fuck it, he was just tired. He hardly got enough sleep nowadays, it was a miracle he was still functioning. He wasn't young anymore, he had to come to grips with that at some point or another. His sleep had only gotten worse when that ship wrecked on the shore a while back.

That ship…

A crackle of static followed by a clear voice. "John, this is Jorge, can we go to two?"

"Yeah, switching." He keyed the appropriate buttons, glad for the distraction as he relayed, "Go ahead."

"John, there's a boat coming in from the west."

"West? You mean east?"

"No, west. I'm looking at the compass now, I'm calling from the northwest tower."

John checked his watch. They were expecting a shipment around four this afternoon, but the weather was beginning to change drastically. Wind was coming in harshly from the west, and on the mainland that didn't necessarily mean anything. But out here in the ocean, the weather could change at the drop of a hat. There hadn't been anything that alerted John or his men as of yet, but he was to keep an eye on the weather forecast and report anything to Amos and the rest of the crew. If a storm were to come in, they would have to bring the guests back and make sure they stay within the confines of the resort, and would have to resort (no pun intended) to other measures of entertainment and counseling for the couples who came here to relax and enjoy themselves.

Also… nothing should have been coming in from the west. That was open water; All shipments usually came in from the mainland unless Crockett notified them.

"It a shipper?" John asked Jorge. "A barge or something from Asia?"

"No, doesn't look like it."

John asked what he was beginning to dread. "Pirates?"

A year ago, some pirates off the coast had come by and decided the tour and snorkeling boats would be easy pickings. There were always someone looking to pawn off some rich family members. The buccaneers had been spotted in time and the boats were brought in immediately and the guests barricaded in the resort. As soon as the pirates reached shore they were surprised by the crew of Isla Bonidada who were all trained in arms and had been able to neutralize the threat so that the coast guard could come and arrest them. There were hidden firearms throughout the resort in case such an attack took place again. Throughout John's many years here there had been only one attack by pirates, and one by some cartel members who had caught wind of the resort. Crockett made sure such events never took place again on his island.

Jorge answered, "No, not pirates I don't think. It kinda looks like a sailboat."

"Sailboat?"

"Yeah, the sail is torn to shit and everything. Roughly sixty or seventy meters off the shore."

Close. "Is it coming straight for the shore?"

"Nah, it looks like it's just drifting."

"Keep an eye on it and report any changes to me. Go back to one for now."

After switching, he called Max Benson and told the sailor to switch to two. Once on the channel, he told Benson the following.

"We have a possible straggler off the coast near the north-western tower. Can you have someone take over for the scuba trip and take a look at it? We dunno what it is."

"Uhhhh yeah, I can have Jessica take over. But a straggler? How big?"

"Small, sailboat or so Jorge says. I'm looking at the camera on that tower now... I see it, although it's smaller than I first imagined it."

"Any passengers?"

"I can't tell. That's where you come in."

"Jesus, where are all these random boats coming from?"

John wished he knew. It would put his mind at least somewhat at ease.

Twelve

Amos had been informed of the strange boat not far from the coast. He was aware that Max was planning to go out for a wellness check, and John was to keep him updated.

With this information in mind, he helped the couples into their proper vehicles so that they could go out and enjoy their time together on the island, meanwhile he and the Whites were heading to the Cove for some (cough-cough) 'professional' marital counseling.

The four-wheeler bumped and bounced the whole way there, him sitting in the front with the driver and the Whites behind them enjoying the scenery of the lush jungle to their left and the beach to their right. Amos turned and flashed a warm smile in their direction as he asked what they thought of Isla Bonidada so far.

"It's wonderful," Cynthia White exclaimed. She placed a hand on her husband's knee, which seemed to surprise Adam which Amos thought was peculiar but he was unsurprised.

It was common for folks to come here all stressed, but eventually they turned to one another for comfort and half the time, counseling was just utter bullshit. Amos thought he was one of the few professionals in the world to admit that. To him, counseling was filler that got the ball rolling and the couple figured things out for themselves; They just needed a little push.

Whatever was going on with these two, they weren't thinking about it, and that was a good sign. They were focused more on the trip and each other. Now it was Amos' turn to make sure they resolved their issues before they went back home and dealt with the everyday stress of life. Sometimes what people really needed was a good night's sleep, no interruptions or distractions from the rest of the world, and most importantly, each other in a place of refuge.

Cynthia was still expressing her love of the place. "The food is amazing, the island is breathtaking, and I'm having a really good time. *We* are having a really good time." A smile for Adam, who was grinning like a fox now.

"Yeah," he agreed. "It's really nice. It was a good idea to come here, even just for the ambience."

Amos nodded. "It is a beautiful place. Can't help but think I might miss it a little. This is my last voyage here. You and your new friends are my last 'patients on vacations' as I'd like to call 'em. I hope you aren't too disappointed that your first official day is with me."

"Not at all!" Adam assured him. "We are excited to see the Cove and get to know you."

"I'm flattered, but it will mostly be me getting to know you and you two knowing each other again."

The two nodded smiling, but Amos could see the hesitation in their eyes. There it was, hiding in plain sight. But they weren't arguing or declining, which was a good sign. Easy first couple. Amos couldn't ask for a better day so far- Provided that business with the strange boat goes well, whatever that was about.

A beautiful gazebo had been set up by the cove shoreline with two comfy plush chairs and a sturdy wooden one for Amos. He preferred chairs that were sturdy and firm as opposed to soft and relenting. He and the Whites stepped out of the vehicle and after thanking Josiah for the ride, he led them to the gazebo where a beautiful brunch of fruit, nuts, bottled water, fruit smoothies with rum, and chocolate fingerlings. He told the two to take a seat and once they were all seated around, Amos settled in without a notepad as he felt that it distracted him from the task at hand. It was a beautiful day, and the sea breeze felt cool and refreshing, the cove as gorgeous as ever.

"Arright," he said getting to the nitty gritty. "I have one question for you two. We are in complete isolation now, no one is here except you two and me, and this is where the true meaning of Bonidada begins."

"Okay..." Adam said, his wife remaining silent beside him but likewise watching Amos nervously.

"Why are you here?"

For a long time, all that could be heard was the churning of the sea, and the occasional squawk of an exotic bird. Adam and Cynthia White looked at each other for minutes, not saying anything, their eyes seeming to read into one another and communicate telepathically. Amos waited patiently, allowing the couple as much time as they needed to gather their thoughts as well as their courage to speak up. As he waited however, he could not help but notice Cynthia's beauty. She wasn't necessarily sexy by his standards, but her small stature and pleasant cheeks made her look pretty enough. Cute was a better word, he decided. His eyes glanced down upon her legs, thinking them a good pair. Her small hands were playing with each other in her lap, wresting as if two sides of her were battling for the first word.

Adam proved to be a responsible guy, and he cleared his throat before talking. "I guess we are here because for some time now... we haven't really been talking."

"Oh?" Amos asked, urging him or even Cynthia to clarify.

"I mean," Cynthia said with a humorless gust of laugh. "That might be an understatement. We haven't been close for over a year now."

"Close as in you guys don't talk, or haven't been together?"

"Well, we still live together," Adam explained. "But, it doesn't feel like either of us are present. We... I, sometimes feel like if I say something we will have another fight."

"Were you two fighting before?"

"We were," Cynthia replied bitterly, appearing more sad than angry. "Our last big fight was... God, I don't even remember."

"Christmas," Adam told her. "We fought on Christmas. I didn't get a tree, you got pissed, I got pissed, we blew up on each other."

Amos stored this little detail in a file cabinet in his mind. "What was the fight *really* about?"

Adam moistened his lips. His hands were clenched into fists, as if he were imagining crushing something within his fingers. Bad memories were stirring again, those had had kept suppressed for so long because he knew that if he spoke his mind Cynthia would get defensive. It didn't matter what Mulderich said, there were some things that could not be brought up for fear of disturbing the peace.

(It wasn't my fault!)

Adam tried to shove that exchange into a corner deep into the back of his head, among the clutter of unnecessary baggage and dust bunnies. He had attempted to try and lock that exchange away and never think about it again, knowing how angry it would make him and how painful going back to that period where he absolutely despised his wife would be. That was a time he did not want to relive.

But would he rather relive the period of hatred and bitterness towards Cynthia, or the period of sorrow and grief caused by her? In truth: neither. But what better place to review old scars than right here, right now?

How to word it though… how to bring it up gently and without losing his temper or shutting down with grief?

"It was…" he started, hesitantly. "Concerning something that had happened. Something pretty bad, and could have been prevented."

That proved to be a bad way to put it and he realized this too late. At the mention of 'prevented,' Cynthia turned on him with the savagery of an angry bear. The woman, Amos didn't fail to see, had a fire in her.

"There was nothing I could do, and you know it!"

Adam turned on her in return, the two glaring each other down like a pair of alley cats about to fight for territory. Amos only sat and watched and listened, taking the occasional note as the couple exchanged their words.

"Then whose was it?" Adam demanded for, what? The Tenth time? Eleventh? Twentieth? Hundredth? Did it matter? "You really gonna blame *him* for what happened?"

"It was an accident!"

"Oh, give me a *break*, Cynthia. Everyone keeps calling it an accident. A fucking 'accident!' Well accidents are supposed to be preventable. You were supposed to be watching him and you didn't."

"You couldn't have done any better!"

"I got to him first, didn't I? If you got off your ass instead of just standing there, Ryan would still be alive!"

"Fuck you, Adam," Cynthia snarled and stood and was ready to leave.

"Wait a minute," Amos called to her, to which she stopped. If it had been Adam who spoke, she was hellbent on just walking away. She didn't particularly care about Amos' outstretched hand as if he were talking to a lion about to pounce on him.

"Sit back down, please. Let's be civil."

Cynthia smiled maliciously. "Fine." She stomped over to her seat and grabbing it by the back, dragged it away from Adam who just shook his head in bitter bemusement even as she sat back down, this time ten feet away from him and nearly sitting on the edge of the gazebo.

"Don't fall," Amos muttered. He cleared his throat and said, "Cynthia, who is Ryan?"

Adam's jaw clenched. He didn't like how Amos directed the question at his wife, but there was a reason behind it. He wanted Cynthia to speak up about it, since Adam was the one who instigated this conversation. Maybe he didn't mean for it to turn into a bout of hostility, maybe he did, but what he said triggered something in Cynthia, and in turn set them both off. He made sure to give Adam a look which said, 'Let her speak.' He didn't want any interruptions, not when this was a fine example of domestic hostility if he ever did see one.

Cynthia, arms crossed as tightly as her thin legs, took her time in answering. She was notably more hesitant to reply, taking that time with a considerate amount of care so that there would be no mistakes or fumbles in her speech. A careful person, compared to Adam's need to take charge and go forward with whatever he's got at the moment. Amos admired her more closely as she thought, thinking what a waste that she was married to a bullheaded guy like Adam. However, there *was* chemistry, anybody could see that between the two, like two business associates able to work well enough together.

Still, Amos sort of wished that there was more of a gap between the Whites. But perhaps, that was his own selfish thoughts coming along, and besides, he had promised John.

Had he promised?

Yeah, he supposed he had.

Focus, idiot, he thought.

Finally, Cynthia spoke up, breaking Amos' concentration and forcing him to play the role of Dr. Love again. "We had a son, Mr. Mulderich. He was our first, and…"

Adam cleared his throat, appearing to feel a need to pick up where Cynthia had faltered. When Cynthia didn't seem willing to or able to continue, Amos looked at him and nodded for Adam to speak up.

"We were having trouble conceiving children. We had been trying for years, and it caused a lot of stress between us. Low sperm count, you know. But we managed to keep going and then we finally got Ryan. Doctor said it was a miracle we were able to have one."

Amos smiled. "That's very good."

Cynthia looked at Adam appreciatively, but then that look vanished as some unspoken pain overtook her gratitude. "Yeah. That's right. Well, there was an accident, like I said. We were in the park, and my son… he went running out into the road. The park was right across the street where we lived, and Adam was home working on the front porch; we were planning on selling it."

"We were moving to New York for my new business," Adam chimed in.

"I see," Amos said feeling a growing ache in his stomach. "And so your son ran out into the road. I think I can guess what happened."

Adam nodded. "When I saw I started running for the road. Cynthia had been talking to one of the neighbors, but she heard me screaming. She was closer, but she got... paralyzed or something. She got scared, I guess. She didn't even try to run for Ryan."

Cynthia fell silent, apparently having nothing to add or defend herself with. Whether out of guilt or because what Adam said was indeed true, she was speechless. She was staring into her lap, unable to do anything else. This of course gave Adam the clearance he needed, be it Amos' request or not.

"Long and gruesome story short," Amos said, "There wasn't anything you could do."

"No," Adam said bitterly. Bitter in the way he looked, and bitter in his tone. "There *was* something we could have done. Sure, I could have been faster. I could have noticed something was wrong sooner. My *wife*," he said it as if he was saying a very offensive derogative. "Could have been watching him better, and caught him before he meandered into the road. But no. She was so caught up and didn't see him and by the time she finally did..."

Adam looked at Cynthia deliberately and with the most venomous look Amos had seen in a long time. "You just stood there like an idiot and watched him get run over like a stray dog."

Cynthia's mouth tightened. No denial coming forth. Not even quite acceptance Amos hypothesized, just self-pity and frustration towards her husband. Understandable, but not healthy, even Amos had to acknowledge that. He could also understand Adam's anger and bitterness, but that didn't quite give him the right to speak to Cynthia in that way. He had to let Adam know that, as well as help Cynthia accept what had happened rather than simply not talk about it or try to use the term 'accident' as merely a way to defend herself. The way Amos could see it, those were the major issues emanating from this couple. The stress and no doubt the doubt of one another during the trial and error of conceiving a child, only for it to end in a tragedy. Now there was the driving wedge of Adam's bitterness and unforgiveness towards Cynthia, and Cynthia's unwillingness to accept what had happened and if Amos was correct, forgive *herself*. Part of that could be due to Adam's treatment of her, but both parties had a hand in this and Amos had to ensure that both worked together to heal together, rather than try to bite and snarl at each other in order to protect whatever tenderness they held dear.

"Adam," Amos said directing his attention towards the husband. *Husband*, he had to remind himself a second time. "This may sound like a very obvious question."

"Okay..." he said skeptically.

"This accident clearly changed everything for you, as well as your wife. Does that include how you view her? Do you blame her that much?"

Adam looked at Amos like he had asked a *stupid* question as well as obvious. "Do I *blame* her that much? Yes, Dr. Phil. She's the one who should have been watching him. I don't care if Ryan just meandered out there, or if the driver didn't see him. It all would have been *prevented* if she had just kept an eye on him. What happened instead?"

He raised both hands up like a gameshow host awaiting the final answer of the contestant. *Name an animal with three letters in it's name,* came to Amos' mind.

Asshole, Amos thought, and this man was matching one perfectly. Although at the same time, he couldn't blame Adam's frustration or anger. He couldn't imagine trying so hard for a child and to lose it. And what happens often with the death of a child? Hostility in order to protect themselves.

"She was busy *talking* to someone," Adam declared and the hands came down. "I don't know about you, doc, but when you are talking to a friend and you are also watching your own child, wouldn't you have liked, I dunno, *glanced* in that kid's direction? Make sure he wasn't wandering too far from the park or too close to the road? Cynthia didn't do that. She let her friend take her full attention. Yes, I understand it was an accident. But accidents can be prevented. What happened with Ryan *should've* been prevented. But no. Our son is dead, and as far as I'm concerned, Cynthia might as well have *shot* him."

Cynthia made a noise in her throat which reminded Amos of how someone gets punched in the gut. The gust of air that rushed out due to the outside force of one's fist.

Adam's fist, meet Cynthia's stomach or chest. Goodbye air, hello look of constricted pain and depression.

Amos nodded sympathetically despite clenching his jaw. That statement had not only been unfair, but absolutely uncalled for.

How to proceed...

"Do you really think that though? That Cynthia murdered your kid?"

Adam looked surprised at that. Caught off-guard or perhaps ashamed when the reality of his words sank in. "Well... no. No, not *really*, but..."

"Then why compare it that way? I understand your pain, Mr. White, but I feel like you are being unfair."

"Unfair?" Adam demanded in a low tone.

"Lemme explain," said Amos with a placating hand. "Your wife may be responsible for the well-being of your son just as you would if you were in her position. But you cannot compare her role into it as if she had *purposefully* killed your child. If you had been in her shoes and someone, maybe your wife, told you 'You killed him. You killed our son!' What would you say?"

Adam clenched his fists again, his gaze directed directly at Amos. Amos held his gaze until Adam's eyes slowly lowered towards his lap. He muttered something under his breath and finally answered, "I'd be pretty pissed..."

"You'd feel awful."

"Yeah..."

"You'd be in more pain then you already had been seeing your son get run over."

"... Yes..."

Amos nodded. Progress was being made. "You are bitter towards your wife, and it is understandable. But doesn't she deserve your support as well? Just as you would need her support if you were in her shoes?"

"She can't even support me right *now*," Adam said spitefully.

Cynthia had started to say "That's-" but then Amos held up a hand, silencing her with both it and a cautionary eye.

"I have no doubt you need support," Amos said to Adam. "But that doesn't mean your wife doesn't need it. She was there too. You both witnessed the same tragedy. She obviously feels just as responsible as you think her to be. What do you think goes through her mind every night when she closes her eyes?"

Adam said nothing for a long, long time. As for Cynthia, whether out of respect or because she couldn't bring herself to say anything, remained quiet and would not look at her husband. Tears had formed in her eyes and began to roll down her cheeks.

Adam's mouth twitched and twisted for a moment longer and then finally he said, "She probably thinks of that day. How she could have... how she could have... Well... Yeah, I guess it... I... I would guess she feels guilty enough..." He looked at Cynthia and asked, "Right?"

Cynthia nodded. She wouldn't look at him still as she brushed a tear away with a delicate hand.

"Do you help her in that regard?" asked Amos. "Help her feel that way?"

"... I guess I do."

Amos nodded, then redirected his attention towards Cynthia White. "Mrs. White, am I right? Do you feel responsible for Ryan's death? Do you feel like you could have done something about it?"

Cynthia swallowed a lump in her throat before answering, "Everyday," in a soft voice, barely above a whisper that trembled as another persistent tear rolled down her cheek.

"But that didn't happen. Ryan got out of view, and by the time you saw what was happening, it was too late."

Cynthia covered her mouth, more tears starting to spill.

Amos looked to both of the Whites. "You both need support, but you need to do it together. Cynthia, your husband ran out there, but was likewise too late. Neither of you could have prevented the turn of events once that started. I don't mean that out of offense or bitterness, but of simple fact. A lot of things happen that are outside our control, and yes, maybe things can be prevented or altered, but sometimes you cannot change anything at all. I'm not saying it was impossible to change anything back then. Maybe Cynthia, you could have been watching Ryan better, or even Adam, you could have gotten there sooner. It wasn't impossible for something to change, but it is now. What has happened has happened. I don't mean slap a bandage on it and move on. But it *does* mean move on. Ryan is beyond your help at this point. But he is still alive in your hearts, and you two still have each other. It is still a blow, but in these sort of times you have to rely on one another. You need to help each other strive through this pain, not hide it or tuck it away, or toss the blame completely on the other. You two need each other. You two can only truly heal when you lean on each other and not keep this bottled up, because if you do, then it's gonna come out anyway and with greater force that could be devastating for you both."

"That's hard," said Adam. "I cannot help but think of what could have been."

"What could have been and what is are sometimes two different things and impossible to have at the same time," said Amos. "You cannot change what happened any more than your wife can. But you can change how it affects you every day. The pain will always be there, but you two can make it more bearable together. Cynthia, you need to learn to forgive yourself for what happened, and Adam, you need to let go of your bitterness towards your wife and let the pain take it's course. You two need to quit fighting over the same life donut and keep each other afloat before one or both of you drown."

Adam laughed humorlessly. "That's quite the metaphor."

Cynthia surprised them both by correcting: "Analogy."

This time, Adam laughed for real. The sound made Cynthia smile. "Yeah, yeah, whatever."

"You're supposed to be a writer."

"Writer, not talker." He looked at Amos with a look which said, *See what I gotta deal with?*

Amos smiled, amused. This was going better than he had expected. There were problems, no counselor could not see that. But there was still a bond, a chemistry beyond the pain these two had gone through. They could work their way out of this. They wanted to, despite their internal conflict with their emotions, they wanted to work it out. Amos genuinely hoped that Cynthia would learn to forgive herself, as well as Adam to let go of his bitterness towards her. That was the only way this marriage would survive.

At least, in his 'professional' opinion.

Professional, not even.

"I'd like to try an exercise with you both," he said. "If you guys don't mind."

"I'm not doing Pilates," Adam declared with a smug expression. This caused Cynthia to smother a chuckle behind her hand.

"Ha-ha," Amos retorted. "No, nothing that requires physical labor. I want you both to share some *good* memories together. It can be about Ryan, sure, but I also want you to mention times you remember most fondly of. Whatever is most significant to you, so that your partner will hear it."

"What does this do?" Cynthia asked.

"Other than be a conversation starter? It helps you both to remind yourselves just why you are together in the first place, and why you love that. But that all depends: Do you two love being together?"

Adam was the first to respond yet again. "Of course! I love Cynthia, and I want this marriage to work out more than anything."

Cynthia nodded in both agreement and content. "Yes, that is why we are here in the first place."

"Well," Amos said leaning back in his chair and with a wave of his hand as if he were presenting something marvelous. "Let's hear it. Just pretend that I'm not here."

Adam blew a puff of air from his mouth. Cynthia looked nervous. Little by little however, the memories came forth. Slowly at first, but then they came pouring out to the point where they were both sharing their experiences together. They were laughing, smiling, and Amos was pleased by their taking of the exercise. Most couples did this naturally, others occasionally needed a little push in the right direction.

The one memory that stood out to him in particular, was the story of the two of them at Mt. Rainier in Washington. They had rented a cabin for the weekend and were intent on climbing the behemoth just as the snow was supposed to be starting to melt off the main trail. He was touched by how tender they seemed to share this memory, how carefully they worded it and corrected one another as if it were a precious treasure meant to be maintained to last eternity. Each person contributing with great care and love to the point where it felt like one story from one person.

"Do you remember when we went to Mt. Rainier for the first time? Yeah, you were scared. You were too, especially when we went on that roadway that banked around the gorge or whatever it was. The trees were lovely though, although I got more nervous when we saw the snow building up. Yeah, by the time we got up to the lodge there were a ton of snow still built up on the sides. Lots of people were there though and I think that's what made it easier. Lots of Asians too. What does that have to do with it? I dunno, there was a lot of them. They were old too. That's true, but they knew what they were doing by the looks of it. We weren't. That's right, we didn't have the right shoes or clothes for it. You went up in your slippers! I thought it was going to be easy! And besides you were complaining about the cold. Didn't bother me for long given how hot I got. We passed the asphalt trail, right? Right, we were going up the slope and there was so much snow! Remember the marmots? Oh yeah, and you were surprised by how big they were and how loud they were. It was a good idea that we came back after seeing that glacier though, I got nervous when I heard the crackling. Those mountain climbers didn't seem bothered. No, that's true. Do you remember what happened on the way down? Ha-ha, how can I forget? You slipped again, this time colliding right into me and slipping beneath me. We both were sliding down laughing and screeching and everyone else just watched and laughed, even that older Asian couple who were shaking their heads at us. Dumb Americans. Yeah, but no one came to help us when we finally stopped and just laid there laughing. I was having a good time. Yeah, me too. That was a good trip. We did it again, and we didn't fall, remember? Yeah, we learned."

They got lost in their memory together, which had to be the greatest feeling shared by a couple.

Amos couldn't help but think if they could learn that back then, they could learn it now. To get back up again and walk the slippery slope that makes up this mountain of a life they lived on.

He looked toward the ocean, across the mighty blue where he saw a single cloud high across the horizon. He frowned. It was far away and it looked to be only one, but looks could be deceiving. His time on the island had proved to him that. John was a better judge than him on this sort of thing however, he would be able to tell if that cloud meant anything or not.

Amos remembered. *Speaking of John.*

"Excuse me," Amos said standing up whilst retrieving his walkie talkie from his backpack. "I need to check in on something. We will continue this soon, you two just… enjoy being with each other." He left the Whites alone to themselves and to their memories. They would be fine, he believed it.

When he got John on the radio, he was delighted to hear that Ben had intercepted the boat out on the shoreline. Turned out it was a small sailboat, with only one passenger.

"He's dehydrated and sick," John said. "We got him in the sickbay now, I'm outside with Jake."

"Is he stable? Is he coherent?"

"No, he opened his eyes, Ben said, but that was it. He ain't from around here that's for certain. It's a Chinaman, or something of the sort."

"Chinaman? He's Chinese?"

"No, he… he looks like a mixture of an Asian and an islander, you know what I mean?"

"Like Hawaiian?"

"I guess, I dunno, when the guy wakes up, we'll ask."

"Where's his boat?"

"Ben has it at the docks. It's an old piece of shit, Amos. Kid's scrawnier than hell too, he's been out at sea for a while I'm willing to bet."

"Shit," Amos whispered. It was a miracle the kid was alive then, a trip in a sailboat across the ocean from Hawaii or maybe even further to this far south? That's a feat worthy of an experienced seaman, not some kid. The boat should have sunk, or the kid should have been dead.

Again, depending on where the guy came from.

"Can you call the coast guard? Have someone come pick him up?"

"Jake says let's see what we can do here. The guy isn't in trouble or anything, he isn't going to die. Just needs some liquids and some food in him. If his condition worsens however, Jake will call. Then from there we'll let someone else take over."

Amos nodded. Crockett might have a heart attack at the idea of someone out at sea landing on his island, but he might also be thrilled at the idea of someone being saved by his island. It would certainly attract attention, which Crockett was always eager to have. John was playing it as smart as he could without risking the kid's life. Still, Amos told himself he would go and meet the kid as soon as he was able.

"Call me if we need anything. Anything," Amos emphasized, and then he and John switched back to channel one. In the time that followed, he checked with some of the other employees who were taking care of the other guests, and when he was satisfied that everyone seemed happy and taken care of, he returned to the Whites and they proceeded with their session, which ended in a couple's swim while Amos read quietly to himself. There was still a lot to do tonight, and he wouldn't find some alone time until he got back to his hut later in the evening.

He still looked out towards the sea where he saw the cloud. It had gotten bigger, meant it was coming nearer. But it didn't seem to bring with it a horde of black clouds that would insinuate a sudden storm. He should have asked John if he could look into it, but he was sure his man would already be on it and would inform Amos in due time. He always had.

A storm wouldn't be the end of the world, but it would put a stop to some of the attraction on Bonidada, and God forbid and Crockett as well that such a thing should happen. It would all work out still in the end, it had before, but Amos would dread having to call Crockett to explain the shut down of swimming along the beaches, or the visits to the grotto, or anything else associated with exposing the guests and employees to possible lightning, heavy rains, and even stronger winds.

4th Letter

Capiz has a dark history dating back to when the Spanish colonized our islands. They brought with them God's message, and practically changed how my people looked at the world and the spirits that walked it.

Capiz was said to be home to monsters, and one would only have to go into the heart of the city to understand that. The people there are all crooks and thieves and even murderers, those who witness this too numb to care. One who enters the city should always keep their wallet in their front pocket, and a knife in the other, and keep well enough away from those who look malicious or anyone who reacts violently should anyone speak in Latin.

I don't speak Latin. I don't have any intention of ever speaking that language. If that was the chosen language of God, then He could keep it with Him and His angels. The priests were all just mimickers, doesn't matter where you come from. They made it a big deal back home, and they still made it a big deal in the rest of the world. Religion like I said is like a curse. A relationship with God is one thing, wanting to have a guidebook, obviously the bible, to help you live the best life, is part of that thing. Forcing it down one's throat, chanting nothingness to the bones of the dead which could be just bleached chicken bones for all we know, forcing prayers towards pictures of the saints, it was all just bothersome filler. It was that religion which had created the abomination that everyone thought plagued our village anyway. I would never have believed it either, if I had not seen it with my own eyes.

    This is something I can never explain to my wife.
How can one explain seeing something so horrible, and
coming back without losing their mind; succumbing to
the madness of seeing something mankind was not
meant to see?
    In Capiz at the time, there had been a lot of crime.
A local church had been vandalized, some kids were run
over in the street by a biker, and a stabbing took place at
one of the homes of an exorcist. At this time too, people
were frantic about the murders, and despite all of this,
seemed to only wish to fuel the supernatural by creating
a sort of ceremony to give peace to the beast. It was
something that would be stopped as soon as my mother
and I left Capiz, and would never happen again as far as
I was concerned. Once I left our islands, I had never
looked back until now as I write these letters.
    There were children, teenagers mostly, but a lot of
them, and they were all in the streets dancing. Dancing,
with their bodies painted completely black, some of them
wearing fake teeth that looked like fangs. Some had
created makeshift wings out of blackened palm leaves, or
even took the wings off a flying fox and stitched them to
their shirts. They looked like demons parading the
streets, and they were often chased off by men wearing
bags over their heads, and whipping themselves with
stingray whips across their backs until they were
bleeding. They took the whips to the kids, and whatever
children were not driven off by the men in bag hoods, the
priests from the local church took care of them as well,
calling them blasphemers for giving in to the ego of the
devils.

My mother, noticing my repulsion of the scene before me, took me to a restaurant that I remember going to with her whenever we come to Capiz. I felt silly being offered such a treat, but there are some things we adults cannot let go, and so I agreed to her offer. We shared a delicious bowl of Hamba and a side of Sisig. The food lifted my spirits like most food from home, and I am happy that I am blessed enough to share this experience with my wife, whom I cook for every weekend she lets me.

After our lunch, we entered the ghetto region of the city, where underground shops and carts were scattered about. Some boys who looked like trouble were watching us, but would immediately shun their eyes when my mother greeted them with the phrase, "Tao po, hindi aswang." This told them that she wasn't a stranger, and had come to seek a fellow shaman, a Babaylan named Ambrosio.

A self-made man, Ambrosio lived in the southernmost part of Capiz where the city just about ends. He lived in a single studio, where he often tells fortunes and blesses those touched by the twelve ministers of the devil. He was crippled, having no legs below the knees, and was ancient. Some say he was over a hundred years old, others claim he was one of the few Babaylan who spoke with the friar Juan de Plasencia, who was a missionary back in the 1500's. A stretch, but many believed that given the shaman's supposed power. Back then, he would have been called a Mangagauay, someone who *pretends* to heal. Still today, he wasn't even close to be considered a Catolonan, one of high rank and power.

But my mother trusted him, and so I held my tongue and kept my knowledge of his history to myself.

She spoke to him in hushed tones, some in Tagalog, some in Latin. The old man's gaze never faltered, and he began to gather some herbs and ashes for her that we didn't have back in our village. He also equipped her with a new stingray whip, as well as a machete made of a sawfish jaw. He then offered us some balut, which I was very fond of although I was also weary of anything this man offered. My mother scolded me, and told me to take and eat. It was delicious, despite my suspicions.

He then looked at me and asked to speak with me, and I will never forget the haunting exchange between us. He placed his old hands over mine, bony fingers of leather that felt cold and inhuman. He told me that I have no faith, and that was what would kill me in the end. Rationality was good, but caution by faith was necessary. I did not question him at the time, but I was disgusted by his proclamation. Thankfully by then, my mother had everything she needed, or so she said, and it was time to return to the village.

On our way out, there were still some people dancing around all covered in black and some with wings and fangs. They were dancing, and some of the youngest children had come up to me laughing and singing. Some were amused, others were disgusted. I couldn't blame the latter. They might as well have been like the American witches of Salem, dancing and singing for the glory of an abomination of the Lord. But as there were no one around to actually step in and stop them, their singing continued unhindered, and even after we had left Capiz at last, their words haunted me the entire way home, as if preparing for me for what I would see upon our arrival.

Thirteen

Matt Winklemann had finished his massage and was now having a light snack of pineapple ceviche which was sour and sweet, along with a margarita from the bar. He was sipping on his second one as he walked the resort grounds, greeting every employee or guest (Matt greeted them but didn't really see them) as he got another look at the place and took in every detail of the building and the surrounding area. He was on a mission, and couldn't afford any delays or distractions.

Like that Tamia girl...

Matt suppressed the memory of the small woman and focused on looking at everything. Every exit door, every fire exit, every generator or water heater contained within a fence roped barbed wire. A path led around the building and around the fence line where the luau spot or whatever it is called sat, and seeing no sign or anyone to stop him, Matt ventured down it his flipflops flip-flopping the entire way.

The power station sat concealed within the tree line. Large metal generators with power arches reaching towards the sky and connecting to power cables that reached the fence and along it down towards the main building and the groundline which powered up the huts. It was smaller than power stations for towns or counties, and Matt considered the amount he would need to cut the power. It would be easier to cut the cable, but he would need to cut the power from the backup generators. A resort on a secluded island would need one, especially in the midst of storms, or worse the aftermath of a typhoon.

Matt stood there for a long time, thinking, and sipping on his margarita. He could pull it off. He could do it, no problem. But even if he couldn't cut the power and plunge the island into chaos, he would still be able to take out as many people as he could before he was either

A) Apprehended

B) Shot and killed and/or wounded in the fray, or

C) Succeed and be arrested or killed by the Mexican Coast Guard.

In any given case, Matt wanted to cause as much damage as possible. One last 'fuck you' to the world just as delightful and exciting as the last 'fuck you' he had given his pathetic wife.

Oh, they had come to Bonidada to fix something all right. And Matt's fix was going to be letting out everything he hated about this world and longed for, onto as many people as possible. Make them suffer as he had suffered, and allow himself to relish in what he had been wanting to do for a long, long time. He had held it in for too long, had worn the mask society had forced upon him and endured it for long enough. Now it was time to unleash the beast.

His earliest memory was being a small boy and being fascinated by pain. Not by pain to himself, he was no masochist, but by the pain of others. He loved movies of what his mother would horrifyingly call 'torture porn.' Horror movies meant to sicken and disgust the viewer but otherwise was meant to horrify the idea of extreme pain and misery. Saw had done it well, but it was never truly done from person to person. Cabin Fever was a little more personal, but Matt always liked it when someone or *someones* would take prisoners and cut them up, slice them open, deform them, make them wriggle and scream and completely degenerate from human beings into something more primal.

When movies no longer seemed to interest him (either he had seen them all before too many times or they didn't seem real enough to him anymore) he turned to animals. He remembered having a kitten his mother had gotten when he was fifteen. The kitten was sweet and took to Matt well enough, and he remembered liking the soft black fur.

He also remembered feeling it's heartbeat, so light and so fast.

His parents had gone out, and little Matthew was alone with the kitten. When he was sure they would be gone for a while, he found the cat sleeping on her cat bed. The kitten mewed and purred noisily as his gentle hands picked her up and carried her outside to his treehouse. There he sat the kitten down on the floor and then taking a pocket knife, a little one-incher primarily used for small cuts, he opened it and when he was sure the kitten was going to stay still as he stroked her back still purring lovingly, he pulled it back and plunged it into her outstretched paw. The kitten screamed and hissed and began to tug on the thing that secured her left forepaw into the wood of the treehouse. Blood was seeping and the kitten seemed hellbent on shredding her paw in order to escape, much to Matt's fascination and pleasure.

From there, he continued to play with the cat. Sometimes with a pair of pliers, sometimes with a small blowtorch Dad often used for cooking on the BBQ. With a sewing needle he had taken from his mother's room, he had poked out the kitten's two eyes, relishing at the sight of the blood and jelly spilling over its cheeks and whiskers and at some point, took some beads in order to fill the empty sockets.

When he had finished playing with the kitten, who was now lying very still and panting heavily, he sat back and admired it. Its eyes were gone, some of its hind claws had been forcibly ripped out and scattered about, her tail sliced off and burned, her other forepaw scorched as well, and a couple of cuts and wounds across her hide. Still, she was panting. Still, she was alive. Little Matt watched her for a long time, realizing that after so long of playing with her, she had stopped screaming and… yes that was what it was. She had stopped screaming, gone quiet, seeming to accept her fate.

He removed the knife from her paw and picked her up. She was trembling in his hands as he carried her down the ladder of his treehouse and strode across the backyard. Little by little, the kitten seemed to calm. Little by little, it began to purr again. She was safe. This human didn't really mean to hurt her. Betrayal was not a thing, he was just as much a mother as her own, and she would no longer be in pain soon enough.

Matt had settled her gently into the pit he and his father had dug for bonfires earlier that summer. The kitten cried and mewed as she stumbled painfully and blindly about, trying to figure out where she was. She sniffed, and no doubt smelling the ashes of fires before her, she began to panic. She winced and hissed as Matt sprayed her with some charcoal fluid he had taken off the BBQ, and with the blowtorch he had burned her with, touched the blue flame to the kitten.

She went up in a ball of orange flames which kicked and screamed as the fire ate away her fur and then her flesh. He watched, relishing in the sight as he felt his penis grow hard and harder still. Making sure no one was around still within the safety of his backyard fence, Matt reached into his pants and began to stroke his cock. He did so even after the kitten stopped moving and crying, and just laid there burning. She burned and burned, her features blackened and shrunken. When he had gone off in his pants, the fire was slowly dying, the stink of burnt fur a waft of incense in his nostrils. Matt dug the pit deeper and buried the burnt kitten deeper within the hole. Then he added some branches and a log off the side of the backyard shed. He sprayed the log, and lit it. Once the fire was burning in the pit once again, eliminating any sign or smell of a burning animal in the area, Matt brought out some marshmallows and roasted them over the fire. His parents never knew anything was wrong when they found him out there.

His mother had been devastated with the kitten's disappearance. Always calling for her, worrying at night, even looking dreadful come morning. His father had told her she might have gotten out and escaped, and when he confronted his son about it, Matt merely shrugged, saying she might have gotten out when he went out to have s'mores. That had been it. If his parents suspected anything, they weren't saying anything.

They should have, Matt thought both glumly and scornfully with morbid delight. His curiosity and pleasures only enhanced from there. Finding animals in the woods, pets from around the neighborhood, he even went through the trouble of adopting a dog from the pound outside of town, only to take the dog to the river and with a cinderblock tied to the end of the leash, toss both it and the mutt into the water. He had masturbated to the bubbles reaching the surface of the river as the dog struggled underneath. He had left it there, no doubt bobbing in the water dead and feeding the fish until someone happened to swim under the bridge and find it anchored like an old underwater mine. He had gone through a lot of underwear that summer.

Well, he wouldn't need underwear this time. This last time, he wouldn't have to be afraid of anyone watching or catching him in the act. They would all be a part of the gorgeous nightmare that he constantly wanted to live and be *free* in. After all, no one here in the world was real. It was all just him. This was all just him, and the world was just one dream trying to follow the rules that no one truly made. He was the different one. He always had been. He had been forced to hide himself like a faggot wanting to be treated equally like straight and normal people. Like blacks when they fought for the end of segregation. Americans when they didn't want to drink tea and eat crumpets anymore.

Matthew Winklemann was no patriot. But he desired freedom. And soon, he would experience true freedom; true ecstasy, and true satisfaction. Like movies, animals just didn't cut it anymore. That was when he had committed his first murder. He remembered her fondly, and was thinking about her still when by the time he was satisfied with what he could find, Matt started his way back to his cabin to rest before the rest of the evening came, and he was expected to join all the others for dinner.

Maybe he'd do it tonight, maybe tomorrow, who knows for certain.

But his first kill... his first taste of true freedom and excitement...

Andes Shoam.

Fourteen

Andes Shoam was someone Matt had met at his favorite bar. While he and his wife did work at the same company they went home sometimes at very separate times.

Whenever Gabbie had a girls night out with her friends, if Matt didn't want to go straight home he went and had a couple of drinks and mingled with a couple of the ladies who would do anything for a quick buck. Considering Matt's position, this was achieved very easily. Sometimes he would have a date or a fling and be home just before Gabbie got back. All had gone well and his wife was none the wiser until the day she caught him flirting with another woman at the same bar. A different story however and was of little interest to Matt then as it is now.

He met Andes one night at the end of the bar table sitting alone and having a gin and tonic. She was a hardbody blonde wearing a blue dress with a black shawl. She was constantly flirting with men who bought her gin after gin until she was too drunk to care and told all the guys to leave her be. Which many did surprisingly, no doubt mentally undressing her as they stared from their positions at their own tables or at the pool table.

At some point however, be it a primal urge or fate itself, Matt stood and sat down right beside Andes who eyed him both curiously and cautiously.

"No other spot look good enough to sit at?" she asked, her voice slurred with drink. It had been difficult to hear with the music and gossip throughout the bar, and so Matt had to read her lips to understand exactly what she was saying.

"Nothing as interesting as this one," Matt said with as charming as a smile as he could muster. His smile had always been a mask however, and a very convincing one at that.

"Well you can skip the pleasantries," Andes said waving him away. "I'm all drunk out."

"I don't think so," Matt said now looking at his Atlas watch and making sure that Andes noticed it. "Still eight o'clock somewhere in the world. The question is, how much will it cost you to have one more pleasant chat?"

Andes' dark eyebrows arched. "I'm not someone who can be bought."

Matt looked her square in the eye. If there was one thing he understood about people in the world, it's that anyone who says they cannot be bought, is a liar.

That was fine, he could deal with liars. Better yet: He can prove them wrong.

"Wanna know what I do for a living?"

"Lemme guess. A broker."

"Not at all. I represent a search engine company here in the city. You know what that is worth?"

"No…"

"A lot," Matt said. "In fact, I got a lot right now to pay for your time."

Andes was intrigued but not quite sure by the looks of it. Matt reached into his pocket and pulled out his alligator-skin wallet. He removed a hundred and placed it on the bar. "Let's do this again. My name is Matt. What is yours?"

He placed a second hundred on the bar with that question, leaving Andes staring amazed at the two hundreds so close to her. Had she ever seen that much money at once given to her so easily? Maybe, maybe not, Matt didn't care. He could drop the whole wallet down on the counter and it wouldn't matter to him. Andes was not going to see a single penny out of the stack he had.

She could have threw the remainder of her drink in his face, tell him that she was not someone to whore herself out to anyone, and to even consider she would be was an absolute atrocity. Matt had this happen to him before, and had been called every sexist thing under the sun and he had been prepared for that outcome to happen when the woman finally looked back at him.

"Andes..." she finally answered.

"Andes what?" Matt asked pleasantly surprised and having placed a third hundred on the bar. $300, three Ben Franklins, all staring up at Andes who looked ready to fall out of her stool.

"Shoam. Andes Shoam."

"Is that European?" Matt asked.

Andes looked at him at last, a smile over her drunken lips. "Matt, how the fuck should I know?"

He bought her two more drinks before taking her into his car. She was so drunk at this point and admiring the interior of his car so much, she did not notice where he was taking her. Outside the city to the farmlands where he could turn down a dirt road and be completely concealed by the corn and the irrigation canal where he could easily dispose of her. She came out of the car easily enough, mumbling about how cold it was and that her purse was still in his car.

She became antsy when he took her to the tree, where he then locked her in a choke hold and held until she passed out, all the while she fought and struggled, and he was careful not to get scratched by her nails. When she was still, he hurried to the car and returned with some rope and tape. When she started to awake, he choked her again and knocked her out a second time. Then he bound her and gagged her, working fast to tie her against the tree by her arms. She awoke as he was tying ropes around her ankles as well. Strapped against the tree she struggled and screamed into the lump of cloth lodged deep in her mouth, which he covered with duct tape before she could spit it out. All of this took roughly two minutes, and another thirty to make sure she was completely bound like a fly in a web. When he was content that she was completely immobilized, the nice rich guy at the bar was gone. He had left the bar and had come home.

He was home, and he was ready to make himself there.

He took off his jacket making sure to check himself and make sure he was unharmed. Then he checked her nails and her clothes, making sure no fabrics or skin was found on her. Not that it would matter, if he did his job properly. He returned to the car where he had the rest of his things, and he took a look back to take in his work one last time. There she was, splayed out with her back flat against the tree, her limbs hugging back around the thick trunk and tied from behind with the rope, her mouth covered and unable to scream, her blue dress looking sexy in the moonlight. Her eyes were bright and frightened, and she was breathing heavily. Good.

When he returned, those eyes turned as large as dinner plates. As large as the kitten's eyes had been before he poked them out with the sewing needle. He had a tool bag in hand, the kind that carried the basic necessities for a house. A hammer, screwdrivers, a few wrenches, a box cutter, handsaw, stud-finder, ratchet, a few different types of pliers, tape measure, and other stuff, altogether was an easy $60 purchase so he could make any small repairs at the house himself rather than hiring someone. Sure, he was rich enough to hire someone, but why do that when humans had evolved with two capable hands and a brain capable enough to figure stuff out? He would leave the bigger more complex projects to the men who charged a lot, but for a scratch in the wall or a screw loose in a chair, he could do it himself.

Or a woman who needed fixing, he thought amusedly. And Andes Shoam was in need of a good fix. Hell, he was too. In the end, it all came down to him winning.

He sat the bag down and after rummaging through it, debating on what to use first, he was delighted by Andes' horrific expression and more frantic squirming when he slid out the pair of pliers first. First, he would play. Foreplay, so to speak. Then he would go from there.

He started with the nails first. Fingernails, then the toes after removing her high heels. The way she jerked and screamed into her gag made Matt feel like he was going to lose his mind before the real fun began. After using a pair of scissors to cut open the front of her dress and bra to expose her breasts, he took the pliers to her nipples as well, pinching and twisting to the point where they were ripped and malformed. He used the slim and long pliers to mutilate her genitals, taking pleasure in watching the blood run down her thighs. She stared at him the whole time, tears in her eyes, seeming to beg for mercy. Like the kitten, she had ceased screaming unless there was pain.

But there would be no mercy. None.

He used an electric screwdriver to drill holes in her ears

(*what do you think of* that, *bitch? An industrial ear-piercing!*)

and with a hammer he broke both hands and continued to strike them until they were black, purple, and bloody. All her fingers stuck out in the wrong direction and they contorted as she wriggled in their binds. Then he smashed both kneecaps in, causing her to hang there like a bastardized crucifix.

Mutilated and hobbled, Andes was easy to remove from the tree and Matt finished his work with the tool he had in his pants. At this point her moans of pain and horror were so quiet that it would be plain to anyone that she was beyond caring what was happening now. Just like the kitten long as the pain stopped, she would let him do anything he wanted to her without a fight. This made it difficult for him to have her, and so he beat her and used a saw across her back to spill more blood, and when he successfully exhausted himself, he stood there looking down at her with contempt as she curled into a fetal position in the dirt. Beaten, bloody, horribly mutilated in some parts and naked in the dirt, Andes Shoam was not the pretty little hardbody she had been at the bar.

Then he got on top of her again, straddling her as if he would violate her again. He had taken up the hammer. He struck her on top of the head once and hard, and she immediately stopped fighting, her head collapsing to the ground. There was a visible dent on the top of her head, and one of her eyes had started to come out of their sockets. She moaned in terrible pain and blood masked her face. Matt got excited again, and proceeded to beat her until Andes was lying in the dirt dead with her brains spilling out of her split skull. He relished at the sight of her, and then got to work once more.

When he was finished with her corpse, he took up the hacksaw and severed the limbs and cut them into two at the joints, and hauled them one after the other in distant intervals into the passing canal. The canal was running fast this time of year due to the irrigation lines being used and so the bits and pieces of Andes would be lost and scattered throughout the river the canal emptied into. The torso was tossed in next, it of course missing the breasts and a good amount of organs having been bisected. Lastly, he took the head and put it in a small Walmart bag to take home with him. With the head he threw both his clothes and Andes' clothes into a black garbage bag. The tools both bloody and not went back into their respective bag. Then taking a broom from the backseat of the car, Matt swept across the dirt and swept more in to cover the blood that was black in the moonlight. He shined his headlights over the spot and did another once over. It looked dark, but the whole area was dark even in daylight anyway. Also, it wasn't like much people came this way anyway. Even if someone did, all they would see is blood and dismiss it as an animal getting eaten. Coyotes or a cougar probably.

Content with his work, Matt washed his hands and face in the canal, making sure he was clean enough to slip into his home unnoticed and from there the shower. From the back of his car he removed a fresh set of clean comfy clothes that he always kept in case he planned to work out at the gym after work. Gabbie would buy it just fine. By the time someone were to find Andes Shoam, she would be decomposed and no doubt fish-eaten to the point of unrecognition. Even if she wasn't, Matt had alibis and he knew he had left nothing to chance.

Once home, he threw his bags of bloody clothes into the garbage bin and in the sink cleaned off his tools. When there was nothing left he sat them aside to dry (the electric screwdriver he threw away), he took Andes' head out to the backyard where he dug out a section of his sod before digging a shallow hole where he placed the head and buried it. The leftover dirt was easy to pack in under the grass. This task finished he went back inside to take a shower. He had missed a few spots of blood and underneath his fingernails looked horrid; he had been lucky that his wife had not come home yet. Once he was clean, he was in bed watching television when Gabbie came home. That night they made love, and she was none the wiser. It was easy for Matt to get off, for while he was having sex with Gabbie in the real world, in his mind, he was once again fucking the corpse of the girl he killed that night.

There had been seven more heads that joined Andes' in that backyard. The last one being the one that Gabbie caught Matt flirting with at the bar. What had resulted was a horrible fight, one that caused Gabbie to leave for a night or two. During that time, Matt had invited the woman back to his house, where he raped and murdered her. This time, he felt no pleasure. Like movies, porn, murdering animals, this had become dull. He didn't even enjoy the look of terror in the woman's face any longer, and this was why he believed he had become careless.

Before, he always made sure the women were single, lived alone, or were so unnecessary that no one would come looking for them. He had met with hundreds of girls and had one night stands with many of them, but only six of them were truly gone from the public eye. His last one, the thirty-something Marsha Lasater, had a husband and son. An investigation had begun upon the report that the woman was missing, and someone said that he had talked to her at the bar. Matt said he had, and that they had been seeing each other until his wife caught him. At this point in time, Gabbie had come back, they had talked, and Gabbie had decided to stay with him. Ever since then however, her trust had been long gone. Matt couldn't care either way, but at least she was back. By then the cops had written him off the list, and he had not killed again since.

Instead, he had been preparing for something bigger. A new bit of entertainment which had become exciting for him whenever he laid in bed fantasizing about it. He had planned to do it back home, one last fling before he left this world with only his name, but this trip had become something else entirely.

Here, on Isla Bonidada, he could do everything he wanted, and however he wanted.

A sound caused him to stop just at the base of the stairs leading up to his hut. He turned and saw a crow perched on one of the palm trees. It was huge bird, its feathers so black it looked like a moving shadow. Its red eyes were bright in the sunlight.

They appeared to be staring down at him.

Matt felt uneasy about the crow. One, because of the way it was looking at him, sure. But also because a crow shouldn't be here. He was no ornithologist, but he knew that crows were not common in a tropical zone, let alone a tropical island. On the mainland, sure, maybe, but not this far from home.

Matt remembered looking towards the docks on the way back here that there was a strange boat that just arrived. A piece of shit that looked like it had spent a majority of its life fishing for some poor village or was stolen and just poorly maintained. Maybe the crow had hitched a ride. Rats did that with boats, so not their feathered brethren?

Matt made a jump at the crow but the bird didn't flinch. Dismissing it with a huff, he started up the stairs. He had stuff to do, and didn't care about the crow either way. What was a bird to him anyway? Just another animal. Just another figure in his dreams just like all the rest. A dream that he was slowly, but surely, taking more and more control over. After all, there was no one else truly here except him. He was the only one who truly existed in this dream called existence. He had discovered that while he was the only one, others could influence the dream; Take it over as Gabbie nearly had and probably would have, should she had been smarter and done away with him sooner. But instead, she had come back an obedient NPC, and her life had ended just as all the rest.

Soon, it would be his entirely. Soon, he would wake up, enlightened.

Fifteen

Winnifred Ashton, Wendy to her friends and family, was having the time of her life.

She and Cain had taken a dive among the coral reefs as well as a beautiful sailing trip around the island with the Jacksons, and now they were returning to Bonidada for some down time before the rest of the evening took place. She and her husband were in the bedroom relaxing and letting the fun of the day run out before they showered. She got up and did just that, afterward going out onto the deck so that Cain could clean himself up as well.

Forty years old and she was out here having the time of her life. She and Cain's life had been good since their joining the Amway corporation and creating a good independent flow of income from their company. They were retired, could go anywhere in the world now, and best of all, they were free all the time to help watch their grandchildren. It had been so long since they had been able to raise their own kids that life couldn't have gotten better. This trip, while necessarily for struggling couples, was really their way of seeing just how lavish Isla Bonidada was, and she and Cain were not disappointed in the slightest. Not a single thing had been wrong or awry here.

Well, except for one incident between her and Victoria Jackson.

Victoria was around the same age as Wendy, just barely reaching the peak of 'the hill,' so to speak. She was married to a very wealthy retailer, and according to her, was simply just unsatisfied with Paul sexually, as was he with her. Wendy tried to gently ask if it was because of their age and Victoria simply said no and refused to answer any more questions. Wendy let it drop of course, after all, everyone was here for something and at any rate it wasn't any of her business in the first place.

But then something happened below deck of the boat as she was getting changed out of her bathing suit to put on a dress for the sailing trip and around the island. She was in the woman's room, and Victoria was with her.

The woman had creeped Wendy out worse than any boy she had ever had the displeasure to know growing up as well as passing through adulthood.

As she was undressing, drying herself with a fluffy white towel, she caught Victoria standing close by, eyeballing her as if she were a juicy steak. She had eyes like a predator, like Gabe Marske from middle school, the wrestling team in high, and the creep with a foot fetish Jeremy Hoyt from college. They all had looked at her the same way Victoria was looking at her now. The very sight of it was so strange and so sudden to Wendy, that she no longer felt forty, but instead as vulnerable as she had been as a little girl. Since becoming that age, men had stopped looking at her so much with lust or desire. Their looks were natural, more respectful, as if thinking 'This is a respectable woman who had done a lot in her life' as opposed to how eyes had looked at her growing up. The kind of eyes that made you feel more like a treasure, but with something sinister about it. A kind of desire that made her as tense as a rabbit being eyed by a hungry beast. Wendy had thought that period had ended for her, and she could finally relax without growing uncomfortable with the heebie-jeebies.

But now, in the current present, she was being ogled at by a woman almost her exact age, and looking like a horny old man with an itch that needs scratching. Men, in Wendy's opinion, were vain and selfish creatures who would mentally undress any girl from the age of 15 to 50 and not lose a wink of sleep over it. To take advantage and steal what wasn't rightfully theirs. Wendy was sure of it, because Victoria had that same look in her eye, and that lewd smile barely tugging at the corners of her mouth.

Wendy had always struggled with this fear of men. It had been an obstacle for Cain who had thankfully overcome it and made Wendy feel safe, vulnerable around him, and trusting of him. Out of all the swinging dicks in the world, his had been honest and true, and Wendy could allow herself to be held by him without the sense of dread and unease she had become accustomed to since she was very little. It took a long time just to let go of everything that had happened to her growing up, and overcome the jittering terror that clutched at her heart the moment she saw a man staring at her, seeming to contemplate of how easy it would be to take her.

Now, presently, those bad feelings began to creep in as if they had never left at all; just waiting for her to leave the door unlocked so that they could slip right back in. It made sense why Victoria mentioned that her husband didn't satisfy her. Now she understood why she was here on Isla Bonidada. This woman and her husband *did* have problems. She could see it in Victoria's eyes, the intensity they held, how severe it really was. The look reminded Wendy of one particular person, who, while no doubt burning in Hell in this moment, felt alive and real before Wendy, and she couldn't help but think almost childishly, *Why are you looking at me like that, Daddy?*

When she *did* speak, Victoria sounded on the verge of losing control. Like someone who slammed their thumb in the car door and had to restrain themselves for screaming or swearing. In this case, like a dog unable to keep its tongue in its mouth. She was restraining herself, but to what end?

"My, my, how *do* you do it?" she had asked. "How do you keep yourself looking so... young and beautiful?"

She had said 'young and beautiful' but it sounded to Wendy's adolescent brain like 'sexy and tasty.' Something a perverted old man would say. Two words that used to traumatize Wendy until she grew out of it. Or *thought* she grew out of it.

Stop it, you are being rude and overthinking it. She is just admiring *you, not thinking... that.*

Still, Wendy felt uncomfortable putting on her panties and bra. In fact, she was in so much of a hurry to get her pants on, her foot got caught in the pantleg for a bit and she had to pull back to release herself and give her more wiggle room. As she was starting to insert the other foot, she froze as she felt hot and boozy breath hit the back of her neck. The familiar scent made her sick to her stomach. Pill capsules and rotten teeth.

She whirled about, nearly tangling herself in the process. Victoria was right there, and Wendy was so startled that her tangled feet caused her to fall back and land on her rump. The impact stung and them numbed her as she sat humiliated and wincing. When she opened her eyes the pain was forgotten as she stared up at the woman now towering over her, still in her bathing suit and grinning like a fox.

There was no doubt about it. If the Jackson family had marital problems, and such problems delve deep in layers and often are a bunch of little things piled together beneath something blatant and huge, Wendy could guess one such problem and she was both disgusted with herself and disgusted with the truth of the matter. Victoria Jackson was as perverted as an old man and had similar tastes. She could see it in her eyes, she could hear it in her breathing, and she experienced it when Victoria stooped down and pushed down on Wendy's shoulders while she was still down, pinning her back to the floor and hanging over her like the disgusting boys who she agreed to go out with in high school, or the men her own father would let into the house to ogle her and mentally strip her. Her own father actually attempting something and Wendy never even knew what was happening until it actually happened.

Victoria *strained* it seemed, and it morbidly reminded Wendy of the old men who came in her presence, jerking off while she was in the pool, or simply wandering around the house, or coming home from school. The look was so repulsive that Wendy felt bile rise in her throat as she began to buck and push Victoria off. It felt as if she were pushing against something heavy in a horrible dream however, as Wendy felt just as paralyzed. Victoria held her still, her face now stricken with panic, breaking like ice across the glee that had previously been there.

"Don't! Don't... Don't struggle, please. I don't mean to scare you, but you are just so pretty..."

"Get off," said Wendy, now beginning to hyperventilate.

"Wait," said Victoria still holding her down. "Wait, I... God, I can't help it. Just relax, please, I just wanna-"

"I swear to god I'm going to scream," Wendy threatened. She had said this a few times in her life before, and had wished she never would have to again. Because she knew when it came to men who had their minds set, they wouldn't be dissuaded. They wouldn't bother with such a threat.

Evidently, Victoria wouldn't either.

"Please, don't," she said. "Look, I've been watching you for a while. You and the younglings, but they would never find someone like me attractive. You're closer to my age. You... I know we just met and this is crazy, but-"

She got no further. In her panic, Wendy managed to get her foot under the woman and kick her off. Victoria flew back arms flailing and her head struck the side of the lockers. She curled up and moaned with her hand pressed against her head. Wendy got up, hurrying to pull her pants on and seize her blouse. She started to leave but then went back and snagged her purse and her flipflops. All the while Victoria laid on the floor moaning and groaning.

"Touch me again," Wendy snarled on the way out. "And I'll report you!"

Such a threat meant nothing to people like Victoria. But Wendy hoped she sounded serene and fierce enough to get the woman to back off. She thought of telling someone anyway, her husband especially, but the idea of describing it made her sick to her stomach and she had to go to the nearest employee bathroom to vomit. She locked herself in and threw herself onto the bowl and spilled her guts as she sobbed and cried. It was difficult to breathe even after she was done and she found herself curling into a fetal position on the filthy floor and not giving a single shit. Her sobs racked her and sent shockwaves through her spine. She had gotten away, but the damage had been done. She laid there for a long time, whimpering and feeling so insignificantly small.

(You're very pretty, Wendy.)

Daddy, what are you-

(Just come here, sit with me. You know I love you, right?)

I love you too, Daddy.

(Good. Good... come here now. Sit with me.)

"Go to Hell," Wendy sobbed aloud in the florescent light that haloed over her as she laid on the bathroom floor. "Go and rot in Hell you... sonofa..."

Her sobs denied her anything else to say as tears squeezed from her clenched eyes. She stayed there for who knows how long.

When she was done she flushed the toilet and went to the sink to wash her face and rinse out her mouth with some water. She was still crying, softer now but crying nonetheless. She had not cried like this since she was a teenager, and she was devastated that in a matter of minutes, maybe even seconds, Victoria had reduced her to such a state that she thought only men were capable of. What she had overcome in order to grow up, learn to trust others especially her own husband, had been shattered completely by someone of the same sex. It completely broke her idea of a deviant, and now Wendy no longer felt safe not just with men, but with women. The illusion of safety concerning her age had completely faded, and revealed the cold hard truth. She wasn't safe just because of her age. She was *never* safe.

When she came back up onto the poop deck, Cain was talking to Paul and smoking cigarettes. The crew on the boat seemed displeased at this but didn't say anything. Victoria was there too, a bandage on her forehead. When she turned to see Wendy, her smile broadened.

"Oh! There she is!" Cain exclaimed, leaving the party and meeting her halfway. There was concern in his eyes but he was smiling. "How are you, hon? Everything all right?" He was looking her up and down, knowing something was wrong. Despite her trying to smile herself, she couldn't hide that from him. He knew her too well.

Wendy's eyes turned from her husband to the woman who attacked her not too long ago. Victoria appeared confused at first and then her face lit up with realization. She looked away, saying something to Paul.

Bile rose in Wendy's throat again, but she managed to suppress her disgust and say with effort, "Yeah, everything is fine. Just... the boat is all." She crossed her arms, not realizing she was hugging herself almost protectively.

She *should* have told Cain then and there, she knew that. She should tell him right here and now, who cares if she put Victoria and Paul on the spot and embarrass them? She didn't feel safe with the woman, and she had the right to feel safe, didn't she? She felt like such a little kid thinking and feeling this way, but goddammit it wasn't right regardless of how old you got; the scars still remained.

"Hon, you've been gone for some time," Cain said in a lower tone. This time he wasn't bothering with a smile to hide his concern. "What's wrong? You look like you've been crying."

She couldn't say anything. She couldn't bring herself to explain what had happened five or maybe ten minutes ago. She knew she should say something, to Cain at least, but she just didn't feel safe enough to do it, not yet anyway. Or maybe it was because Victoria, like herself, was a woman. It had been easier back then, growing up Wendy had detested men, and Cain had been the only guy she had actually allowed inside both physically and emotionally. Trust came hard for her, but he had pulled through and helped her heal from her past. What she felt right now, was indeed the past, the past which had been ruled by the nasty men and boys in her life, and at that time, Wendy never trusted anything with a dick, plain and simple. Women she could trust. Women she could understand. Women, like herself, she vowed to protect.

But this time, the woman was a lesbian, and had come onto her as easily as a man would have. Hesitant, yes, but many of them had been hesitant too, and the initiation was just as bad as the actual act. However, because of this, not only did it not feel safe exposing Victoria, but it also felt wrong. She felt like she would be betraying that little girl who managed to survive that sort of childhood. Wendy felt like she was betraying everything she had stood for back then, as wrong as it was, given how Cain had practically saved her from herself and her (understandably justifiable) prejudice. Because of this, her tongue had been tied in a not and her jaw locked tight.

(you won't tell your mother, will you Winny?)
Oh god...
(you're such a sweet girl... come here...)

"Winny?"

It was Cain. His voice, comforting and soothing, commanding no power this time, only concern. Upon hearing his voice, Wendy audibly shuddered, and said she was fine. "Just seasick," she told him, hoping her eyes told him to be patient and he would be told later.

Cain got the message and hesitantly said, "Okay."

He had led her to the edge of the ship in case she had to vomit and Wendy appreciated that. She was still hugging herself defensively, and had to resist the urge to pull away from Cain's comforting hand. He understood that stance immediately. The protective hugging gesture Wendy did as a subconscious method of comfort and safety. She had done it a lot when they had been going steady in college and throughout his small-time IBO stage in Amway. Part of her healing had been being in a safer environment, but also just being around him. He respected her boundaries, was patient when she cried or was defensive and tried to send him away, and in the end everything had paid off. Even through marriage she had her moments, but little by little, she learned to trust herself as well as he, and she had gotten over that terrible childhood that Cain knew everything about and respected her for making it out. 'For surviving' he had called it.

Seeing her in this protective mode again however, made him nervous. What had happened that had caused her to degenerate in a matter of minutes? She had been just fine earlier, happy and free.

Now, it felt like to Cain as if he were looking at a younger version of Wendy. Still pretty, still smart and caring, absolutely. But also untrusting, haunted, and scared.

To pull her aside again and persist to ask what was wrong was out of the question. When Wendy was like this during the earlier parts of their relationship, she responded with defensive hostility in order to protect herself. As much as he always hated to do this, Cain would bide his time and simply stick close to her without breaking any physical or mental boundaries. Inaudibly let her know that he was there, and as long as he was there, the monsters of the past would not get her.

And so he did, and she stuck with him the entire boat ride back to Isla Bonidada. Other than a one or two word response or a small hint of a smile, she didn't say much. She only sipped her drink somberly, and chewed softly on crackers and cheese. Cain only placed his hand close to hers on their seat, not quite touching her but close enough to feel her body temperature, and she no doubt feeling his. This brought her comfort, and at last she responded and took his hand in her own. Small, bony hands in his thick and leathery fingers. He gave them a squeeze, and she squeezed back.

Whatever it is, this gesture always said. *I got your back.*

And he did, even when they had kissed and he had tasted vomit. He had asked no questions, only looked at her curiously before quickly washing his mouth out with his drink. As funny as it had been, Wendy appreciated him.

Thinking back on what had happened now on the balcony of their hut, Wendy felt her stomach clench and unclench like a giant fist. When Cain got out of the bathroom, she would tell him. They wouldn't go out and about like all the other couples who were no doubt taking advantage of their free time before dinner, they would discuss what had happened and what to do from here.

She looked towards the beach and saw someone walking up the boardwalk and stairs towards their hut. By the uniform, it was someone from the resort. She waved him up, and he arrived just as Cain had gotten out of the shower. Giving him time to get dressed, Wendy met the man out on the front porch.

"Mrs. Ashton, yes?" the man asked, his accent thick and Caribbean. His chocolate skin made his teeth pop out sparkling and white like piano keys. He was strong, and had long dreadlocks that were pulled together with a rubber band between his shoulder blades.

"That's me," Wendy replied. "Can I help you?"

"Just wanted to inform you and your husband that dinner will be an hour late. I'm going down the beach and letting everyone I see know. If you need something to eat beforehand, please call the kitchen, otherwise I would save your appetite for tonight. Ms. Lewis is going to be making something spectacular tonight."

Wendy smiled. "Well, if it is anything like last night's meal, then I think we will wait. Thank you for informing me, Mr...?"

"Campbell, Ma'am," Mr. Campbell replied. "And thank *you*. Enjoy the rest of your afternoon."

"We will," Wendy said while thinking at the end, *We'll try*. By the time Cain came out, Campbell was already making his way back to the beach.

"What was that about?" Cain asked.

"Dinner will be late," Wendy answered, and she turned to look at her husband. Married for over twenty years and counting. He was still as handsome as ever, and an overwhelming feeling of love spread through her chest like a fever.

"Hmm," Cain replied. "Well, what do you want to do until then? Wanna try that bocce ball court we saw last night?"

"Later. Cain, can I talk to you?"

Those had been the magic words. Cain ushered her inside, and they went into the safety of the hut, and she discussed what had taken place between her and Victoria Jackson.

5th Letter

Our return home had brought no joy or relief as it often does when returning from the city. We had come home to what words can only describe as a catastrophe. One of the huts had burned to the ground, the residents who had been inside reduced to charred bone and ashes. We found everyone around this pyre praying or lamenting among the ashes.

Upon asking what had happened, someone said they saw something feasting on the family inside the house. A woman who had no legs and wings. It was devouring the pregnant mother who was inside, the husband and daughter already having been killed and would no doubt be fed upon next. Before I could get a chance to get a closer look, several men from the village had converged on my mother and bound her with rope, beating her with bolos and dousing her with holy water. When I tried to rush to her aid, I was held back and beaten, and forced to the ground where I watched as she was stripped and hung naked upside down in front of the entire village. Like the woman before, she was stationed above a boiling cauldron once it was finished, and was violently spun around like a top; all the while getting whipped despite her pleas and mine. For the longest time they spun her around, but they did not eject a black bird from her system. They then took me and stripped me and performed the same ritual on me, hoping for the same result, all the while ransacking our home and what we had gathered in Capiz. I remember spinning around for what felt like an eternity, the blood in my head making me grow dizzier and dizzier and thus unable to comprehend the pain as I was whipped and beaten nor the heat rising up from the bubbling caldron that I thought for sure would be my doom.

When they found nothing circumstantial, they let us go, but still remained weary simply because we had gone to Capiz in the first place. They had no suspects as to who the woman in the hut with the Abarro family was, nor did anyone wish to take responsibility for setting the fire. No one trusted one another, and things were starting to get much worse. I remember helping my mother into our home, our bodies covered shamefully with pieces of tarp to hide not only our nakedness but the bleeding wounds we had received for our unspoken crime.

The next highest priest had taken my mother and I in to treat our wounds. My mother requested a blessing to be bestowed upon them, but the priest only acknowledged her in Latin, trying to get a reaction out of her. Trying to see how my mother and I would react to the ancient language. All of our stuff had been taken from us, everyone seeing a need to protect themselves more than we who had risked going to Capiz in the first place. We needed refuge, a blessing from God, anything to protect us from the evil that has settled into the village like a dark plague.

The priest did as he was asked, for a price. I was sent away, allowing him to use my mother how he pleased. I never felt less of a man than when I allowed that to happen. Only then were we allowed to stay within the church, a luxury not many in the village could afford. But we were no safer in the church than we were outside. Because the devil that they thought would not step onto holy ground, did just that. It was this very night that my hatred for the village was extinguish, and all doubt about what sort of person the killer was along with it. Because it had entered the church, and tried to kill my mother and I.

What I am about to describe is very hard, and I am sobbing as I take the pen to this paper. Even now I see stains from my tears smearing some of the ink. But I will write it down. I will write it all down and I will conquer this demon, once and for all if I can help it. I refuse to let it haunt me any longer than it already has.

We were asleep in the back room just behind the sanctuary. It was a storage area with tables and chairs and some boxes of decorations for holidays and events. My mother and I slept on some emergency cots the church had in case of disease or some other catastrophe. My mother had been sound asleep, but I was wakeful and would not sleep for more than an hour or so. Throughout the night through the thin walls of the backroom I could hear the chitter of flying foxes, beetles, and the occasional croak of a frog. Thinking back on it, I remember all sounds waking me up, with one sound in particular seeming to grow further and further away. A rattling clicking sound, like hollow stalks of bamboo striking one another or the clicking of bones. I can remember it distinctly because it always came in patterns, which I assumed was because of a nearby beetle. Every time I heard it when I awoke in the night, it became quieter and quieter, slowly fading away as if the perpetrator was moving far from the church to the point where you could no longer hear it. I remember ignoring it too, because my mind was fitful with the anger at my people and what had happened to my mother and I, what she in particular had to do just to gain sanctuary in a place that practically blamed us for the deaths of that family.

Tikitik-tik-ka-tikitik-ka-tikitik... Tikitik-tik-ka-tikitik-ka-tikitik... Tikitik-tik-ka-tikitik-ka-tikitik... Tikitik-tik-ka-tikitik-ka-tikitik...

I still hear this sound in the dead of night even to this day.

When I had fallen asleep for the last time that night, I could barely make out the sound. The next time I awoke, blinding moonlight was shining through a hole in the roof, the palm leaves that filled the spaces between the timber having been pulled open to let something in. I heard a sort of clucking sound, along with something that sounded like a slug squirming across pavement. It was right behind me, and my back was to my mother. I remember breaking into sweat, feeling very afraid for whatever I might see. It was if my body knew something my brain did not, and refused to let me turn to look at what was making the sound between me and my mother. What monster now had her.

Except when I finally *did* manage to turn, I would see what many would have gone mad at the very sight of.

I am sorry, my hand trembles at the memory of this night. I must call it quits.

Sixteen

By the time Amos got to the infirmary, John had met him at the door and wouldn't let him in without talking first.

"First off," the old man said. "His boat is locked away. Second, we need to talk about what sort of man he looks like. I think he's a pirate."

"That so?"

"It's so. On board, we found a rifle, and something that looked like a machete. Also, he had a whip coiled at his hip."

"A whip? Like for a bull?"

"Maybe, but it isn't an iron-tip. I don't know what it's made of, but it ain't anything I'm familiar with."

Amos frowned. "Did the guy talk?"

"He hasn't woken up yet. Guy is dehydrated to a fucking crisp. He's getting liquids injected, but it will be a bit before he gets up."

"Any identification?"

"None."

"Hence why you think he's a pirate."

John nodded.

"What do you think?" Amos asked. "Should we call the coast guard?"

"Might bother your guests," John said. "You know how Crockett is with the coast guard."

Amos nodded. The last time someone needed medical attention, the coast guard had blocked off the beach to ensure they had plenty of space to remove the injured worker and get him off the island. Someone, one of the guests, complained that he couldn't go for a swim that day, and Crockett got wind of it. Ever since then, if the coast guard *were* to be called and that was *only* if the doctor on Isla Bonidada couldn't do anything for the patient who was not a guest, then the coast guard had to be told to come at night. Guests were one thing, but workers were another in Crockett's eyes. It made it difficult for the crew to feel safe here, especially when working in an environment where anything could go wrong, from a kitchen burn or accident, to a shark attack on the coast, which was exactly what happened to the worker who was snorkeling around the area collecting coral for souvenirs when a shark mistook him for a seal. And what had Crockett said to Amos that day?

"I want that man *fired*, Amos. He disrupted our guests, and his talk of a shark might not get anyone to swim in our waters again. Also, have John sweep the beaches. I don't want any sharks hunting anywhere near the shore."

Amos had done the second part, but not the first. He had simply called the man while he was in a Mexican hospital, and told him to come back under a different identity. They would go through the interviewing process again, and he would be able to keep his job if and only if he used a fake name and told his closest friends not to call him by his real name. It was dangerous, but Amos was not going to fire a guy who almost got his leg ripped off by a shark. Fuck that.

And Crockett too, he thought even now.

"Okay, so we wait until the guy wakes up," Amos said sarcastically. "Then he never wakes up, we end up with a dead body and get in deep trouble with the American Resort law as well as Mexico for not helping a man in his time of need."

"Not quite," said Jake who was stepping out of the infirmary to meet with the men. The man in white was as old as John, his leathery skin thick and tanned. He wore thick glasses which he took off to clean as he shut the door behind him. "There is no point in calling the guard anyway because the man's life isn't in danger."

"You sure about that?" Amos asked.

"As I told John," Jake said patiently. "Let me see what I can do here, so that Crockett doesn't blow a gasket. I saw what I could do, and I say the man needs rest. Moving him isn't going to make him any better or worse."

"John said the guy might be a pirate."

"Could be," Jake agreed. "But that isn't our concern. My concern is making sure the guy wakes up coherent and healthy. When he does, we ask him what he wants us to do. If we jump the gun, not only will be attracting unnecessary attention that could cause Crockett to worry, then we have to deal with the Mexican politics despite being *technically* U.S. soil. I already discussed the situation with Crockett myself, and he said, and I quote, 'Get him better and then get him off the island with the crew going home for the summer.'"

"Make it look like he never just arrived here out of the blue," Amos said unbelievably. "Doesn't he care about how dangerous that might be if not for that drifter, then maybe, I dunno, *us*? We don't even know who the heck this guy is."

John scoffed. "You're talking about someone who wanted us to fire Campbell for getting attacked by a shark."

Amos shook his head. It would do none of them any good arguing about Crockett, so he changed the subject. "Our new guest, is he gonna be all right?"

"Right as rain," Jake said. "Needs rest, and food. We'll figure the rest out as time goes. There was really no need to delay dinner for this gentleman, Amos. Everything was fine, as I told John."

"I want someone watching him still," John said. "Not on cameras, but in the room as well. We don't know who he is or where he is from, and that makes him a risk. If he doesn't wake up tomorrow, doctor, then I'm sorry but I'm calling the coast guard."

Jake shrugged, not seeming to care either way. "Do what you must. As long as Crockett doesn't get on my back about it."

"Then I might as well call," Amos said. "Not like I'm gonna be here much longer anyway."

John smirked. "Going out with a bang, eh?"

"Crockett is an asshole, he might as well be told so," Amos reasoned. "At the same time, we might be saving not only that kid's life but our own skin as well."

"Agreed," John said.

"Gentlemen," Jake said excusing himself to head back inside the infirmary and leaving the two outside.

"On a different note," Amos asked his friend. "Any news on our missing workers?"

John nodded. "Come to the office. I want you to look at something."

At the security room, John replayed the clip of the female worker and Winklemann. Amos didn't see any significance other than the guy going into a restricted area, until John zoomed in on the worker. His eyes widened.

"Tamia?"

"Keep watching."

They did, and when it was the dog that came out and not the missing girl, Amos grew even more puzzled. "What in the world?"

"No one was in there either. We checked."

"She didn't just *disappear*, John, so where the fuck did she go?" Amos realized the frustration in his voice and was instantly ashamed of himself.

John shrugged, seeming not to notice. "Beats me."

"Where is that dog now?"

"With some of the boys working on the pit out back. It's been sitting there watching all day. Nothing seems out of line for it."

"How did *it* get in, and how did Tamia get out?"

John wished he knew. He had an idea, a minor thought, but he wouldn't speak it. Amos thought it too, but the idea was too nutty to comprehend. For one, it wasn't possible, plain and simple. Secondly, it was improbable. That Tamia and the dog were one and the same. But that was just silly thinking, and both men mentally dismissed the idea without even so much as discussing it.

"Keep your eyes peeled for her and her boyfriend," Amos told John. "I want them found and in my office this morning."

"Yes sir," John said with a halfassed salute.

Just then the radio crackled, and John picked it up. "Yes? Go for John."

A Hispanic voice answered, asking him to go to channel four. He switched, and then asked what was going on.

"I have a Cain Ashton on the line, he wants to talk to you as head of security," said the man on the other line.

"What's the problem?" John never took direct phone calls unless he knew the details as to why. Amos couldn't blame him on that.

"Says there was, eh, unethical conduct, so to speak."

John immediately looked at Amos, at first accusingly, and then curiously. "With a staff member?" he asked. Amos gave him the finger, and the old man grinned despite the seriousness of the situation.

"With another guest."

"Aww, Christ," Amos moaned.

"Patch him through," John said. "Back to one." After changing channels John picked up the receiver of his office phone. After dialing the transfer number, he paused for a moment and said, "This is John, how can I help you?"

He listened for a while, grunting and nodding and occasionally saying "I understand." Other than a question or two which he wrote down on a nearby pad, he didn't interrupt the man. When he was finished, he thanked Mr. Ashton and hung up. He leaned back in his chair with a sigh, as if exhausted.

"Well, this is a new one," he finally said.

"What? A youngling going after an oldie?" Amos said smiling.

"Heh, something like that, if the age is correct."

"So what is it?"

"Let's just say, a female guest got pretty handsy with Mr. Ashton's wife."

Amos couldn't believe his ears. "No shit."

"No shit," John confirmed. "Shook the missus very bad according to her husband. We'll have to make sure those two families are separated indefinitely. It's up to you however what we do with the Jacksons."

"Victoria Jackson did it?"

"Yup."

"Shit… Does the husband know?"

"Not yet, I told Ashton to leave it to us and according to him, he hasn't said anything to Paul or Victoria."

"Hopefully he keeps it that way. In the meantime, we'll keep them separated and I'll have a talk with the two of them after dinner. Give them a strike. One more incident however, and we will have to figure something out. We cannot tolerate harassment like that between guests."

"Agreed."

Amos sighed, thinking about his booze back at his hut. This day just kept getting better and better.

Seventeen

Dinner while delayed was greatly anticipated, and when the time came exceptionally executed in reception.

Everyone gathered outside and after a stellar introduction from Kyra Lewis who came in after the fire jugglers were sent away, the food was brought out in huge heaping plates for each table which housed each couple, with the exception of Matt Winklemann whose wife was still sick. Jake had to inform Amos that Mr. Winklemann had refused aid from Jake's part since his wife wanted to be alone. Amos absently told Jake that if the wife doesn't request help by tomorrow or after at the latest, to check in himself.

The first dish served was *tacos de langosta*, a fried lobster in tacos with fresh vegetables and delicious sauces for all palates. This was served with a bed of soaked Mexican rice and octopus ceviche, which was an acquired taste and required a lot of homemade tortilla chips. This was accompanied with margaritas, mojitos, and other authentic drinks from Mexico. Most of the older couples were hesitant to try something so new, but they warmed up really fast once they tried it for the first time, and all praised Kyra and her crew for yet another smashing success in terms of food. For dessert, keeping up with the tradition, was deep fried ice cream with a thick cinnamon shell which Cynthia in particular, absolutely fell in love with and had a good chunk of Adam's portion along with hers. After which, music played over the broad speakers and everyone was invited to dance as the DJ stepped onto the stage and played music which got even most of the employees dancing along with the couples who were intoxicated with drink and food.

Before the event, Amos took it upon himself to not delay and pull both Paul and Victoria Jackson aside. He informed them of the situation and told them what was expected of them in the following weeks on Isla Bonidada, and if they believed that they were the victims instead, to please tell him now. Victoria apologized up and down but Paul simply looked shocked, and so their side while not needing to be told, was told regardless. Amos had been concerned about the guy, and watched him even as he danced stiffly with Victoria out on the sand. He watched as they were the first to leave, and after radioing someone to go and watch them, he went back to his drink and watched the other guests. At some point, Kyra Lewis walked up to him, her smile wide and just as intoxicating.

"Hey, handsome," she said. "Come here often?"

"Every night," Amos said with just as much good humor. "What's up? Everything okay?"

"Just fine. You are just sitting here looking as sour as John is." She pointed at the old man who was at the bar having some drinks of his own.

"He works hard, cut him some slack."

"Bullshit, I work hard," Kyra retorted. "We all need to loosen up. So how about you come dance with me, since sourpuss over there declined?"

Amos had to laugh. "Did he now?"

"Yeah, now come on."

Relenting, Amos allowed himself to be led to the dance floor. Kyra was right, they all worked hard, and he was almost done. Soon he would never see Isla Bonidada or deal with Mr. Crockett again. He might as well enjoy the good things about the island. The music, the food, drink, and wonderful company and crew. In the end, there was no doubt that this was the best job in the world, despite all its flaws. He still looked forward to early retirement, but it was good to dance, drink, and be merry.

Markus Williams had been working at the Isla Bonidada Resort for almost two years now. His father had gotten him the job after moving out of Brazil, saying how wonderful it had been for him to work on the island, and the twenty-something had no argument otherwise. He enjoyed working for Amos Mulderich, he liked Mr. Hopper, and most importantly, he liked working for Benjamin Franklins who was his primary leader. Other than the big three, Mulderich, Hopper, and Lewis, there was Mr. Franklins, Ms. Novarez, and Mr. Mendez. All three were the best bosses Williams ever had, but Franklins was his favorite, wherever he was. When Mulderich asked him to follow the Jacksons and make sure they returned to their hut safely, he got up without question, downed the rest of his mocktail, and followed at a close but otherwise respectfully distant pace.

He drifted closer to the ocean, letting his feet get struck by the tide which proceeded to wash out the sand that was caught in his sandals. He loved the ocean, loved how the air smelled, loved the warm waters, loved the fish and the seabirds. As a child, he always liked taking a little raft out and pretending to be a pirate. Now he was on an island, working for a fantastic resort and had been trained like a majority of the employees on Isla Bonidada to be prepared in case *real* pirates ever did show up. One bit of training which had to be done in the outskirts of Mexico, was learning how to shoot firearms safely and efficiently. It was required for those who were entrusted with this knowledge to take a course once a year, and renew their handling license for legal purposes concerning the island. John Hopper oversaw that process every year when he took his three months off.

He was on the shore, trudging softly through the ever-arriving tide, when he noticed that the Jacksons were heading up their boardwalk. He stopped and watched them make their ascent while having a private conversation. Once they were inside, he would radio Amos and head back to the resort pit. Then the rest of the evening would commence and he would be able to rest before leading the trip at the Crockett Grotto.

He was about to turn to head back when he caught something in the corner of his eye. A flicker of movement across the water roughly four meters away from the shoreline. He stared at the softly rolling waves until he saw it again, a dark figure seeming to leap a few inches over the water's surface only to descend again and disappear from view. A big fish by the looks of it, not a shark for Williams didn't see any fin. But he stood there fascinated that something was out hunting this late at night. Most jumpers, regardless of size, started to come out during the early morning hours. There were more insects and smaller fish often patrolled the reefs for food as well, making good eating for the bigger fish and so on and so forth. But it still was unnatural, for the reefs were further away from the shore, not as close as it was now.

So what in the world was feeding this late at night, so close to the shore?

Then it came out of the water, and remained as such, slowly shifting like a piece of driftwood. There were some clouds in the night which momentarily blocked the moon, and so Williams had a hard time understanding exactly what it was until the cloud passed, and silver moonlight shone down like a halo upon the creature who stood up from the water dripping and unnatural.

It was a girl. It was no one that Williams recognized, but he was barely able to process such a notion. For the woman was standing waist-deep in the water as naked as that painting of Venus in the shell. Her breasts were clearly visible, and her long dark hair went down to almost the small of her back. Williams couldn't believe his eyes, and the woman who was now staring at him with an intensity that made his stomach hot and heavy in his gut, curled a finger at him, gesturing for him to come. Her bright eyes, bright and luminous in the light to almost a dim red color as if she were in an old photograph or wearing contacts that reflected the moonlight differently, seemed to draw him further in.

Something about those eyes made Williams feel lightweight, as if he were just getting the feeling of getting high. He had not smoked since last night but the feeling was about the same, and the longer he looked upon the woman the more sensational she appeared; Her form unbound by clothing and instead the sea, her raven hair catching the moonlight and that gorgeous face seeming to want him and only him, made Williams lose his concern of a strange woman being out in the water at night entirely, as well as any other concerns that plagued his mind.

He smiled, allowing the drawing to take hold as he began to wade into the water, first sinking to his ankles, then his calves, then his thighs. It was as if he were an insect being drawn to a light, under a spell which drew him closer and closer. Questions of who this woman was and where she had come from and *why* she was out here, were damned. Indeed Williams was unable to say a simple 'hello' let alone even an 'are you okay?' All that mattered was the sensation of those breasts in his hand, the plumpness of her rump, the taste of her kiss. This primal force alone was all Williams knew, as he came chest-deep in the water and approached the woman. She had to be almost taller than he to still be sticking out of the water as high as she was. He was now eye-level with those breasts, and he puckered his lips to kiss and to suckle.

That was when the woman smiled broadly, displaying several rows of jagged shark-like teeth, and the spell on Markus Williams was broken.

Panic began to surge in his blood, fueling it with adrenaline, his brain telling him to flee but it was too late, for the woman pounced on him and dragged him under the water. He screamed as a burst of bubbles escaped his mouth as the woman pulled him deeper into the wake and looking upward he could see his air escaping towards the surface, now mixing with the crimson wafts of his own blood. He felt sharp dagger-like claws sink into his chest, anchoring him down onto the ocean floor and then something thick and warm drove into his mouth like a wriggling penis, causing him to panic. He couldn't close his mouth however for his jaw was fully extended, propped open by the loathsome thing that was now driving down his throat, causing the walls to tear all the way down to his chest cavity. His vision turned red and hazy, slowly diminishing into an inky blackness that shut out all light, and all Williams could feel was pain, and then numbness.

He couldn't breathe, and the blackness became spotty bubbles rose, as well as waves of crimson which too were lost in the void.

Meanwhile Paul Jackson was having a drink on the balcony. He had not answered Victoria who was asking him what he was thinking the whole way back to the hut. He didn't want to talk to her, and she finally gave up and went inside. He didn't want to think or feel the pain he felt now. All he wanted was to drink and forget. The whiskey burned his throat and boiled in his stomach along with the tequila he had from dinner, but he didn't care if he puked. He didn't care if he blacked out and slept the night out here on the balcony or got so drunk he'd just jump off it. He would keep on drinking so that the world would just disappear and him with it if that was what it took. He felt betrayed, hurt, it wasn't just men he had to constantly feel worried about now, but *women* too?

Christ, it was enough to make him sick on that alone; can't even satisfy her enough that even women were better than him. *Women!*

He downed another, then refilled it halfway up the glass. It took him three gulps to finish this one, and he sat the glass down and sighed as the burning sensation escaped him like dragon's breath. He burped and winced as some of it was caught in his throat making it burn. Another thing to add to his self-pity.

And why not? Does he not deserve it at least for a moment? There would be a time to deal with this, a time to be an adult and figure out where to go from here. He had been strung out too far and he had only himself to blame for it. He had let the bitch have him and his life and he had no one else to blame but himself. The shame and embarrassment of it had been tolerable or so he thought, but now? When Mulderich came to them and expressed concern, what was he supposed to do? That had been the final nail in the coffin, and once this trip was over, he'd have to get rid of her. Plain and simple.

But when does anything that sounds simple ever get executed?

"Well, that's it then," he muttered. He looked at the empty glass, thought of throwing it as hard as he could into the night and waiting for that satisfying sound of glass shattering. However, that would have changed nothing about what has happened here tonight.

He looked behind him. Victoria was out now, reading something from the bookshelf provided in the hut. Acting like nothing happened. Seeing her going through the motions filled Paul with so much rage that his grip tightened on the bottle, threatening to break it.

He poured himself another glass, this time releasing the bottle once he put it down and he quaffed the drink all the while glaring hatefully at the woman curled up and reading a goddamn book.

Fuck it. She didn't care, so he wouldn't either. He wasn't going to let this go on anymore; He didn't care if he went fucking bankrupt, he was a man goddammit, and he was not going to deal with this anymore. It was time he started to act like a man; It was time he cut out the cancer.

He returned his attention to the beach, where he saw someone walking down towards one of the huts. He squinted, thinking it had to be one of the workers. Or maybe that was Matt Winklemann, the sleaze. Cain had told him to keep an eye on that creep, that he had been eyeballing Wendy earlier, as well as some of the other women. The guy didn't seem to have a type, didn't care how old or young the women were.

Like Victoria...

Paul hadn't realized he had been squeezing his hand into a fist, the glass still in his grasp. It shattered in his hand, glass slipping into both his palm and sprinkling the deck. He felt the satisfying sting, and looked at his hand where the blood was starting to drip. A nearby mosquito had been buzzing about, and at the scent of blood, it handed on his hand and seemed to scuttle across it, probably thinking it didn't have to work so hard to get it's food, the little parasite.

Parasites...

Women.

Victoria...

Paul closed his hand around the mosquito, felt it's little body crumple and grind. He imagined it being Victoria, her limbs twisting and turning to dust, her insides squirting out and mixing with his own blood.

When she tried to talk to him and ask about what happened to his hand, Paul ignored her. He just went to the sink, pulled out some of the bigger shards stuck in his hand, and washed it. He then wrapped it in a towel and simply got another glass from the cabinet before going back out onto the deck. Victoria didn't bother to follow him; showed how far she was willing to go to talk to him. After a moment's thought, he poured some of the whiskey over his hand to disinfect it. Then he poured himself another glass and drank.

The person he saw on the beach was gone. And Paul didn't give a shit one way or another, and was just glad for the blessed silence that joined in his drinking.

No more, he vowed. No more.

Eighteen

Who Paul saw on the beach was indeed Matt Winklemann.
He was returning to his hut for the night after the music
was shut off for the conclusion of the evening. Some
couples were still there, but he wanted to sleep. He had a
big day tomorrow, and he wanted to make sure he got
plenty of rest.

He climbed up the steps, hearing the weathered
boards creak beneath his weight and he walked up to his
hut and stepped inside before locking the door behind
him. His mind was a blur of the evening as well as the
anticipation for tomorrow, and all he could truly think
consciously as of now was getting into bed with his
deceased wife and falling asleep beside her. He had never
slept so peacefully with her before.

He stopped when he realized the kitchen window
was opened. It was letting in the cool breeze which had
gotten stronger as the nights went on, a precursor for the
storm some of the workers were talking about earlier.

He stared at the window puzzled. Had he left the
window open? He didn't think he had. Nevertheless, he
closed the window, shutting out the breeze and left the
kitchen. He entered the master bedroom shutting the door
behind him and went straight for the bed. His wife was in
the bathtub where he had left her draining. He didn't want
to sleep in a bed full of blood and urine and so it had been
the best place to put her when not in use.

At the bed he stooped down and pulled out his
duffle bag. He pulled out his clothes and his toiletries, and
then sat back looking at the item he had smuggled in
through the Mexican border and onto the Santa Bonita

before getting it into Isla Bonidada. He placed three fingers
upon it, gently caressing it like a woman's smooth thigh.
Even the thought of what this would be used for was
giving Matt and erection, and he grinned in the gloom of
his room.

He was still staring at it when he heard a creak. He
looked up, eyes looking towards the bathroom. The door
was shut. Had he closed it before?

Yes, he had. Gabbie was in there, her storage area
for when he felt the need to have her company again. Her
body was getting colder but that had only increased his
excitement with her, especially when he thought about
what he would be doing tomorrow. Kind of funny, really,
as it had been years since Matthew had looked at Gabbie
the way he had this past 24 hours.

That creak sounded again on the other side. Matt
thought about the window he had closed and he
immediately grew serious, the lump that had been
developing in his pants slacking only to hang as nothing
solid.

Someone was inside.

Not taking his eyes off the door, Matt reached into
the duffle bag and after feeling around he found what he
was looking for and pulled it out. He then reached into one
of the side pockets of the bag, and removed the
appropriate magazine that went along with the .45 he had
brought on his vacation.

The pistol Gabbie knew about. Matt never liked
leaving home without it, saying it was always for
protection and he would rather have it and not need it
rather than need it and not have it. Gabbie had agreed,
and the pistol had proved to be more useful in things

other than protection, for he never had to truly use it to defend himself. But right now, knowing that someone was in the bathroom with his dead wife, he thought it would be high time to use it for that very purpose now. The other thing in the bag Gabbie had not known about, and it was to be used tomorrow.

But that depended on how Matt could handle this intruder and the aftermath that would follow. With the gun loaded and the safety off, he pulled back the slider to place a round in the chamber and he took aim at the door. He stood up and slowly made his way towards the door with the gun aimed right at it with both hands that held it firmly, and with purpose.

He crept slowly towards the door, heart pounding and temples burning. His hands did not tremble, and he did not hesitate as he neared the door and raised a foot to kick it in. His heel connected with the space right next to the knob and the cheap lock gave in. The door swung wide and crashed into the large tub on the other side.

What he witnessed paralyzed him completely, and inarguably.

It was a demon. That was all Matt could process as he stood before it. A demon sent to him from the depths of Hell by Satan himself. He had been watched, he had been tried, and now he was going to pay for the sins he had committed against those women and his wife. The winged monstrosity looked up and snarled at him with a mouthful of sharp teeth, her tongue long and red was down Gabbie's throat, and when it came out it was holding something red and dripping blood at the end. It disappeared down the demon's gullet like a worm in a hole along with the organ it had taken. Gabbie laid on the ground, appearing deflated like a dead balloon in the dim lighting of the bathroom nightlight. Her face was ghoulish, her bones pushing against her skin with nothing else to hold her together, and her skull had been cracked open with the brains inside appearing gone. It was a gorefest that Matt would have liked to be a part of, but given the current circumstance, he might very well receive his judgement here and now; there was a special place in Hell just for him, and this demon was going to be the very thing to take him there.

Matt felt his knees begin to shake, his hands holding the gun quivering. In his maddening terror, he let his bladder go, his pee warming the inside of his thighs and sending a pungent odor into the air that made the demon hiss distastefully.

Oh god, oh god, oh god…

But God wasn't here. He was somewhere far, far away, and even if He was here, He probably wouldn't lift a finger to save Matt's life. He was on his own as the demon turned towards him completely, rising like a snake over Gabbie's corpse with eyes burning bright and red like polished rubies.

He should shoot. He should put a bullet right in between those hellfire eyes of the demon. But would that even kill it? Were Matt's chances better if he were to fall to his knees and beg for mercy? Would it have any?

Why hasn't it come for me yet? Why is it just sitting there?

It occurred to him that the demon was speaking to him. It surprised him, for it sounded nothing like he was expecting. The voice was soft, melodious, and calmed him enough to get hold of himself and grip the weapon tighter and stop the shaking. He told the creature to keep back, and the demon asked it's question again. It was a language he couldn't understand, but it somehow sounded morphed or compressed into the English language to form a barely comprehendible sentence. It was as if the creature was speaking in all tongues rather than just one, and somehow, despite not understanding the words themselves, Matthew Winklemann understood. The more he looked into those hellish red eyes, he understood.

Understood, and began to feel at ease.

This both confused and scared Matt. He still felt locked in paralysis as his terror would not let him go. And yet as he looked upon those burning eyes and heard the words coming from the demon's mouth, he could not help but feel relaxed, tranquil.

The demon asked it's question a third time, and this time Matt answered, but his mouth was so dry; his saliva had dried up completely so that his voice cracked and he had to try again. "I killed her because she got in my way."

The demon stared at him, taking him in. The gaze was so unwavering that he felt as if the demon was picking at his brains, reading his mind in order to dig out the truth. He risked another look at his wife's corpse. How gruesome it looked. How defiled it had become. Had it really been eating her insides? Or was it lapping up whatever was left of her retched soul?

"Wh... who..." He licked his lips, feeling as well as *hearing* his dry tongue scrape against his drier lips. "What are you?"

The demon didn't reply. It only stared at him, studied him as if he were an interesting new species of insect. It disgusted Matt and filled him with revulsion, but at the same time that morbid curiosity of his made him wonder. What had Gabbie tasted like? He had licked at her blood, but what would the rest of her taste like? Her heart for example?

I'm going crazy, he realized. *I am going crazy; I will scream, and everything will be gone. I'll wind up in a padded room if this thing doesn't take me now.*

The demon asked another question, and Matt felt no need to lie for fear that if he would, the demon would know and charter his soul to the underworld. Little by little, Matt lowered his gun, feeling almost hypnotized into doing so. Was it the demon, or was he simply allowing himself to be approached? Even with the threat of being shot momentarily out of range, the demon didn't shift or move. It did not flee, and it did not attack.

It...

Just...

Stared.

The languages swirled and mixed. Bubbled and frothed. Pulsated and *breathed.*

Mahal mo ba ang kamatayan?

¿Amas la muerte?

Você ama a morte?

Mahal mo ba ang kamatayan?

Aloha 'oe i ka make?

Mahal mo ba ang kamatayan?

Amas mortem?

Mahal mo ba ang kamatayan?

Do you love death?

"I..."

I...

What had he said on the day of his and Gabbie's wedding?

(Do you take this young woman to be your lawfully wedded wife? In sickness and in health, for rich or for poor, until death do you part?)

How she had looked then. Young, innocent, pure in heart and none the wiser. Believing in another version of Matthew Winklemann, the one he had allowed her to see; allowed her to fall in love with. The one that didn't know about his true self, and never even came close to it until her own death.

(Until death do you part)
Until death do we *part…*
Do you take this young woman
(do you love death?)
to be your lawfully wedded wife?
(do you love death)
All the blood, that ghoulish face, the woman he had raped as she gone cold. Raped of her reality she had been made. How she looks now…

In sickness and in health, rich or poor, until death
(do you love death, Matthew Winklemann?)
do you part?
"I do," he finally answered.

The demon seemed to have moved, for it was now right in front of Matt so close that should it wished it could have kissed him. It stared at him, those eyes absorbing him more so and him standing there dazed like a deer caught in spotlights for a second, two, three, four…

On the fifth second, or was it five minutes? Time seemed to have stopped completely. But on the fifth second, or what Matt believed to be the fifth, the demon grinned. An evil, large grin, with sharp serrated teeth that were stained pink. Shark-like teeth, stained from his wife's blood.

The next question was easier to answer. Why are you here?

He gave his answer in a voice that sounded hollow and husky, as if his body had stopped functioning and it were his own ghost that was doing the talking for him.

The demon rose, black wings shrouding any source of light behind her. It then spoke, it's authority unmatched.

Matthew listened. He no longer had a choice. His free will had been taken entirely just like the lives of those he had killed. He stood dumbly and entranced, captivated by the demon's words as it spoke. In the maddening circle of words that made commands, Matthew Winklemann was lost to the world as well as himself.

The world didn't belong to him. It never had. It belonged to this thing, and now he belonged to it.

Nineteen

The following day, Adam awoke surprised to see Cynthia was not with him. He climbed out of bed and ignoring the thudding in his head from last night's drinks, got up and was pleased to see coffee already brewed on the kitchen counter. He poured himself a cup, and then stepped out onto the balcony where Cynthia stood, her own creamer-filled cup in hand and wearing a bathrobe.

"Hey you," he said coming up behind her and planting a kiss on her cheek. How long had he said that to her, his usual catchphrase when he saw someone he loved. Between her and Ryan, it used to be so often. Not so much now.

"Hey-hey," she responded in kind and turned her head to give him a kiss. "How are we feeling today?" she asked as he came up alongside her.

"Might've been overserved," he admitted.

"'Might have' huh?" Cynthia asked with a cocked eyebrow. She squealed as he pinched her thigh affectionately. Another first in a long time.

"Doubt I had as much as Ethan though," he claimed. "He is probably feeling it worse than I am today."

"That's true," Cynthia agreed.

"Jesus, what do you think they put in those margaritas?"

"Tequila, I would assume."

"Oh, well, thank god for that."

Cynthia laughed. It was good to hear her laugh on this beautiful morning.

They stood there on the balcony in silence, sipping their coffee and listening to the waves crashing against the beach. A couple was already there, but neither could tell who it was. In the distance, the blue sky which was speckled with white clouds broke off to an immense gray which Adam took for a storm coming, especially with where the wind was blowing. He voiced his thoughts to Cynthia, who asked what the resort would do if that was the case.

"I'm sure they are prepared," he answered. "I'm sure they get random storms like this more often than not."

"Hopefully," Cynthia said. She wasn't looking at him, and appeared distracted.

"You okay?" Adam asked.

"Yeah…"

"Cynthia?"

She looked at him. Her expression was stony but it wilted a bit under his gaze. "I've been thinking…"

"Yeah?" He turned to face her completely, give Cynthia his undivided attention. Gone were the sounds of the beach and the smell of coffee and saltwater. All that was here was Cynthia, all that would be heard was what she had to say.

"Look, I… I realized something yesterday while with Mr. Mulderich."

"Okay."

Those tiny lips pursed, loosened, then pursed again as she shifted her words around in order to manufacture the proper words for the proper sentence.

"I think he is right."

"Mulderich?"

Cynthia nodded.

"About what?"

"That you are bitter towards me, and I was unwilling to accept that what has happened happened."

"Well, that's why we are here isn't it?" Adam asked not feeling comfortable at all now. "To heal? To learn?"

"To *realize*, you mean," Cynthia countered.

"Sure, I guess."

Cynthia shook her head. "You don't get it..."

"Cynthia, what the hell are you talking about?"

Cynthia took a deep breath, released, and then looked Adam straight in the eye. "I was up all night last night and I figured something out. You're the reason why I cannot move on. You're the reason why I am stuck where I'm at."

"I thought this was already established yesterday and we were gonna work on it."

"Well I figured out what *will* work," Cynthia said. "Adam... I think we need to get a divorce."

Adam stared at her slack-jawed in shock. He felt as if he had knocked back a couple of drinks and his head was currently spinning, and for good measure someone struck him in the chest with a hammer. The world seemed to go out from under his feet, leaving him weightless, suspended, not knowing how to touch back down. He felt an ache surge through his chest, and his lips had gone numb.

"Wh... what?" was all he could muster to speak, his mouth was so arid it felt like he had swallowed sand.

Cynthia looked genuinely hurt by her statement but she stood firm. "I'm sorry, but I don't think I can ever really accept what has happened when you breathe down my neck the way you do."

"I haven't since we got here!" Other than maybe the session with Mulderich, but that shouldn't have counted. "I promised I would try to take it easy on you. It was an accident and I needed to understand that- And I do now!"

Cynthia shook her head miserably. "It doesn't matter if you understand or not. How much time have we lost since Ryan was killed? When we go back, how long will it take until we end up in that loop again? I think about it, and I feel... I feel so sick, and I don't want to deal with that anymore. Even if you mean what you said and keep your word, how will I know you are not thinking all of that still?"

"You can't be serious," Adam said now with more vigor, fueled by his frustration and disbelief.

"I am though..."

"Cynthia, you can't read my mind anymore than I can read yours. You never could! You thinking we divorce because you can't tell if I'm mentally blaming you is like you divorcing me because you don't know if I'm thinking about another woman or not."

"Have you?" Cynthia demanded looking him square in the eye.

Adam was appalled. "How could I?" he demanded. "My son was *run over*, Cynthia. Looking at other women was the *last* thing on my mind."

"You *never* thought you would be better off without me?"

This time Adam didn't answer. Because he *had* thought that. He had never thought of cheating on Cynthia, she was still his wife. But on more than one occasion since that terrible day, he had thought of how much he would be better off if she were gone. Not necessarily for his own sake however, but because of hers. Because if she was not still his wife, if she had not still stuck around, he would probably be dead.

He recalled a time when Cynthia went out on a camping trip with some friends. Five days out in the Colorado mountains. She had taken her own car, and Adam would be alone for that time, which he primarily spent that time working or getting completely and utterly plastered. One night he even smoked some weed to go with his whiskey and it ended up a helluva lot more than his stomach could take. In the end, it only depressed him more, and he actually almost did it. With Cynthia gone, it was easier for him to go upstairs to the master bathroom and fill their two-person jetted tub with water. He had gotten in, and next to the tub was the toaster he had brought up from the kitchen. It was plugged in, and ready for him.

Without Ryan, his life felt utterly empty like a cold pit; a never ending void of darkness and hopelessness. He had laid in that tub for a long time, thinking, his head swimming from the drugs and alcohol. In fact, he was in there for so long that the water had started to become chilled. Finally, he reached over the edge and scooped up the toaster. He sat up, holding the toaster in the space between his legs. He would drop it, and it would electrocute him and this nightmare he could never truly escape would finally be over.

It was there, when he finally broke and wept.

He sat there hunched, snot and tears dripping from his nose and chin and into the water and occasionally on his floating cock. He cried there, toaster in his hands and the chilly water around his lower body. With a horrible cry that sounded almost animalistic, he threw the toaster to the side and across the bathroom floor, it crashed and screeched across the tiled floor and had cracked the outlet he had it plugged into as it yanked its cord out. He crossed his arms over his knees and allowed his head to rest on it as he cried and cried some more, rocking back and forth like a baby. He cried for Ryan, he cried for himself, and then he cried for him and Cynthia.

Him and Cynthia, regardless of what could have been done to prevent the death of their only son, they were dealing with it together, and yet they were alone. They were both all alone, and Adam had felt horrible. He had drained the tub when he had nothing left to cry about, and he curled into a ball inside the now-empty tub and in his fetal position, he had fallen asleep.

When next he woke cramped and stiff from the tub, he got up and went into the shower. There he washed himself and paid no attention to the kitchen appliance still on the floor. When he was done, he took the toaster downstairs and threw it in the trash. He would get another one later that day, one that didn't have a bunch of dents in it. He hadn't bothered with dealing with the outlet though, Cynthia wouldn't notice it or so he thought. She would ask about it one day about a week or two later, but would just as easily dismiss it as Adam had.

Cynthia had come home, and she had told him about her trip. He had listened, and then told her about how work had been here. She then mentioned she had been thinking, about Ryan, and mostly about them.

Not long after, Cynthia had suggested their trip to Isla Bonidada.

She had suggested it, because she believed their marriage could be saved, she said. He and she had both come here, willing to give it all one more try and give it their best shot in order to have it all come back to normal. Maybe not completely, maybe not the exact same, but to the point where they could lean on one another once more.

Because they were lonely, and needed to fix what had been broken.

But now…

"You're giving up," Adam demanded bitterly. "Just like that?" He was so angry he shoved the mug off the balcony, didn't even watch as it fell to the sand below. Cynthia started to complain but he cut her off.

"That's what you mean, isn't it? You're giving up? Just like *that*!?"

"Please don't yell," Cynthia said looking past him.

"Fuck those guys and everyone on this island," Adam snarled. "Talk to me, Cynthia, *please*. If this is what was gonna happen then why are we here?"

"We came here to try to fix it," Cynthia answered sternly. "And I believe that this is the only way."

"Bullshit," Adam swore viciously.

"Please, Adam, stop it. You're making a scene."

"You're the one starting this 'scene,'" Adam snapped. "Don't worry about them, worry about us right here right now."

Cynthia crossed her arms and looked at the weathered boards visible between her feet. "I shouldn't have said anything yet…"

"What? Were you thinking of just filing without so much as a warning to me?"

"No, I'd never do that."

"Yeah, I don't believe that," Adam said waving his hand at her and turning away to put his hands on the balcony railing. He was livid, and he wanted to take this railing and rip it off and crush it into a thousand pieces. To destroy it because if he turned his anger on Cynthia or someone else he might hurt them if not verbally then definitely physically.

Because he wanted to destroy. Yes sir, he wanted to take his anger out on something rather than someone, because he felt like he was going to explode. His whole body was vibrating with his anger, which never since the time he spent with Cynthia after the incident had he felt so powerfully destructive.

"It doesn't matter if you believe it or not," said Cynthia. "I don't think we can go on like this, not knowing exactly what the other is thinking? How can I fake a smile, when you might be doing the same thing? How can I trust you really have forgiven me when in your heart you might have no intention of doing so?"

Adam looked at her, not turning away from the railing. "You wanna know what I'm thinking right now, Cynth?" Only then did he turned, his body square with hers and his back straight as if he were about to shove her. "I think you are a cowardly selfish *bitch*."

Cynthia winced at that word, exactly as Adam hoped she would. Good. Let her feel pain, let her be hurt. "Adam-"

"*Bitch*," Adam emphasized, the word clearly taking a toll on his wife as her words had taken theirs on him. "You, are, a, *bitch*. A bitch for deciding this marriage is not worth saving after we came thousands of miles to this goddamn island, a bitch for stringing me along and making me believe that it can be saved, and a bitch for running over my little boy!"

Cynthia moaned miserably, covering her face in anguish as her husband berated her and scolded her.

"Yeah, that's right. Cry. Cry until your fucking head explodes. Scream even, *that* will bring Ryan back, won't it? That will fix everything. Bitchy Cynthia crying and sobbing and hoping the world will just leave her alone so she doesn't ever have to face the truth that she is an unfit murdering mother."

"Adam, please..." At this point the tears were streaming down her face, dripping off her chin and crashing to the boards at her feet. She was shaking her head back and forth, trying to deny it all and yet was unable to.

"Oh, I'm sorry," Adam drawled now getting into Cynthia's face, looking her in the eyes between her wet fingers. "Want me to apologize? Apologize that I'm being so mean to you? Well tough shit, you bitch. Where's *my* apology goddammit? Where is *Ryan's*?"

That did it. That finally did it, and with a wail, Cynthia spun on her heel and rushed for the safety of the hut. She slammed the door shut but it bounced off the bracket and swung back open. Adam watched as she fled to the bedroom where she slammed it shut and locked the door behind her. He stood there feeling numb staring at that closed door, hearing Cynthia's cries on the other side.

Fine. Let her hide in there like she did back home. Let her have her pity party. Adam didn't care anymore. If she was giving up, then why the fuck should he?

He glanced to his left and saw the couple down there staring. He still didn't know who it was and didn't care. "The fuck are you looking at!?"

They both turned away and Adam stormed into the hut himself.

He stomped to the living room and picked up the bedroom key. He then arrived at the bedroom and unlocked it, stepping in and announcing to the Cynthia laying on the bed with her head in the pillow that he was grabbing his clothes. Grabbing whatever he could find, he stepped out and changed right out there. She could stay in here all she wanted. He might as well get his money's worth out of this fucking island.

He didn't need her to live his life. He hadn't needed her during the months after Ryan's passing, and he didn't need her now.

He was done.

Twenty

The couple that Adam and Cynthia had spotted were none other than Matt and Gabbie Winklemann. They were both enjoying a stroll along the beach when Adam and Cynthia were fighting. They didn't know what was going on and didn't care, for they kept on walking along the beach.

Both were well dressed but whatever tan they had upon coming to Isla Bonidada was gone, leaving them looking pasty like mayonnaise. But they appeared in good health, and any passerby greeted them and wished Gabbie in particular good health since she had been bedridden for almost three days. Even Matt seemed relieved, Cain had noticed while having breakfast with his wife, that the creepy man did not stare at most of the women working or even those as guests on the island.

That was because Matt's mind had been broken; driven mad by the night he had spent wandering around the island with the demon that had chosen him and offered aid in his quest for pure destruction and death.

He moved in a doze-like state, the kind that made one look like a zombie after a long night without rest or spent too long in the office without seeing anything other than his/her cubicle. He walked stiffly, slowly, and often relied on Gabbie who was more awake and alive and smiling than he. She wore a black skirt with a white shirt that made her look absolutely stunning, and whenever Matt started to falter in step or mutter to himself incomprehensibly, she would guide him with a gentle hand and kiss him on the cheek. To the average eye watching this, it was a tender sight. To Matt, he felt revulsion, as if the place on his skin that had been touched by his wife's lips were toxic or contaminated by some disease; a dark sort of bubonic or even Covid-19 that instead of ailing the body ailed the soul and state of mind. But no one was the wiser of this reaction of his as his body outright refused to act and so he went on stumbling about dreamlike with a tranquil smile on his face despite how much he wished he could scream.

As he walked along the waters of Isla Bonidada with the thundering clouds still a good ways away in the distance, Matt was thinking about what he had seen last night, what he had to do, and he would think about it again and again and again; never ending as if his mind was a broken record player, the needle stuck in a single loop that went on forever, and ever, and ever. However, whenever he tried to think about what Gabbie- What the thing is impersonating Gabbie really looked like, it became a blur, a haze as if he had been drugged.

Each step he took was a heartbeat, each heartbeat the things he had seen and experienced on the longest night of his life.

He remembered going up into the forest and following the demon's instructions he had gone up the pathway to the Crockett Grotto. She tells him he will be watched but to not worry for she will be there to protect him. He makes his way up and once he is inside the grotto, the smell of fresh geyser water had momentarily relieved him and he crosses the bridge to the location the demon had told him about. A tree tilting towards the water like a hand reaching to grab a drink, where a hollow had been dug out at the base among the roots. Matt had crouched down, wincing at the flutter of birds and scuttle of bugs as he neared the hollow. He was told that what he would be looking for would be stored there deep in the base. How the creature was able to dig so deep, Matt didn't know. But he heard the flapping of heavy leather wings somewhere above him and with a deep breath he stooped and descended beneath the tilted tree.

His hand brushed something smooth and he yelped as he felt something crawl across it. Digging into his pocket he removed his cellphone and after finding the flashlight widget, he turned it on, and screamed.

He saw bones and mangled flesh. Bones stained crimson and cracked for the marrow, with bugs and other vermin crawling over the remains. Skulls were cracked open for the brains and were grinning at him it seemed, with centipedes and worms wriggling in the space provided. There was a dog's corpse close by appearing completely intact until Matt was able to see that the mutt had been gutted, it's insides removed and now making home for many restless maggots and beetles. Human clothes had been stacked in one corner, torn and bloody. Further back, he had found what he was looking for, but to reach it he would have to crawl deeper under the roots of the tree and that would mean touching the scattered remains of human bones and discarded tissue.

Feeling something crawl on the back of his neck Matt yelped again and swatted at the spot mercilessly. He was about to turn and get away, but the demon was there watching him with keen and sharp eyes glowing bright and red like windows filled with hellfire. It would not let him pass, and if he dared to try, she would rip him apart. Her claws dug deep into the dirt and tree roots, and her teeth shone bright and sinister in the flashlight. She had threatened to kill him and save him for later, as she would all who lived on Isla Bonidada. Then she would escape on her own, and Matt's offer of escape after the planned massacre would rot along with his corpse.

So, he turned around, and on his hands and knees, he began to crawl. He shuddered with everything that squished beneath his knees and hands, yelped at the touch of tiny feet crawling across his hands and back, cried at the touch of small roots ticking the top of his head. Crawling into the hole which felt like it could be his very own grave slowly broke Matt down to the mind of a child.

At last, he reached what he was looking for, and grabbing it by the foot, began to drag it back towards the entrance of the hole. He smelled something then so pungent that he had to turn and vomit. The insects detecting warmer food began to slither towards his half-digested dinner. Still, he crawled back dragging the thing in question through the mess as well and not caring. When at last he felt nothing brushing his lower back, he realized he was out and he pulled the item in question out and shuddered at the very sight of it in the pure moonlight that shone down from the opening of Crockett's Grotto.

It was the lower half of a human torso. It was naked which revealed it's sex, which was female, the space in question hairy and unkempt. The small feet were dirty, the legs short and a pale tan in color. The hips were small, the belly button tinier, and less than an inch or two above that was where the body ended. A jagged cut clear across the top which was hollow and empty with the skin looking like it had been pulled apart rather that cut in the first place. The spine stuck out of the crimson muck within the body, jagged and ending somewhere that the small of the woman's back might have been.

Disgusted and yet unable to stop at this point, Matt tucked his phone away and picked up the lower half which felt heavy in his arms. Then making his way carefully off the side he crossed the bridge and continued down the path back to the beach, knowing well that the demon was following and watching from above.

What scared him the most however was how the legs felt as he carried them back to the hut under the cover of darkness. Something he did not consider until he was practically off the mountain and walking across level ground. It was the simple fact that the legs did not feel *dead*. Here he was carrying the lower half of some corpse or whatever and it didn't feel dead. Gabbie felt dead shortly after he had killed her, the body having cooled to the point of satisfactory especially when he had sex with it. The women he had killed before had felt dead after their torment was over and they had finally passed on. Cold, the temperature of death. He had held severed breasts in his hands, tried to juggle them in fact. He even once heled a woman's severed head and forced it to perform fellatio on himself. He had carried and bundled arms and legs like they were tinder for fire, stripped and kept the vagina lining of five of the women in a box where they dried and remained back at his house. All of those parts, all of those bodies, felt as dead as they were.

And these legs and lower half did not feel dead in the slightest. They felt *warm*, alive, with blood still flowing through the veins despite having no connection to a heart. The skin felt so warm, the buttocks plump and full, and yet despite should have been feeling cold and otherwise dead, they did not. They felt alive, and half the time Matt wondered whether or not those legs would start kicking.

Yes, maybe they would. Maybe it would start subtly. A wriggling of a single toe, maybe all of them. A twitch of the foot, and then all of a sudden the knee would extend the fibula and tibia out to make the leg straight. Maybe it would kick all the way, swing it's hips and kick him before landing on both feet and running off into the night.

Dear god, if they do that...

Sweat had accumulated. His heartbeat had increased in pace. Gooseflesh erupted on almost every pore in his body, and Matt realized he had begun to cry. He could not remember the last time he had cried. His father had beaten any tears out of little Matthew's body; or so he thought.

(don't be such a pussy, Matthew! Goddamn baby)

The jingle of a belt buckle, the silence of a bat or a tool like a wrench.

(stop crying goddammit!)

He tried, but he couldn't.

All his years of forcing others to cry for him, all his years of letting out all his anger, all his hatred, and he had been reduced to this. Carrying the severed half of some woman and it didn't feel the least dead in the slightest.

What am I doing? What am I doing here; Oh dear god help me now what in god's name am I doing here? Oh god...

God didn't help. But the demon did, it helped him make it all the way up the thirty-something steps that felt like a thousand towards his hut, all the way up all muddy and covered in filth and possibly blood. He carried the severed corpse all the way up and then having to set the body down, letting it lean against him like a drunk needing support, he opened the door and dragged the lower-half in.

Then he placed it on the floor against the couch in a sitting position. The image would have been comical but considering the circumstances, Matt couldn't laugh.

The demon was there. She crawled over to the pair of legs and pushing itself up with her arms, her dangled herself over the severed legs. Matt was about to ask what she was doing, but it answered already with actions instead of words.

Matthew's eyes widened. He had been momentarily numbed by the demon's strange powers, but now his brain seemed to unlock in the most awful of ways. The creature and what it was doing, changing shape before him and becoming something else, something that looked human, made his mind crack at last. An involuntary hand came fast and hard over his mouth in order to stifle the scream, his face stretched in a look of terror so great that nothing mattered anymore. He was long, long gone, and there was no one to pray to, no one to ask for salvation.

When the process was over, a woman sat on Matthew's floor, naked, covered in dirt and gore, and other than that appearing every piece as normal as any woman could. She looked Mexican or maybe Filipino.

She looked up at him, slanted brown eyes sparkling almost.

"So," she said in perfect English. "Shall we begin, *Mahal*?"

Now they were here, walking along the beach, pretending to be Matthew and Gabbie Winklemann, husband and wife. In reality, it was a demon masquerading in Gabbie's image, and Matt was her obedient and broken dog to do her bidding. Incapable of any thought other than repulsion and a desire to die, and yet his mind was far gone from his body which proceeded to masquerade, just like her.

Oh god, kill me now...

But God wouldn't. He simply wouldn't do that. Man has free will after all, and free will includes dealing with the consequences of his actions.

And Matt was no exception whatsoever.

6th Letter

It's been three days since my last letter. Every time I return to this notebook I feel like I am going to vomit, my hand refuses to obey my commands, and I cannot help but break down and cry at the very memory. All I remember was going completely mad during the time everything happened, and it still drives me mad today. I cannot help but believe that once someone is driven mad, they are almost irreparable. I would never be able to behave as I did before the events of that terrible night. I would not be the man I am today if not for that night. Scared, constantly suspicious of sounds at night, mortified by the night terrors that leave me screaming awake while my wife tries desperately to wake me and show me that I am safe and sound. But I will never be safe, at least not in my heart.

I will never be truly sane, until I can overcome this. Years and years later, and this nightmare must end. I must remember what I chose to forget. I must push on, and face the demon that plagues my mind to this day.

I remember turning on the cot I was sleeping on, turning to face my mother who should have been on the cot beside mine. The moon was shining through the hole in the ceiling, and it helped to better see the monster that was devouring my mother.

It was a terrible black thing, with glowing red eyes and outstretched wings. It held my mother in place with long black claws that dug into her shoulders, a long proboscis-like tongue deep in her throat as if it were a mosquito. Rows upon rows of shark teeth encircled the tongue

I cannot do this. To even remember the shape of that thing that took my mother and sister away, it makes me so sick. I'm sorry, but there are some things that no one should be able to know. To bear witness on such an abomination is... disheartening because of how little we humans truly matter.

Tao po, is all I can really say. For I am human, and am not a monster. But during that time, as I sat in that house for days if not weeks, I felt like a monster. Alienated, and lost in my own thoughts of misery. I would not break for a long time, and by then, half the village would be destroyed, and it would be time to try and make a final stand without the help of any village. My village had been marked as the monster's territory, and no one was going to come to help I soon realized. We were on our own.

Soon I would be on my own too.

I hear my wife calling. My current reason to live now, and my greatest blessing. Without her, I do not know if I would have had the courage to live on. I don't know if I would have been able to tell my story. I will continue this story, even if it kills me. I will end this for now, and return when I have the strength to pick up the pen again.

Twenty-One

The day went on without much incident. At one point after their couple's massages, Ethan and Shawlyn Duncan had returned to the resort and were talking to Anton and Jessica Bateman.

Everyone at the resort held the same opinion of Anton: He was cold, quiet, and intimidating. While everyone agreed that Matthew Winklemann was a creep, everyone was intimidated by Anton. His build shouldn't have been possible at his age and whenever someone asked what his secret was, he never answered.

Ethan was particularly interested if the man served, and when he inquired Anton grunted, soft-spoken and polite. Ethan was surprised that the guy was actually answering.

"I did," he replied. "Four tours in the Middle East, Navy Seal, retired."

"No shit," Ethan said impressed. "Why didn't you become a drill-instructor or something?" He was in study-mode now, the way he often got when he met new or interesting people. He was taking mental notes with the intention of jotting it all down the moment he had the chance, so he could try to integrate Anton's personality into a book one day.

"Jessica got sick," said Anton. "Ever since then I invested what I earned into stocks, and we became rich and I was able to stay home more often. It was for the best, by far the best decision I made since marrying her."

Shawlyn, who had been conversing with the almost-catatonic Jessica, asked, "What brought you to Isla Bonidada? You two seem like a very loving couple."

Jessica nodded softly, and Anton voiced for them both, "We are. We are here because Jessica might not have long to live. It was the best deal we could get under short notice, and I wanted her to go to as many places that are as acceptable of her condition as possible. This was the best in the Western seaboard, and so here we are."

"Doesn't it bother you that this is technically a counseling island?" Ethan asked.

"Not at all. People keep their business to themselves and everyone seems to enjoy one another when we are not on our own. If we did have problems, we more than likely would not have told you. By the way, it was rude of you to ask what we are here for." He said this to Shawlyn who looked ashamed.

"I'm really sorry, I did not mean to pry."

Anton shrugged. "Didn't matter in the end so don't worry about it. Just trust I'm not gonna ask you two why you are here." He looked at Ethan again and asked, "Anyways, you write books?"

"Yes sir," Ethan said with a touch of pride. "Wrote three series and four stand-alones."

"Impressive. What do you normally write?"

"Crime fiction, mostly. Although one of those stand-alone books was a young adult novel about a kid joining a band while dealing with a personal death."

Anton was more interested in the crime novels anyway. "Have you served then?"

"You mean police? No."

"At all?"

"None whatsoever."

"Did you serve overseas then?"

"No..."

"Security even?"

"No, I have no experience in working in law enforcement or military."

Anton frowned. "How are you capable of writing crime fiction then? You have no experience in the field."

"I talk to people. I have friends in the police department where I live, and I listen to stories and procedures. A lot of my books are dedicated to those who help me in my writing. All I really do is come up with the story, the rest, the nitty-gritty details, I leave to the experts."

Anton nodded but he still didn't seem happy or satisfied with that answer. "What is your most recommended work? Perhaps I will read it one day, see if your research is commendable."

Ethan felt a touch of irritation at the big man's word of 'commendable.' You didn't have to be in NASA to write a story about space. The man had never even read one of his novels, didn't even know the stories and already he was criticizing him.

Still, he managed to smile and say, "Well, my personal recommendation is the stand-alone novel 'When in Doubt.' It's about a serial killer who gets a job as a groundskeeper at a detectives home in order to get close enough to kill him. One day the detective's daughter almost drowns in their pool and the killer saves her only to flee and never return. When doing a background check, the detective finds out who the man really is."

"And then what?" asked Anton.

Ethan flashed his smile he usually saved for questions such as this. The kind that makes it easy for him to say as thus: "You'll have to read it to find out."

"Hmm," Anton sounded and took out a napkin from his pocket. "You got a pen?"

Ethan took one of his pens out of his shirt pocket and handed it to the man who jotted down a note before returning the pen. The rest of the conversation turned to how Anton made his investments and how he knew when to cash in or stay. By then, it was lunch time and he and Shawlyn made their excuses and returned to the ballroom where a simple lunch of smoked salmon and wild rice was being served for those who would eat at the resort. The fish was splendid, although Shawlyn's pregnancy only made it easy for her to eat rice. For some reason, salmon was one of the things the baby didn't want her to eat.

At some point Ethan got up and announced he was going to the men's room. He told Shawlyn the salmon didn't sit right, and she hesitantly told him to hurry back. He rushed to the men's room and was bummed that it was a public one but he didn't want to get out and look for a private or family one. So he selected a clean stall and after dropping down a sheet from the cover dispenser dropped his pants before sitting on the toilet.

He did not need to go, at least not in the way that the restroom was designed for. Instead, he reached into his pocket where he kept his little notebook for notes he would use for his books, the latest being what Anton had told him about his time in the service as well as some key components Anton was discussing concerning the stock market. He continued to flip through the pages quickly though, into the white area where there were no notes to be discovered just yet. He had known that Isla Bonidada would not allow cellphones on the property, and Shawlyn had been thrilled with the idea and made sure to put both his and her phone away in a little lockbox they kept at their house. She had done this not just because she liked the idea of not having connections with the world while on vacation, but it was also an unaccusatory way of keeping her own husband in line.

Well, her own husband had stored some nuts for the winter, and he finally came across the printed pictures he had made before the trip hiding them within the confines of his notes. Staring at each one, he spat into his palm and began to masturbate.

Shawlyn was eight months pregnant. The baby could come at any time at this point, but it hadn't come soon enough for Ethan. Ethan himself had been living a lie, a lie he had thought he had done pretty well for himself. He was a writer after all, lying was part of the craft. But sooner or later it caught up to him, and it wouldn't matter how he explained it to Shawlyn in the end. He had done it before here and there, when Shawlyn wasn't in the bed with him and he didn't have to pretend as he conjured up images of what he really wanted. He loved her, loved her dearly.

But women, just didn't satisfy him, not completely.

He had known what he was when he was in high school. All the stories of finding love, a girlfriend, his friends and even his own father pressuring him to find a good woman, all of it having been done but purely out of the sake of those around him. It was bad enough he never played any sports, for after the blood sweat and tears went into whatever sport he was in, afterwards in the locker room, he would be exposed to so many naked boys his age. The first time this had happened and he got an erection, he quit the baseball team then and there and never played again. His father had given him hell for it, but he never backed down from it. He just allowed his father to be disappointed in his son. It was better to be disappointed because of a lack of sports, rather than being disappointed at having birthed a-

(goddamned faggot)

homosexual.

A faggot, his father would have called him just like all the other people of the gay community. If he were alive today, Shawn Duncan would feel like the world had gone insane.

Who he really was, Ethan had always managed to hide it. He managed to hide it and only experience his desires in privacy. He would do it every so often just to get that sort of satisfaction that Shawlyn just couldn't give herself. It wasn't her fault and he had never meant to harm her. He had always been so careful whenever he decided to do it, and on the day Shawlyn went shopping and he decided, 'Why not?'

That was when it all went to shit.

He had been in the middle of it when Shawlyn walked in on him. She knew he often worked hard and didn't like distractions, but this time she simply wanted to ask if he wanted some ice cream on that hot summer day.

The look on her face was both scary and heartbreaking to Ethan. The betrayal so stark on her face that there was pain radiating from her and sinking into his own chest. He had broken her trust, cheated on her so to speak. He had looked at other women and jerked off to them as if she never existed. She was so furious she threatened to throw him out. They had talked it out, and Shawlyn had forgiven him. The way she saw it, it was too late to back out of the marriage, especially with their child. But she had made it clear that she had no intention of staying with him after the boy or girl was eighteen. They would be stuck with each other for another eighteen years and by God she was not going to have that shit happening behind her back.

"You're still my husband," she said. "And I'm gonna make sure you act like one otherwise you can leave and be a fag elsewhere."

It wasn't the word that hurt. Ethan understood more than anyone that words were just words and there was no such thing as 'bad words' or 'bad language.' It was the context that mattered. It was the context that hurt him so.

It was understandable from her point of view. She had come from a broken home where the father had one day gone out for a beer and never came back home. That steeled her resolve to ensure her children would never be put through such a thing as an absent father again. But at the same time what Ethan had done was unconscionable. She could forgive him, make sure both of them were together for their son or daughter's sake, but she would be damned before she allowed him to get away with it again; and if anyone *was* going to have to leave, it sure as hell was not going to be her.

Yep. Make Ethan the one to choose to be the good guy or bad guy, the good father or the deadbeat. Either way, it was a suitable enough threat under the circumstances and Ethan had no trouble agreeing that Shawlyn was right. He had wronged her, by all accounts she should quit on him, but because of their unborn child she was not going to, and neither would he for the baby's sake.

But ever since then during the time before their departure for Isla Bonidada, life at the Duncan household had become stressful, tense, and simply uncomfortable for the both of them.

For one, Shawlyn didn't trust Ethan alone for more than five minutes. Whenever he went into his study to write and he didn't leave the door wide open, Shawlyn would shout and point her finger accusingly at him, calling him all sorts of nasty things even after he complied. Even then she would hound him and he would never get any work done. Not only that, but if he were in the bathroom for more than five minutes she would beat on the door and demand what he was doing. Even when he showered she had barged in on him to make sure he was indeed showering and not doing anything else. If he left the house for groceries or to pick up prescriptions, Shawlyn would always want to come with, and if she wasn't with him, she would call and shout and scream again. All of this broke him down little by little; his whole life had been put on surveillance because of his actions.

He couldn't blame her, but at the same time, he couldn't stand her. Despite him deserving such a suitable response from Shawlyn, he found himself resenting her. This only made him feel worse, and he found himself resorting back to his addiction. If a woman was called a prostitute long enough, wouldn't she give in to what everyone viewed her as? Just say fuck it and go? That was how Ethan felt, anyway. It was only made easier when he and Shawlyn's sex life would most likely have ended indefinitely, or so, that was what he told himself every time he snuck in a quickie.

It had been easy enough, despite Shawlyn constantly going through his phone or checking up on his history on his computer or even on TV. There were still pictures he could come across. In this day and age it was easier to get ahold of something to get off with. It was just too good to pass it up since Shawlyn was no longer giving him any attention other than the all-seeing goddess who had rightfully stripped away his privacy.

Deep down though, he knew that he was only telling himself that. Shawlyn was doing everything she could to protect herself as well as his marriage, and he knew that perhaps after the child was born, things could go back to normal. Deep down, he had tried to quit, to at least try to do her right and in his actions whether she believed in them or not, things could go back.

But he eventually found himself unable to stop. Found himself doing it several times a day every chance he got. Even now as he sat in the Isla Bonidada restroom, he had come here just to do it again. Relieved and now full of shame, Ethan rested his head back against the wall above the toilet tank relishing in the self-disgust he had with himself. It had felt good once before, but now he felt nothing but shame. And yet that shame didn't seem to give him the chance to stop. It had become a part of him, a part of his routine.

Making excuses for yourself, again.

Maybe he was, but it was too little too late.

He came in about a minute or two, fast given his time and practice. He would clean himself up and flush away the evidence so to speak and after making sure every drop was out, he would clean up and step outside like nothing happened. Shawlyn would see him, give him a kind enough but still suspicious smile as he approached, ask him how it was, and he would say it was good.

As he had twice already while here on the island.

"You gotta knock it off," he told himself in the mirror as he washed his hands. "Just knock this off..."

How many times had he told himself that? How long was he going to continue living like this? How long was he going to resent Shawlyn for how she was treating him now, only to feel shame whenever he committed this act of self-indulgence again and again?

Isn't that why you're here?

This was also true. Because deep down Ethan knew that he couldn't blame Shawlyn. There was no one to blame. At the end of the day, just as his shame would tell him every single time, he was to blame. Understanding this was more than likely the motivation for him to suggest this trip in the first place. Shawlyn had been delighted, wanting to get away for one but to also see what they could do to make their lives together a little easier; Even if they didn't make it past their child's 18th birthday. Most of this would be just talking with Mulderich as the pivot between them, and Ethan's hope was that if Shawlyn could be hopeful again, perhaps that would make it easier for him to eventually quit. He couldn't ask for an intervention for that would reveal his dirty secret. He would have to be honest of where the problem began, and would have to remain somewhat honest in the time since. The rest he would do in the shadows, fight tooth and nail, and hopefully gain some insight as to what to do to stop entirely without giving Shawlyn any idea of what had still been going on since that day.

To this as well even as Ethan finally emerged from the restroom, he felt shame. A deep pit that expanded in his stomach and felt to have swallowed him up entirely leaving nothing but a pathetic little man.

Shame on you, Ethan, you sad little man. Pathetic little closet-fag.

Ethan couldn't help but chuckle with remorse at that. He couldn't even lie to himself and call himself a man at all. Maybe that's why he did it after all.

Or maybe, that was just another excuse.

Twenty-Two

Today, it had been Derian and Carla Anderson's turn to speak with Mr. Mulderich. They had just gotten back, having learned more about themselves than they ever had before in their lives.

It had just been an hour since, and Carla was deep in her cups. She had asked to get a drink at the bar and was already working on her third Lavender Cosmopolitan. Derian was still sipping on his first Jack and Coke, not sure what to do as of now. It wasn't that the session had gone bad, quite the contrary, really. Carla had stated her piece that she didn't feel like she could trust Derian because she believed he was out at night because he was with other women. Derian had held his tongue and let her spill her arguments and when she was finished, he had no questions for her. Amos looked like he was full of questions, and Derian said it would be explained when he told his story.

"Mr. Mulderich," he had said. "Are you liable to disclose any personal information regarding the two of us?"

Amos said that he was not. That his sessions were considered medical and therefore he could not disclose any such information. That everything was private, an open book until the two of them had left the cove and then it would be closed. This of course caught Carla's attention who was watching her husband wondering what was going on.

"That include criminal pasts?" Derian asked which looked to have surprised Carla even more than before.

"Even then," said Mulderich.

"You've never been to prison," Carla said staring at him. "You expect me to believe you have been serving time only at night?"

"That isn't how that works," Derian said amused to the point of actually releasing bemused chuckles. That seemed to soften Carla up a bit which made it easier for him to add, "It's nothing like that at all. What it actually is might be a shock to you. Hence, Mr. Mulderich, I ask that you do not discuss this information with anyone. That this is private."

"You have my word," Amos Mulderich declared.

And so, Derian told his story as to why he was out many nights sometimes for days.

When he had finished, Carla had no questions. In fact, she had nothing to say at all. She only stared at him, at first disbelievingly but the fact that she wasn't arguing or accusing him of lying meant that she was indeed believing him. The only one with questions was Mr. Mulderich but purely at first to satisfy some of his curiosity. When he was done, he had asked Derian how it felt finally letting it out and Derian was honest.

"It's not what I had thought it would feel like," Derian said. "I feel like I just got the elephant off my damn chest."

"So that's why you are understanding what Carla would think you were having an affair or two." It was no question.

"That's right. I had always denied it and took anything else as an excuse because I didn't want the truth to be revealed. But I'm retired now and I'm finally able to actually live a life with the woman I married. And I didn't want that to be ruined by what she thought of me so I decided on this trip I would tell her the truth."

This time, Carla actually did speak. "Why couldn't you tell me this before?" Amos who no doubt thought the same thing, merely watched as the bystander he was clearly supposed to be.

"It never felt like a good time. Also, if I did, we would have to move. That's why I had also been looking at houses out of state. You remember that? You had asked if it was to house my second family?"

Carla winced and looked away, pained by that memory of her accusation.

"Do you think you two are in danger?" Mulderich asked.

"Not here, hence why I wanted to talk to her here. Because after we leave Bonidada, I have no intention of returning to Miami. I want to go somewhere else, we have the money and we have the bare necessities. I want to start anew, Mr. Mulderich. I want to give my wife the time and love she deserves. Because for so long I had been distant to keep her safe, have endured being called a liar and an adulterer, all for her sake."

Now Carla began to cry. Not loudly, but silently, with tears slowly rolling down her cheeks without so much as a hiccup.

When Mulderich was done telling Carla to consider what Derian had said and for Derian to give Carla the space she would need, the two thanked Amos and left the cove. The counselor had watched them go, Derian noticed, clearly mystified about whom he had just met and no doubt either feeling honored or scared by the matter.

Now they were at the bar, and Carla was still not talking to him, still drinking her now fifth cosmopolitan. Derian had finished his first, and was now staring at the bottom of his empty glass. When the bar tender had asked if he wanted another, he asked for two glasses of water. Carla had finally downed the last of her drink and said she was done, and thanked him for ordering the water.

Now with an actual hydrating beverage in front of them, Derian dared to speak to her, making sure to approach her gently and tenderly, as to not frighten her or upset her.

"Are you angry with me?" he asked.

She didn't move, only stare into her water. "I don't know…"

"I uh… packed our wedding album, in case you were wondering."

She didn't respond.

"Carla…"

"I don't know if the album matters," she said. "I didn't marry the man in those photos…"

That stung, but Derian endured it. "I'm sorry. I know it doesn't make it better or fixes anything, but I'm sorry."

Carla shook her head slowly, appearing to debate something. "All this time…"

Derian didn't speak. He allowed her all the time and space in the world to say what was needed to be said.

But no words came out. Just that vacant stare into nothingness of which Derian had never seen on Carla's face before. She was beyond shocked and amazed and angry and confused. She was beyond all of that and then some.

"Where would we go?" she asked.

"Anywhere we wanted, really. I always wanted to go to Colorado, personally. But didn't you want to go to Texas?"

"I did," she admitted.

"We can go there if you'd like."

"What about work?"

"You usually work from home anyway, right? If you have to travel you do anyway. But when it comes to Miami… we can't go back."

"What about our family?"

In truth, it was only her family that was left. Derian and his family had a horrible falling out growing up, he and his siblings practically hated each other and when their old man died and Mom got all the inheritance, there was no room in her heart for her children. He knew he had relatives but he didn't care much for them. Carla's family was his family now, and he was grateful for them.

"We'll tell them I got a new opportunity somewhere else, it didn't affect your job that much so it worked out. Easy."

Another miserable shake of the head in wonderment. "Easy… It has never been 'easy,' how can this be any different?"

"It would be a new start."

"Maybe… with a different man it seems."

Derian frowned. "Carla, that isn't true." He made to reach for her hand but she pulled it out of reach before he could so much as touch her. He let her go though, allowed her to have her space. "I'm the same man you married, I promise."

"The man I married didn't seem the type who would *kill*."

Derian didn't have an argument for this. She was right to be this way, right to question him. Everything he had her believe had been a lie to save her from the truth. Now that the truth was out, the danger gone, it was indeed as if he was a different man. But he had always been the same, he just finally took off the mask he had been wearing for so long and the poor woman had fallen in love and created memories with that mask. Not him, and he was just as hurt as she was by the cold hard truth of it. It was like waking up one day and finding out your husband or wife was a pedophile; you began questioning everything about that person and even ask yourself the god-awful question, 'How did I not see it?'

In Carla's case, she <u>had</u> seen something, she had just been wrong about what it was the whole time, and Derian had argued and argued but gave her no ledge to grasp onto for the truth until now. He had waited until they were out of Miami, waited until they were at Isla Bonidada, waited until he finally pulled the plug and took up his retirement.

But was it too late?

He hoped to God it wasn't.

Derian sat forward in his seat. "I don't know what to tell you about that other than the truth. I didn't enjoy it, but it was the only chance I had when I was younger. I didn't care where I was going or if I even survived."

"Oh, god," she groaned.

Derian nodded, not shying away from the truth. "Then I met you, and to be honest... you saved me. I wanted to do something else. I put all my money away and saved up for you. I tied up whatever loose ends I could find just so that I could get away with you, and give you the life you deserve. Now we can start a new life, and I will never have to go back to that lifestyle again.”

"How do I know that for sure though?" she asked. "In movies those people always get caught."

"This ain't a movie, it's reality," he told her. "I know I'm asking you a lot, but you would have to trust me on that. You believe me *now* about the affair thing, right? That I never cheated on you?"

"I don't know which is worse though…"

"They're both pretty bad, aren't they?" he asked with a harsh chuckle. He couldn't help it, Carla's statement had indeed been ironically funny.

Unfortunately she didn't have the same opinion. "Derian, what is it that I am *supposed* to think? My whole world is turned completely upside down and I don't know what to do or think."

"What does your heart say?" he asked genuinely.

"Don't pull that sappy crap with me."

"I'm being serious. What is it that you want?"

Carla was quiet for a long time. Minutes in fact, that Derian began to think that she either hadn't heard him or had no intention of answering in the first place. At last she released a heavy sigh that seemed to lay heavily on the air around them and she gave her reply.

"I obviously want what's best for us, and I… I do love you, really. That is why I've been so hell bent on getting you to admit your… your affairs with me so that maybe it would prove that you do care for me. When you kept denying and denying it only made me feel more distant. But now that the truth is out... It really is the truth, isn't it?"

Derian turned to face Carla completely again. "Carla, I give you my solemn word that everything I said was true. I didn't say anything in order to protect you. And... I guess also myself. I didn't know how you would react knowing that you were dating... and eventually marrying a... a..."

Carla nodded, understanding. "I can see that. Well... do you really think it would be a new start for us? Or would it be a new start for you?"

"It would be a new start for me no matter what," Derian said. "I have no intention of going back to Miami. I will go somewhere and start anew. My only wish... My only wish is that you would come with me. You married me, but you are not obligated to someone who never really existed. I only ask that you give me another chance to prove my worth to you. My life will change no matter what, but regardless of how it does, I want you there by my side. I made that clear on our wedding day, and still mean it now. So, will you come with me? To the ends of the earth if that is what it takes?"

Carla chuckled. "You make it sound so easy..." she said again.

"Well, at least you know how it really would be," Derian admitted. "It won't be easy. Accepting who I really am isn't easy, and I don't want you to feel pressured into anything. Will you at least think about it? We have until the end of our vacation anyway."

"You think it will take me a couple of weeks to make a decision?"

"I want to make sure you have all the time in the world, Carla. I love you, and I cannot imagine a new life without you. I want you to come with me, but I will respect any decision you make. Even if it... even..."

Carla looked at him suddenly. "You really aren't the man I married, Derian. I thought I was marrying someone social, someone who was kind and wouldn't hurt a fly. When I thought you were cheating on me, I... I couldn't bear the thought. Now that I know the truth... it isn't something I can just easily accept and forgive because I can't help but wonder... Just what went through your mind at the times."

"You want the truth?" Derian asked. "It was awful. Terrible."

"You never enjoyed it?"

"No. I did it because it brought in the dough. A lot of it. Now that we have enough, I decided it was time to call it quits. I wanted to start fresh. When my family abandoned me, I didn't have anything else or anyone else to turn to. I took on the job, because I felt there was nothing else I can really do. But then I met you, and I decided I was going to put an end to it all. I was going to quit and make sure we could both walk away from it completely independently and sustainably. I took longer than it should have, the boss wouldn't let me go. So, that is why I want to run away. Do you understand?"

"What kind of boss was he like?" Carla asked not answering his question.

Derian produced a humorless chuckle. "Ruthless. An asshole, but powerful. He had a lot of connections, and a lot of enemies. I was the one who helped clean up the messes."

Carla looked at his hands then. "Those same hands I used to hold so often, the hands that held my sister's baby and craft birdhouses, are the hands of a killer."

Derian winced. "Yeah... that's right."

Carla looked back up into his brown eyes. "My husband was never cheating..."

Derian nodded.

"You killed people..."

"I did."

Carla shook her head. "And you think I can just accept it like that?"

"No. That's why I want you to carefully think about it. I don't want you to do something you believe you'll regret, although you are probably regretting it all right now. One way or another, I have no intention of going back. I can't, Carla. And I want you to come with me, as my wife still. I know I made a lot of mistakes and I know knowing the truth about me is unforgivable, it will take a long time before even I can forgive myself. But we have a chance for a new start, and I want you there by my side still. That is, and only if, you still want to be by my side. Just think about it, okay? I will respect any decision you make. I promise."

Carla was quiet for a long time. They had ordered a snack of freshly-caught and fried oysters and a couple more drinks. Other than the occasional question concerning Derian's old work or to comment about the resort, Carla didn't seem in any hurry to speak about it. Until finally, she did, and it surprised Derian more than anything in the world could have thrown his way.

"You are done, completely, right?"

Derian looked at her. "Yes. I don't ever want to go through anything like that again, and I don't want to be a part of our family history. I want to bury it, completely."

Carla nodded, understanding. "Well... that is all right, isn't it?"

Derian smiled softly. That used to be such a common phrase of Carla's. Whenever she was happy for him, thoughtful, or liked a suggestion or accomplishment that she was proud of him for, she never said 'good job' or 'sounds great.' She always simply said, 'that's all right, isn't it?'

Hearing it again, made Derian think just that. "Yeah, I guess it is."

They talked some more, as patrons came and left at the bar, one of which included Adam White, who was deep in his cups considering the conversation discussed between him and Cynthia. He had gone to the massage parlor alone, for Cynthia had not left the hut and preferred the isolation rather than getting touched by a stranger, even if it was meant to help heal. Derian had noticed the man, and made some small conversation with Adam, who merely just wanted to be left alone in his misery.

It was not hard for anyone to guess that not everyone can heal on Isla Bonidada.

Twenty-Three

John had searched the pump room himself that day after still thinking about the missing Tamia in that room after the dog had left. He had checked all around and even in some of the panels that hid some of the fire extinguishers and tools used in the room. It was here where he found Tamia's uniform, indicated by her name badge. When Amos was back from the Cove, he showed it to him in the security room.

Amos stared at the pile of dirty clothes that looked like Tamia had gone rolling in the mud somewhere on the island with distaste. "This still doesn't explain where she went," he stated.

"No shit," John said grumpily as he took out a hookah pen and smoked it. It was against the rules to smoke in the security room but not vape; if they were outside, he would have taken out his pack of American Spirits and smoked two.

"And still no sign of the boyfriend either?"

"Nada. They seem to have just vanished."

"People don't just vanish, John."

John jerked a thumb in the direction of the consoles. "Explain that then." He then pointed at the clothes in question. "Explain that."

Amos stared at the clothes again. Where the fuck had that woman gone?

"Do we know where the dog is?"

"Nope. No one has seen it. Talked to the workers already from Bunk C. They haven't seen the dog around. Think that gook brought a tiger to the island?"

"Jesus Christ, John a *tiger*?" Amos stared at his friend disbelieving.

John shrugged. "You can't explain the pump room here, but what about the boyfriend? The mutt?"

Amos shook his head tiredly. Sometimes John's dry humor was just what he needed, whether the old fart intended to make him laugh or not. "Tamia had to have gone in through the vents then..."

John looked up at the nearest grate and barked out a laugh. "She wouldn't fit."

"Then you give me a better excuse for her being gone, John," Amos said now exasperated. "I'm all ears."

"I don't know, this is a mess I never dealt with or experienced. Nothing makes sense other than the fact that she is gone. The boyfriend is just missing, but Tamia is *gone*. Poof. Vanished."

"People-"

"Don't vanish. Yes, we've established that. But what else could have happened?"

"I don't know..." Amos was frustrated now. The more he tried to figure out what happened to his employees the more upset he became. Every logical explanation had been tossed out the window, leaving a big gaping hole in the question of where Tamia had gone. A hole that was deep, dark, and unexplored.

"All we can do is keep looking," he finally decided, wanting to just not think about Tamia Gonzalez at all at the moment. Besides, he had other fish to fry. He got up and started for the door.

"You coming?"

"You gonna see our newest arrival?" John asked. When Amos said that he was, John took one more puff out of his hookah and pocketed it before standing. "Let's go."

As they walked Amos decided to break up the mood by saying, "By the way, you ain't gonna believe the shit I heard from the Andersons."

"I'm all ears."

"No telling, got it?"

"Who would I tell?"

So Amos told him, and by the time they reached the infirmary John's jaw was damn near dragging across the floor. "You're kidding."

"Nope. Word for word."

"No way. You believe that shit?"

"We've seen crazier here. Remember that raghead from Iran?"

John did remember. He never liked that particular guest who thought Bonidada was a simple private resort. He felt particularly bad for the ten year old he had with him. Needles to say once the coast guard caught wind of the man, they were quick to come and pick him up. Crockett might be tolerant for a lot of things, but his island was still U.S. territory and the island customs therefore not tolerant of such practices.

The man in the infirmary had been awake for almost two hours and while delirious upon awakening, Dr. Jake Mendez, was able to calm the man and get him to drink some water and eat some soft foods courtesy of Kyra. The man who had begun to scarf down the cottage cheese and peaches was instructed to eat slowly while Mendez did another checkup on his eyes, ears, and blood pressure. Other than a few nicks and bruises, the man was otherwise healthy. Probably in his mid-twenties, the kid (for he was small and terribly malnourished to the point where it was difficult to tell his exact age) said very little other than his own language which Mendez couldn't understand. Once the boy seemed to understand that he was in the presence of someone who spoke English, he was able to say a few words in terribly broken English but it was still comprehensible nonetheless.

"Where... where...?" the boy had asked.

Mendez who was jotting notes down on a clipboard with a blank sheet of paper answered, "Isla Bonidada, off the coast of Mexico. Who are you?"

The boy thought about it for a moment, as if he were asked to solve a complicated equation for calculus. "J... Joshua... Josh."

"Last name?"

"Last?"

"That's right."

"Uh... Ramos. Josh Ramos."

"Ramos, eh?" Mendez thought the names were peculiar, and not at all what he had expected. He had expected something like Tao or Kirito, with a last name like Wong or Wang. Which meant that this boy was either somewhere off the Americas or was an islander from the Pacific, with the latter being the most likely.

"Are you Hawaiian?" Mendez asked.

"Hawaiian? From... Hawaii?"

"That's right."

"No... No, I am from Capiz."

"Capiz?"

"Yes, Capiz. I am Pinoy."

"Pinoy..." Mendez turned to his computer and after a quick Google search, discovered what the boy was saying. "Oh, you're Filipino. You're from the Philippines..."

That means the kid travelled over 8,000 miles to get here... holy shit...

Joshua nodded. "Yeah, that's right."

Mendez returned his attention to the boy. "Done eating? Would you like some more water?"

"Please," the boy said and after giving him some, Mendez proceeded with some of his questions.

When he and John arrived, most of the questions Amos Mulderich had were about the same as Mendez's although not all of them were medically-related. John kept quiet, studying the boy who took a liking to Amos almost instantaneously upon his arrival. After figuring out his name, where he came from and how he was feeling, Amos got to the very heart of the issue.

"Kid, what were you doing out in the ocean?"

Joshua pursed his chapped lips deep in thought. He was twiddling his fingers between his legs, as if debating whether to tell the truth or a lie. "I got lost..." he simply said.

"Lost? You're a long way from home, kid. I find it hard to believe you got lost after setting sail."

"Where is my boat?"

"We'll get to that. We just wanna know why you were out at sea."

"Amos," Mendez said softly. "Take it easy."

Amos ignored the doctor. "Are you a pirate?"

"Pirate?"

"Yeah, you know, pillaging and plundering? Yo-ho?"

"Yo-ho? No, no... not pirate. Fish."

"You a fisherman? That why you were out at sea?"

"No..."

Amos told John to take out the whip and machete-like weapon and once they were produced, they showed it to the boy whose eyes widened at them. "What are these?"

"Those..." the boy swallowed hard. "Those are mine."

"No shit. What *are* they?"

"Amos," Mendez warned again.

The boy swallowed again and pointed to the whip. "That is a whip. Made of... dahunan."

"Da-hu-what?" Amos asked as Mendez typed it into the computer.

"It's made of a barb of a sting ray," the doctor announced.

"That's pretty cool," John said, the first time he had spoken.

"And this?" Amos asked waving the machete.

"Bolos," the boy said. Before Mendez could check he added, "Dagger."

"Helluva dagger," Amos commented. "Why do you have these?"

"Protection."

"You had guns too, they were in bad shape."

"Protection," Joshua repeated.

Amos didn't question further. Maybe the Filipinos thought they needed more protection out in the jungle other than guns. Which was to be expected. Also, out at sea there were probably more pirates than along Mexico's border, so it made sense why the boy had them. Also, the kid didn't look like a buccaneer or meant any of them harm. He was scared, hungry, and thirsty, that is all.

"Do you know how long you've been out at sea?" he asked Joshua.

Joshua shook his head.

"Was anyone with you?"

Again, Joshua's head shook. "I went out alone."

"Alone for what?"

The head shook a third time. The steadfast look in the boy's eyes made it clear to Amos that Joshua wasn't going to answer that one.

"What do you think?" he asked turning Mendez. "Is he okay?"

"He seems healthy, like I said just really dehydrated. He just needs water and bedrest."

"What do you wanna do with him?"

"He should be good to go after a week or two. By then he can probably be picked up by the coast guard and they can figure it out from there."

Amos looked at the boy. "When you are feeling better, we can give you to someone who can help you get home. Would you like that?"

"Home…" the word sounded so sad in the boy's words. He was staring at the floor, between his sandaled feet.

"You don't wanna go home?" Amos asked, thinking that the kid was a runaway, hence why he didn't take anyone else with him out to sea.

"My home is… is destroyed."

"Oh, I'm sorry to hear that. What happened?"

The boy shook his head, not wanting to talk about it.

"Okay," Amos decided. "Last question and I'll leave you alone, okay?"

"Okay," Joshua said robotically.

Mendez shot Amos a warning glance but the counselor ignored him. "Where were you going? Were you trying to go somewhere?"

"No," said Joshua.

Amos nodded, respecting the lack of clarity. "Well, it ain't none of our business and as long as you don't mean danger to us we won't be a danger to you. Doesn't mean we trust you, got it?"

"Sure," said Joshua coolly.

Amos nodded again, this time smiling softly. "Well, you'll be in good hands here. Kyra is one helluva cook, she'll make sure you are healthy by the time we give you to the coast guard."

"Coast guard?"

"It's like police, but they help those lost at sea. You're just lucky you wound up over here, you could have drowned or died of starvation."

The boy nodded, unspeaking.

Outside, leaving Mendez to the boy as well as a newer patient who had been bitten by a poisonous spider, John and Amos discussed about the boy outside the ward.

"Professional opinion?" Amos asked him.

"Kid looks sick and filthy, needs a bath and a good meal along with some whiskey."

"Other than that, John."

John shrugged. "Kid seems harmless. Doesn't look like a pirate or a soldier to me. Probably weighs ninety soaking wet."

"Joshua Ramos though," Amos mused. "What kind of Asian is called Ramos?"

"The Philippines was once under the control of Portugal," John said. "Hence most of the Spaniard surnames."

"Didn't know you were a historian."

John shrugged again. "I have a life too, you know."

Amos chuckled, amused.

"But I digress," John said with a smile. "The kid seems harmless. I don't see any reason to hurry the coast guard. Not like they can get here any sooner than a day or two. You see that storm brewing to the north?"

"I did, yeah." Amos said all spirits low now. He hated storms that happened out here. They slowed down everything and gave Crockett a reason to call just to bitch and moan.

John, seeming to understand Amos' thoughts, placed a hand on his friend's shoulder. "Don't sweat it. Crockett ain't gonna do anything. What's he gonna do when you subject the guests indoors for a time? Fire you?"

Amos laughed out loud at that, a loud barking sound that startled him. "No, I'm worried he might take it out on someone else."

"He ain't that cruel."

You don't know him like I do, Amos thought.

"Worst case scenario," John added. "You can always give me the phone."

"Hell no."

The decision regarding Joshua closed, the two went out of their way to prepare for the rest of the night. They never spoke about it or agreed together on it, but both were internally glad that they had other things to worry about other than Tamia Gonzalez and her missing boyfriend. It was another night at the Bonidada Resort, and time was money.

Twenty-Four

Dinner was in forty-five minutes. They were sitting at their respective table together, their drinks untouched. It was then when Matt Winklemann was told by his wife, "I believe it is time."

"Yeah," he muttered dreamily, his eyes appearing sunken now more than ever. It was as if throughout the day he had become slowly drained by some parasite sucking away at his lifeblood. He stood up from his seat almost robotically while Gabbie was flashing him a beautiful smile that to him was grotesque.

"Magsaya ka," she told him.

He said nothing as he left her there. Without looking back he knew she too was rising, leaving both of their drinks at their table as she started for the resort entrance as elegantly as his wife normally would. Outside it had become grayer as the day went on, and already the muffled boom of thunder could be heard across the sea. A storm was indeed coming considering the chatter from the employees Matthew passed by, and Matthew was willingly allowing himself to become a precursor for things to come.

'Have a good time' indeed.

Through his glazed eyes as he walked towards the hall where the restrooms were, he could see what the demon was seeing as she slipped out the resort doors and breathing in the salty air tinged with ozone from the distant clouds she was looking out at. Through her eyes he could see her slipping into the brush heading towards the power station. When she had taken over she no doubt must have seen the station through Matt's eyes and were now integrating one of his thoughts into action, and would therefore be his signal to act.

He knew further down the hall near the pump room that one of the locked doors was going to be the security room. The demon had told him that John Burrows or someone just as high (Amos Mulderich for example) would be the only ones capable of unlocking it. How she got this information he didn't understand, probably the same way she had plucked everything about him out of his own head, opening him up like a book as she dug her claws deeper into his consciousness. Now he was in the restroom sitting in one of the stalls, waiting for the power to go out. Here he was going to have to wait for her signal and once he saw John Burrows, he would have to play his part and hope that no one would be around at the time, otherwise he'd be fucked.

He sat there on the porcelain throne like a mute king, his pants still on and his hands folded neatly in his lap. This was not a mannerism that Matthew Winklemann ever expressed as he thought any man who held his hands together for any reason was just a front; a pussy who wasn't truly comfortable or confident with himself. That was what his daddy-

(stop being such a goddamn baby)

had taught him. His father had been a bastard, but he had a hand in making his son who he was today. After all, he was the fire necessary to hone the true being of this world. Nobody else was truly real, and although the beatings had been real, they were a necessary evil just like every other obstacle in Matthew's way. Any boss he had to please in order to get ahead and make his life better, the caution he took when committing his murders as he did not want his world to end in a jail cell. He had been in jail long enough as a child, and he truly believed he wouldn't be caged again. This demon had come into his life seemingly as just another test, when in reality it had taken over completely. The one person who was actually real, and it had come for him. It had come, and had essentially hijacked his plan to end his life and in turn this world on his terms. As he got older Matthew became more and more aware that he just might not be the only person in the world, and this was supposed to solidify the fact that he always had been.

Well, who he *was*, up until he was founded by the demon who like his old man, had caged him like a bird.

How could this have happened to him? This was Matthew's world,

Deep inside, Matthew Winklemann was screaming. His screams resounded only in his head, and in the glaze of his eyes tears had begun to well. If he had been conscious of his own body he might have angrily wiped the tear away, furious with himself for crying. If his old man could see him now, it would be an absolute travesty. Matt never thought of his father so much in his life until last night, and he had no doubt that like with everything else, the demon was using the ghost of his father to torment him as he sat in the restroom stall completely comatose, even as at last, the lights went out.

Adam White was at his designated table with Ethan and Shawlyn Duncan who had seen him come alone and offered to sit with him. Helping Shawlyn into her seat, Ethan then took his own beside Adam and noticing his new friend's disheartening look, asked what was wrong.

"Nothing," Adam said no longer drunk but dealing with one bitch of a headache. He had vomited all the free booze not even an hour ago and was already paying the repercussions that came with sobriety.

Ethan frowned, looked to his wife who shrugged. All around them the employees were serving the other guests, with Paul and Victoria Jackson being the closest to Adam's table with Victoria having a wicked sunburn and Paul drunk to the point of red-faceness himself. Derian and Carla were visiting with Anton and Jessica as well as Brad and Leslie Woldemontt. All that was missing were Matt and Gabbie Winklemann, although some had heard about Gabbie and didn't think she would make it tonight. Cynthia had been a surprise, although both Ethan and Shawlyn figured that her absence had something to do with Adam's current mood.

An employee came by the table and asked if the Duncan's would be joining Mr. White, to which Ethan took the initiative and said they would be delighted to. Adam looked at Ethan annoyed but his expression softened when he took a moment to consider his friend's action.

"Splendid," said the dark man with a Caribbean accent. "Will you three be having anything to drink?"

"Apple cider for me, please," Shawlyn answered.

"J and B on the rocks," said Ethan.

"Bloody Mary," said Adam. He needed all the salt he could get into his body. "Along with three glasses of water please."

The man then asked if they would like appetizers. "We got a special dinner planned this evening, beef wellington and a sweet potato puree. Appetizers are a bean salad, clam chowder with fresh dill and tomatoes, seared tuna with black pepper, and a personal recommendation: lobster risotto made with homemade pork broth.”

“Risotto,” Adam said with no hesitation. It was his favorite dish, the kind Cynthia used to reserve for his birthday. Both Ethan and Shawlyn ordered the bean salad for them to share.

When the waiter had gone, Shawlyn took up the harness and spoke to Adam.

“Adam, what’s going on, love?”

Adam glared at her. “No offense, but you don’t know me and I don’t know you. You’re probably not gonna remember me when we are through with this vacation so why do you care?”

Shawlyn looked hurt and so Ethan stepped in. “Because we’d like to think of you and Cynthia as our friends. You two seemed like a nice enough couple and we enjoyed getting to know you earlier this week.”

Adam scoffed. “Don’t tell Cynthia that. She might stab you in the back later.”

Shawlyn and Ethan shared a quick glance at one another. There it was. Now they just had to get Adam to talk about it; vent if he needed to. Shawlyn would step in for Cynthia if need be just as Ethan would for Adam.

“Did you two have a fight?” he asked his friend. “You and Cynthia?”

“Something like that,” Adam grumbled.

“Wanna talk about it?”

Adam thought about it. “Oh, well, not like it’s gonna matter one way or another. She wants a divorce, long story short.”

This caught the Duncan's off guard. "How come?" asked Shawlyn. "Something happen yesterday?"

"Yeah, we actually decided to talk about our dead son. Made her think she's never gonna have closure with me and so she's just gonna give up. We come all this way to try and fix our marriage and she just throws her hands up and say 'oh well.' Fucking bullshit, pardon my French."

"Oh dear," Shawlyn said sympathetically. "I'm so sorry, Adam, that's too bad."

"We didn't know you had a child," said Ethan.

"Yeah, 'had' being the operative word," Adam muttered. "Doesn't matter now, that can't be changed. Because of that it drove a wedge between Cynthia and I, and I'll admit that I really hated her for it. It was an accident, but I always berated her for not watching him. I even admitted to my behavior and apologized and promised to do better. Nope. After a night, she decided it wasn't worth it. That the marriage and I simply aren't worth it."

He then laughed humorlessly. "It's kinda funny, really. I did everything with her, and yeah, I treated her very poorly in the time she needed me just as much as I needed her, and when it is all said and done, we can't even last a whole twenty-four hours trying to make it work. She just gives up. Just like that."

"I'm sure she doesn't mean it," said Shawlyn.

Adam wasn't swayed in the slightest. "Oh, she did."

Ethan asked what exactly was said and Adam told the story about what happened concerning Ryan, and then what had happened yesterday and today. When he was done the appetizers and drinks were there, and he fell silent as he began to eat and drink again. The Duncan's picked at their salad quietly, digesting what they had heard and thinking how to proceed from there. Both sympathized with Adam and wanted to help, but both were thinking completely different things along with it, particularly, their own marriage.

While both truly sympathized with Adam, both the Duncans had very different opinions on the circumstance, and as selfish as it was, they couldn't help but think of their own problems as well. The White's issues resulted in the lack of keeping an eye on their only child, which caused the boy's destruction. Adam of course blamed Cynthia who at the time was left to guard little Ryan White, and Ethan understood Adam's frustration. He felt truly bad and believed that Cynthia was not as good of a person as he had believed. Like he and Shawlyn, the Whites had hidden their problems well, their privacy a shared treasure until that bond was broken by Cynthia threatening to break that marriage. She really was a sleaze if she was going to just give up on Adam when he was trying to hard to let it go and forgive her for her mistake. If he were in Adam's shoes, he doubt he could forgive Shawlyn as much. In fact, if Shawlyn had done such a thing, she'd probably try to brush it off and talk about Ethan's own struggle and temptations just to get it off of her. Whenever Shawlyn was in the wrong, that was always her playing card: Bring up the moment she had caught Ethan in the act of masturbation, and she was once again the perfect wife in the eyes of the world.

At the same time, Shawlyn thought differently of Adam's situation. She sympathized with him to be sure, but at the same time she could not help but think he was getting what he deserved. Cynthia made a mistake, true. A terrible mistake, but to cut her out the way he did (if he was telling the truth) and hold that sort of resentment towards her was uncalled for. She couldn't blame Cynthia for not wanting to deal with such a thing anymore. If Ethan had dared to try to hound her for whatever reason, she would have left him on the spot. But then again, there was her own unborn child to consider. Cynthia was lucky in a way, she had no other family members to tie her down to such an abusive man. If she wasn't pregnant to begin with, Shawlyn would have dumped the cheating bastard known as her own husband; the fact that he himself has to look at other *men* to get off while she was carrying a child!

To Shawlyn, it didn't matter one way or another. All men were the same, and while she expressed her sympathy towards Adam as tenderly as she would with any soul on earth, she mentally cursed him and believed Cynthia to be the victim. She planned to go and find Cynthia the moment she had the chance to talk to her, and comfort her the way her husband should have long ago; convince her that she was doing the right thing.

Before anything else could be said between the group however, the lights suddenly went out. The music ceased, and everything plunged into black chaos.

Joshua had wanted to get up and walk around and Mendez believed it presented the perfect opportunity for him to mingle with everyone and get used to walking. It would do for a good meal as well. After allowing him to shower and clean up, the boy came out looking like a new man. Mendez had Novarez bring him a fresh pair of clothes. Rachel Novarez was one of the newer managers for Isla Bonidada and she had come to check up on

Mendez which led to her asking for a favor. She was young, younger than most women were when it came to management. She was reported to be Amos Mulderich's replacement once the guy left, and she was learning everything she could about the island. As far as Mendez was concerned, she was fit for the task and was unafraid of work or being put to work.

She arrived later with a pair of shorts and t-shirt and a pair of shoes and after expressing great gratitude to the young woman, Joshua began to dress. He was notably happier, and Mendez didn't fail to catch on that.

"She's a pretty thing, ain't she?" he asked the boy.

"Uh, well…" The boy looked embarrassed, and Mendez laughed good-heartedly.

Deciding to spare Joshua the good doctor said, "We'll head down to the ballroom before Kyra delivers the food. I hope you are hungry for something marvelous."

They both walked to the room together, where after greeting a few employees who were hard at work to deliver an exceptional evening for the guests, they came across Amos Mulderich and John Burrows talking near the bar with a young black man in a suit and tie. He greeted Mendez and offered him a drink, but the doctor turned it down. Joshua only asked for water, and he accepted it as the three men spoke and then shook hands with the boy.

"Surprised to see you up and about," said Amos. John Burrows only smiled in greeting, saying nothing. He was intimidating Joshua, and everyone was aware.

"You can join us in the corner," Amos said pointing out a collection of bare tables and chairs. "Kyra will be joining us too; It's gonna be a good one. Do you like Wellington, Joshua?"

"I've never heard of it," Joshua said a little embarrassed. He didn't know a lot about American cuisine other than hamburgers and hotdogs. He knew about Spanish cuisine but didn't think it mattered to bring it up.

"It's really good," Mendez assured him. "It's a beef tenderloin wrapped in a mushroom and parma ham mixture and baked in a puff pastry. It's like a bread with meat in it."

"Like siopao?"

"I'm not sure," Mendez admitted, likewise not having any clue what Filipinos ate. "There is also risotto, a sort of rice, and a bunch of other stuff too. At some point we will have dessert."

"Okay," Joshua said smiling for the first time in forever. He couldn't remember feeling this calm before. He was still uneasy, and that was no surprise to the men around him. Kid was lost at sea for who knows how long, anyone would be as cautious and untrusting as Joshua.

He's only been in bed for a day or so too, Amos thought to himself. *Kid's strong if he can be walking or even thinking about food at this point in time.*

Little did the men and women who ran Isla Bonidada know that Joshua Ramos had seen more than what the sea could ever show him.

"Rachel's on her way," John announced, and they all turned to see Ms. Novarez coming to meet with them. Joshua noticeably turned a shade redder at her arrival and the young woman said it was nice to meet him again which caused the kid to clear his throat in embarrassment.

"Glad to see you are actually joining us this time," Amos said.

Rachel nodded happily. "Same."

All this time, Rachel Novarez had been working in the office doing some online training that Crockett would not take no as an answer for. She was to do all 120 sessions and pass with an 80% on all 20 tests on top of a 75% on the final exam which she had yet to take. She was about three quarters of the way through her training, and then the actual hands-on training for managing Isla Bonidada would begin. Amos wasn't worried about her counseling training however, the woman had a degree in psychiatry from Harvard and had worked in a lot of clinics as is. She would be just fine in dealing with strained couples as opposed to stressed and suicidal students.

Not only that, but everyone genuinely liked Rachel. Sure, she was offstage for a majority of the time here on Isla Bonidada, but whenever she did come out she was always eager to learn everyone's names and learn how they do their job. She had been left out of the missing persons situation however although Amos had made it a point to get her in on it as soon as possible so she doesn't deal with any backlash if any would occur. John even said he would take care of it all if it ever came to that.

Ironically however, John was the only one who did not like Rachel Novarez. He never necessarily 'liked' anyone but he also never disliked anyone. Rachel, as he had told Amos one night, was the exception. It was when the girl first arrived and Amos had announced her as his soon-to-be replacement. At the end of the meeting that night, John had pulled him aside and told Amos of his opinion of her.

"She's too young to run a place like this," John had said. "Look at her! She's barely out of her twenties."

"She's twenty-nine, John."

"That doesn't matter, she has to do more than psychiatric bullshit to appease sex-deprived couples. There is a lot of paperwork, a lot of reliability, does she even know how to drive?"

"She's a smart girl, I interviewed her myself after she passed Crockett's test. What's your deal with her?"

"Uh, other than she's a goddamn girl?"

"Kyra's a girl."

"She's a *cook*, not someone in charge of a whole island."

Amos looked at his friend. "Didn't know you hated women in charge."

John snorted. "I love women in charge in the right places. An island isn't one of them. Workplaces aren't one of them. If this was back in the eighties she would be kicked off the island. If this was when pirates sailed the seas she'd be tossed overboard."

"You aren't going to toss her overboard and neither is anyone else. She's a smart woman, you gotta give her a chance. Times have changed, John."

John grumbled and said, "Yeah, and pigs can fly."

Other than that though, John had never spoken ill against Rachel again as far as Amos knew. He never brought anything up to him and he hadn't heard anyone else saying John was talking bad. Even to her face John was tight-lipped but polite, telling her she is doing a good job with her training and even offered to answer any questions she may have about something technical or mechanical that she didn't understand. He was tolerant, and that was all Amos really cared about. Although he wondered if the old man was also thinking about retirement.

They were still talking when suddenly the lights went out, plunging them into the inky blackness of the night as the oceanic winds howled all around the Bonidada Resort.

Twenty-Five

"Goddammit," John Burrows snapped upon turning on his iPhone flashlight. All around them guests and employees were speaking in surprised tones while standing perfectly still. The only light in the building other than John's phone as well as some employees who defiantly brought their own were the fires left over in the kitchen which were gas.

"Hey!" someone shouted. "What the fuck is going on?"

"Derian!" called out another, and then someone else hushed the woman.

"Sorry folks," Amos called out in a calm but commanding tone. "Power's out, storm must have knocked it out. We'll get it back on in a moment, give it two seconds." He then turned to John, eyebrows raised.

"I'm on it," John said without hesitation. "Mendez, wanna come?"

"Hate the dark?" Mendez teased as he started walking with the old man.

"Yeah, just need someone to hold my hand."

"Funny."

They apologized to a few men and women who were asking questions as well as gave some instructions to employees who looked absolutely lost, and then stepped out of the ballroom and started making their way through the reception area. There they saw Matthew Winklemann, probably waiting for his wife now looking worried as he groped through the dark.

"What's happened?" he asked the men.

Mendez answered, "Blackout. Sit tight, we'll have the backup generator on shortly."

Once in the main hall, they made their way to John's office so he could grab the access key for the backup generator at the end of the hall. Right where the pump room is at.

And where Tamia disappeared, his mind reminded himself.

Stop it. Focus on the now. Fix the lights.

Using his keycard John opened the door to his security office and while grabbing the keys asked Mendez to check the status of the main power grid. Leaving the doctor to the monitors John hurried down the hall towards the pump room where he could get the backup generator online. The damn thing should have been able to turn on automatically, but Crockett the cheap prick decided to stick with the old generator that had been on the island since it's purchase in the 70's or 80's. He stepped inside and using the key he needed to get into the panel, he revealed the old whore of a generator. It was an old and rusty thing, with a chord used to start it up like a lawn mower. He was just about to grab it, when John Burrows was instead grabbed from behind.

An arm had snaked around him, strong and thick. John had grabbed it with both hands, the intention being to throw off the arm so he could turn and strike at his assailant, but then a sharp pain punctured his back and pierced his left kidney. A choked sound like a pig getting stuck escaped his throat and he thrashed as he felt himself being stabbed a second time in the lower back. He managed to twist about so he could get his own arms around the assailant but the arm around his neck curled and forced him to stoop like an old man. Then the stabbing continued in his gut and chest, blood spilling onto the floor in great rivulets with each bite from the knife that was bloody to the hilt with the hand holding it just as spattered with gore. He tried to scream but another plunge of the knife stuck him in the jugular and he made a gurgling choking sound as his mouth filled with blood.

Then John felt himself being released and shoved to the ground, his head striking one of the thick water pipes on the way down. He laid there, gasping and choking as blood pooled all around him and laying on his back his hands now crooked claws around his throat, John was able to barely see Matt Winklemann standing above him, a look of dissatisfaction on his slack face.

He fell to his knees, each on either side of John's body, straddling him like a horse. With both hands the man stabbed John Burrows again and again in the chest, blood spraying and flying in thick droplets with each time the knife was withdrawn. Blood spattered Matt's face, and still he looked neither fierce nor angry, just simply unsatisfied as John continued to kick out and try to stop him, even to the point of getting his hand stuck by the knife so that the point was sticking out the back of it.

To John's fading gaze, he looked like a dead man walking, a ghost.

And just as quick, John Burrows became a ghost himself.

Oh Jesus, it hurts...

But it didn't hurt for long.

Mendez was able to see what had happened on the monitors. The solar transformers were okay, the generators which took in heat from the thermal activity deep underground were fine, the problem was not caused by the wind or the rain. Instead, he found the problem at one of the power boxes used to turn power on and off for the island during the times Isla Bonida were shut down. The generators there had been shredded, the metal latches tossed aside and the interior shredded to the point of unrecognition. Sparkling wires were sticking out, motherboards were snapped, someone or something had gotten into the panel and chewed on it. John Burrows was gonna have a row, and once Crockett got wind of the damages, there would be even more hell to pay.

He stepped out of the security room, making sure to shut the door behind him. He stood there waiting for John to come back or for the lights to come back on, whichever came first. This was Mendez's first semester on the island and he didn't know what to expect concerning blackouts such as this, especially if it was done by the way of sabotage.

When John hadn't returned, he started towards the pump room, calling the man's name. When he came to about ten feet from the opened door which led into darkness, Mendez suddenly stopped. Primal instincts deep inside the recesses of his being were flailing alarm bells, warning him to get away. Never mind the why, just get away. He felt blood circulating through his body, and on the back of his neck sweat had broken free and was starting to run down his back. He suddenly had the urge to turn and flee, run as fast as he could as far away as he could. Leave the building just get out of the resort, just get the fuck out of there.

He started for the door again, peeked his head in. "John?"

Quick as a flash, a bloody knife arched it's way around the doorframe and collided with Jake Mendez's left eye, popping it like a ripe grape and spilling blood and jelly all over his cheek. He had no time to process what was happening even as the blade grinded against the bone of his inner eye socket. He cried out as the knife was ripped out and his deflated eye began to tumble over his face but Mendez wasn't seeing that. He was seeing the bloody man coming at him with the knife again, and again, and again.

Matt stood up staring blankly at the murdered man at his feet. He looked up barely glancing at the other whom he had killed first. For a long time he stood there, breathing in the scent of blood as his heartbeat slowed.

Though it had begun how it was supposed to, he still felt nothing. He felt no joy in this as he had planned on, nor did he believe he would enjoy what was to come. Dropping the knife carelessly, Matt Winklemann turned around and trudged down the hall returning to the reception area. He went to the spot where there were some lounge chairs in front of a high window, and in his hiding spot, he pulled out his duffle bag. Now the real fun could begin.

Well, it would have been fun, if he was really in control. His own hands moved as if they were being puppeteered, his knowledge now belonging to the monster who led him like the puppet master she was. There was no point in fighting her, she had him literally by the balls and wouldn't let him go. She had seen something in him to aid her in her bloody desires, and had taken control of him as easily as he had taken control of the lives of all those women, that dog, the kitten.

From the duffel bag he takes the pistol he would have used on that very demon and tucks it into his belt. He also takes a Mossenburg 12-Guage with a strap, and he puts it over his head and right shoulder to sling across his back. He then takes a Bushmaster semi-automatic and loads a magazine into it. From the duffel bag he takes six more clips and tucks it into every empty pocket in his pants along with some additional shells and magazines for the pistol. He loads the rifle and turns the safety off. Then he stands, and turns as he started for the ballroom, hands which would normally be sweating with anticipation feeling as cold and numb as if he were in deep snow. He walked zombie-like towards his soon-to-be victims, uncaring about the world and his own safety.

He only prayed that someone would end this soon.

Twenty-Six

The first to see that something was wrong was Leslie Woldemontt who with her husband sat waiting patiently at their table closest to the ballroom doors.

They had left their companions when orders for appetizers and drinks were given out, and were discussing what they would do upon their return home. Brad was thinking of writing a song specifically about the beauties of Isla Bonidada, as well as the love of his wife that had blossomed significantly on this trip, as most of their vacations did. Leslie, flattered by this idea, had begun to help Brad jot down key notes about the island itself (no doubt it would've grown longer as time went on) when the lights had gone out. Now they waited patiently in the dark to which their eyes had slowly begun to get used to. The few employees with cellphones were using flashlights and others used actual flashlights to calm and ensure the guests that everything was okay.

Then she saw the man in the ballroom doorway standing there like a hulking statue. He was cradling something in his hands and there was something sticking over his right shoulder like a spike. Leslie remembered being a school teacher and telling the children a story about Jack and the Beanstalk, when the giant was thudding throughout it's castle in the clouds. How big it had been, how intimidating it had looked in the minds of children and adults alike.

Fee-fi-fo-fum,
I smell the blood of an Englishman,
Be he alive, or be he dead
I'll grind his bones to make my bread.

The shadow that was visible in the darkness had taken the very shape of that giant, and Leslie chuckled to herself how ridiculous of a comparison that was despite the rolling feeling of despair growing in her chest. The chuckle in fact being a sort of reaction to the warning signals going off in her head. When a stray flashlight came across the figure, in that blink of a second Leslie saw Matt Winklemann standing there with a gun in his hand. Realizing what was happening, she had opened her mouth to scream.

Then a blinding light from a LED shoulder light began to flash bright and white, blinding her and her husband and everyone close by. The flashes continued even when the gunfire erupted loud and commanding. Whether the flashes were from the light or from the muscle of the rifle no one could truly tell, not even Leslie who took three bullets to the face while her husband was hit in the neck, shoulder, and chest. Both fell back to the ground as everyone began to duck and scream as more bullets flew over them and into the crowd. Leslie had died before she struck the floor, her husband screaming in pain and terror beside her as he called out her name over and over and over again.

"Les? Leslie? LESLIE!?"

Be he alive, or be he dead

I'll grind his bones to make my bread.

Matt Winklemann stood dead and stoic as he felt the kick of the rifle going off again and again. Using the light on his shoulder he was able to pick out all the muddling people in the ballroom. He shot at those he saw carrying lights to help make it easier to confuse and frighten people, and if anyone tried to run past him, he only had to shoot them with a short burst and they would fall back onto the floor screaming. One man was trying to crawl away, Brad Woldemontt he realized from the upturned table after shooting them. A bloody trail was being left behind as he dragged himself across the floor, and Matt put the poor man out of his misery with a burst to the back of the head which sprayed brain and skull fragments across the elegant carpet.

A gaggle of employees close to the wall to the right had their hands up screaming in Spanish, French, and some other language but Matt showed them no mercy. After he had finished reloading his weapon, he swept the rifle across the four of them and they all dropped like sacks of laundry. Those who tried to hide under their tables he unloaded clips as he delved deeper into the ballroom. Now they were all running back towards the kitchens, not straight forward when they might have had a chance.

It was exactly as he had imagined it. Exactly as he had planned it, and Matt would have been excited if not for the dead glaze over his eyes. To any who dared to look and see his face through the flash of his LED light and the rifle, they saw nothing but a statue, a husk of a man who might as well be wearing a mask. Even to himself Matt felt like a husk, continuing to be led like a dog as he killed again and again.

A sharp pinching sensation spread throughout Matt's gut and he had stopped shooting, hearing the report of another gun going off to his left. He turned as stiff as a board and at the bar table, the tender was up and with both hands shooting a pistol in his direction. His body seeming to ignore the pain, Matt fired a burst in his direction but the man ducked behind the counter, and glasses and bottles exploded on the impact of the bullets. Matt watched the bar sharply; he hadn't expected any of these assholes to be packing.

As soon as the bartenders head popped back up again, Matt unloaded the rifle. The man's head broke apart and split, getting completely destroyed as he fell back with the gun still going off in his hand. The current threat eliminated, Matt turned his attention to someone else running towards the kitchens. He turned and shot the woman in the back, relishing at the flowers of blood erupting across her blouse. When his rifle was out of ammo, he knew he had dispensed the last of his magazines and he tossed it to the floor where it bounced and landed on a nearby body. Dead bodies were everywhere, their blood soaking into the carpet. Reaching over his shoulder, Matt removed the shotgun and pumped a round into the chamber. He raised it towards one woman who was making a rush towards the fire exit past the bar. Two more had gotten through he had noticed, but he could at least stop her.

One man, Anton Bateman, surprised Matt by leaping out from under a table and swinging a steak knife at him. Matt turned to face him and shoot but the old bastard was *fast*. He ducked beneath the barrel of the gun and threw his shoulder into Matt's wounded stomach, tackling him to the ground and plunging the knife between his ribs.

Matt stared blankly up at the man his face expressing no pain which to Anton was absolutely terrifying. This momentary scare made it easier for Matt to reel his fist back and strike at Anton's face before kicking out at him, hitting him in the knee and throwing him off. With the knife still stuck in his side, Matt raised the shotgun and a deafening boom sounded throughout the ballroom. Anton's front shirt was shredded and the flesh beneath it was punched inward as he was thrown back and over another dead body. Matt pumped another round into the chamber and started to get up. He stumbled over to the old broker and putting the barrel directly over Anton's face and pulled the trigger. Blood and bits of skull fragments had splattered everywhere, momentarily blinding Matt as some got into his eyes. He wiped at his face and pumped the shotgun again, this time seeing Jessica Bateman still in her wheelchair not far from the table. She hadn't moved, but her eyes were on her husband. Tears of pain and sorrow were in them.

Matt turned like a robot in her direction and without any indication of pain or remorse, shot her dead.

Jessica Bateman's death served two purposes. One of course was Matt's drive despite not being at the wheel at all to kill. Unable to flee herself she was sacrificed like a lamb so everyone else could try to get out via the emergency exit or the back kitchens. For the moment the gun went off Matt wasn't noticing the man rushing for him from behind. While everyone was fleeing, only four people managed to hide to get the jump on Matthew and now they were springing a trap of their own.

Lucas Powell had laid down among the dead and had remained still as Matt was starting to head for the kitchens. While he was occupied with the Batemans, he had gotten up and charged at the man from behind. He threw all his weight at Matt and together they fell to the ground. He managed to get the shot gun away from the shooter but Matt pulled his pistol and was about to shoot the employee when Amos Mulderich threw himself on top of Matt and held him down so that Ethan Duncan could move in and help. They all struggled and wrestled with Matt, trying desperately to get the gun out of the man's iron grip. The weapon occasionally went off, deafening the men with every blast which barely missed one or the other's head. At this point, Matt had thrown his head back into Amos' face and broke the man's nose, forcing him off. Now he and Ethan were standing, both now fighting for the gun while Lucas threw his arms around Matt and tried to pull him down. All the while Matt wrenched and kicked like a wild animal, howling and snarling like one as well.

Then someone shouted "Get down!"

Ethan saw something Matt didn't and released the man before throwing himself to the ground. Matt jerked his elbow back and it connected with Lucas who stumbled away. Matt was just about to shoot Ethan with both hands gripping his weapon tightly, when four reports sounded behind him, and he stumbled forward as Derian Anderson shot him in the back.

Derian had a concealed weapon in a concealed holster in his jacket, and after making sure his wife was safe and hidden in the dark, he had pulled it and started for the shooter. When the scuffle broke out, he got closer with both hands gripping the gun tightly to steady his aim. When he barked out his order he thought he wouldn't have time to save the brave men who rushed Matthew Winklemann, but he squeezed the trigger again and again as the man stumbled and jerked and swayed.

There was a momentary pause and then Matt had turned, his back already bleeding profusely. His eyes still had that dead sheen to them but now his face appeared contorted almost. His lips twisted into a snarl and in the dim light as Derian shot again, he saw that Matthew's teeth were irregularly large and sharp, with his canines exceptionally longer. His shot had struck Matthew in the cheek and already blood was seeping through the hole. Still the man was turning and taking aim with his own pistol. He fired blindly in Derian's direction, and the gunman fired three times more.

Matthew's body jerked but his face remained a monstrous grimace adorned by the blood as Derian's shot got him three times in the head. One struck him right in those pointed teeth while the other two were driving into his forehead. Speckles of brain matter glistened in the sudden shots and still Matthew Winklemann was firing his weapon and succeeding in hitting Derian in the shoulder. Ignoring the fire in his shoulder, Derian kept squeezing the trigger over and over again until he had spent all his rounds and only clicking could be heard. Likewise Winklemann's gun was clicking, his face a bloody death mask.

A strange gurgling sound escaped Derian's destroyed face and then the man quite comically fell straight back, crashing down to the floor with a loud thud. Some of the men started for him but Derian told them to stay away as he reached into his belt and removed another clip. In just a few seconds the gun was reloaded, and he approached Winklemann with his gun aimed directly at the prone man.

"Careful," Amos Mulderich was saying but Derian could see Winklemann was not going to be a danger anymore. The man was laying perfectly still, his breath wheezing in his bubbling mouth. Already the other men were circling the body and Winklemann's eyes rotated in their sockets to admire each and every single one of them.

"You got him," someone else was saying. "You got the sonofabitch!"

Derian stared at Winklemann who likewise was staring back. The man had tears in his eyes which rolled down his ruined cheeks and soaked into the carpet along with the blood of his victims.

His mouth opened, his teeth now a ruined mess of ivory, and from Winklemann's dying breath uttered the word, "Thank…"

And that was it. All the men who stayed while the others fled stared down at the dead man, not believing what had just happened nor could they believe Matthew had been able to still stand after being shot and stabbed so many times. Already Luca was coming back with an assault rifle but the carnage was over. All around them the dead bled, the wounded crying softly.

And Matthew Winklemann, was set free at last.

Twenty-Seven

Derian lowered his gun allowing his other hand to clamp onto his shoulder where he had been hit. His suit had been ruined and Amos Mulderich took noticed of it and asked

"I'm fine," said Derian. "Don't worry about it."

"Shit," said Luca gripping the rifle he had managed to grab stiffly. To Ethan he said, "You okay?"

"Fine," said Ethan now standing and rubbing the back of his head. His clothes were bloody but not because of himself. They all looked around with Amos' flashlight at the carnage that was the ballroom.

Dead were everywhere. Twisted bodies destroyed by a gunman all bloody and torn. Chairs and tables were laying askew, the bar and bar table destroyed by the gunfire, and bullet holes and casings could be found everywhere. The four men stood in silence as the clamor of the survivors in the kitchen came from the opened window. Finally, Derian broke the silence and shook everyone back to reality.

"Duncan," he said to Ethan. "You're bleeding."

"Wha-" Ethan looked at his left leg which had turned crimson with blood. He had been shot after all. "Oh. Oh... I... I don't even feel it..." He was starting to panic, his face turning to the color of cheese.

"Relax, sit down," Derian said tucking his pistol into his belt. "It's adrenaline, you're in shock. Hold still." He got to work taking a part of his shirt and stuffing it into the man's pants.

"I've been shot," Ethan said almost dreamily.

"So has he," Amos said having left the group momentarily to grab a bundle of napkins from an overturned table. He handed some to Derian to use on Ethan while he began to cover Derian's wound.

"It ain't that bad," said Derian not looking. "Just grazed me."

Amos didn't respond. When he was done, he said to Lucas, "Where the hell were the other guns? Why was Jacob the only one to first respond?"

"I dunno," said Lucas appearing perplexed. "Everyone seemed surprised by the blackout. I doubt any of the cooks were prepared either, especially once people started heading out the back."

Amos nodded, but this still didn't make him any less angry especially as he looked around at all the dead. People who he had worked with for a long time, people who've lived on this island and have handled plenty of trouble in the past. In the gloom lighting of the flashlights, he saw all of their faces frozen in places of pain and terror, some with their eyes wide open staring doll like at the elegant ceiling that was shrouded by the blackness.

This shouldn't have happened, he kept telling himself. *We shouldn't have let this happen...*

"Mr. Mulderich," Lucas said noticing his bosses expression of gloom. "We couldn't have known."

"Doesn't matter," said Amos feeling sick to his stomach. "Jesus, what a mess..." He went for his radio and keyed it. "John." He waited, watching as Derian finished working on Ethan's leg, his own sleeve having been stuffed with the cloth napkins which were already soaked.

John didn't answer.

He tried again. "John, do you copy?"

Nothing. He tried for Jake Mendez. Again, all that responded was the silence of the radio and the distant clamor of guests. A dreadful pit began to form in his stomach, and desperate to become distracted he looked at the other men, the wounded having stood up from where they had been working on themselves.

"We gotta get all the survivors together," he said. "Lucas, can we go get them?"

"Yes, I think that is best."

Derian had left Ethan then and was back at Winklemann's body. Amos shuddered at the sight of the man who had still been standing when he had gotten stabbed and shot so many times. There was no way he was human; Anybody would have dropped after getting hit several times in the head. He was suddenly struck with two conflicting pieces of himself, part of him glad he never had to sit down with a man capable of such monstrous things, and at the same time wished he was so that if there was any sign such an atrocity would happen, maybe something could have been done.

Don't blame yourself, Amos told himself. *Crockett and the family members of these people will do that enough. Get these guys out of here and calm down the other survivors.*

"We need to go," he said to both Derian and Ethan.

"Okay," said Derian who was now using the barrel of his pistol to raise Matt Winklemann's upper lips. Seeing the weapon made Amos want to ask how he managed to get that piece here on the island and through customs, but a more important one came to mind.

"What are you doing?" Lucas asked beating Amos to the punch.

"Nothing," said Derian obscurely. He looked both confused and disturbed by what he saw. As far as Amos could see Winklemann's teeth had been punched in by Derian's shots. The jagged pieces that were what's left of his teeth shone in the light of the flashlight, with some bits having landed in the back of the man's throat shining like bits of quartz in a fleshy mine.

"Come on," Amos said again and this time, Derian let the shooter's lip fall.

He followed the others out of the bloody room, the haze of blue gun smoke shone in the flashlight's beam like dense fog over the bloody floor, and Lucas was helping Derian walk Ethan out in front of Amos as they left. Walking over the sea of ruined members of their little community, their family, Amos felt grief nearly trip him as he nearly stepped on the face of a dead servant. He recognized the man as Jaque Malona whom had just started earlier this season. The guy was barely in his twenties, and the thought of such a short life being cut off almost instantaneously was a cruel tragedy.

But Jaque had died from bleeding out. It had not been instantaneous, and Amos could see that from the amount of blood and how the man laid curled as if he had a stomachache. Tears stained the man's cheeks, and as he passed over him, Amos felt his own tears streak his own.

Twenty-Eight

Everyone was clustered and panicking in the kitchens, and Kyra, try as she might, could not get everyone to calm down. It had been scary enough the moment the lights went out, worse even when the gunfire erupted.

Every single one of her crewmembers were trained in firearms and they had some emergency guns stashed in a few of the ceiling panels away from the ventilation. The moment her boys got to them however that was when people came flooding in, causing pots and pans and carts of food to go everywhere as people stumbled into darkness. Some poor guy even crashed into one of the stoves where cast irons had been used to sear the tuna. He had placed his hand right on it and howled like a banshee, causing the already cluster-fuck of panic to erupt instantaneously. Her men struggled to help the man while others tried to turn off everything as the stoves were all gas and not electric. Needless to say, Kyra was glad to see Amos finally walk in and call the room to order.

Between Amos and Lucas with surprisingly the assistance of the guest Derian, they managed to get everyone to go through the back doors and into the main hallway. It took some doing but they had managed to do so just fine and clear out the kitchens. As they led the survivors to the reception area of the resort, Amos asked Lucas if he was willing to check the pump room for any sign of the backup generator coming online, especially to check on John and Jake. Once everyone was in the reception room, they were all asked to sit and wait for further instruction. There were some people who were badly wounded, but they would survive.

There were nine guests left in the reception area, and eight regular employees after the headcount. Including Kyra Lewis, Ben Franklins, Joshua Ramos, and himself, Amos counted twenty-one survivors and who knows how many stragglers. The wounded consisted of Paul Jackson whose seared hand was heavily bandaged and Ethan Duncan from his wound to the leg, along with four of the employees. Kyra suffered from a head injury she didn't even notice when everyone had started to shove their way into her kitchens.

Everyone else was dead, or missing. Those who survived looked to whom they regarded as the ringleader of this whole island for explanation with some even shouting at him.

"Everyone stay calm," Amos repeated for the third or fourth time his hands raised like a preacher beseeching the crowd. "We are trying to get a clear headcount, everyone remain calm. Please."

"How are we supposed to be calm?" demanded Adam angrily. "We just got fucking *shot* at!"

"Mr. White, calm down," Amos demanded. "Getting angry isn't going to help anyone."

"I can't find my wife, don't tell me-"

Derian had moved in and placed a hand on the distressed manager's shoulder. "Relax. We'll find her." *Hopefully.*

Three more stragglers had come in. One had been Rachel Novarez, her shirt torn and dirty from her escape through the fire exit, and one employee who had hidden among the dead with a gunshot wound to his shoulder. The last and final person did not come from within the resort but from the huts, and Adam screamed the woman's name out as she came in looking surprised and bewildered.

"Cynthia!" he cried out and rushed for his wife. He had tackled the surprised woman with a mighty hug and kissed her forcibly on the cheek. When she managed to get him off she asked what had happened, seeing the people who were injured and bloody but especially the horror now mixed with relief on her husband's face.

"We were attacked by a shooter," Adam explained. "Guy went fucking postal on everyone in the dark. Power went out. Oh Jesus, Cynthia, I'm so glad you're okay..." He hugged her again, looking like he was about to start sobbing.

Cynthia hugged him back, appearing very shocked and very confused. "It's okay, I'm okay... I came thinking I was late, it got so dark outside and windy and I didn't want to be in the hut alone..."

"Thank god you didn't come," Adam said. "If you had been there, I don't know if anything-"

"Hey," Shawlyn said coming up to them. "Nothing happened. We are all safe. They'll figure out what to do from here and we will be fine."

Kyra Lewis, who had overheard the conversation over the clamor, sincerely hoped so.

She came up to Amos just as Lucas Powel had returned, looking green and sick.

"John's dead," he announced in secret between the two. "So is Jake."

"Sonofabitch," Amos swore miserably. He turned away from everyone and stopped at the reception desk running his hands through his hair. He then brought a fist down hard on top with another curse that sounded animalistic even to himself.

"Amos, don't!" Kyra said immediately at his side and grabbing hold of his hand. It didn't matter though because he didn't bring his fist back up off the table. He was trembling so bad she could feel his skin vibrating through her own hands.

Clenching his teeth, Amos tried to get ahold of himself. His good friend had been killed, same as the doctor, who was sorely missed at this time with all the wounded. He shook his head miserably as if trying to clear it.

He turned to Lucas and asked hoarsely, "What about the generator?"

"Not on. I checked John but he didn't have any keys."

"Winklemann must have taken them to keep us in the dark," said Kyra.

"Why do that if he planned on shooting everyone?" Ben asked.

Rachel, throughout this whole thing, only stared at the guests blankly, especially at Shawlyn, the poor pregnant woman who missed death by a hairs-width, same as her husband. The four remaining leaders of Isla Bonidada, were now having to figure out what to do from here; the worst disaster the island had ever seen.

"Who knows and who cares?" said Amos. "We need to get that generator back online so these people can have good shelter for the night. With the storm outside we better keep everyone in. Also, we need to feed them still. Ben, can you take a few of our able guys back into the ballroom and find Winklemann's body and check for the key, please?"

Ben looked appalled at the idea but said he would round up some guys.

"Kyra, as soon as the lights go back on can you get food out to these guys?" He jerked his head towards the guests. "Whatever we got."

"Of course."

"Lucas, come with me," said Amos. "I need to get on the radio and have someone come out here to deal with this mess. Hopefully we can get a signal out with this wind. If not, we'll have to wait until the storm passes."

"I'll wait here with the guests," said Rachel. "Everyone should be here now, right?"

"I hope so," said Amos and with Lucas he left, along with everyone else with their tasks at hand.

Rachel looked over everyone, and smiled softly, encouragingly, despite the unfortunate circumstances that had fallen upon them.

Adam had taken Cynthia back to where he had been sitting along with the wounded Ethan and Shawlyn Duncan. With the few remaining survivors talking amongst themselves, Rachel Novarez watched over them all and answered very few questions, occasionally looking outside which was revealing that the sun was almost completely down. She had applied to this job with excitement and a desire to help others while living on a tropical island almost year-round. She never expected to deal with a shooter literally during the period of her training. She saw that soon the stormy gray outside would be a world of blackness which would converge on the resort which would hopefully return to brightness.

Which it did, the lights went back on and a few people actually applauded at the concept of brilliant light returning. They seemed to be growing in spirits, despite the horrible atrocity that had taken place. Some were even standing and sharing smokes, but the celebrations did not last as someone noticed something off and began to scream incoherently and yet understood among the survivors.

It was Shawlyn Duncan. She had felt a pain growing in her belly. A mild popping sensation that burst only for a brief moment, and then she felt a wet trickle between her thighs.

Her water had broke, and she was screaming something about her water breaking, but in the midst of her excitement, it came out like something guttural.

"Shawlyn? Shawlyn!" cried Ethan.

"Holy shit," someone said. "Her water's breaking!"

"Put her down here," someone else said and Shawlyn felt hands gently move her away so she could sit down. It had been Adam and Victoria Jackson, and her husband was close beside her, his pantleg removed and his wound wrapped in pieces of cloth to stop the bleeding. He was grasping her hand, and she gave it a squeeze.

"Seriously?" Ethan demanded laughing hysterically. "Right now?"

"I don't know," Shawlyn said at last. The stress had finally gotten her to the point of her baby finally having enough of it's mother's anxiety and wanting out; to be free of the womb and enter the world a new being.

"Is there a doctor in the house?" Cynthia cried out. When no one stepped up she said it again. "Anyone?!"

But no one was a doctor. The only doctor on Isla Bonidada had been Jake Mendez, and Jake was dead in the pump room with John Burrows courtesy of the gun-wielding maniac.

That was fine though, Shawlyn kept telling herself. It would be fine that there wasn't a doctor in the house. She may have to give birth here or someone can come from the mainland to help. After all, mankind has given each other births since the dawn of time, right? Even so, she may be in labor for hours so what could possibly go wrong?

What went wrong, was Rachel Novarez, who while wanting to wait until it was safe to move, was drawn by the possibility of losing her favorite food. So with a howl that seized everyone's attention, the woman began to change in a drastic and hellish manner.

Not everyone saw when it began, but those who did didn't understand it at first, and in the aftermath wished they didn't understand at all.

The woman's upper body seemed to pull free from it's lower, separating just above the hips. Skin stretched and tore, muscles and veins burst, bones cracked until the woman's entrails were exposed. Someone screamed as they began to lash out like tentacles in a sporadic movement that was a blur sending blood sailing everywhere. At the same time, bony protrusions broke free in the woman's back just behind the shoulder blades, her fingernails fell away to give way to claws that stretched thick and black. By the time black leather wings broke completely free from Rachel Novarez's back, her upper torso was freed from the lower, and she rose with her entrails dangling beneath her. A horrible sickly grin stretched across her face; a mouthful of shark-like teeth beneath eyes that glowed like the fires of Hell itself. Any resemblance of Rachel Novarez was gone, replaced with a pale expression of a monster as ancient as time itself.

Now people were screaming, many fleeing towards the hall to get away from the wretched thing that appeared out of nowhere. Even Adam and Cynthia fled at the guttural roar of the monster who took flight and circled the room, snarling and cackling like a witch. Shawlyn was still on the ground, and Ethan was hovered over her protectively.

"Hey!" he cried out. "Someone help us! Help-"

The creature drove him into the ground, her claws digging deep into his back and with a mighty heave she lifted him up and hurled him at the receptionist desk where he crashed over the table and landed on the other side with a sickening *crunch.*

Shawlyn lifted herself up staring wide-eyed at the monster who unleashed a horrible high-pitched shrill past those monstrous teeth. The scream seemed to break her free of her paralysis as she began to crawl backwards to get away from the demon who held herself suspended in the air directly above her, grinning that terrible smile.

"Oh god, oh god, oh god..."

The demon tucked it's wings in and landed on top of Shawlyn, roaring into her face and taking horrible pleasure at her terror. Then it backed up, it's mighty hands closing tightly around her ankles as it lifted her legs up and spread them.

"No! No!" Shawlyn screamed not knowing what was going to happen but scared nonetheless. Anything that forced your legs apart like that did not mean anything good, and she thrashed and tried to kick to break herself free but it did her no good and she watched in horror as something snaked it's way out past the set of shark's teeth in the demon's mouth.

It was thick, red, and sharpened into a barb at the end. It wriggled above her spread legs as if taunting her and Shawlyn knew immediately that it was a very long tongue. Then like a viper striking at a mouse, it plunged through her exposed panties and into her privates and went deep into the womb cavity.

Shawlyn *screamed* as she felt the creature's tongue wriggle inside her. She threw her head back crying and screaming for help, but no one came for her aid. Immense pain spread throughout her womb and even deeper still, all the way to her chest cavity which felt like something was alive inside of her and was bouncing around her ribcage. Ethan, who had survived the thrashing had gotten up and witnessed the creature's tongue bulging between Shawlyn's thighs and like a chunk of fruit being sucked up by a straw, something went up the tongue and into the monster's mouth. More and more joined, as the creature first devoured the unborn fetus, it's favorite food, and then the rest of Shawlyn Duncan's internal organs. She gasped and choked and blood spilled from Shawlyn's mouth until at last she stopped trying to kick, stopped trying to fight, and laid still dead and staring at the ceiling, her stomach and chest deflated like a dead balloon.

"Oh Jesus," Ethan croaked covering his mouth with his hand. He felt all that he had eaten threatening to come out, and he cried out Shawlyn's name as the monster retracted it's tongue. It slid right back into it's mouth and it snapped it's jaws with a satisfactory click before the barbed end stuck out again and licked it's lips almost savagely before turning it's horrid gaze towards him. It had waited almost too long, and now it was time to feed.

It rose, ready to pounce on Ethan but someone was screaming and charging at the demon with a tall lamp clutched with both hands as if it were a club.

Ethan didn't know the boy's name as he had never met him, but it was Joshua Ramos. He had not run like the others, he had been cemented in place, paralyzed by his disbelief and fear. When he had finally broken free, he had charged at the monster and taking it by surprise, swung the lamp which connected with it's head which shattered the bulb and bent the shaft. The monster growled at him and swiped at him with his claws. His shirt was torn and bloody furrows appeared on the flesh beneath.

"Hindi!" cried Joshua who was on his back and clutching at his chest. The monster was now hovering over him, ready to pounce on its's next victim.

That was when someone else was coming back from the main hall and was taking shots at the monster who barely flinched as bullets bit into it's hide.

It was Derian, who after making sure his wife was safe had come back and was down on one knee and shooting the monster with the accuracy of a sharpshooter. The monster roared at him and taking flight it swooped in to attack him from above. That was when another employee came out with a rifle and took a shot at the monster who veered off course and with a shrill scream that sounded like a curse, and swinging in it scooped up it's lower half which had collapsed near the door and it flew right threw the glass window above it. Glass fell tinkling like icicles across the floor as the monster fled from the resort and into the night.

"Oh, fuck," Derian said now standing and reloading his weapon, his face a stretched and pale mask. He was rushing for Shawlyn but Ethan had beaten him to it.

The guy was bawling and screaming for his wife, but Shawlyn was dead. She had been eaten alive by the monster, as was her unborn child who would have been a boy, and they would have named him Samuel. All the while the storm outside blew into the resort, a horrible howl that doomed the people inside to the long night ahead.

7th Letter

I have been thinking. Thinking back on that night brings tremors through my very being. It is impossible to write everything without feeling like I am going to faint.

My wife, knowing I had been writing in my journal, begged me to stop and just rest. It pained me to see her so worried, and so I had her lay beside me and I told her that there is a reason why I am going through this torment one last time. When she didn't understand, I did what I never thought I could do to myself or to her: I let her read what I had written. I haven't written a lot, only six dates along with this one, but by the time she finished she looked old, haggard, and worst of all, disbelieving. She asked if I was okay, if I was possibly under a lot of stress because of the drugs. She knew I had sailed across the ocean to America, she knew I had struggled finding my way through Mexico, but she didn't understand how a notion of monsters came into place.

So, I showed her my scars again. I remember her admiring them after our first night together, inquiring about each and every single one. While most of them had been truthful, gunshot wounds, a knife wound in my cheek while I was crossing the border, a scar on my knee I got when I fell from a tree as a child, all of it easy to explain enough. What was easier to shrug off, were the lies. The lies about the four deep furrows in my back, which I told her was from a jaguar who had been hunting me. The cut went from my left shoulder down to my right hip, and there was a hideous bite mark between my neck and shoulder right along the shattered and resealed collar bone which I told her was from a shark attack. I had been attacked with one with shark's teeth, but not an actual shark. The puncture scar in my belly, was not of me walking into a pole, but from being impaled by the knucklebone of an enlarged bat-like wing. I told her that these were not scars from something created for the beauty of this world, but of something sinister, something only the devil could be capable of. She was still doubtful, but as she could see no lie in my words, asked what exactly it was.

So, I told her what I will write to you now, what I was told while I was laying in a cot after finally awakening in the church. The priest had been there, along with someone else. The Babalayn from Capiz, who had hurried here upon the word of my mother's demise. Her body was burned, but it was not the first.

I had been asleep for almost four days, and in those four days, my village had become a nightmare of biblical proportions. All the livestock and animals had been killed off, all of them having their fur and feathers taking on a darker hue which is a mark of the beast. People were walking around with bulat in their sacks, carrying bolos and other weapons and vials of holy water and ash. Some homes had been burned down, and many had either fled or had been slain by the beast that now stalked the land. Apparently, even a family who had attempted to flee was caught in the middle of the night, and was slaughtered with their bodies left hanging in the pathway as a warning: No one was to leave. The monster had claimed our village as it's herd and it the shepherd. I took all of this in without remorse or pity. My family was dead, the monster responsible having been so close to the point where I could look her in the eye. Nothing in the world mattered anymore, I have laid eyes upon something no man was meant to see, and not even the bread and water I was given to eat while I was told what happened could make me care.

What did catch my attention was when the Babalayn asked the priest to leave us be, and when we were alone, he took out his pipe and lit it. He asked me if I knew the story of the woman of blasphemy. I answered for the first time upon awakening that I did not.

There had once been a woman who turned her gaze away from the Holy Ones, and away from God the Father. She had no love for Him, nor the people of her village. She only had love for a man. This caused her to be shunned by the people, who hated her from defying the laws of womanhood and disregarding tradition, but she would not listen. She cared for nothing but the man. She was passionate for him, and was willing to do anything to gain his devotion. She was willing to rebel the strictures of women for her village, and show herself as herself to someone who just might have possibly understood her. The passion was so great and so painful, that it made what was to become of her all the more terrible.

She was denied by the man, rebuked by him even, for she did not follow the laws of her village. She was disregarded, just as her God had been. Because of her denial of the religious codes and sense of morality. This rejection, awoken something within the woman, and the pain was so great, it tore her apart. Her upper and lower half split apart, spilling blood and entrails, and her body contorted into that of a monster with huge black wings, and a mouthful of shark teeth and claw-like fingers of deadly magic and ill will. She flies away, taking the man with him to drop him from the sky, all the while leaving her lower body on the ground. In her rage, she had laid waste to the village, and satisfied her lust and hunger with the blood of man, and the flesh of the unborn.

When she at last returned to her lower half, she reconciles what she now finally understood from another level, and what she has become. She tried to understand the pain and suffering she had caused by her bloodshed, but she could not. She could not understand from a human level anymore. She could not reconcile, and she could not release that passion and pain. From that day forward, every night, she takes flight and eats, and curses. She walks in plain sight of all around her, and at night, she pulls apart from her human side or what shall always remain on the ground, and her demonic side takes flight free, and hungry.

This story did not make me sympathetic towards the monster. Nor did it make me feel like I could, given like her, I too had struggled with my faith. But not out of sake of vainness nor corrupt passion. No, I could understand what had created the monster, but I could not understand the seed from which it had been planted. I could look upon it like a bloomed flower and understand both it's beauty and ugliness, but I would never be able to look at the seed and find it relatable, nor could I find sympathy for it. I didn't have it in me. All I felt towards the monster was rage, and hatred.

Because of that, I was able to ask the Babalayn something I never would have asked before. Something I refused to believe in despite hearing about it all throughout the village. My faith wasn't what was driving me forward, as it never truly had. What drove me to ask were the facts, what I had witnessed, and what I felt.

"Tell me," I implored the old man. "This thing, is it aswang?"

The Babalayn looked at me incredulously. "In part, yes. It is one of the devil's twelve ministers. Surely you know what it is without me saying?"

"Am I right though?"

"Yes. Your village, your family, was and is plagued by the Manananggal."

Twenty-Nine

Everyone was gathered in the conference room and given a chair. Kyra Lewis and her boys had brought in water and some of the food meant for the feast that hadn't been ruined in the panic. Everyone was attending to one another as best as they could. Ethan was in a state of shock and was given one of Mendez's shots to put him to sleep, and he laid across Adam White's lap as everyone listened to Amos Mulderich who had arrived just in time to see what was happening.

He and Lucas had seen what Derian had been shooting at, and neither could believe what they had seen. Everyone was in a state of shock and panic; as if a shooting wasn't bad enough. Now there was something out there, and it had attacked and eaten Shawlyn Duncan and would have killed her husband as well if given the chance. When they tried to all discuss it, outrage erupted between the guests and the employees who were now all armed, having taken some guns from the various stations hidden throughout the resort in case of an emergency.

In case of an emergency, Amos thought bitterly. *We weren't ready for Winklemann. We weren't ready for any of this.*

Rachel…

"That wasn't a monster!" Cain Ashton said viciously.

"Then what was it then?" demanded Paul Jackson cradling his burnt hand like a precious worry stone.

"I don't know, had to be a mistake!" someone else cried.

"Jesus Christ, did you all not see that woman pull apart in *half*!?"

"What did Ethan say again? It did *what* to his wife?"

The arguments, justifications, sympathy, and outrage went on, and on, and on.

"Everyone, stop it!" Ben Franklins barked. His voice was loud enough and commanding enough for everyone to stop for at least a minute. "Fighting is not going to solve anything. We need to calm down."

"Calm down!?" Paul Jackson almost screamed. "We all just got our asses shot at by a maniac and now we got something flying around the resort and it *ate* someone!"

Amos was now looking at Joshua Ramos who had seen the creature as well. Had actually charged in and attacked it, as Derian Anderson had put it. The kid had been quiet since their coming to the conference room, and had not spoken since the attack.

Why didn't he run too? he wondered. *He didn't have a gun or anything. Went at it with a lamp. A fucking* lamp!

"Amos," Kyra Lewis called his name and reaching for his side. "What is going on? What are we supposed to do?"

He cleared his throat and told everyone to shut up. He had to maintain order here, that was the only way anything was going to get moving around here.

"Everyone, listen up," he called out. "What happened with the shooter is a tragedy, but we got another problem. Someone or something has attacked us right after, and might still be lurking around outside waiting for us to come out. We don't want to get outside, obviously. The storm is getting worse and it's night time, we wouldn't be able to see jack-shit out there. Therefore, we are going to sit in here until someone catches our distress signal and comes out to look for us. Maybe when the daylight comes out we can attempt to make a break for one of the boats but for now it's best to stay on the island until the storm passes."

"How long will that take?" asked Cynthia.

"We don't know," admitted Amos.

"You don't know!?" Paul Jackson demanded exasperated.

Victoria tried to talk him down. "Paul-"

"Shut the fuck up you goddamn dyke," Paul snarled. Victoria winced as if expecting a blow and Paul ignored her. "This shouldn't have happened in the first place; you people shouldn't have let this happen!"

"Well, it did," Kyra Lewis barked her no-nonsense attitude coming out of the kitchen at last. "It could have happened to anyone anywhere. So you listen you-"

"Don't," Amos said to Kyra who looked outrage. There was no point in arguing with someone who never had to deal with such a thing like this. Someone who could afford to place a bubble of security around him and never suffer any harm the outside world had in store for mankind. While there was a lot of good in the world, there was enough bad to go around, even to the rich and seemingly untouchable.

Too bad Crockett isn't here, he thought bitterly.

"For now, we sit and wait," said Amos to everyone. "Someone will pick up our signal and pick us up hopefully by daybreak."

"*If* day even breaks," muttered someone in the crowd.

Amos ignored them. "We have plenty of food and we will make sure that-"

"What if that thing comes in here?" asked Winnifred impatiently. "What if that... that *thing* breaks back in?"

"Whatever it is it'll have to get through us first," said Ben who gestured to those with semi-automatic weapons. All eight employees were armed to the teeth, the five men and three women, all garbed in fancy serving attire and looking like the followers of some mafia boss.

"What if it isn't enough?" demanded Paul Jackson.

"It *will* be enough," said Derian still brandishing his pistol. His wife huddled close to him, seeming to take greater security being by his side. "We will get through this, we just gotta wait it out like the boss says."

"What the fuck was that about anyway, darkie?" Paul demanded. "You special-ops or something?"

"Not even close," said Derian. "Little of concern to someone like you. Just sit tight and we will make it through this."

"Is Ethan here gonna be okay though?" Cynthia asked as she crouched next to her husband and the man in question.

"He'll be fine, he just needs to rest and get over his shock," said Ben. "He'll wake up right as rain."

"I hope so," said Adam.

"So what? Just wait?" one of the employees asked, Gregory Carson if Amos remembered his name correctly.

"Yes sir," said Amos really wishing he was anywhere but here now. "We wait."

"Waiting will do us no good," Joshua Ramos said breaking his silence for the first time.

"Excuse me?" Amos demanded now losing patience. He took a deep breath though, allowed himself to calm down. It had been hell for them all, he didn't need to lose it now.

"Josh," he attempted again. "What do you mean by that?"

"It won't matter where we wait," he said. "It'll come for us. We cannot hurt it with guns."

"You talk as if you know what this thing is," Kyra demanded with crossed arms.

Amos realized something. "Josh," he said. "Do you know what that thing was? What we saw out there?"

Joshua hesitated, but then nodded miserably.

"Well, what is it?" Paul demanded angrily. "Tell us!"

"Calm down," Derian warned the man. "Leave the kid alone."

"If the kid knows what it is then he may have something to do with it!"

"Do you even *hear* yourself right now?" Adam demanded. "He tried to save Ethan, weren't you listening!?"

"So the man with the gun says," Paul said bitterly.

"Knock it off," Amos barked at them all and then returned his attention to Joshua. "Josh, talk to us. What are we up against? What is out there?"

Josh looked at Amos miserably. "Will you believe me though? I didn't, not at first, and that is what got everyone I knew killed. That is how it managed to escape me, and why... and why I went out after it."

"What do you mean?" asked Ben.

And slowly, miserably but with effort, Joshua told his tale of the monster known as the Manananggal.

Thirty

Everyone sat in silence, taking in all that they had heard.

They had all listened to Joshua Ramos with enough respect simply to hear him out. If they had any questions or arguments, they kept it to themselves. Paul Jackson in particular thought it was all a crock of shit, but he was biding his time and waiting for his turn to speak. But it annoyed him how the kid barely spoke enough English for his story to make any legitimate sense.

When his tale concluded, ending with how he ended up on the island, Joshua looked at everyone and waited for their response. Which took a while for anyone to express, for they all sat in silence and digested this story with the cynicism and criticism worthy of police detectives.

At last someone broke the silence, bringing everyone out of their own thoughts and back to reality. The grim reality where they were in some resort out in the middle of the ocean miles off the coast where a massacre had just taken place. Now they were having to deal with something purely monstrous, and worst of all, hungry. Regardless of their individual belief's of what exactly they had seen, all could agree that something was out there in the darkness and the wind which had finally blown in some rain, and they were trapped until help arrived.

All of this, was brought by none other than Ben Franklins in an uneasy, relatively disbelieving voice.

"That is… well… It's quite the story."

"I'll say," said Derian. He was sitting next to wife and shaking his head slowly, still absorbing it all. "Christ, when you think you've heard it all."

"A manan… what is it again?" asked Victoria beside her husband who was frowning disbelievingly.

"Manananggal," Joshua answered. "It's a breed of Aswang, a… how do you call it… a ghoul or vampire of some sorts. Ancient, and dangerous."

"You don't really believe that, do you?" one of the employees asked. It was Jennifer Strohm, and she looked skeptical, as did most who sat at the conference table or stood close by.

"The story?" Derian said. "Not particularly, sorry to say, kid," he added to Joshua. "But I also cannot deny what I saw with my own eyes."

"It had to be a hallucination of some sort," reasoned Cynthia. "Something because of what had happened."

"I know what I saw, ma'am," Derian said slowly, respectfully, but more importantly, patiently. "I saw what I saw. Poor Ethan saw what that thing did to his wife, and I checked the body after. It ate her baby, probably most of her guts too. Josh here went after it with a fucking lamp, and I got a few shots at it."

"Regardless of what it is," said Adam likewise in a strange state of disbelief mixed with that primal fear of the unknown out in the stormy dark. "If we can wound it, it should stay back, right?"

"It won't do any good," said Joshua. "It won't stop until it kills us all. Then we will all be stored for meat until she has to move on."

"'She'?" demanded Paul Jackson feeling as if he was going insane throughout this entire discussion. "I can't believe this; You all are out of your goddamn mind."

"Mr. Jackson," Amos started but Paul cut him off by slicing through the air with his good hand.

"No, you people are fucking nuts. Monsters that look like people, tearing themselves apart and flying. *Flying*! Next you'll be telling us whatever this thing is has tentacles!"

He turned to Derian. "I dunno what you or this gook saw, but it has to be some sort of animal, that is *all* it can be. Monsters don't exist out here in the real world, buddy. And you, kid, in the jungle you may get scared and have your little stories to explain it all, but over on this side of the world, we understand that monsters don't exist."

Amos regarded Paul with a grim expression. "Given what happened in the ballroom, mister, I don't agree with that statement."

"What are you talking about?" Paul demanded.

"Monsters *do* exist, look at Winklemann. We are just dealing with a different one right now." He of course was talking about what Matthew Winklemann was doing, and not what it felt like Matthew had *become*. He was still stuck on what Derian saw when looking at the man's teeth.

That, and the red sheen when the flashlight was close to his eyes...

At any rate, Amos' words had shut Jackson up good and proper, and he frowned with irritation and crossed his arms.

"Regardless of *what* it is exactly," said Lucas taking note of the looks on everyone in the room. "That thing killed and ate a human being. Mr. Ashton, you said you shot it. Do you think you killed it?"

"I don't know," admitted Derian.

"You *can't* kill it," Joshua insisted in despair. "Not with bullets. The Manananggal will only absorb and heal, and the more it has to heal the more it will have to eat."

"Let it try," someone said raising his machine gun. "We'll blow that horror back to whatever Hell it crawled out of." This was accepted with barks and murmurs of agreement.

Joshua looked at Amos imploringly. The kid was terrified, and Amos couldn't blame him. Even if half the things Joshua mentioned were actually true, it was still a horrific concept; a difficult pill to swallow. The way Derian described it too, and Joshua hadn't corrected him or added any other detail that would have given Amos more doubt. But the fact of the matter was that whatever it was, it was still out there in the rain, and they were inside where it was safe.

Safe, or safer? his mind plagued him.

"All right, listen up," he called out regaining order. "Doesn't matter what it is that is out there. The important thing is, we are inside, and it is outside. Means we have the upper hand. If we stay inside, keep our heads low, continue to call in someone from the mainland, help will arrive and we can all just go home. And who knows, maybe when daytime comes it will be easier for us to roam about. Ain't that right Josh? You mentioned it doesn't like sunlight, right?"

Joshua frowned, and then admitted that was true.

"Almost like a vampire," someone commented.

"Jesus fucking Christ," Paul Jackson groaned. "Do you people hear yourselves right now? *Vampires*, hmph."

"Will you shut up?" Adam White snapped, losing patience with the man. "Unless you got something helpful to add, shut the fuck up."

"Agreed," said Cain in an exasperated tone.

"It'll all work out," Kyra said soothingly. "We have a kitchen full of food, water, and we got emergency cots somewhere, don't we Amos?"

"We do," said Amos. "We'll get everyone settled in and then just play the waiting game."

"Sure wish we didn't give up our phones," muttered Winnifred. "Would have liked to play Farmville to kill time."

"How can you think of a game at a time like this?" demanded Cynthia. "You guys barely made it out of a mass shooting and now we are stuck here by the storm and whatever it was that got Shawlyn and Ethan?"

Winnifred frowned, pained. "Sorry, that's not what I-"

Cain placed a hand on the woman's shoulder. "Don't worry about it. We are all on edge. That's all."

"True that," said Adam, having already discussed Cynthia's behavior before responding. Cynthia apologized to Winnifred, and then Amos took the stage again.

"Everyone just sit tight, we will get the cots; and Kyra, can you and the boys bring in some food and water just in case? Also, no one is to go anywhere near the ballroom at this time. We... we oughtta leave *them* alone."

Them. The dead. The ones that couldn't get away from Matt Winklemann's rampage. Amos didn't want anyone to upset themselves by seeing what was left of the ballroom, especially in the light where every graphic detail could be seen. But he also didn't want to disturb what had officially become a tomb for those unfortunate to be caught in the line of fire.

"Ben," he then regarded his captain. "Can you take a couple guys and fetch the cots, please? Let's make everyone here comfortable as we can. It's gonna be a long night."

"For sure," said Ben. He quickly hand-selected a few employees and together they left, followed later by Kyra and what was left of her cooks. That left Amos with the guests and the few injured employees alone in the conference room. He did not know what to expect at this point.

Nor did he feel comfortable with the grim and ghostly look in Joshua Ramos' eyes.

Thirty-One

Kyra Lewis took her two boys into the kitchens through the side door rather than go through the ballroom again.

After gathering some totes used to ship food to the island, they began to fill them with some dry goods and anything canned and yet easily accessible. There was a discussion on cooking something but with the massacred ballroom right next door, Kyra didn't feel comfortable cooking among the dead. It just felt wrong cooking right next door to a massacre; It was like painting a picture of a beautiful field or garden right next to a forest fire. You couldn't keep our eyes what was beyond the borders.

Despite being encouraging to the boys who were obviously uneasy being so close to the site of the massacre, Kyra was discouraged herself. How had everything gone so wrong so soon? In the case of the pirates that had come a while back ago, there had been a warning. The island could be prepared, and the resort did not lose power right before it happened. Ben or John or someone would have spotted the strange boat coming in if it wasn't too stormy, just like they had with that Joshua kid. Here, the attack had happened within, and this time, it had succeeded with deadly consequences.

Having been one of many survivors of a school shooting back in Colorado, Kyra Lewis knew how these sort of things went. She remembered being just a kid in the late seventies, the shooter in question was one of those hot-headed kids no doubt influenced by their parents or maybe even society, who believed that blacks didn't belong at his school. When he had been expelled from beating on one of the black boys, he had taken his revenge on the entire school, successfully murdering five students and injuring twenty before he was taken down, shot and killed by the gym teacher who had ran out into the parking lot to get his hunting rifle. Every day since Kyra would wonder how many more people that Chrisopher kid would have murdered if not for Jon Hughes that day. She had nightmares about that incident even beyond going to college for culinary arts, and had only made peace with what had happened two decades ago.

Even so, the end result of this shooting had caused her to remember those bad memories, and she tried her best to comfort the survivors as best she could.

So many dead too... Oh, Lord, why must these things happen?

She was grabbing a casepack of chips when she noticed something in the walk-in pantry. The pantry was often lit by a natural ray of sunshine coming in through a small window in the very back. At night the window would be opened to let in the cool breeze and the overhead light would be turned on. Kyra was now looking at the opened window, watching some raindrops that had accumulated against the glass drip off the edge and land in a growing puddle on the floor beneath it.

Had one of the crew opened it up once the sun had set? Or had it been closed? Had it been opened recently? If it had been, was it the storm, or something else?

Kyra shuddered at the thought. No, someone else must have opened it. They wanted to have a breeze going through the pantry which would normally be a sweltering hotbox especially at the peak tropical summer.

(But it had been windy earlier. Rain had only now started. Why would they open the window if it wasn't that hot today?)

This was what made Kyra pause in the doorway, casepack of chips tucked in one great arm and her face a grim portrait.

Had it been one of the others?

Or something else?

She remembers the story The Window from those children's books, Scary Tales to Tell in the Dark when she herself was a child, before the school shooting in Colorado. She remembered that story scaring her, as the creature with the yellow eyes began to approach the little girl's window. She had feared her own bedroom window after that story, and always drew the curtains when the sun sat, and the moon rose. It had become a ritual all the way until she had left for college, a necessity in order to simply believe that the curtain would keep whatever was outside outside. That whatever evil existed would be deterred by it as if it were a force field. Even until she became an adult she still did it, and only didn't stop until she was in the third story dormitory at college, as if subconsciously believing that if the yellowed-eyed monster or something similar did exist, it couldn't climb up to the window or fly to it.

Fly…

Kyra berated herself, angry at her childish thoughts. *Stop it, you're not a kid anymore and this isn't some scary story.*

Kyra moved forward, keen on shutting that window to prevent any more water from dripping into her pantry. She just wanted to stay the storm, and nothing more.

What if a pair of yellow eyes stare back while you do it?

(The creature would never come back. She was sure of that)

There is nothing out there. Nothing!

(... Margaret was awakened by a scratching sound at the window)

She reached up and with nimble fingers, took the hook that was used to lock the window and she began to pull the window down to shut it.

(When she opened the eyes, there was the same shrunken face staring in at her)

The window closed, and the rain pounded the glass. Her shirt was wet, and the howls of the wind became muffled once the window was gone. Blackness was all she could see beyond the droplets against the glass.

(Margaret was awakened)

Kyra turned the lock to secure the window. All at once the pantry felt too hot, too cramped, it made her feel claustrophobic, as if the walls were closing in on her, the shelves meaning to pin her in place.

(Kyra was awakened...)

A pair of yellow

(red)

eyes looking back at me...

"Ma'am?"

Kyra jumped, a scream almost escaping her lips but she clamped a hand over her mouth, dropping the chips in the process. She turned about, seeing Frantz in the doorway of the pantry, looking startled himself because of her reaction.

"Putain de merde," Frantz said exasperated. "You scared the hell out of me."

"Well hell *yourself*. You scared me!" Kyra retorted and immediately started laughing with relief. This caused Frantz to laugh as well. She was being silly for being scared. It was silly to be scared, and deep inside, whatever Frantz was thinking, he knew he was being silly too.

That was when the ticking sound suddenly came, causing the two cooks to freeze and listen. It was so loud and so close, Kyra herself felt like the sound was coming from inside the pantry with her.

Tikitik-tik-ka-tikitik-ka-tikitik...

The sound was so loud and so close that Kyra felt gooseflesh erupt on every square inch of her skin. Her neck became clammy as if a fresh breeze had caressed it.

But I closed the window...

The monster Derian Ashton and Joshua Ramos described came to mind. It was here. It was inside the pantry with her, and was biding it's time, ticking like a rattlesnake ready to strike should she try to flee. Frantz heard it too, and keeping his eyes locked on Kyra's, he began to slowly back away.

Tikitik-tik-ka-tikitik-ka-tikitik. Tikitik-tik-ka-tikitik-ka...

Kyra cried out at last, unable to take it anymore and she bolted for the pantry door. She expected it to slam shut on her and plunge her into darkness where she would not be able to see what was happening to her. Frantz turned tail and ran, and she ran after him out of the pantry, through the kitchens and out the double-doors into the hall.

By the time they got there, the ticking sound had stopped. They stood there watching the kitchen doors panting and scared. Then the door flew open and they screamed as Elbi came out looking at the two confused.

"What are you two doing?" he demanded just as confused. "Y'all are screaming like a buncha banshees out here!"

"I... we..." Frantz started but he looked to Kyra for help.

They were okay. They were alive.

There was *nothing* in the pantry, she realized. It wasn't big enough for more than three people in there, so it would have been obvious is anything else was in there. She felt so stupid for getting so worked up, and she had scared poor Frantz in the process.

She was about to explain and apologize, when they heard Amos screaming for them down the hall.

"KYRA! GUYS! GET OUT OF THERE!"

Without looking or asking why, they ran in the direction of Amos' voice, unaware of the danger lurking far behind them.

Thirty-Two

Ben Franklins had taken Lucas and the others into the supply room which was on the second floor of the resort at the end of the hall. The supply room was really just a suite that had been integrated into a storage facility with cleaning supplies, emergency kits, and even stored kayaks and inflatable tubes for the beach. Some old fishing gear were stowed in a chest in the far corner and on more than one occasion Ben had wanted to take the antiques and sell them on the mainland.

But of course, he wasn't here to look for fishing gear.

The other two with them were Jaquie Hansen and Chris Ontario. All four of them scoured the supply room for the emergency cots including flashlights and more first-aid kits for the wounded. They were packing it all up in crates they would take down together with two carrying each stack, when they too heard the ticking sound seeming to come from everywhere and nowhere.

Tikitik-tik-ka-tikitik-ka-tikitik... Tikitik-tik-ka-tikitik-ka-tikitik...

"You hear that?" Jaquie asked nervously. She was holding onto her weapon tightly now, no longer letting it hang loosely on it's strap.

"I sure do," said Ben uneasily. "Everyone keep a sharp eye out. Chris, get over here and help me."

Chris moved in and taking the other side of the tote Ben was next to, helped him team-lift it up and take it out into the hall where they placed it and then continued to stack more boxes. All the while the ticking sound which was an annoyance at first became gradually quieter and quieter, taking with it whatever discomfort Ben felt growing in his beating heart.

"Think it's that thing?" Lucas whispered to Ben. "The Manana… mann…"

"Don't know," Ben said sparing Lucas the pain of pronouncing such an alien word. "Just forget about it for now, we need to get this shit out of here."

Manananggal, he thought. *Just what sort of world do we live in where such legends exist?*

Although he supposed that was why so many nations were still third-world countries; they refuse to move on with the rest of the world and realize that monsters and myths were nothing but stories.

(But that Derian guy said…)

Nothing. He is stressed; we all are.

Tikitik-tik-ka-tikitik-ka-tikitik…

"Jesus," he murmured.

"Ben?" Jaquie said nervously.

"Just ignore it," said Ben. "It's getting quieter so it's obviously dying down or going away. We got everything?" he then asked Chris.

"I think so."

"Good. Everyone load up, let's get back to the others."

With the totes stacked three high, each pair took a stack and started their way slowly down the hall. Sure enough true to Ben's word, the ticking sound slowly died down until there was nothing left but the faint whisper of the wind outside, and the groan of the resort as it stood in defiance against it. Ben was about to say something when Lucas the dumb bastard suddenly lurched forward, causing

Ben to fall back and the totes to crash to the floor and spill it's contents.

"Goddammit, Luke," Ben snapped looking at the boy on his hands and knees. "What the hell did you trip on?"

"My toe skipped across the floor," Lucas said embarrassingly. "I'm sorry."

Ben sighed. "Fuck it, don't worry about it. Just help me get-"

"AHH!" Chris screamed as something charged out of the nearby restroom and crashed into him, striking him against the wall and then thrashing about with him like he was a rat being tossed about by a cat. An overhead light shattered and went out, dimming the hallway around them. Ben and the others watched in horror as the thing in question dragged the screaming man to the floor and drove a probiscis-like tongue into his right eye. Blood and jelly squirted everywhere and the man twitched and his screams ceased.

Then the Manananggal reared it's ugly head toward the trio, it's lips stained with blood and jelly. It's red eyes glowed hellishly, and when it grinned at them, shark-teeth glimmered pink in the dim lighting of their flashlights.

It's grinning, Ben thought his mind becoming frayed with terror. *Oh Jesus, it's grinning at us!*

"Oh, *shit,*" whispered Lucas and Jaquie screamed out loud and open-fired on the monster.

Click-click-click! the gun sounded in quick succession. Jaquie stared dumbfounded at the weapon and realized too late that she had forgotten to take off the safety on the rifle. By the time she figured this out, the monster was upon her, claws digging deep into the flesh of her chest and shoulders and she opened her mouth to scream which was her final mistake. The proboscis-like tongue slithered out and shot directly down her throat, tearing the walls of the esophagus all the way down into her stomach where it began to eat it's way out and suck up all the internal organs of her very being.

As the monster fed on Jaquie, for she was four-weeks pregnant and it could not resist the taste of an unborn fetus, Ben and Lucas both scrambled to their feet and forgetting the supplies and their own weapons, fled just as Kyra and her boys stumbled out from their scare. Amos was at the far end of the hall coming towards them, and without having to warn him, Amos saw what was happening behind them. The Manananggal had risen to the ceiling, and using both it's wings and it's claws, it was crawling across it like a salamander towards the fleeing men as well as Kyra and her cooks.

"KYRA! GUYS! GET OUT OF THERE!"

Thankfully the cooks did not look back or question why, because they turned and ran towards Amos like a flock of bats out of Hell.

Ben ran faster than he ever had in his life. He had always been comfortable at sea other than land, and as a result had developed his legs to master the sea and not running. He had never joined a track team nor had he any reason to actually run in his life. But at thirty-five and in good-enough shape, he was running pretty fast; even his endurance was something most his age would kill for.

Still, Lucas was younger and had a lot more energy. Plus, he was built for the land, and so he outpaced Ben and was gradually leaving him behind. Ben panted and his lungs burned with the effort to double his speed and gain another burst. He did not know how far behind the Manananggal was, but the more he ran the more he could swear on his brother's grave that he could feel it's rancid breath tickling the back of his neck. This of course was not true or even possible given the height of the ceiling, but Ben was right to be fearful, for the Manananggal had gotten closer and had forgotten about crawling altogether and dropping from the ceiling took flight after him, it's claws outstretched for him.

That was when Ben finally became aware of the heavy metallic thing bouncing against the side of his ribcage. He still had a weapon; he still had a chance to fight back. Lucas was already far ahead, and Ben didn't want to lead the Manananggal to the others. So, grasping out with his hands as he ran, Ben managed to catch his weapon and after checking the safety and ensuring the magazine was secure in it's slot, Ben cried out and dove forward while at the same time twisting his body in the air so that he could face the monster who was coming upon him.

The gun went off in a loud burst of fire, the kick of the weapon making his fall onto his back all the more painful. He managed to shoot the Manananggal twice in the chest, once in the right wing, and again above her eyes. The demon tackled him as they fell and the gun was pinned between her and Ben and it roared into his face defiantly, for the gun was useless against her. She looked up, saw Amos running towards them with his own gun aimed at her. She hissed at him like a cat, and then looked up. Ben, still pinned beneath her, saw that it was staring at one of the ventilation ducts in the ceiling, and without warning, extended her wings and propelled them both up and into it with a metallic *crash*.

"Help!" Ben cried as he was dragged into the cramped and dusty vent. He felt like a kid being forced into a cat tube by their older sibling. "Help me!"

But it was no use, he was being dragged down the throat of the vent to who-knows-where. It became little concern to him however for the monster, needing to heal itself from the bullet holes that oozed black blood, pressed it's mouth against his as if to kiss him. Her shark teeth tore and shredded his lips and he felt his throat becoming penetrated by the tongue of the monster and felt it go deeper still as it began to feed.

The only sign of where exactly Ben was a few droplets of blood coming from one of the vents further down the hall. Amos managed to see but a glimpse of the crimson drops but by then he had stopped, believing it too late to save his friend from his grizzly fate.

"Oh god, oh god," he moaned looking down at the dead further back. Finally losing his grasp on his control, Amos stooped over and retched.

8th Letter

I had to stop writing last night for I was tired and could write no more. I was not filled with dread as I had the other nights. Just exhaustion.

That is good. It means it is getting easier to talk about this. All the more easier now that my wife will be reading my letters after I have read them. We had agreed to not discuss them unless I had to, or she had a general question for the monster I had witnessed. For this has surprisingly become easy for me, describing every little detail of the beast. From the color of her hair, the color of her dangling entrails, how long her wings are, how many rows of triangular teeth were in her enlarged maw, every excruciatingly dangerous detail, even to the lore and legends surrounding it. How it is a shapeshifter, and can take any form it chooses as long as it has the capability to be convincing. Clothes it would need to borrow in order to blend in, but that was of little consequence to a creature as cunning as the Manananggal.

It doesn't make what had happened in the days after seeing such a terrible creature any easier, but my wife just simply listening even if deep down she believes it to be insane ramblings of an imagination that just wouldn't die just yet, it made me feel less alone, less afraid.

That day, after discussing it with the Babalayn that day, I came out of the church blessed by the priest and given my own vial of holy water. That night, I vowed to stay out and challenge the beast to come and face me. Everyone saw me as crazy, suicidal, and perhaps I was.

But no one was going to stop me, either by fear of me given my connection with the creature, or they simply didn't care. Too many had died in the village, and I was going to stand my ground even if they weren't. I look back on my decision then, and I sometimes wonder if I really was that stupid. But then again, maybe I wouldn't be here today for making such a stupid decision.

And so I stood alone in the center of the village, a torch in hand, a whip in the other. I kept my eyes to the sky, my ears alert for any sort of sound. This was not difficult, for it was something that while used by the Manananggal as a way to confuse and capture her prey, it could also be her downfall. Because the clicking sound she expressed was warped in human ears. If the clicking sound was loud, she was really far away. It was when it became quieter and quieter when one should be weary. Because those who think that it is quieter because it is far away, are doomed when they see they have been tricked and are devoured.

I heard the clicking at last, and at that moment, the Babalayn had come out to join me, a bolos at his hip and a rifle in his hands. I knew other villagers were watching us, no doubt with guns of their own. They were willing to wait and ambush the beast at last, rather than leave me and the Babalayn alone to face it. Again, I didn't care. All I cared about was what I was hearing, which was the clicking sound. Loud at first at the arrival of the beast, growing steadily more silent as it realized I had no intention of fleeing, and began to approach.

Tiktik-ka-tiktik-ka-tiktik…

Over and over again I hear that clicking. Sometimes in a different order, sometimes at a different pitch, as if the vocals of the beast were somewhat questioning or threatened. Quieter and quieter they became until I could hear nothing at all. Nothing, except for the heavy beat of wings.

That was when it attacked us, starting for the Babalayn who was the oldest, and perhaps in it's mind, the weakest.

The air had been cut by the swift flapping of wings, and the sound afterward I will never forget. A wet, <u>shredding</u> sound that can only be described using that word. To me it sounded like a bunch of wet paper being torn down the middle, when in reality, it was really human flesh being ripped and sliced. The Babalayn had screamed, and I turned to see that he had been pierced through the back by the claws of the creature, both sets having come out the front and speckling me with his blood. The monster then reared it's head in a horrible cry of victory, teeth flashing as she bit down and hard onto the Babalayn's head. The skull caved immediately, the top of his head bitten right off and leaving only the lower jaw and some of the nose. Blood had erupted in a geyser, which the creature lapped up as she retreated and released the Babalayn who dropped dead and capless. The sound afterward was just as terrible, as the Manananggal chewed with her shark-like teeth, the crunching, grinding sound of sharp teeth powdering bone, and she <u>swallowed</u> the bits of skull and brain matter. The horrible sound was like a child chewing on an American jawbreaker.

With a cry that sounded more animal than human, I reared my arm back with the stingray whip and it arched through the air and cracked against the side of the Manananggal. She screamed as the gash in her side bled, and to my astonishment hissed black smoke. She roared at me and I snapped the whip again, trying to get her to back away from the Babalayn who laid dead in a pool of growing blood and brains, and the whip actually got caught inside the entanglement of intestines. It hurt her, no doubt, but I could not pull away, and she used this to her advantage and lunged for me. She lashed out with both wings, and one of the protruding knucklebones stuck me in the belly.

Hot pain had swept through me, as if I had been stabbed. I doubled over and was forced to my knees as I felt blood escape through my fingers. Then she went for my head with her claws and I ducked to avoid the worst of the blow, which raked across my back and opened it like a fillet knife across a fish. I howled in pain and collapsed to the ground, face in the mud and blood pouring from the four deep gashes in my back. She was over me, balancing herself on the knuckles of her wings, her entrails brushing the back of my head as if they were hair to tickle a laughing baby. I heard nothing of the creature, only my own labored breathing was real. Only my pain was real.

I did not hear the cracking of gunfire. I did not feel the hot blood that felt like acid speckling my head. I did not hear the Manananggal's shrieks of pain. I lifted my head, eyes hazy from the pain, and saw that the monster was no longer looking at me. It was snarling in defiance and challenge at the unseen attackers. It 'crouched' which can only be best described as it lowered itself to the ground so that it's hands touched the ground. The wings stretched out, and it prepared to take off into the night. Seeing this had filled me with a new resolve that I must not let her go. My grip on the stingray whip tightened, and with my other hand I reached for the Babalayn where his belt was, where his bolo knife rested. I seized the handle of driftwood, and as the Manananggal started to take flight, I pulled down hard on the whip, startling it and howling in menacing victory as I pulled myself up and brought the bolos up. My aim was true, and I stabbed the she-demon in the back. It howled as the blade got stuck between her ribcage and I was momentarily surprised by the belching of black smoke from the wound. She turned on me, seized my arms with her hands and lunged out with teeth snapping. I had pulled back, but she still managed to bite me on the right shoulder. Those horrible teeth had scissored their way down the bone, and still with my hand on the bolos I twisted the blade, and forced her to release me. Hot blood poured down my arm until finally she did take flight, and the awkward positioning of my arm forced me to let go and I felt myself drop. I seized the whip with both hands this time, and allowed myself to be dragged across the ground as she took flight and tried to escape amidst the gunfire and approaching torchlights.

    I do not know how far she dragged me. Like everything, it too was something I would never remember at least not completely. Thinking back on it now, all I can remember is the pain. The warmth of my blood and the cold chills I gained. The taste of blood in my mouth where I had bitten my cheeks and tongue. All I remember was holding onto the whip as if it was my one and only lifeline, and then I closed my eyes, and woke up back in the church with the priest healing my wounds. He had explained that we had ran the monster out of town, and that a group of men were going into the woods to search for the Manananggal who would no doubt be wounded enough to kill at last. For once, I had hope that we would soon be rid of the demon that plagued this village and murdered my family.

We never saw the group of men again, and that left only a few more villagers, mostly whatever women and children were left, a few older men, the priest, and I. Around fifteen people in all, all against the approaching night which has proved the most deadly of times for us humans.

It is late, I must stop for now. I will continue tomorrow. I have to finish this.

Thirty-Three

Amos dropped the gun now covered in speckles of blood from the impact between the Manananggal and Ben onto the nearest table in the resort reception area. All present stared at the weapon and him with their faces ten different shades of pale if it was ever possible. Amos, his lips still stained with his vomit, looked at them all with a dreary expression.

"Chris and Jaquie are dead," he announced in a voice that sounded hollow even to himself. "Ben too. It got them all. Lucas was the only one who made it out alive."

Three more, dead as doornails, he thought morbidly. *How many of us now... Christ, only fourteen. Most of 'em are guests. Guests.*

With most of the Isla Bonidada group gone now, there were very few people possibly trained on firearms and Amos didn't know how he was going to get everyone out of here safely. He didn't think these rich folk knew how to fire pea shooters let alone machine guns. That Derian guy, definitely, but the rest? Amos felt like he was a teacher among a bunch of toddler students incapable of protecting themselves always relying on others to do so. In the back of his mind, Amos wondered if it was worth it or if he should just go into hiding himself, he and Lucas and Kyra's crew. Let the rich people fend for themselves for the first time in their lives.

But then again, Amos didn't believe he would be able to live with himself if he did that, and he pushed the thought as far back as he could, with very little success.

"Did you get a good look at it?" Paul Jackson asked already looking cocky and ready to argue and debate. "Was it really a monster or-"

"Listen you," Amos said his patience as thin as a dry hair. "I don't give two shits what the fuck it is. All I know is that it killed three more of my people. People who were *armed*. This thing doesn't give a shit about being shot, and it won't stop even if someone else is coming in to fight back."

"I told you," Joshua Ramos said quietly at his corner. "I told you, but you didn't listen."

Amos started for the kid his hands opening and closing as if crushing something, but Kyra stood in front of him, her expression stern. "Amos," she said.

"Get out of the way," he told her.

"No. Leave him alone. He didn't have anything to do with it."

"Maybe not but he's still running his goddamned mouth."

"Then *listen*. Maybe he knows what he is talking about."

Amos stared at her for a long time. Kyra's stare never faltered. She was right, and he found himself relaxing not just because of Joshua's sake, but her own. A small smile tugged at her lips in gratitude.

A snort came from the group and they looked at Paul Jackson. "What does this third-world gook know that is actually *helpful*? What is he gonna do, throw rocks at the thing, whatever it is?"

"Shut your goddamn mouth," Derian warned him.

Paul Jackson marched to the tall man and got into Derian's face. "Listen you fucking-"

Fast as lightning Derian had grabbed Paul by the arm and looping his way underneath it like a ballerina, twisted the arm behind the now-screaming Paul's back and threw him against the wall, his face squished against the wallpaper and his burnt hand now clasped tightly in Derian's other hand which he squeezed to cause Jackson more discomfort.

"Come at me again," Derian warned. "And I'll break your fat neck. You got me?"

"Get off!" Paul snarled thrashing like a fish and wincing as Derian applied more pressure on his bandaged hand. "Victoria! Someone, help me goddammit! Motherfucker, I'll sue!"

But no one helped. They only stared at the two men as Derian twisted the arm further, causing Paul to wince and curse all the more.

"Do you understand me?" Derian asked again.

"Kiss my ass, fuckhead!"

Derian twisted just a little more to the point where he was afraid he might break the stubborn man's arm. He didn't dare to harm the burnt hand anymore but he would if he had to. He still held the thrashing man firmly as Jackson proceeded to curse him and threaten to sue him and everyone present for not helping him.

As last out of tiredness or pain, Paul shouted, "Fuck! Fuck! All right! All right just lemme go you crazy fuck!"

Derian released him, letting Paul drop to the floor. He stood there for a moment staring at the man who was rubbing his arm and bad hand before going back to his wife, all eyes on him for only a moment longer before

Amos finally spoke to Joshua, having his time to calm down during the altercation.

Paul, still fuming, was glaring at not just Derian but everyone in the room. Amos had already considered this guy a problem, but now he knew for certain that if anyone needed an eye kept on them, it was Jackson and maybe his wife too, given how quiet she was and how she wouldn't look at her husband. A young wife and an old husband, both in a shitty situation with a bunch of strangers and already on bad terms on top of what was going on.

Amos cleared his throat and said to Joshua, "Josh, do you know how we can kill this thing?"

"You can't," said Joshua. "Not with guns anyway."

"But you hurt it, didn't you?" asked Adam. "Back on the island?"

"I *did*," Joshua replied hesitantly. "With my bolos and my whip. You still have both of them, don't you?" he asked this of Amos.

"Yeah, they are in John's office," Amos said hopefully. "We can get them and-"

"I don't know if it will be enough to kill the Manananggal though," Joshua said miserably.

"But they will hurt it, right?" asked Cynthia.

"Yes. It would be best if we had holy artifacts, but yes, it would hurt it."

Amos grinned. "This is a resort. It's like law or something to provide a bible in every room."

Winnifred asked, "Would that work?"

"It might," Joshua said.

"This is a load of horseshit," Paul muttered.

"No, it ain't," said Amos patiently glaring at the man. "If we all go together and get the kid's weapons-"

"Woah, woah," Carla Anderson said with her hands raised. "What do you mean 'we' will go?"

"We all gotta stick together," Kyra said backing up Amos almost immediately. "We can't risk being split apart. That thing attacked a group of four, so hopefully with all of us together it might be more hesitant."

"And what about them?" Cain asked jerking a thumb to Ethan and the rest of the wounded. "Are they in any shape to go? They can barely stand as is given what happened earlier."

"Shit," Amos swore bitterly. He looked at Joshua. "Even if we get all this stuff, what will actually kill this monster?"

Joshua swallowed, collected his thoughts, and then answered. "To kill a Manananggal you have to stab it in the back with a blessed bolos. Mine was blessed by the Babaylan who tried to help my village. You can also sever it's head with a good strike of the stingray whip, or hang it upside down until it coughs up it's evil soul. But the best is making sure it cannot return to it's other half before sunrise."

"Wait, so the other half of the Managal is *attachable*?" asked Victoria for the first time.

"Manananggal," Joshua corrected patiently. "And yes, the lower half can be separated and attached at will, that's how she achieves her transformation."

"How do we stop it from reattaching?" asked Adam, appearing pumped now that they were learning how to stop this thing. Beside him, Ethan groaned in his deep sleep.

"We need holy water, which we don't have," said Joshua. "But spices like sugar and salt, and fresh garlic rubbed on top of the lower half will prevent it from returning to it's lower body which will stop it from turning human. It will also stop it from... what's the word? When they can change their appearance?"

"Shapeshift?" asked Cynthia.

"I guess," said Joshua unsure. "It can look like anything or anyone it wants. Animals, even people. If that happens, we might not know who is who."

"Which means," Paul Jackson said miserably, eyeing everyone untrustingly. "Someone in here could be that thing and we don't even know it." His eyes stopped at Amos, who scowled at him.

"Don't do that," Kyra said pointing a finger at the man. "The last thing we need is turning on one another."

"Just like in *The Thing*," muttered Cain.

"So we stop it from reattaching before sunrise," said Amos. "What then, Josh?"

"We hope it makes a mistake and end up outside while the sun is up. Or we will be able to kill it before it kills us all. Whichever comes first."

Amos regarded everyone with a look of confidence and decision. "Well, I plan on dragging that bitch out into the sun if that is what it takes. Problem is we all need to stick together. We can't risk splitting up again."

"I can stay with the wounded," said Derian. "If anyone else knows how to shoot, we can board up in here still until the rest come back."

"That could work..." Amos admitted.

"I'll stay too," said Lucas. "Sorry, boss, but I ain't going out there again."

"I don't blame you," said Kyra. "My cooks and I will go though. We need stuff from the kitchens anyway.

Which means there are four of us. We need some of you to come with us." She looked at all the guests, hoping one or some of them would volunteer other than Derian, who offered to stay first.

"Fuck that," said Paul Jackson with crossed arms. "I ain't leaving this room."

"Don't want you to go anyway," said Adam standing up. "I'll go."

"Adam!" Cynthia hissed.

"We gotta help each other if we wanna get out of here alive, Cynthia," Adam said calmly. "I don't know much about guns though..." he admitted.

"Hopefully we don't need to use 'em," said Frantz already strapped up.

"I'm coming then," Cynthia decided.

Adam started to argue but Cynthia shut him up with a raised hand.

"I'm not leaving you again. You go, I go."

"If it's all the same," said Carla. "I'd like to stay here with Derian."

"That's fine," said Cain. "I'll go with them. Winny, you coming too?"

"Yes," Winnifred said without hesitation. The last thing was to be separated from her husband, as well as be stuck in the same room with Paul and Victoria Jackson, no matter who else was in this conference room."

"All right," Amos said doing a quick headcount. "That should be enough. You guys will be okay here on your own for a bit?" he asked this of Derian, who he thought was the best person to leave in charge here.

"We'll be fine," the man assured him. "When you get here, say, 'No bruja here.' I'll know it's you if that thing decides to shapeshift."

"Got it," said Amos feeling the phrase was pretty funny, under the circumstances.

"Go, quickly," Derian motioned away towards the door. "Come back as soon as you can, and we can work out a gameplan."

"Pfft," sounded Paul Jackson. "All you guys are gonna do is get yourselves killed. It's best if we all just stay here."

"For how long?" said Amos. "Until the guard comes? They don't know what is out there, they might get hurt or worse."

"Or," Joshua added grimly. "The Manananggal will... shapeshift into someone else and will make it's escape again."

"We'd notice, wouldn't we?" asked Paul.

"Maybe," Amos agreed. "But what if we don't make it?"

Paul threw his hands up in frustration. "This is stupid. Stupid and reckless."

"No one is asking you to go," said Derian. "You'll be safe in here."

Paul scoffed. "Safer than them, maybe."

"Um..." Victoria said her voice soft and nervous. "I think I'm gonna go too. I... I want to make sure we can get out of here."

Paul stared at her. "Are you fucking kidding me?" Then he threw up his hands. "You know what? Fuck it. Go on. Run off again."

"Is now *really* a good time for this?" Kyra demanded impatiently. "Can't you two save whatever is up with you both until after we get out of this alive?"

"Shut up," said Paul.

"Leave it," Amos told Kyra. "That's fine, Mrs. Jackson, you can come. The more the merrier in this situation. Mr. Anderson-"

"Just call me Derian."

"Fine. Will you be okay here on your guys' own?"

"We'll be fine," he assured everyone. He took his wife's hand and gave it a squeeze. She squeezed back, tenderly. "When should we expect you?"

"When should you worry you mean," muttered Paul."

"Will you just shut up?" demanded Lucas. "Jesus, you're annoying."

Paul opened his mouth but immediately closed it blessedly.

"If we aren't back in an hour," Amos said. "That's when you should worry. Bunker down and hope it's safe by the time the guard shows up."

If *they got the broadcast*, he reminded himself but didn't dare say aloud.

"All right," Cain said with a sigh and a glance of unease at the door of the conference room, and the unknown dangers lurking within the walls of the Bonidada Resort. "Let's get it over with."

Thirty-Four

The group going out moved quickly and quietly, every set of eyes checking every corner and every nook and cranny for any sign of life or movement. Familiar walls within the resort were no longer friendly, having turned into a deceptive maze where it could hide it's monsters. The now-invaded Bonidada Resort which had been familiar for so long to the point where it felt like a home was no longer theirs anymore.

Amos wanted to check the radio while they were in the security room and while he did that, Joshua moved to the locker where he was directed to. Using the key provided by Amos, he unlocked it and took what was his. His whip, his *buntot ng pagi*, uncoiled as he pulled it out, the five-foot length of leather and barb feeling familiar in his hand again- More comforting. It made him homesick being able to actually look at it again. His bolos he took and tucked into the belt of his new pants. It was awkward, but it worked.

He noticed the others watching him and he asked, "What is it?"

"Nothing," said Winnifred. "Just... just hard to believe, that's all."

Joshua grunted. "I agree. Oh, I agree..."

Amos returned then. "Nothing coming back in. Hopefully they got the message..."

Another groan sounded throughout the resort against the wind, causing everyone to freeze and listen. When nothing happened, only then did everyone visibly relax, only to jump again when thunder rose like a great roar of a lion.

"Can anything get out through this storm?" asked Victoria.

"Hopefully," Kyra answered who had been constantly peeking over her shoulder ever since they left the conference room. "For now, we should keep moving."

Adam White nodded. "Agreed."

They got to the kitchen where Kyra and the others raided their spice pantry. Coming back made the cooks nervous, both Frantz and Elbi working vigorously while Kyra held a small plastic tote for them to fill as quickly as possible. The last thing they wanted was to relive what had nearly happened less than an hour ago. Boxes upon boxes of course salt and containers of all types of sugar went into the tote, from pure cane to light and dark brown, coconut and palm sugar, sanding and coarse sugar, and more. While Kyra primarily expected fresh garlic to be used, there were still a couple of plastic bags of garlic power and granulated garlic, all of which was added as well. For good measure, the boys took up their knives and quickly minced all the cloves they had and stored them into small mason jars. The paste was fragrant, and everyone welcomed it for it masked the smell of death literally in the next room. No one had forgotten about those who couldn't escape Matt Winklemann's wrath, but no one was willing to talk about it.

Winnifred in particular was thinking about the Woldemontts and the last conversation they had together. What had they talked about? With everything going on, everything else in the world or the past seemed meaningless. It would remain meaningless until she could return to some sort of normalcy, and yet she knew she was only fooling herself into believing such a thing.

Kitchen appliances, she and Leslie Woldemontt were talking about kitchen appliances, what they wanted for their Kitchen Aids, their favorite brand of knives, what china they like to display in their cabinets. All seemed to have happened so long ago, when it was really only less than a day. The whole day was gone, almost instantaneously, under the strain of pain and horror.

To think a man was capable of such destruction… did that make Matthew Winklemann worse than the monster now lurking these very halls? Winnifred tried to sympathize with the monster, trying to think that all living creatures on earth served a purpose in some way shape or form. Matthew simply wanted destruction, the Manananggal was only trying to eat.

Human beings, she reminded herself, and Winnifred reasoned that both of the monsters set loose at this resort were evil. Maybe in different ways, but evil nonetheless. If what the others said was true, then that meant the Manananggal was cunning as well as vicious. She had taken this chance to eliminate them all, and feed on them all; even going so far as to attack right in front of them to get to Shawlyn, and her unborn child.

Such a concept made Winnifred sick to her stomach again, she couldn't imagine such a fate for herself.

"Um, Mrs. Ashton?"

Winnifred turned and her stomachache heaved at the sight of Victoria who had come to talk to her while the men were helping Kyra and the others load up the totes. She looked sick herself, paler, and definitely frightened.

"I uh… I want to apologize for what happened between us."

"Victoria-"

"No, it was an awful thing to do. I'm not apologizing for Paul, it's for you and me."

"Is now really a good time?"

"No," Victoria admitted. "But I don't know if I'll get the chance to again."

Winnifred could hardly take it now. "Don't even think about that," she scolded the young woman. "Quite frankly, I don't care about your apology. What you did, what you tried to do, was unforgivable."

Victoria looked pained. "I know you're mad-"

"Just go away. Go away and leave me alone. We got other things to worry about other than your apology to me."

If you don't leave me alone, I'm going to be sick. If I get sick right here, it will prove how capable I really am. Cain needs me, as do the others. I can't let them down. I can't let this tramp try to destabilize me. I won't!

Now Victoria was looking at her not just with sickness and fear, but also scorn. Her face was trembling like a loose mask, but her eyes narrowed at her. "I said I was sorry," she said.

"Good for you," said Winnifred. Sorry's never worked for her, and it wouldn't now. "You wanna show how sorry you are? Help us get out of here alive and don't do anything stupid like your stubborn husband. You come near me again and I won't hesitate to hit you."

She meant it too. She didn't know if it was necessarily because of the situation at hand, the raw feeling of being capable of doing whatever was necessary for her own safety, but Winnifred meant it. If she thought that the Manananggal was after her, she would run or fight to her very last breath. If anyone else still alive at the resort, including Victoria Jackson, tried anything with her, then she was not going to let it break her. She was going to get out of here alive. She and Cain both were leaving Isla Bonidada alive and unscathed.

Victoria, outraged and hurt, turned and marched towards Amos and the cooks, who were now grabbing kitchen knives for additional protection. Some were given to the others, Cain wielding his own sharp knife and handing another one to Winnifred.

Joshua didn't look happy with the kitchenware. "I don't know if that will work at all…"

"It's the closest thing to a 'bolos' we got," said Frantz. "Besides, as long as we can hurt the fucker, we should be good, right?"

"It'll have to do," said Amos quickly. "Good news is we don't have to go outside to one of the huts to get a bible."

"Really?" asked Adam. "Where do you have one?"

"Upstairs in the old lodgings. They are primarily used for special guests or cooks during the inactive months but right now they are mostly for storage. The suites all have bibles in them, we can just clear them all out together."

Delighted with the plan, everyone followed Amos out of the hall and towards the stairwell leading to the second story of the resort. On the way there Winnifred noticed that Victoria was stealing glances at her, quickly averting her gaze every time Winnifred looked. But she wasn't being fooled. That girl had her cogs turning, and Winnifred worried what that would turn up.

Meanwhile, back in the conference room, Ethan had regained consciousness. He had awoken, feeling muddy and confused. When the pieces of the puzzle slowly fell back into place one by one, he began to sob despairingly. Carla had taken it upon herself to comfort the grieving man to the best of her ability, while the others all sat uncomfortably around watching.

Lucas was with the wounded, and Derian was by the door, his pistol drawn and hanging limply in one hand. Paul Jackson was in his corner, glowering at the sobbing man in disgust. Fucking crybaby. They weren't dead yet, were they?

He looked to Derian who was watching the hallway through the glass window, occasionally tensing as he heard something the others didn't. It seemed even when he appeared relax, he was a spring-loaded board ready to move into action. Paul's eyes glanced downward toward the man's gun. If only he had a weapon of his own.

"What are you, exactly?" he asked. When Derian looked at him, he repeated his question. "Were you in the army?"

"No."

"Cop?"

"No."

Paul gritted his teeth. *Be patient.* "What then? Come on, tell me."

Derian thought of it for a moment, his eyes never leaving Paul's until the end. He looked at the others, his wife especially, who was listening but not looking at them. The others appeared more interested, trying to act like they weren't.

"I was a hitman in Florida," he finally answered. "I worked for some of the mafia bosses along the coast."

Paul scoffed. "Yeah, and I'm Robert Downy Junior. The *third*. C'mon, are you shitting me?"

"No."

Paul ground his teeth together, more annoyed than ever. "You weren't a hitman. I don't believe you."

"Okay."

Paul eyed him for a long moment and then, "All right then. Explains why you are Mr. Tough Guy and all."

Derian said nothing.

"Leave it be," said Lucas. "He obviously doesn't wanna talk to you."

"It's fine," said Derian without looking.

Paul turned his attention towards Carla. "What do you think of it, miss?"

Carla's mouth went tight.

"Leave her out of it," said Derian now glaring at Paul.

Paul grinned wolfishly back, glad he managed to find a soft spot on the asshole after all. "A hitman then. Like Agent forty-seven?"

"What's it to you anyway?" asked Derian.

"Just curious is all. Anyone would be given your... demeanor and calm. Must be difficult for the wife, being married to someone who *hits* people."

"You might be right," said Derian unwilling to disclose any information of the sort. To push him further might result in severe consequences, if not from him than the rest of the group who were now staring daggers at Paul.

"Did you enjoy it? The job, I mean."

"No."

"What made you do it?"

"Why does anyone work? Money."

Paul grunted. "Explains why you could afford to come here. Quite the predicament though." He turned to Carla. "Ma'am, I'm sorry if I upset you. Also to you all, sorry if I'm causing trouble. I'm just stressed…"

It was the truth, but Paul wasn't sorry in the slightest. He was stressed, stressed as anyone could be in this circumstance, but he wasn't the least be sorry in the least. He felt he owed this anger and frustration, this hatred of his wife and the people he is stuck here with. He didn't give a rats ass about anyone else here, all that mattered was himself. He was focused on him getting off this god-forsaken island alive. Everyone else could rot in Hell for all he cared. Derian, Amos and his third-world rejects, and especially Paul's wife.

He had to look out for himself. He couldn't risk relying on anyone, no matter how useful some of them could be individually.

"That's okay," said one of the wounded at last. "This whole thing is a clusterfuck."

"Amen," said another.

Lucas grunted in response.

"Don't worry about it," said Carla. "I'm not upset."

She's a liar too, Paul decided.

Derian cleared his throat. "What made you decide on investing in retail?"

"Everyone needs toilet paper, right?" asked Paul. "Should the world end, inflation, all that shit that could result in people unable or unwilling to buy more than they need, what are the best investments to be involved in?

Not Mercedes, not Apple, but anything regarding gas, food, or toilet paper. If people are struggling, they aren't going to invest in all the big businesses that offer cars or luxury jewelry, they are gonna want what they need. Because people are still gonna eat, and still gonna wipe afterward. Also, we rely on cars now. So, naturally, retail was the best option. Started small, now a big chain."

"That's admirable," said Lucas.

"It is," Paul agreed. "It's sustainable, and it will last forever."

"Hopefully it does," said Derian. "I sincerely hope it does. Hopefully you can get back to it. Hopefully we can all get back home."

Paul grunted. "Yeah."

He stood up and approaching Derian joined him at the door. He wanted to talk to the hitman personally and without a crowed. The others were watching, but he didn't care. As long as they couldn't overhear the two of them, in case Derian bares his teeth.

"Serious question for you," he said to the man.

"What?" Derian was looking him square in the eyes, unblinking, absorbing. Paul didn't like that, he didn't like how Derian wasn't just looking him in the eye, but merely absorbing him. It didn't feel like he was looking at a fellow man at all.

Paul swallowed his pride and his discomfort. "How much do you care about them? The guys who left?"

Derian's eyes narrowed. "What do you mean?"

"Well, we are in a safe place here, aren't we? They are the ones risking getting caught when that thing is out there."

"What's your point?"

"My point is, screw them. Leave them behind. They are acting like we are stuck when we can't be. That Franklins guy had a boat he brought us here on, and he also took some of us for cruises around the island. Don't you think it's odd that they didn't think of using the boat?"

Derian smiled bemusedly. "You seem to have forgotten that there is a storm out there, as well as something dangerous."

"No shit. I'm saying if it's dangerous on the island why not risk it and get the hell out of here?"

"Because the storm is bad. Listen. The winds are *howling*. If you heard winds like that in Florida, you wouldn't go out on a boat. Believe me."

"We aren't in Florida though, pal. We are *here*, stuck on an island with something hunting us and we are split up. We are just sitting ducks here, it's better to take our chances getting away."

"And get capsized and sunk never to be seen again?" Derian demanded. Between the two men, no one else was speaking up to either join or argue. This was purely between Paul and Derian. "No thank you. If it wasn't that bad outside I'd agree, but because of the storm, not a chance."

Paul gritted his teeth. *Patience, patience...* "The weather could get better in an hour or something..."

"It also couldn't," said Derian. "Look, I know you wanna leave. We all do. But I'm not risking us going out and getting caught in the storm. We have the others to think about as well."

"That's just it," Paul insisted. "We don't. We don't owe these people anything."

"They are taking care of us as best as they can under the circumstances" said Carla speaking up at last. "We have to trust that Amos and the others know what they are doing."

"We couldn't even trust them to keep the island safe from that psycho Matt!" Paul said angrily. "Don't you think it's funny that they didn't even check the fucking bags? They let him on this island with a fucking arsenal."

Derian said nothing, clearly agreeing with Paul on that account.

Paul went on. "We couldn't trust them with that and now look how many people are dead now because of that guy. So why should we trust them about what's considered agreeable weather to sail in? I'd rather us take our chances of getting away rather than sitting here and doing nothing. You agree with me, so you should-"

"Be quiet," Derian said sharply, his head tilted now.

"No, listen. We need to-"

"Shut the fuck up!" Derian hissed. "Everyone, quiet!" he then barked at the others who immediately stopped their murmuring. Everyone listened now, and Paul understood.

Above them, creaking and groaning was coming in through the ceiling. Nothing that sounded like footsteps like how one might hear at some cheap hotel and some fatass was waltzing around the room above you. It didn't sound like normal movement at all. It was a faint clicking sound occasionally broken by a sort of faint but sharp scrape, like fingernails against metal or stone. It would stop for a moment, and then continue, followed by that faint scraping as if something was being dragged.

"Is someone upstairs?" asked Derian.

Lucas answered, "You wouldn't be able to hear them if they were. The floors are thick."

"Then what's that sound?"

"Could be the airducts..." someone else said nervously.

The sound was now closer to the backwall. The scraping persisted, now sounding closer than ever. That was when they heard the ticking sound again, the sound they had associated with the monster. But it was faint, far away.

"That sound again..." said Lucas now trembling with fright. He was facing the conference door though where Derian and Paul stood, for the sound was coming from the hallway. They all turned towards it, ignoring the shuffling in the walls and ceiling.

All except Derian whose eyes trailed the faint shuffling sound which was now in the ceiling again. He focused on the square vent in the ceiling and pointed his gun at it even when the shuffling stopped and the *tikitik-tik* sound persisted outside. The others started to glance around once they noticed Derian focused on the vent, their eyes darting to and fro in fright, especially those incapacitated on the floor.

"It sounds like it's coming from out there," said Paul anxiously, his eyes glued to the conference room door.

"Why are you looking at the vent, mon?" asked one of the employees.

"I don't like this," said Derian. "We need to leave."

"But it's out there!" Lucas said pointing outside the conference room. "Can't you hear it?" He was now inching towards the door along with Paul, leaving Derian directly under the vent and the others along the back wall.

"Lucas, get over here," he told the man. When he came he asked, "Are there other vents in this room?"

"Uh… uh…" Lucas thought hard, thinking until he finally said, "There is one under the table so that the people's legs could get some air. It gets humid sometimes."

Was it humid now, or was Derian just breaking out in cold sweat?

Derian asked Lucas to take a peek under the desk. Nervously, timidly, the man did so, stooping so that he didn't have to get down on his knees. Everyone watched him and Derian frozen in place. For a long time nothing happened. No sound, no movement, just the faint *Tikitik-tik-ka-tikitik-ka* happening outside somewhere in the resort. No one noticed Paul cracking the conference door open and peeking outside except for Derian who was aware of the clicking of the lock being unbolted. He mentally thanked Paul for checking the hall, just in case something *was* out there.

He moistened his lips, and told Lucas to get up as he lowered his gun. Now standing, Lucas regarded Derian with a haggard expression.

Carla had left her spot on the floor and approached them. "What do we do?" she asked clearly too afraid to think for herself. They all were looking at him more directly now, expecting him to have a good-enough answer. He was in charge here, there were no questions asked.

"Paul," Derian said turning to look. "You see anything?"

"Nothing," Paul said keeping his head out the door. "Nothing at all." He turned to the others and said, "This is crazy, we need to stop arguing and just get the hell out of here." He no longer cared if others heard, it was high time to get out before they got killed.

"I told you," Derian said as patiently as he could muster. "We aren't leaving without the others. For crying out loud, we aren't sailors we won't know what to do if we are out there."

Paul turned and stomped towards Derian like an angry T-rex. "It's better to take our chances out at sea than just hide here. Don't be stupid!"

"*You* are the stupid one here," Lucas snapped.

"Shut it," Derian said to Lucas now eyeing Paul carefully, analytically it seemed. Carla started to go for his arm but he shook her off gently, telling her to back off. Paul's one good hand was opening and closing, the man's stance unstable and jittery with the desperation flashing in his eyes.

"Look, murder-boy," Paul said bitterly. "You need to be smart for once. We need to get out. Fuck learning how to sail and fuck those who might get stuck behind. We need to look out for ourselves. Think of your wife!" He pointed at Carla with a finger that was almost accusing.

"I am," Derian said in a low and terrible voice. "Are you?"

"She ain't here," Paul snarled. "We don't know where they all are, so I say leave them."

"And them?" Derian said jerking his head back towards the wounded who were all sitting up now, anxious and concerned.

"They will slow down the monster too," said Paul bitterly.

"You're awful!" said Carla in disgust.

"No, I'm only telling the truth," said Paul. "Now I'm leaving. Anyone else coming, or are you all gonna be stuck on this island?"

Derian raised his gun and pointed it at Paul's head, causing the man's eyes to widen but his face remained stony, defiant. "You aren't going anywhere, Jackson."

"Or what?" Paul demanded with hands outstretched, his face a grimace of a smile as if trying to hold in a burst of nervous laughter. "You gonna murder me? You really gonna do that in front of all these people?"

Derian's eyes narrowed. "Lucas, help me grab him." They both started to converge on Paul Jackson who was waving his fists in front of them, as if he was about to box them.

"Get away!" he yelled. He struck out with his bad hand and Derian smacked it away. He cried out as if he had placed it on a hot cast iron again.

That was when the vent in the ceiling was kicked out and what came crawling out like a loathsome spider was the Manananggal. It had taken the distraction and dropped down and fell upon the wounded who were now screaming as they were torn into by teeth and claws, pieces of fabric and spatters of blood sailing and smacking against the nearby wall.

The female worker screamed as her head was pulled back and her throat was bitten into back to the bone. The monster ripped out the chunk of flesh and like a cat tossing a mouse the glob of bloody meat hit the back wall as it turned and clawed into another employee. With them all badly hurt, they could do nothing against the apex predator who despite Derian turning and shooting into it, did not care for the bullets burrowing into it's skin. It's wings were a flurry of blackness, it's teeth and claws razor sharp, and by the time it turned and roared at the remaining group viciously, the wounded had joined the dead. Blood was everywhere, the walls, the ceiling, chunks of flesh and organs scattered, and even across the monster's body as well as it pulled itself up onto the conference table using it's hands and wing knuckles for support, it's dangling entrails dragging across the hardwood as it started for them.

That was when Derian heard the door shut behind him and he quickly turned with the others and tried to pull the door open. Paul was on the other side, grinning at them madly behind the glass window.

"Paul! Open the door!" Derian bellowed as Lucas and Carla crowded around them.

"Fuck you!" Paul screamed as he held the door handle with both hands, keeping the group trapped in the conference room with the monster. "Fuck you! You can slow it down too! Nice knowing you 'hitman!' Fuck you and your-"

Derian, desperate for the monster was coming now, raised his gun to the glass window right in front of Paul's face and pulled the trigger. The report of the gun was deafening and he felt chunks of glass bite into his face as the window was punched through, and Paul flew back and landed in the center of the hallway clutching at his face where he had been shot right between the eyes. The group started to fall out of the conference room and that was when Derian realized it was just he and Carla out, for

Lucas was now grappling with the beast who was thrashing and throttling him across the conference floor in a bloody fury.

"Lucas!" Derian cried rushing for the man but he could see upon reaching the door and the man was dead, his neck twisted and his head facing the wrong direction. The Manananggal looked up from her kill on the floor, and snarled at Derian who at the last minute grabbed the door and pulled it shut, pulling all his weight down into it to keep the monster trapped inside as she crashed into the other side. The force jarred Derian's arms and he released the gun and used both hands to hold the door shut as one of the Manananggal's hands reached through the broken glass and made a grab for him. He felt talons dig into his shoulder and he screamed out at Carla to get away, to run as fast as she can and escape this horrible nightmare.

He looked at the glass window and saw the Manananggal on the other side, grimacing and snarling with teeth flashing as it tried to force Derian to release the door and let it out.

It was terrible, looking into that terrible and twisted face. Seeing those serrated teeth gnash and bite at empty air, with pinked spittle flying across the glass as it thrashed and snarled. Those hellish eyes burned into Derian's very soul, and he could see his terrified expression which was upside down in the reflection of those red orbs. The black hair of the Manananggal flayed every which way, making it appear deranged and wild. It's talons dug deeper into his shoulder, shooting up terrible pain throughout his arm. From the monster's maw a long red tongue lashed out and slithered through the gaps between it's arm and the shards of glass which occasionally scraped against it. It lashed out at him and he seized it with his injured hand, feeling the pain in his shoulder all the more. It wriggled and bucked, trying to throw him off balance and the tip tried to reach his face but barely nicked him across the cheek as if it was a razor blade. All the while he pulled on the door, holding it shut despite the monster's strength. He was not going to allow it to get out. He was *not* going to let it get to Carla who he hoped to God had gotten away.

But she hadn't. She had ran off, yes, but she had returned with something red and bulky which whooshed past Derian's blurry vision and struck the creature on the arm. The demon howled in frustration rather than pain, but then Carla had shoved something black between the glass and the tongue that was coiling around Derian's arm. With a scream, Carla pulled the pin off the fire extinguisher she got off the back wall, and pulled the trigger, blasting the creature in the face with the aqueous film-forming foam.

The tongue that Derian held jerked and pulled back, nearly dragging his hand through the glass. The claws still stuck deep into his shoulder and he felt the creature thrash as it swallowed up the fine metallic powder and was blinded as well. Carla continued to spray into the conference room until finally Derian felt relief as the talons pulled back and out of his shoulder, the gnarled hand retreating into the room as Carla continued to spray it.

Taking up his gun and ignoring the blood that was pouring from his shoulder and soaking his arm, Derian told Carla to run and together they turned and fled towards the back of the hallway not knowing where they were going but understanding that come Hell or high water, they must flee. They leapt over the body of Paul Jackson, and fled as the monster barreled it's way out of the conference room angry and covered in yellowed dust.

Derian dared to look back to look at the yellowed creature, her face a snarling grimace of frustration as the foam bubbled down her chin as if she were rabid. With a shrill growl, it leapt up and climbing along the wall, chased after them.

Thirty-Five

Amos and the others had been in the hallways when they had heard the Manananggal's calling. They had finished gathering some biblical texts and were about to regroup with the others when the ticking began. All stood frozen in the middle of the second-story of the resort. Joshua had gripped his whip tighter, as did everyone with their own weapons.

"It's quiet," said Kyra.

"Is it downstairs or outside the resort?" Frantz asked. "It's difficult to hear it."

In fact, it had been hard for anyone to hear it. It had been Joshua who had stopped and told everyone to do the same and listen, and only then could they hear the quiet and far away ticking of the Manananggal.

Tikitik-tik-ka-tikitik-ka-tikitik...

"God," Cynthia moaned and moved towards Adam for comfort. "That sound..."

"Don't be fooled," said Joshua sternly, his eyes on the entrance to the stairwell leading back down into the main hallway. "It's using a trick."

"What do you mean?" asked Adam gripping his carving knife almost feverishly with Cynthia holding onto his shoulders behind him.

"When a Manananggal makes that sound, it is using... what is it called, when bats use sound?"

"Echolocation," said Amos.

"Yes, that. They are searching for their prey when they cannot see them. Also, it *throws* it's voice, if that makes sense. When you speak far away, you sound far

349

away. But when a Manananggal speaks far away, it sounds *closer.*"

"How does that work?" demanded Victoria who was hugging herself with her hands clasping her elbows nervously.

"I don't know. But if it sounds close, it is not. When it sounds far, it is not."

"So, the closer it is, the quieter we hear the sound," said Adam shaking his head. "God…"

"No 'God,'" said Joshua. "Nothing God made would be like this…"

"So where is it then?" asked Elbi.

Before anyone could answer, that was when they heard the screaming followed by gunshots. They all rushed for the stairs, pounding down each two at a time until they reached the bottom just as Carla and Derian Anderson were bulldozing their way past. Joshua turned first, and then immediately stepped into the center of the hallway and when everyone was out of the stairwell, they saw what he was facing.

The Manananggal was there, now on the ground holding itself up on it's clawed hands and bony wing knuckles. It looked almost like a spider trailing it's guts, and everyone stood frozen while Derian and Carla stopped at the end of the hall once they realized their pursuer had stopped in the presence of everyone else.

"Holy shit," Amos whispered pointing the gun at the demon, forgetting what Joshua had said.

"Keep back," the kid said uncoiling his whip and snapping it against the wall. The creature hissed at this, but did not attempt to move forward and attack the group. All the while the resort continued to groan and ache against the unstoppable winds outside.

Something caught Kyra's eye in particular past the monster. Something was moving, getting up off the floor and then hurrying down the opposite direction towards the resort's reception area. Good. Someone was still alive and was getting away. Hopefully they can find a place to hide until help arrives. She would tell the others later, but for now, like them all, she was planted, seemingly frozen in the presence of the Manananggal who swayed from side to side on it's hands and knuckles, hissing and wriggling it's loathsome tongue past it's teeth.

Then Joshua began to speak to the monster. It was in Tagalog, nothing the group could understand. They were more interested in the monster's reaction, as it glared at Joshua as if it could understand him. He had said this in his native language, barking it out like a wild animal challenging a predator.

"I've found you! You will not take anyone else tonight. I will find you, and I will kill you. Come! Come to me and fight!"

The monster hissed at this, a low growl always present in her jugular. It crouched as if to spring and attack, but instead it remained low, it's wings slowly extending, making it appear bigger and more threatening. Adam and Cynthia both took a step back, as did Kyra, but no one else backed down. No one dared to move, less they give the monster a reason to call their bluff and charge. More importantly, Joshua stood his ground in front of everyone, whip and bolos in hand, he was willing to risk his life to end this nightmare, and finish what had been started back home.

"Josh," Amos spoke up. "Get back. Come join us."

"I'm not afraid of you," Joshua said instead to the Manananggal, again speaking in Tagalog. "Do you hear me? *Hindi ako natatakot sa iyo!*"

Surprisingly, the Manananggal responded to Joshua's bold statement. "*Ikaw ay magiging.*"

Then it stretched it's wings out all the further and charged at the group who ducked or fired their weapons. Joshua cracked his whip, but the tip of the stingray barb barely nicked the creature's belly, causing a thin tendril of black smoke to belch from it. It continued to fly past them and then crash through the rear emergency doors and out into the night which poured in through the shattered glass rain and wind. Everyone looked at the exit like they were the gateways to the worst circles of Hell ever imagined. A place that was dark, and full of monsters.

Thirty-Six

Paul's eyes had flickered open while the Manananggal was facing the others. He started to sit up, and placed a hand upon his head. It stung, and when he removed his hand it came back bloody.

The pistol Derian Anderson had brought with him was a standard-issue .22, something small and easily transferable when it came to international crossings. When they had gone to Mexico for the trip, they had gone by car, therefore making it easy to carry the weapon. It was a pea-shooter in all honesty, nothing compared to the weaponry Derian had access to, but he had wanted to travel light and carry a weapon that was easily concealable not just from authorities, but his wife. At point-blank range through a glass window no less, when the bullet struck Paul Jackson between his eyes, he had been just at the right angle so that the bullet glanced off the front of his skull and penetrated the ceiling above him, leaving a deep gash across the bridge of his nose and up to his hairline.

Upon realizing he was alive, having been shot and still breathing, Paul Jackson felt his bladder let go, the pungent odor of his alcohol-steeped piss hitting his nose like a sledgehammer and he began to chuckle madly at the very idea that his life could have ended then and there.

The moment he had spotted the Manananggal, he tried to get up shakily, a hand pressed to his head again as he stumbled for a moment. He got back up he fled down the corridor and into the resort, leaving the others to deal with the monster. Fuck them all, he was getting out of this resort and off this island.

He stumbled out into the wind and rain, eyes squinted to stay the sea spray and sand. He trudged towards the direction of the docks, not knowing if he would need a key or not for the boat. The wind was so strong that it nearly knocked him off his feet, and the sting from the salt it carried with it was felt all over his face but especially his eyes and the gash in his forehead. Once or twice he *did* fall into the sand, cursing and spitting out sand as he dragged himself to his feet and kept going. When he finally arrived, waves had soaked the entire dock and the boat was rocking against the side, it's ropes tight and frayed. Without checking for anything, Paul used a pocket knife to cut the line and he leapt into the boat, slipping into the water accumulated by the rain and landed on his side. He cursed, but got back up and started up the stairs towards the stern cockpit. There he dug around the glovebox until he found a second set of keys. He thanked God for them, and he inserted the key and started the engine.

It did nothing for a moment. Turning it again and again, Paul listened to the motor churning deep below deck only to sputter and cough and die. He kept going at it however, hearing the engine go just a little longer and all the while telling the piece of shit boat to wake up. At last the engine roared to life, and he smacked the wheel victoriously.

"Fuck yeah!" he crowed and putting the boat into gear as he would with his own fishing boat back home, he pulled away from the dock and started in the direction of East via the compass on the dashboard. The sea rocked the boat and the wind was terrible, causing takeoff to be slow and menacing. But eventually he was able to get out into the current and leave the island a good hundred yards behind him.

He had made it. By god, he had made it!

He looked back at the island which was shrouded in the mist of the rain, making it appear no longer a tropical paradise he remembered coming in to see just a few days ago, but a black lump that stuck out of the sea like a disgusting tumor. Lightning flashed directly above the island and the boom that followed rattled the windows of the boat and damn near blew out Paul's eardrums. In the blinding light he could see the island and he laughed as he thought he saw a face staring at him disappointedly from the side of the island's mountain, where the caves and waterfall appeared to be a pair of eyes watching him go.

"FUCK YOU!" Paul bellowed like a viking sailing away from a pillaged village, his plunder being the very life he now carried with him and no doubt would still carry upon returning to the States. "Fuck you all- And FUCK YOU VICTORIA!"

This could not have turned out better than Paul Jackson could ever hope. He had been planning after all after this vacation to get rid of Victoria once and for all; Find some loophole in his relations with her and make it out of the marriage with enough money to keep his business afloat. He doubted if that was possible and if not he would just take his chances and leave her anyway; He had started this business once and he could start another. Because of this situation however, he was now free of her forever and she could feed that monster's belly along with the rest of the doomed vacationers and crew. He could return to the States, tell them what has happened and come out of this a hero as well! His business would be saved for one and he would also have the fame of surviving the Bonidada Massacre as he was already imagining in his head as he gripped the steering wheel with white-knuckled vigor. He could already see the headlines now: Retail Giant escapes a paradise-turned-nightmare. There would have to be some details left out or outright changed, of course, but he had been lying to the cameras with Victoria for so many years that he could easily come up with at least one more, maybe two if he could come up with a good story about how he had tried to save the others. After all, if that monster got them all, who was going to dispute that? Certainly not Victoria, Paul sure hoped.

As he was thinking all of this however, the current he was now riding was *not* on his side. Unbeknownst to Paul Jackson who was not a sailor in the slightest, the accumulation of the winds churning up the sea as well as the speed of the California current was pushing him further south despite his direction going east. Because of this as well, the pressure against the boat on top of the wind became too much, and quickly Paul was realizing he was losing control of the ship and he had already put up a considerable distance between him and Isla Bonidada. The steering column went spinning without his control, and the engine was even overrun by the pressure until it eventually gave out below deck, causing smoke to bellow up from the deck's hatch.

"Shit!" Paul cried out in disdain upon seeing the smoke. He had tried to go for the wheel but it was moving too fast and strong for his one good hand, and he didn't dare try to grab it with his injured.

By that point it didn't matter though, for a large wave had come up and Paul saw it coming. It was a behemoth monster, rising over fifty feet above the tallest mast of the ship. Looking up at it coming towards him, Paul had felt so significantly small in comparison to the vast ocean that was between him and freedom. This stormy wave which came in like a great black wall, crashed into the side of the boat, throwing Paul off his feet and causing him to crash over the side of the stern cockpit. By then however, the boat was already capsizing, and another wave had snatched Paul Jackson before he even had a chance to take in a breath of air to scream. He was taken under, and the waves refused to let him surface until eventually, all that was left of any proof that he had existed, was the rapidly sinking boat which was the final legacy of Ben Franklins.

Both it and Paul Jackson were never seen again.

Thirty-Seven

"Oh god… Kyra, girls, get back."

Amos and the others were looking inside the conference room, hands covering mouths and faces turning green. Everyone who was left behind was dead, their entrails spilled across the flood and the stench of blood filling their nostrils. The body of Paul Jackson was missing, as well as Ethan Duncan. Kyra had taken the women back so that they didn't have to look at the grisly scene. Joshua was with the men, crossing himself as he admired the dead.

"Where the hell is Ethan?" asked Adam after vomiting. "Where's Jackson?"

"Who gives a shit about him?" Derian asked. "As for Ethan, he was right here when that monster attacked. Only Carla and I got out other than Jackson, and I shot the bastard in the head."

Cain looked at the bloodspot on the lavish hallway carpet. "Apparently not enough," he muttered.

"Forget about him," said Amos bitterly. "Ethan might be alive somewhere."

"Or the Manananggal came back and got him…" said Joshua.

"Don't do that," Amos snapped pointing a finger at the kid. "We don't know that for certain. There is no way in hell that thing is fast enough to go around the building and come back."

"Air ducts…"

"Still doesn't matter. We just… we gotta… oh god…" He covered his eyes in despair, dropping to a crouch and bouncing on the backs of his heels as he did so. "Oh god…" he moaned miserably.

Adam and Cain both looked at each other uncomfortably. This really was a despairing situation. Things just seemed to get worse and worse even as it had looked like the Mannananggal was hesitant to take on the rest of the group and immediately turned and ran into another room, disappearing entirely by the time they had arrived.

Derian returned from checking on Kyra and the girls, and he asked in a low tone, "What's the plan now?"

Amos removed his hands, released a sigh. "Nothing has changed. We need to kill this thing." He turned to Joshua. "Can we though?"

"I hope so," said Joshua.

"I don't want an 'I hope so,'" Amos said standing. "I need a 'we will.' So can we or can we not?"

This time, Joshua didn't hesitate. "We will."

Amos patted the kid on the shoulder respectably. "Good." He brought everyone out into the hallway and with the girls regarded them all with a sober expression.

"We have all that we need, or what we believe we need. We now have to search the entire resort to find the lower half of this monster's body. We find it, dump all we got from the kitchens onto it, and then find the upper body and destroy it."

Joshua cut in. "We might not even have to do that. The Manananggal will die if it isn't in it's one-form by sunrise. It doesn't have to be out in the sunlight for it to work, it will die."

"So we don't have to fight it?" Cynthia asked hopefully.

Joshua hesitated. "I don't know. If it is guarding it, or finds out we severed it's chance for survival, it might come after us again."

"The sun won't be up for almost four hours anyway," said Frantz checking his watch.

"What?" Carla asked in disbelief. "What time is it?"

"Three-o-eight," said the cook.

"It doesn't even *feel* that late," said Cain.

"I'm sure we'll feel it tomorrow," said Adam.

"If we live that long," Victoria said bitterly.

"Hey," Kyra said glaring at her. "We will make it. Don't think like that."

Victoria frowned, unconvinced. No one blamed her though for being dishearten. Her husband, as great of an asshole as he was, was taken away from her. They all sympathized with her, even Winnifred, although she would never admit this out loud.

"So here's the plan," said Amos getting back on track. "We are going to go from room to room and search this entire resort up and down. We hear something, we check it. No one goes anywhere alone. Got it?"

Everyone said they did.

"Good. When we find the body, Josh and I will take care of it. The rest of you will watch our backs.

"Amos," said Kyra. "The cameras."

Amos' shook his head. "Cameras are dead like the rest of the island. But... Holy shit!"

"What?" Adam asked nervously at Amos' sudden excitement.

"We have more walkies in there. And should we manage to get some power back online during our search...

"Then whoever is in there can check the cameras and watch everyone," Kyra added smiling broadly.

"Woah, woah," said Adam with raised hands. "What happened to no one goes anywhere alone?"

"It makes sense," said Cynthia and while it seemed to calm Adam down, he didn't look convinced.

"It'll work," said Amos too excited to not worry. "That door is able to be locked tight too, nothing can get in there. Besides, if power does come back on, then hopefully that means the distress signal will get boosted as well which we would need someone there to do so anyway." He looked to Kyra and said, "Would you be willing to sit in the security room? You're the only one other than me who knows how to use them."

"Of course," said Kyra. "I doubt I would be much help anyway, given my age."

"Thank you, really. Someone will go with you and-"

"No," Kyra shook her head. "I will sit in the security room alone. If I secure the door nothing can get in."

"What about the vents?" Derian pointed out.

"They're small, unless that thing can turn to mist-"

"Which it *can*," Joshua cut in but immediately said when all eyes turned on him, "But only in it's human form! It can't do it when it's flying!"

"Well, that's *some* relief," muttered Cain.

"Even so," Kyra said. "It should be the safest point in the entire resort. After you get rid of the lower body, if what Josh said is true, then we can all hide in there together- *Hopefully* with help on the way."

"That's what I was thinking," said Amos nodding with approval. "That sit right with everyone?"

"I don't feel right leaving her alone," said Elbi. Out of all her cooks, Elbi held Kyra at a high pedestal, the guy learned everything he knew from her and thought of her like a grandmother or mother he never had the pleasure of having.

"I'll be fine," Kyra assured him. "We need to get rid of that thing and make it out of here alive."

Elbi nodded but he still wasn't happy with it.

With everyone ready, they all began their search. They first escorted Kyra to the security room where she went in and locked the door behind her. With the radios from there as well, she and Amos could communicate as she tried to start the cameras up again.

At last, they officially all began, starting with the second story and working their way downstairs.

Every suite was checked and every closet was gutted. But they could find nothing that could mean the Manananggal was around. They had managed to check the backup generators and after some tugging on chords and cursing, Amos finally managed to get one going. Some of the resort's lights began to flicker and the vents began to exhaust a rancid odor along with fresh air all throughout. According to Kyra who was now on the cameras and watching the group's projects

(*watched over by the all-seeing African goddess,* thought Amos)

she didn't see any movement throughout the entire resort, even in the ballroom where the massacre took place. It had taken a moment for her to turn on the overhead lights and search all across the floor that was still strewed with the dead. By the time the group was downstairs and checking the other rooms along the main hall, she spotted something entering the front entrance and into the receptionist lobby.

It was Ethan Duncan.

She reported this to the others who hurried down the hall and met with Ethan in the hall, and all men aimed their guns at the man who held his hands up looking bewildered, his wounded leg stuck out as he hobbled towards them. His clothes were soaked with rain and blood, his hair a rat's nest. He had some fresh wounds on his back and chest from the attack in the conference room, and he was giggling hysterically.

"Guys! Guys!" he giggled. "I got out... That thing almost got me... but I got out! Paul did too! I saw him take the boat! The boat is gone! *Looong* gone!" He broke into another fit of laughter as if it was the funniest thing in the world, his teeth appearing larger and sharper than Adam specifically remembered.

"Goddammit," grumbled Amos lowering his gun. "Come on, we gotta-"

"Hold up," Derian said not lowering his own weapon. "Didn't Josh say the Manananggal can shapeshift?"

When inquired Josh said, "Yes, that is true, but only when it is in it's whole form."

"Do you know that for certain?" Derian asked.

Joshua hesitated, then admitted he didn't know for sure.

"I saw Ethan getting ripped apart in the conference room," Derian said. He was eyeing Ethan with distrust, which upon hearing his name, threw the man into another fit of hysterical laughter. Lightning flashed outside and in the light his large teeth shone like white neon, and his eyes had a red sheen to them like how they would appear in a camera shot. When the thunder roared overhead causing the windows to rattle, he began to laugh some more.

Ethan began to blurt out, "Ulan, ulan, umalis ka…" over and over broken only by fits of giggles.

"What the fuck…" Amos muttered bewilderedly. Derian's eyes were wide and scared now, the sight of the man's teeth and eyes having reminded him of Matthew Winklemann.

"His body wasn't in there though," Carla pointed out. "Derian-"

"The Mananangal could have taken him," Derian said his voice quaking a bit. "Make it seem like he got away and then come back to deceive us. Maybe that's why we can't find the lower half of the body."

With this hypothesis, everyone was now hesitant. Some of the men kept their knives close, those with guns took aim at the man again who was completely delirious. Even Amos took aim, unsure of what to do now. If Ethan really was the monster, it was doing a pretty bad job at convincing them it wasn't a threat.

"I… I just don't know…" he said now trembling.

"It doesn't get hurt by bullets though, right?" asked Derian. It was more like a demand. Joshua said that was true, then the man said, "I'm not taking the risk."

"Wait!" someone screamed. It had been Adam, but by then it was too late.

The report of the gun was hushed by the roaring wind, but the impact was still severe, causing some ringing in the others' ears. Ethan flew back as he was shot in the head, which like Paul Jackson resisted the .22 caliber, but this time with devastating consequences. What had happened was the bullet struck Ethan in the head just above his right eye. The angle of his head in the midst of his hysteria, caused the bullet to travel downward whilst caught in the folds of the skin across Ethan's temple and jawline. It then struck him on the side of the neck where it stuck right into his collarbone. He fell back laughing still until his body struck the floor and he laid in the center of the lobby coughing and gurgling arterial blood. Everyone stared in bewilderment as he was still laughing.

They all rushed for him, but Carla had most of them back up so that Derian and Amos could inspect Ethan. Despite this, Adam shoved his way through and inspected his friend who had a gaping hole in the side of his throat which looked like a budding flower gushing crimson nectar. Derian sat on the other side of the man and lifted his head with one hand and covered the hole to slow down the blood from the other.

There was no black blood, no black smoke, and Ethan was not retaliating. As Derian stared into Ethan's now glassy eyes, he could see his reflection was upright and normal; nowhere near what he had seen in the conference room.

"Oh shit," he swore. "He's real…"

"Of course he's real, you asshole!" Adam snapped angrily.

"How can you tell for certain though?" asked Amos wearily, likewise shaken by Derian's decision. Behind him, Joshua was watching with a stunned and mournful expression.

Thinking fast, Adam turned to Ethan. "Ethan, can you hear me?"

"I hear you…" his words were muffled by the blood
which was now bubbling from his mouth which was spread
in a clown's smile. His large teeth shone sharply making
him appear like a vampire.

"Don't make him talk…" Derian started.

Adam ignored him. "What was the last thing we
talked about? Before the shooting? Do you remember?"

Ethan nodded, choking. "Your wife was missing…
you were mad. Mad as a hatter." He broke into laughter
again.

"Shh… shh…" said Derian as if he were dealing with
a fitful child. He looked to the others for help.

"I'll grab something, hold on," said Amos as he took
off running down the hall. Kyra told him not to go alone
and then told Frantz and Elbi to follow. They did so
without hesitation.

"Ethan? Come on, man, stay with us," Adam
begged as he sat there feeling helpless. Derian had lifted
the shirt to inspect the wound as more blood gushed.

"Probably cut his curated artery," he muttered.
"Keep pressure here."

Adam did as he was told while Derian accepted the
med-kit Amos had returned with. Seeing some gauze he
balled some up into a makeshift plug and with Adam's
help, shoved the gauze into the wound and causing Ethan
to wince in pain. They reapplied pressure onto the shirt
and Derian asked Amos if there was a cot nearby. The men
hurried off and returned with one, which with effort they
carefully loaded Ethan onto it. Frantz and Elbi took either
side and lifted him up so that Derian and Adam could still
hold onto him.

"Put him down!" Derian suddenly said and the boys did so. They were down the hall close to where the security room was. Kyra had stepped out and was watching with a hand over her trembling mouth.

"What's wrong?" Adam demanded. Ethan's complexion was pale, and he was less responsive than he had been before, at the very least he was no longer giggling like a maniac.

"Ethan? Come on buddy, wake up," Derian said lightly slapping the side of the man's face. Ethan's eyes fluttered open and he moaned something incomprehensible.

"There you go, pal. Just stay awake, okay? Stay with us..." He checked the pulse and Derian's face turned grim.

"What is it?" asked Victoria looking green around the gills herself.

"Derian?" asked Adam.

"Keep pressure there," Derian said. "Ethan? Ethan, look at me."

The eyes turned, barely focused. The smile remained.

"Can you talk?"

Ethan moistened his lips with a tongue that was turning arid. "Barely..." he croaked. His eyes began to flutter again, closing more and more with each passing blink. "That was... really mean of you..."

"Ethan?" said Adam. "Ethan, come on, man, don't do this to me..."

But Ethan had no more choice of the matter than anyone else did at the Bonidada Resort. His eyes closed,

Derian checked his pulse and felt it fade in and out like the tide, and then stop completely. He was gone.

When Adam realized this, he began to scream and shake Ethan. Derian sat back, allowed him to have his moment of grief and didn't let anyone else come close to him.

Then Adam turned his attention to Derian, his eyes blazing and furious and brimmed with tears. "You motherfucker, you killed him!"

Cynthia tried to say, "Adam-"

"YOU KILLED HIM!" he bellowed angrily. He had grabbed Derian by the front of his shirt but the man only stared back unafraid, which angered Adam more.

"It was an accident, Adam," Derian responded calmly.

"Fuck you!"

Amos stepped in. "Derian didn't know anymore than we did. If he hadn't, I might have. Any of us could have. We just don't know for certain."

"We do now," said Joshua.

Adam glared at him. "Why didn't you know for certain!? I thought you knew all about this thing?"

Joshua looked down at his feet.

Cynthia reached Adam's side. "Don't be so harsh. No one could have known. He..." She was crying because of Ethan, but she was trying to be there for her husband's sake. "We are all doing the best we can. Hopefully... hopefully he's with Shawlyn now..."

"Hopefully," said Derian still held hostage by Adam. He returned to Ethan and after checking his pulse said in a low voice, "I'm sorry..."

But even as he said this, he was looking over the man with undisclosed distrust.

Everyone remained around Ethan for a long time, no one willing to move or speak. It really was just one thing after another. Now someone was dead by their own hands. They had killed him, simply because they didn't understand the legends entirely, and in their fear, Ethan Duncan had joined his wife once more.

That is, until everyone began to look at Ethan's teeth more and more. Now that he was still, no longer laughing, Ethan's teeth did look longer, more sharp. When Derian peeled back one eyelid and shone a flashlight against it, the brown in Ethan's eyes were once again tinged with red.

Amos was the second person to notice this and he looked at Derian. "What do you think?"

"Just like Matthew Winklemann…" He looked to Joshua who was staring at the eye with a dreadful expression. "You know anything about this?"

Joshua shook his head. "I… I don't know."

"'Course you don't," said Adam callously. He regretted it immediately by the way Joshua looked away guiltily. Cynthia shot him a cold glare and Adam muttered, "Sorry…"

Joshua shook his head. "It's okay…"

"Josh," Amos said speaking up turning his eyes away from the long teeth and red gleam of Ethan's face. "Are you sure you don't know anything about this?"

Joshua still unsure said, "He… he could have been turned into aswang."

"And what is *that*, exactly?" asked Frantz nervously, remembering Joshua mentioning the word before as he told the story of his village.

"We believed them to be shapeshifters like the Manananggal. Vampires primarily."

"Oh, great," muttered Cain morosely.

"But now I wonder," said Joshua uneasily. "If they were really just people being controlled. Manananggal… their gaze, maybe they change people's bodies as well as their minds. I don't know what would happen if he lived still, I never got the chance to see what happened after back home."

Amos looked to Derian and said, "Least we know what to look for if anyone gets stared at."

"Bad enough that it can fly and make noises sound everywhere and nowhere," said Cynthia numbly. The more they dealt with this Manananggal, the worst their situation seemed to become.

"But why Ethan?" asked Adam. "Derian said he saw-"

"I *thought* I saw," said Derian cutting him off. "I think I was just scared to see him alive. There's a good chance Ethan slipped away while that bitch was coming after me and Carla. Maybe she caught him, and decided to use him as a distraction. Maybe even give away our position with all that laughing."

Everyone shuddered at the thought. Ethan was completely out of his mind when they found him, and they all feared what would happen if they were caught by the Manananggal and *weren't* immediately killed. What happened to their state of mind once plunged under the gaze of this Filipino monstrosity?

It was only when Kyra said she saw something when they finally stirred. When Amos asked her to say again, she spoke feverishly almost.

"One of the cameras outside caught the bitch flying back," she said. "She was coming back from the hill!"

"The hill..." Amos muttered to himself.

"So it was never in the building to begin with?" demanded Cain. "Where is it's body then?"

"I think," Amos said. "I think I might know. Come on, we need to get back to the security room, and fast."

No one was willing to leave Ethan behind, especially Adam. "I want him put somewhere."

"The closet across the room will do fine," said Frantz. He helped Adam with storing Ethan's body away, in hopes that it wouldn't get caught by the Manananggal. After a brief argument, Adam managed to get help in retrieving Shawlyn's body as well, and they put her with her husband in the closet where they could be together until help arrived.

As they hurried back to regroup, they heard the loud calling of the Manananggal, hunting them all once more.

Tikitik-tik-ka-tikitik-ka-tikitik...

9th Letter

I'm going to get to the heart of the matter tonight. I have decided to stare my fears in the eyes and relinquish control of my shame and my pain. I must not let this linger any longer. I must rise above this.

The final attack on the village had finally destroyed all of us. It had attacked while we were all sleeping, save for the few men who stayed up to keep watch. Even then it mattered little as the men were either picked off like sheep to a wolf, or had gone mad by the monster's piercing gaze. Men would stand idly, giggling and even raving even as their friends and family were slaughtered before them. If left to their own devices they would have fully transformed into Aswang, and the village would no doubt become overrun. These men were killed by their own kith and kin, sometimes in the most brutal and savage of fashions for fear of they too wandering the night and preying on the weak. We all believed it would go out to the men patrolling the yards, seeing as it wouldn't be hiding in their homes like difficult prey.

Instead, it had broken into one house and slaughtered the family inside. Then it went to another house, and devoured the old woman living there, keeping ahead of the hunters including myself who went from house to house trying to catch this thing. At last it was just us and the Manananggal who had snatched up one man and dropped him from a great height, breaking his neck by the fall. Then it went after Tetsa, who didn't stand a chance. The monster had gutted him, slitting his belly open as easily as one would fillet a fish. Then it went after Ralph, then Jesus. Then at last, me.

I struck at it with my whip with all my might. I wanted revenge, revenge for my family, revenge for my mother, revenge for taking everyone I knew and cared about out of my life. But we were at the mercy of the monster now. Without our defenses, without our faith, we had crumbled and were no more than mere lambs to the slaughter. It had dispatched me, and threw me into the dirt. Then it clawed me in the back, and bit me in the hand to force me to release my whip. Then it held me in the dirt, and I looked into those hellish eyes that reflected my face upside down in her gaze. It held me there, and roared into my face. I cannot describe the horrible smell coming from the monster's gullet. A fishy smell, which I associated with fresh blood. Human blood. It had made it's point, it's plague was over.

But it was not done with me. As I looked past the rows of shark teeth in the Manananggal's mouth, I stared directly into death itself. With a horrible cry, I bit down onto the small vial I had held in my mouth. I felt glass break between my teeth, ground between then and shred my gums and mouth. I spat at the creature, my blood and the mixture of the coconut oil and holy water splattering it in the face. It reared back and howled in pain, covering it's face as it burned before me. Then I took up my whip and cracked it across her flank, forcing her to retreat. It hissed and snarled and bit at me, but I forced it back, forced it into the light so I could look into the face of the one who murdered my family and destroyed my village.

It wasn't the face of the demon. It was the face of my own mother, begging me to spare her.

Three days we have fought this demon off. Three days she has picked us off one by one, until I, the faithless one, became the last one standing. Standing before me, mocking me it seemed, was the face of my own mother, looking distraught as if I betrayed her. It was a trick, I knew that, but my heart still ached at the sight. Then it shifted to that of my sister's, then the Babalayn. Then at last, it revealed myself. Faces upon faces looked at me, pleadingly. Almost mockingly.

But I had suffered too much to have any sympathy for a monster such as this. I was outraged it would try to use such a deceitful tact against me. So with a war cry worthy of my ancestors, I struck at the monster again and again, relishing in the deep and bloody furrows that hissed black smoke from the tip of the whip. Scooping up the bolos, I swung it viciously and severed the right wing of the Manananggal. It spung about like a top as it tried to take flight and then crashed to the ground. Then it crawled away like a wounded animal, barking and snarling throughout. I had moved forward, believing I could end it once and for all.

But the worst sort of luck had befallen me. I had been careless with my whip, and it had coiled around my ankle, tripping me. Seizing it's chance, the Manananggal doubled it's efforts to flee, and it was escaping towards the docks. Hissing and cursing, I managed to uncoil the whip from my leg and stand, breaking after it as fast as I could. By the time I had reached the docks, I had been too late. The Manananggal was gone. I searched high and low for it, and then I saw something in the distance beyond the shore. A boat sailing off to the east. Horror had stricken me then; the demon had to have been on that boat. It was escaping the island. It was escaping me.

I could not let that happen.

Taking one of the fishing boats, I had loosened the sails and made haste in the direction the boat was heading. It was dark, and the Manananggal needed no light to see no doubt. It's wing could heal, but it would need time to do so. Also, it would need to return to it's body, I knew that. I knew not whether it had hidden it's body in one of the boats to make it's attack this time, or if it was taking a chance to lose me at sea, but I was not going to be taking chances. I was going to chase that monster down to the ends of the earth if I could.

In the end, in a strange sort of way, I had.

I remember screaming towards the boat, begging for whoever was on it to stop and to turn around, to warn them of the danger that they were in. But the boat continued to drift further and further away into the haze of the distant ocean, which eventually took me too in it's unforgiving embrace. That was when I had become lost at sea.

This, was when I had lost my home, permanently.

Thirty-Eight

Back in the security room, Amos told everyone to get comfortable. Then he asked Joshua to sit beside him and he then began his brief interrogation.

"Where would the Manananggal most likely hide itself?" he asked.

Joshua looked uncomfortable with answering. He shifted in his seat and played with his hands. "I... I'm not sure..."

"You don't have *any* idea at all?"

Kyra started to say, "Amos..."

"Hold on," Amos said waving her away.

A pause, and then Joshua answered, "Somewhere safe, I know that for certain..."

"No shit," muttered Cain which earned him a glare from Amos.

"Do you know where it hid itself last time?" Amos asked. "Back where you came from, I mean?"

Joshua swallowed hard, and everyone was surprised to see that the boy was crying now. Tears rolled down his dirty cheeks, leaving wet and somewhat cleaner streaks across his face.

"Yes," he finally said. "Yes I knew where it hid itself."

"Where?"

"Outside the village..." He was struggling to speak now, seeming torn up by some conflict with himself or the mere memory of it was too horrible for him to try and relieve. But the kid stuck through with it and finally answered, "It hid itself away in a nearby cave by the river. It liked the river."

"So it likes damp and dark places?" asked Cain.

"Y… yeah, it… she does."

Amos slapped himself on the knee as if he had just discovered the solution to a complicated math problem, or had just rediscovered a love for a hobby he had once forgotten. He patted Joshua on the back, surprising the boy.

"Atta boy. If that is the case, then I have an idea of where it could have gone."

"Where?" asked Carla, excited now.

"The Crockett Grotto," said Amos. "A couple of nights ago two of our workers went missing. They had gone up to the grotto but only one of them came back down. That one I am pretty sure was that Manananggal pretending to be her though, but that isn't the point."

"Isn't the point…" Cain started but Amos was on a roll.

"I think… I think that it got them up there. I'm thinking if maybe that's where it went when it came, however it got here."

"That strange boat," Kyra mentioned suddenly remembering.

"Yeah, that's what I think too. But that's what I'm thinking, maybe it went to the grotto once it realized it might not be safe to be anywhere near the resort in case we went looking for it."

"How would it know that we know what can hurt it?" asked Cynthia.

"Him," Amos said pointing at Joshua. "It only makes sense. Besides, if Joshua was able to find it before, it would take extra care to make sure he couldn't again. Which means if it gets the chance," he added looking at

Joshua grimly. "It might go after you just to pull your plug."

"Pull my plug?" Joshua asked not understanding the reference.

"Kill you," Derian said insensitively.

Joshua replied with a pathetic "Oh."

"So, the grotto then," Victoria said. "Up the hill?"

"That's right. Unless it went out of it's way to hide it somewhere else, although it had been gone for a while if our cameras are right. Kyra, can you bring it up again?"

Kyra scrolled back on one of the monitors to the point where she saw the Manananggal take off. The picture was hazy from the rain and the creature was moving so swiftly it was a mere black blur on the computer screen like a splotch of ink across the ruined canvas. It was impossible to tell for certain whether or not it was carrying something, but it was heading in the direction of the grotto. Another camera was brought up when a flicker of movement went across the camera on the pathway leading up to the grotto itself. The camera had been shaking in the wind but it managed to catch a glimpse of a shadow passing overhead. Five minutes later another shadow appeared, then Kyra brought the first camera back where they could see the Manananggal returning to the resort near the rear.

"Gotta be it," said Amos feeling a buzz going on in his head from excitement, almost like he was making the bet of a lifetime before he took back a Las Vegas jackpot. "The grotto."

"So, we go up there and look for it then?" asked Adam.

"No," Joshua said shaking his head. "If it sees us it'll move it. Might even use the darkness and the open space to attack us. No, we must not go up there all together."

"Then what are we supposed to do?" demanded Carla.

"I was actually about to get to that," said Amos. "This room is the safest on the entire island. Nothing can get in so the Manananggal won't be a problem in here. Kyra can stay in here, but someone else needs to go out and lure the Manananggal away. We need to keep the bitch's attention so that the rest can hurry up the grotto and find the body. Once they do, they destroy it, and hopefully it's enough to hurt or even kill it."

"Won't it be suspicious if it sees only one of us out there?" asked Derian. "This thing isn't stupid, Amos. We all know that for certain."

"Then a few of us, maybe two or three, that way it doesn't think anything of it and might even be bold enough to attack."

"Who's gonna do it though?" asked Elbi.

"I am," said Amos to everyone's surprise. Kyra tried to say something but Amos silenced her with a shake of his head. "I'm gonna be the bait. I'm gonna do whatever it takes to kill that thing if it gives us the chance to find it's body and destroy it."

"If it's even up there," Adam pointed out.

"Yeah, that's true. Still, I need someone to come with me. Who's coming?"

Everyone was looking at one another now, no one willing to volunteer themselves or another person for a long time. The room had gone dreadfully silent in the seconds that followed.

Finally, someone spoke up. "I'll go."

Amos immediately turned on Joshua. "No. You are needed for the body, to make sure we do it right."

"I have my whip-"

"Hand it over," Amos said holding his hand out. "If it will really hurt that thing, I'll give it a good thrashing if it rears it's ugly face towards me."

Joshua didn't looked pleased with this idea, not at all. He didn't say anything however, only frowned bitterly as he surrendered his sting ray whip.

"I'll go with," said Derian as Amos coiled the whip around his shoulder.

"No!" Carla exclaimed. "No, you're not going out there to be *bait*!"

Derian looked at his wife sadly. "Someone has to, Carla. I'm the most fit, so I have a better chance. Someone has to watch Amos' back."

"If anything," said Amos. "I'd rather you be up on the hill with the others. We need someone who knows what they are doing if someone gets injured."

Derian didn't look happy, but he muttered, "Fine."

"Where you go I go," Carla then said hooking an arm into her husband's. "And don't argue with me. We are doing this together."

Frantz cleared his throat. "I'll go with you, Mr. Mulderich."

"You sure?" asked Amos in a serious tone.

"I'm sure. I'll watch your back."

"Frantz," Kyra said sadly.

"I'll be fine, ma'am," Frantz promised with an assuring smile that looked forced. "We'll make it back."

"I'll see to that," Amos promised as well.

Kyra turned so that no one would see her cry.

"All right," said Derian. "Then I'll need Adam, you and Cain to come with me. Victoria?"

"I'd rather stay here," said Victoria.

"We'd have a better chance of surviving if you went with either Amos and Frantz or us."

Victoria crossed her arms. "Maybe Paul was right. Maybe we should have just left."

Amos scowled at her. "Your husband decided to just leave us stranded here. We don't even know if he even made it out alive."

"He could have…"

And if he did, Derian thought bitterly. *That chucklefuck better not let me catch him alive.*

"That isn't the point," said Adam taking up Amos' side. "The point is we are still here, and we are only gonna get off this island alive if we work together. So who are you going with? Us, or them?"

Victoria grumbled and then said she would go with Amos and Frantz. "I'm not going out there in the wind and rain."

"Then we are coming too," said Cynthia taking Winnifred's hand. "We'll come to the hill with you."

"Winny," said Cain softly.

"Where you go, I go," she said taking her husband's hand as well. Despite their predicament, she was glad Victoria was not going to be going with them.

"That settles it then," said Amos. "The three of us will cause a distraction and as soon as we have it after us, that's when you guys will make a break for it. Any questions, concerns, comments?"

Everyone had all of those, but no one spoke up. After a momentary pause Amos turned to Joshua, saying, "We are gonna finish this, right?"

This time, there was no hesitation. "We will."

"Would..." Amos cleared his throat. "Would someone like to... say a prayer?"

Kyra looked at him thoughtfully. "I never thought I would live to see the day when you would ask such a thing, Amos Mulderich."

Amos smiled softly. "Never thought I'd live to fight against some demon yet here we are."

Kyra nodded and asked if anyone had any objections. There were none. With their backs against the wall, much had changed in the hearts of these men and women, and the concept of a God listening and watching over them was not far-fetched in their haggard minds.

Kyra had prayed for everyone's safety, and that the hand of that God would carry them to victory, and get them all home safe when the night was over. To be with the souls who had been unjustly taken in this place that had once been paradise, and to bless the men and woman willing to risk their lives in order for the rest to destroy the monster. In the end, all religious and not had responded with "Amen."

Thus, they got it on.

Thirty-Nine

Amos, Frantz, and Victoria all decided to return to the ballroom to plan their attack. Seeing the dead again and having their stench fill their nostrils made them all sick, but they worked fast. The ticking of the Manananggal was loud, indicating that it was far enough away for them to work.

Unless, Amos thought fretfully. *She's fucking with us...*

They laid out their trap, and thus Amos stood among the dead his whip ready in one hand and his pistol in the other. Before he began, he walked over to the bar, and after a quick look at their inventory, removed a bottle of scotch off the shelf. He uncorked it, and saluted everyone who had died in the shooting, and took three deep quaff's from the bottle. It burned his throat and set his senses on fire, but he relished the drink. It would very well be the last thing he would ever have touch his lips, and goddamn if he wasn't going to leave this world without one more drink. The other two saw him but he didn't care. He saluted them as well.

"Well, Crockett," he said after gasping for a gulp of soothing air against his throat. "Hope this place turns out exactly as you planned it to be, especially after this night."

He took one more drink and then poured the rest of the alcohol over his head, letting the bitter smell soak into his clothes and once the last drop was gone, he tossed the bottle aside where it landed somewhere with a satisfying crash. Joshua had said that while the Manananggal relied on it's sense of hearing more than anything else, he hoped it's sense of smell was just as strong, if not stronger, so that it would smell him and only him and not the others.

Then, in a loud and commanding voice, he bellowed to the ballroom ceiling, screaming like a bugling moose alone in the dark somewhere in the arctic wastelands. "ALL RIGHT, YOU BITCH! I'M HERE! COME GET US!"

The other two did the same, shouting and calling for the Manananggal. Frantz was gripping his rifle tight in his hands, his gold crucifix dangling around his neck. Victoria had her knives, and her eyes darted around every entrance to the ballroom, hoping to catch a glimpse of the creature before it saw them. She was scared, looking like a frightened rabbit, but Amos appreciated her coming with him and Frantz. He only hoped the three of them would make it out of this place alive.

He looked at a small bowl they had placed on one of the tables that had not been overturned. It was a small thing they had taken from the kitchens and had filled it with what Joshua had mentioned would be helpful. Inside the bowl was liquified coconut oil that Kyra often used to fry some Caribbean fries. It remained still like a stagnant pool of water, and he eyed it from time to time while repeating his challenge to the Manananggal. All the while, he didn't fail to notice the ticking sound of the monster getting steadily more quiet and quieter as time went on.

Then, his eyes caught sight of it, the coconut oil starting to boil in it's bowl. When he had heard of this tactic, Amos had laughed bemusedly at Joshua. However considering all the things he had witnessed tonight, he decided it wasn't completely far-fetched. Therefore he decided to go through with it as they prepared the ballroom for their attack. He could barely believe his eyes, the oil was *boiling* as if a hotplate had been placed beneath the bowl.

As if on que, the ticking stopped all at once. Something burst into the room and began to circle the ceiling above. Her black wings shrouded the light, her entrails dangled and whipped from the flight, and her burning eyes were glowing with glee.

"All right," Amos said and he cracked the whip against the ground. "Come on, you *bitch*."

The Manananggal swooped down talons and teeth bared and reaching for him as she came for him. He leapt back and struck out with the whip, causing her to change course to avoid getting hit. He snapped it again, keeping her attention on him and not the others who were now shouting and waving their arms to confuse her despite them being told to lay low among the dead.

Frantz let loose a war cry as he shot at the monster who jerked and hissed at the shots it took. It turned on him, wounds belching black smoke and as it rushed for Frantz, the boy reached behind him where a bible was tucked into his belt and he held out the biblical text and began to say a prayer against the unholy in French. It did the man no good however, for the Manananggal tackled him to the ground and with her claws, rip his lower jaw off and toss it aside. He fell back with his tongue dangling among the torn flesh and the monster finished him off with a jab into his eye with her writhing tongue.

"Jesus Christ," Amos muttered as he rushed for her. He cracked the whip against her back, and the monster howled in pain and it backed up hissing and clawing at him like a wild tiger at a circus against it's trainer. Amos cracked the whip against her again, creating a deep gash across her left temple which belched more smoke. Her shrill shrieks nearly deafened him.

"HA!" he barked victoriously. "How do you like that, you fuck? Take *that*, you bitch!"

Victoria was rushing in as well, her knives up and ready to plunge into the monster's back. It heard her coming or something however, for it whirled about and with it's bony wing knuckle, punched Victoria back and sent her sprawling across some dead bodies. The bone had punched a hole into Victoria's chest and it glistened crimson in the lamplight. Amos cracked his whip across the monster again and forced it to get back as he put himself between it and Victoria.

Victoria moaned as she sat up, her hand over a spot on her chest. Blood was staining the front of her blouse, and Amos told her to get up and move. The monster was about to take flight and Amos raised his gun and unloaded the weapon into it. It didn't seem to hurt the monster and instead of taking off it charged right at him again, getting past the whip and tackling him to the ground. The two wrestled as Amos punched at it and tried to hold it back from biting him or using that loathsome tongue on him. To her astonished disgust, Victoria saw that the entrails dangling from the creature's abdomen were writhing, coiling and snagging at Amos like an octopus would with tentacles. Ignoring desire to become sick, Victoria had come up behind the creature and swung a chair at it, breaking it against it's back and forcing it to retreat. Once he was back on his feet, Amos cracked his whip at the Manananggal again, and this time it hissed and took off straight to the ceiling where it hung from it like a bat and snarled at them from above.

"Come down here!" Amos shouted. "Come down here you chickenshit!"

The Manananggal then took a deep breath and unleashed a hellish high-pitched screech that tore at Amos' eardrums and forced him to wince. The high-frequency had shattered the bowl of coconut oil as well as some of the nearby windows and liquor bottles. With him distracted, the Manananggal dropped down and charged at him, but despite being deafened by it's audible attack, Amos cracked his whip and forced it to change course where it proceeded to tackle Victoria to the ground and drag her to her feet. It held it's claws against her throat as it stood behind her using it's knuckle bones to stand.

"No!" Amos said holding a hand out as if he could grab the demon and stop it.

Victoria was whimpering now, the Manananggal's tongue coming out and wavering, caressing her cheek and *tasting* her it seemed. All the while it did not cut her throat or do anything to harm her. The goddamned thing was using her as a *hostage*, Amos realized.

Christ, just how intelligent is this thing?

The Manananggal bared her teeth and hissed at Amos threateningly, the talons pricking the sides of Victoria's jugular but otherwise not puncturing skin. It knew exactly what it was doing, and it was showing Amos that it meant business.

"Let her go!" Amos shouted, wishing he had taken more than one pistol with him. He didn't want to say anything to Victoria, and hoped she would be smart enough to do what was necessary. The bibles weren't doing anything, so that left one more thing which Victoria had in her possession.

But the poor girl only stood there, crying and trembling. She was scared out of her wits and little by little, Amos began to doubt that they would be able to get out of this alive. They had already lost Frantz as swiftly and unfairly as the shooting that took place here not that long ago. Amos had a chance because of the whip, which the Manananggal appeared to fear. But how long could he keep it up if he was the last one standing?

Hopefully the others are doing well, he reminded himself. He knew why he had come to this final conclusion. He had made his decision for the better of everyone, and he was going to see it through, consequences be damned. Frantz even knew the risks and Amos was not going to let his death go in vain.

But did that mean Victoria would die? She hadn't wanted this, but she had stuck through and fought back to the best of her ability. If there was any way to save her, to give her the chance she deserved, then he had to take it. But not at the risk of putting himself in danger. The Manananggal feared the whip, so he had to make sure it remained a fear for this dreadful monstrosity.

The Manananggal had begun to back up, slowly dragging Victoria with her. It bared it's teeth some when Amos took a step forward, warning him to stay back. Victoria, understanding what was happening, began to go hysterical, kicking and screaming and the monster appeared to lose some patience and lowered the talons from Victoria's throat in order to drag them across her belly. The sound of tearing fabrics and skin were audible past the screams and Amos felt his blood boil when he saw Victoria's spilling from her belly.

When at last the creature spoke, it's words were gargled and faint, as if it were struggling to formulate the words as a mimic of human speech. To Amos it sounded like many voices at once, many languages at once, all the while the language he was most fluent in sounded as if it were coming deep underwater.

"Drop your weapon, hinayupak," it said drawing more blood as it dug it's claws into Victoria's belly. The words rang in Amos' ears, made him sick to his stomach and nearly made him do as he was told.

This however seemed to rattle something within Victoria for she dug into her right pocket where she had cradled a fistful of salt and sugar. The plan was to add garlic as well but they had no idea if the Manananggal would be able to smell it or not. Still, the effects were still satisfactory for when Victoria slapped the monster in the face with the salt and sugar, the Manananggal reared back and screamed like a banshee, releasing Victoria and covering it's face which was hissing and burning. Victoria had fallen to the floor and was crawling away by the time Amos rushed the creature, his whip ready as the Manananggal removed her hands and snarled with a ruined face. Where the salt and sugar had landed, speckles of burnt marks as if she had been hit in the face with hot oil were visible, and one eye was bleeding black pus down one cheek. It made the face look strained and more horrifying but Amos steeled his nerve and with all his strength cracked the whip against the monster's right wing. The scream that followed seemed to shake the entire room and then the Manananggal in blind fury Amos realized, met his brutality with her own.

This time, with a familiar face that was still scorched by the salt and sugar, but otherwise still completely recognizable to Amos Mulderich.

Seeing his father immediately made Amos momentarily pause. The likeness was so uncanny that he felt himself lost in the eyes of his father who glowered at him with the same disdain he had always carried. His father rose to his full height, towering over Amos like a great beast about to lay down some divine justice upon him. Even his voice which once spoken was so perfect that it caused Amos' spine to tingle with chills. As long as Amos looked into the eyes of his father, he was lost to everyone on Bonidada.

With a cry that sounded shrill and desperate, Amos forced himself with great effort to snap the whip. The stingray barb struck his father across the left cheek, causing a great gash to appear as suddenly as a paint stroke and black smoke belched from the wound. A shrill scream came from his father's face which momentarily blurred like a TV buffering and then the Manananggal was there, the spell it had tried to cast as broken as it's face which snarled in rage and came at him with the ferocity of a leopard.

Freed from this spell of familiarity, Amos snapped the whip again and retreated from the grasping claws only to snap and retreat again and again, all the while keeping pace with the monster who crawled like a rabid panther and struck out at him with flashes of her talons and reaching tongue. Where she occasionally missed deep furrows were made in the floor and furniture, and once or twice she managed to get a small bit of Amos, spilling blood across his thigh and once across his chest. Still, Amos attempted to force the monster back but she was not allowing him to have the chance and so forced him to continually retreat and use the whip as a defensive mechanism rather than offensive. Very quickly this drained him and left his limbs feeling heavy and rubbery. His chest burned with the effort to breathe and when the Manananggal actually took flight in order to get in close and not be so limited on the ground, he had to fight the urge to run away in fright. All the while he had to leap and bounce in order to keep himself from tripping over a dead body and falling. Sweat and blood had accumulated on his forehead and a drop had slithered into his right eye, blinding him there and so forced him to keep it shut while his left eye remained focus. If he slipped even once, he was dead. He was grateful that Victoria was able to get away, and only hoped that the others were having better luck than he was.

They better find it, he thought. *I can barely keep this up...*

His whip connected with the side of the Manananggal's jaw, sinking deep and seeming to melt into her flesh and stick to her bone. It looked painful but the monster used that to her advantage to move in and drive the talons of both hands into Amos' gut. He felt the air get punched out of him as he was lifted up and *thrown* across the room. He managed to keep his grip on the whip purely because he could not process the idea of loosening his fist for the pain in his belly felt like molten lead. He landed and slid across the floor and smacked into the back wall next to the kitchen entrance with a huff, and he gasped as he sat up placing a hand on his belly. He felt hot and wet there, and he was afraid to look down at himself as he felt something slimy slip out of him and into his hand.

Get up, you sonofabitch, get UP!

He dragged himself to his feet using the wall for support, and his legs threatened to buckle beneath him he felt so weak and dizzy. He wiped the blood and sweat from his eyes so he could see the Manananggal clutching at the side of her face in great pain, her talons crimson with his blood. When she saw him rising, she removed her hands from her ruined face and snarled at him again, appearing outraged that he was still up and moving. It began to crawl over the bodies and the overturned tables, it's crimson eyes full of hateful fire.

"Come on, you bitch," he said through clenched teeth, his free hand still clutching at his belly. "Come and get me…" He staggered through the kitchen doors and entered the kitchen. The smell of last night's dinner was still fresh in here, and disturbingly felt more present than it had earlier which frightened Amos.

Just move, he told himself as he stumbled down the length of the kitchen using the counter and butcher's block for support. *Just, fucking, MOVE.*

Blood was dripping everywhere he stepped now, and where his hand rested he left dark handprints. He was losing a lot of blood now, and he started to lose sense of surrounding to the point where black stars danced across his vision and he couldn't even hear the Manananggal burst through the kitchen doors, eager to finish what had been started.

Sensing her prey's weakness, the Manananggal took her time chasing after him even as Amos turned and cracked his whip menacingly at her, despite it sounding not nearly as dangerous as it had earlier. His strikes were weakening along with the rest of his body. He cursed and howled in frustration as it hopped onto the counter and continued to crawl toward him, entrails slithering through the bloody handprints behind her. The horrible grin on her face never left as those teeth opened and closed on each other, ready for fresh blood to rinse with.

"Get... back..." Amos said cracking the whip again. He grasped out at a stray pot and hurled it at the creature who merely shifted it's weight to avoid getting hit. He threw several more cooking utensils at the creature, finally settling on a carving knife sitting next to a warmed and rotting piece of fish. His leg struck something, one of the totes left behind and he collapsed to the tiled floor, crawling back and still whipping at the air as the Manananggal dropped to the floor and crawled toward him. She was relishing in his weakness, relishing in him dying.

He finally came to an abrupt stop, the back of his head smacking against the back wall and he cursed as he felt himself stopped at last. His belly was still spilling out his insides and his blood was pooling, and he gripped the carving knife and pointed it at the creature who was still approaching him with deliberate calm.

"Fuck... you..." he managed to gasp out, striking out with whatever strength he had left with the whip only for it to land limply on the floor before the Manananggal. She stepped down on it, seeming to climb up it before she took the wrist of the hand holding the whip and twisted it so that it was pinned to the wall above Amos' head. He tried to stab her in the face with the carving knife only to have it grabbed and held it up as well, making him hang there like a medieval prisoner.

Her face was mere inches from Amos'. Her eyes burned with hatred and pus, her smile wicked and her breath smelling of decaying flesh. Her tongue slithered out thin and red, and caressed the side of his face as she proceeded to mock him in his weakness. It didn't matter that he had the whip, didn't matter what he had anymore; She had *him* now.

Amos ground his teeth bitterly and he spat into the creature's face, surprising her for that moment. Then she hissed and groaned as where he spat on her began to sizzle and smoke, a result of the garlic salt he had poured into his mouth just after he had entered the kitchen before the Manananggal had given chase after him. It didn't have the same effect as it had when it was dry, but it still appeared to hurt the creature enough to cause discomfort. It turned those hideous eyes back to Amos, growling with newfound hatred for the defiant prey.

"Fuck you," he said again past his clenched teeth.

The smile returned, that horrible tongue wriggled downward and toward his belly. It went in, and Amos' vision went hazy and red and hot pain flushed through his entire body. In the haze he watched as the tongue retracted, and revealed to be coiled around one of his intestines which she was pulling out not for food but for the sake of tormenting Amos in his final moments. It's eyes gleamed at his pain, at the tears in his eyes and the sounds he made as he was disemboweled slowly, and painfully.

"Fuck you..." Amos said once more, but more weak than ever. He tried not to look down at his belly and what the creature was doing to him. In fact he tried to keep his eyes on the Manananggal just to spite the creature, as well as keep himself from fainting.

This proved to become Amos' downfall, for with nowhere else to turn to, he found himself becoming absorbed into the gaze of the creature who held no remorse as she proceeded to torture him, and make him suffer for his insolence. Her eyes took him in deep and somewhere far below, and her face which remained spread in a grimace, morphed into that of the one man whom Amos had dedicated his whole life to, and was thus tortured all the more by his presence.

"You have heart," said James Crockett. "I'll take that too…"

Forty

While Amos fought off the Manananggal to the best of his ability, the rest of the group had made it to Crockett's Grotto.

For almost twenty or thirty minutes they stumbled about blindly through the darkness their flashlights catching every sway of trees or thick raindrops. The mud on the trail made it exceptionally difficult for the climb and as a result many of the party had made it to the top of the hill with scraped and muddy knees. All the while they worried that they would not be able to hear Kyra on the radio should she have to warn them about some monster returning the dark and looking for them. On more than one occasion, the radio had sparked with electric barking that was incomprehensible and whenever someone tried to answer back begging for Kyra to repeat herself, all that came back was more static.

This only made their predicament all the more terrifying as the group were constantly jumping at shadows, believing themselves to have seen something the others didn't who in turn would become just as frightened. Every sway of a tree was a flapping wing, every howl of the wind a hungry screech. Cynthia in particular thought she saw something in the corner of her eye, something shifting and following them in the dark. Every time she mentioned something however, it proved to only be another tree fighting against the harsh pacific winds. The whole entourage became so feverishly convinced they were becoming stalked that they all had become speechless as they continued their climb, the chatter on the radio a distant language they could not decipher, nor did they seem to care to attempt.

At last, they made it to the entrance to the grotto, and quickly ducked into the cavern and got out of the rain and winds. All were soaking wet down to the bone, and all were shivering and miserable. But they had made it into the grotto, which was quieter inside as the winds howled and made whistling sounds through the opening in the top and two sides of the grotto. Birds and other animals were crying out in fright at the sight of the newcomers, but were immediately silenced against the raging winds that persisted.

The group discussed looking along the paths but in the end decided to split up and look all around the cavern individually. The Manananggal could have hidden her body anywhere, and so they didn't have much time to find it. Joshua in particular felt it in his gut that they didn't have time, but didn't express why he felt that way, for he feared that if he was right...

No, he had faith in Amos. Amos had faith in him, so he had to have faith in the resort overseer.

Carla had screamed when she caught sight of a centipede among some hibiscus flowers. By the time Derian got to her however, she said she was fine and continued the search. All the while she kept an eye out for other insects taking refuge in the grotto. A surplus of bugs had to mean the Manananggal's body had to be near, and so while she wanted absolutely nothing to do with the dreadful creatures, Carla continued to search on much to her husband's gratitude.

As time went on, it became unofficially declared that everyone would work in groups of two, the unease of what could happen should the Manananggal decide to come back once it found out no one else was in the resort, if Amos and his group were even still alive. The search by then felt agonizingly slower, but there was little they could do. Adam and Cynthia White in particular were glad they managed to stick together almost as naturally as it had been during the height of their marriage.

"Ever thought you'd be doing this on vacation?" Adam asked trying to lighten the otherwise dreadful mood.

Cynthia shook her head, her hair a wet mass like a used mophead. After a long time she smiled and muttered, "Next time *I* get to pick where we go."

That sentence made Adam pause in step for a moment causing him to fall out of line with Cynthia and he had doubled his pace to catch up with her. She looked at him confused at the hesitant smile tugging on his lips.

"Next time, eh?"

"Yeah," Cynthia said confused. "And?"

Adam shook his head. "Nothing. It's just…" His hand had been reaching out and upon touching Cynthia's own he went to hold it. At first it was just his hand over hers but she then laced her fingers between his and held it tight.

"What?" she asked him.

"I guess I'm just glad you want there to be a next time."

Cynthia said nothing, her eyes falling forward.

"Hey," he said giving her hand a squeeze. "I'm sorry. For what it's worth whether we get off this island or not, I want you to know that. You don't have to accept it and I don't expect you to. I just want you to know I'm sorry, Cynth."

She stared at him for a long time, her gaze only breaking when they thought they found a good hiding spot and began to sift through the damp leaves and vines. For several minutes Adam didn't think she was going to say anything at all and even told himself to not expect her to. He had said some terrible things to her out of anger, whether she truly meant the prospect of divorce or not still a painful thing to consider. He even went so far as to consider that they were only feeling this way because of the real danger they were in, and that everything could end up being exactly as it had been before coming to Isla Bonidada should they survive this trip.

Still, he meant what he said and he hoped that she believed him. He also hoped deep down inside, that even after they survive this whole thing, that they could somehow work it out. That they could process this whole nightmare together, because if Adam had to deal with it himself... he didn't know if he had the strength to do it.

At last as they were looking through some transferred plots of large ferns, Cynthia said, "I'm sorry too, Adam."

He turned his face towards her, saw it coming towards him and he received her kiss with he same tenderness and love as he could muster. When they came away from each other the two chuckled slightly and began rubbing their noses together as they used to whenever they caught each other staring at each other after a kiss.

"We better make sure we get off the island then," said Adam.

They searched for a little longer, and at a hollowed out stump, Adam had started for it thinking it another potentially empty but worthy place to check for a hiding spot. Upon coming close he had sworn and gagged as he pulled away from the hole he was looking into. He wouldn't let Cynthia look, but Derian ducked his head under and swore. Inside, illuminated like Halloween decorations in the beam of his flashlight, were bones. Two human skulls were visible among the femurs and ribs, and one dog or some other animal. A pile of clothes were nearby, some bloody, some messily washed.

"Christ," he muttered to himself brought himself out to take another big gulp of breath. Cynthia watched him fretfully as he stuck his head back in only to come back out shaking his head in disgust.

"It's a mass grave in there," he told her. "But the body isn't in there."

"Are you sure?" asked Cynthia.

"Yes," said Adam, and he wasn't about to go back in there to check a third time.

"Should we tell the others?"

"If we see them, sure, but not right now. Let's look around a bit, it can't be far."

After a few minutes of searching around, it was declared that the Manananggal had not hidden it's lower body with it's feeding area. After a while, the while group had all began to lose hope. Maybe the Manananggal had not come here after all, and Kyra and Amos had been mistaken. It had hidden it's body somewhere else, and now they were wandering in the dark, helpless and defenseless.

Finally, it was Winnifred who had stumbled upon it. It had been the smell that had caught her attention. For so long the smell of salty rain and hibiscus flowers had been the only thing the group could smell, but then Winnifred had come across something sweet-smelling and yet gross, like leftover pork left out overnight. It was behind one of the trees closer to the rear of the cavern which led out to a cliffside that was blocked by a guardrail so tourists can take in the view of the sea beyond. There was nothing to see out there beyond the dark, save for how vast and violent the ocean had become with each crash of lightning in the distance. When she first saw it, Winnifred thought it was a survivor hiding beneath the tree, until she moved in closer and when she parted the limbs that obscured her view, she saw that the legs ended at the hips and she screamed for her husband who was ten feet away inspecting some more foliage.

"HERE! HERE! I FOUND IT!"

Cain was obviously the first to arrive, and then one by one they all gathered around the lower torso of the Manananggal with grim expressions. Some were staring at the perfectly normal-looking legs, some were staring at the severed flesh and protruding spine at the top. What only Adam noticed was when a bug, a beetle of some sort, was crawling over the body, it had gone to the top where the stench of blood and meat was emanating. Once it reached the top however, feeling it with it's antennae, it had fallen over and rolled off the body where it landed beside it dead. Whatever prevented the lower half of the body from decaying without the rest of it, clearly protected it from wildlife as well.

"What do we do now?" asked Cain to Joshua who was looking green at the sight of the lower body. The kid shuddered and swallowed, and then approached the body, stooping to a crouch before it and looking like he was going to throw up.

He took the jar containing the mixture of salt, sugar, and garlic. The others had jars of their own, but he figured one would be enough at least for the lower body. If he was wrong, he was wrong, and they would apply as much as necessary in order to put an end to this nightmare. As for the legend, he hoped and prayed that he was right, and that he had not made a mistake or anyone else who had faced such a monster before him. He hoped it was not some superstition as he once believed, and prayed that they were doing the right thing now.

With a muttered prayer, he tilted the jar towards the top of the body, with everyone watching with bated breaths.

The moment the powdery slur touched the upper body, it sizzled and bubbled, with smoke coming from the spots as if he had touched it with hot wax or a hot metal poker. He poured it until he was about near the spine when he ran out, and he asked for another. By then, Derian had already come in with his own jar and applied his own. Together they poured the mixture all over the upper body until they covered the entire section where the Manananggal would normally reattach itself.

By then, in the distance, over the thunder and rain, came a screeching sound so horrible that everyone turned towards it's direction where the lights coming through the windows of the Bonidada Resort stood like orbs in the black. The horrible sound went on forever it seemed, until just as quickly it died down as if someone had flicked a switch and ended the screams of a loudspeaker siren.

"Did we do it?" asked Winnifred breathlessly. "Is it dead?"

"I don't know," said Joshua. "I just don't know…"

"What do we do then?" asked Derian. "Go back?"

"We can't stay here," said Adam taking up Cynthia's hand again for both comfort and to comfort her as well. "Let's head back, keep an eye out, and lock ourselves up with Kyra like planned. Hopefully Amos and the others are alive still."

"And if they aren't?" asked Cain and everyone winced at the thought.

"Then we help him finish the job," said Cynthia taking up Adam's hesitation. "Whatever it takes."

Forty-One

Victoria Jackson had fled the ballroom the moment she had gotten free of the monster. Whatever was to happen be it the will of some cruel god or fate was of little importance to her. The fire in her belly fueled her desire to live, and so she fled for her own sake, Amos Mulderich being a faraway thing of little concern in the heat of this dreadful moment.

She ran down the hall, not knowing which hall she was in nor where she was going. She was sobbing bitterly, her hands hugging her belly as she staggered almost drunkenly out into the hall. She tried the first door and when it refused to open she wailed miserably before staggering off to the next, and then the next.

In her terrified stupor, all Victoria could see was that wretched face, smell that tainted breath of death, feel that loathsome tongue that contaminated her skin. None of this should have happened; She never should have agreed to go with Amos and Frantz- She shouldn't even have stayed behind when her husband began to flee. As she finally came across a restroom, she gasped out with immense relief as she threw her shoulder into it and stepped inside.

She stopped dead in her tracks, terrified by what she saw and covering her mouth in order to stifle the scream that tried to escape her.

There was a Bonidada employee lying prone on the bathroom floor. She looked like a hula dancer or one of the actresses from one of the dinner's events. She was face down on the ground in a pool of blood, the back of her head opened and speckled with bloodied gray matter. There was blood spatter on the bathroom counter and some skull fragments on the stalls directly behind her. Looking between the counter and the gun that was clutched in a death grip in the woman's right hand, Victoria registered the suicide and proceeded to vomit in the nearby trash can. When she was done wiping bile from her mouth, she heard a terrible shrill scream in the resort and covering her ears she slid down to the floor with her back to the bathroom door with her face pinched in a terrified expression of terror and grief. Had Amos been killed and it was roaring in victory?

I want this to end! I want this to end! I want this to FUCKING end!

She shouldn't be here. She never should have been here in the first place, but she didn't deserve to be stuck here still. As horrible of a man in both their life before this whole thing and during, Paul was right. They needed to just get out of here, and she should have left with him when she had the chance. She sobbed for herself, sobbed and cried for being such an idiot and putting herself in danger. Screw Amos and screw everyone and everything, she was not going back to deal with that *thing* again! If there was no way off the island, then she would hide somewhere rain or shine until help arrived. Someone had to, right? This nightmare had to end soon, right?

She looked at the dead woman. She shook her head in disbelief. How many guns did they have on this island and how in the world in the midst of the shooting and the monstrosity that followed, did this woman managed to not only find a pistol but take the chance to take her own life? Victoria had to give the victim one piece of credit, she was certainly onto something.

When the shrill screams of the monster died at last, Victoria removed her hands from her ears listening intently. It had to be searching for her now. Could it catch her scent like a bloodhound? Scared out of her mind, Victoria dropped to all fours and began to crawl over to the dead woman. She placed her hand on the gun, nearly puked again at the touch of the cold hand still grasping it, and whimpering like a child touching something absolutely revolting she began to peel the fingers away from the gun. She didn't know what the weapon was nor did she know how to use it, but she wasn't going to take the chance of just waiting for that monster to come and get her.

She was onto something...

She finally managed to wriggle the gun free from the woman's grasp. It was difficult but now Victoria clutched it tightly in her hands. She skirted around the body to the other side of the restroom and using the untainted side of the counter for support, pulled herself up to her feet. The weapon felt lighter than she had expected, and looking over it she felt repulsed to even be carrying it. Still, it didn't look too difficult to use and if this random girl who probably spoke no English was able to use it, why couldn't she?

She looked up and stared at herself in the mirror, nearly gasping at the sight that beheld her. She was way beyond her prime she understood, but the state that she was in made her feel so alien to look at herself. Her makeup was smeared, her clothes filthy and stained bloody. But it was Victoria's eyes that made her feel so alienated. They were not the eyes she was used to looking back at her through the mirror with the confidence of one who would say, 'Go get 'em!' whomever 'em' might be.

Now those eyes which had seen horrors unimaginable stared blank and dead back at Victoria, as if to say, 'What now?'

What now, indeed...

She started to lift the gun, wondering how it would feel should she put the barrel into her mouth as the woman no doubt had. On there barrel she thought she saw blood but then wondered if it was lipstick. She looked down at the body, thought of looking at her lips, and decided against it. She started to lift it up more.

Just don't think of it like a gun, she told herself as she trembled violently. *Think of it as a popsicle, a cock, anything except a gun.*

The tip of the barrel poked her lips. She moistened them, opened her mouth wider and then-

Tiktik-ka-tiktik-ka-tiktik...

Victoria whirled around staring wide-eyed at the bathroom door. That horrible sound had jolted her out of her almost hypnotic movement and she stood rigid near the counter clutching the weapon now with both hands in a clumsy sort of grip common to those unfamiliar with firearms. That thing was now out there, no doubt looking for her. Swallowing a large lump that had materialized hard and dry in her throat, Victoria pointed the weapon at the door. Her trembling had gotten so bad that the barrel was bouncing in her blurry vision. Sweat collected on her brow and she felt her bladder swelling and threatening to burst.

Oh god, oh god...

At last her bladder did go, when she heard the voice of Amos Mulderich, singing. Singing in a language that Victoria didn't understand.

"¿A donde irá… Veloz y fatigada…La golondrina que de aquí se va?"

It was so uncanny and so close that Victoria didn't even realize she had peed herself. The smell of urine wafted before her nose, causing her eyes to water which she mistook for fear. There was something about the way Amos spoke,

(What was that? Spanish?)

made Victoria feel that it wasn't a person speaking them, let alone the goddamn counselor. His voice was highly pitched, warbled almost, broken up by a series of giggles that echoed, which while combined with that dreadful ticking sound, made Victoria conjure the ridiculous image of a maniac laughing as he worked on a ticking time bomb.

"Por si en el viento… Se hallara extraviada- Hehe, Buscando Abrigo, y no lo encontrará!" Insane howling filled the halls on the other side of the bathroom door, the sound louder than ever before. Victoria now envisioned Amos twirling around in the hall just outside, the whip the kid had given him spinning about him like a ballerina's wand.

Had Amos killed the Manananggal or had simply gotten away? The ticking meant he hadn't, but the way he sounded so bold, insane, made Victoria wonder what exactly happened. She felt it her duty to go out there, to ask him what was going on, but that laughter made her sick to her stomach, so distrusting of the man who promised to protect them all, that she remained frozen in place. Frozen, save for the wavering gun before her.

Her heart stopped when a series of loud banging's came upon the bathroom door. Removing her left hand from the weapon, Victoria covered her mouth to hold back the scream that nearly escaped her. Tears proceeded to roll down her cheeks at a feverish rate. For some reason her mind went not to her husband whom she wished she was with right now, but with Winnifred Ashton. All at once Victoria wished she could have apologized better to the woman, and prayed that should she get out of this she never take someone for granted again.

"Mrs. Jackson?" Amos called out from the other side. He giggled, hiccupped, and then called her name again. "Are you in there?"

He knows! her mind proceeded to blare out like an ongoing alarm. *He knows! He knows! He knows!*

"Victoria?" Amos called in again. "May I come in?"

"No," Victoria moaned into her mouth, the word lost to everything beyond her own ears or so she thought. When nothing happened at first she actually believed she had managed to stop the word from reaching the man on the other side.

"Why not?" asked Amos sounding concerned but then he began to giggle. "C'mon, I just wanna show you something..."

"Go away," Victoria said lowering her hand. Her voice sounded so cracked and so hoarse she felt pathetic upon saying so. Nevertheless her terror willed her to add, "I got a gun!"

"A gun! What fun!" Amos began to laugh at his own little rhyme.

"Mr. Mulderich," Victoria called out. "What's going on with you?"

"Nothing! Nothing, nothing at all! A little lightheaded but I feel great!"

"Where's the monster?" Victoria demanded. She felt her head slowly turning as if invisible hands were forcing her to do so. She tried to keep her eyes on the bathroom door but then relented when she finally thought of something she hadn't considered before. Behind her on the wall opposite of the bathroom entrance was one of those hatch windows, the long ones about six inches wide. Too thin for her to escape through, but perhaps not so thin for-

She turned around violently, her back slamming into the stalls to her right. Now with her back to them she could see both the window and the bathroom door. She kept the gun pointed at the door but found herself constantly glancing towards the window which was now speckled with rainwater. A flash of lightning illuminated the glass outside and two seconds later a rolling thunder shook the resort.

Perhaps finding this funny, Amos suddenly brayed out more insane laughter. "I'm coming in, Mrs. Jackson, I need to show you this!"

"Don't!" Victoria begged. She was shaking so hard now she doubt she would be able to shoot the door let alone the man if he forced his way in. She should have barricaded the door with something, somehow...

"Ready or not," Amos said in a singsong voice. "Here... I... come..."

The door swung inwardly slowly, deliberately. Amos' face poked through the crack, a wide grin stretched across his face in a painful grimace. Around his cheeks and across his forehead and chin were deep indents cut into his face. It reminded Victoria of how a shark's bite looked upon a surf board after an attack, or a victim who barely managed to escape.

"Here's Johnny!" Amos chuckled and he shouldered the door open the rest of the way. Victoria screamed and the gun went off, momentarily blinding her and causing her ears to ring. Amos was still standing and much to her horror, she was able to see what exactly he wanted to show her.

His belly had been ripped open entirely, his entrails dangling before him like a gory apron all the way down to his knees. Thick ropes of gray all lumped and coiled and dripping blood and pus. In his hand was the sting ray whip, which he brandished like some cowboy with a bray of more insane laughter, the bite marks on his face spreading and causing his skin to split in some areas.

Victoria screamed, her hands tightening claw-like around the pistol. The gun went off several times, the explosions that followed just as deafening and kicked violently in her hands which would have dropped it if Victoria wasn't so stricken with horror and disgust. Holes erupted in the bathroom door and the adjacent wall around the gutted man but nothing struck him. Perhaps laughing at her bad aim or just by the sound of the gun, Amos started for Victoria, his whipping arm raised and ready to strike. As he approached Victoria saw in the flash of the gun that the man's eyes had a red sheen to them, and the terrible grin he wore was decorated with a pair of elongated canines which made his once handsome features monstrous.

Victoria screamed. Amos brayed a victorious laugh. The gun went off once more as he fell upon her.

What perhaps saved her life happened in the mere seconds as Amos struck out with the sting ray whip. The tip of the whip had been caught in the bathroom door as it began to close, the metal closer having snatched it as it had come over the frame. When Amos struck out the whip did not go where he was aiming, and as a result his arm was yanked upward and his body turned just enough so that at the moment the gun went off, a bloody hole erupted in the man's side. He let loose a surprised gasp as he released the whip while collapsing to the floor, but the smile still remained.

Victoria screamed again pointing the gun at Amos and still squeezing the trigger. But she had exhausted all the ammunition from the weapon and she couldn't hear the faint clicking over the constant ringing of her ears. Blue gun smoke wafted across the ceiling leaving an acrid smell in her nostrils which eventually got her to stop. She sat there still clutching the gun with tears streaking her face while Amos laid on his side right beside the dead dancer clutching at his side and chuckling weakly.

"Ow… ow…"

"Oh, god…" Victoria groaned as she tried to get to her feet. Her legs felt like rubber and her knees so wobbly that she actually collapsed onto the body of the employee, much to Amos' gleeful laughter.

He then lunged for her suddenly, his hands reaching for her throat and grasping her tightly. His thumbs drove into her jugular, cutting off her airway and causing her eyes to bulge out as he straddled her to pin her down.

"GOTCHA!" he practically screamed in her face, his spittle falling like scattered rain upon her brow and cheeks. "GOTCHAGOTCHAGOTCHA!"

And over his heinous screaming, the Manananggal's call was heard by Victoria's ringing ears.

Tiktik-ka-tiktik-ka-tiktik...

Forty-Two

At the sound of the dreadful ticking, Victoria howled like a banshee, throwing her hips up in desperation to get Amos off of her and cease his strangulation.

Amos was giggling manically now, seeming to adjust himself in order to avoid getting thrown off while at the same time continuing to ride Victoria as if she were some ride one would see in front of a supermarket. "Yee-haw!" he cried out over and over again which only made Victoria double her efforts to try and throw him off.

Victoria could feel the erection on Amos Mulderich and her revulsion and terror of the beast no doubt coming for her now made her fight all the harder. Never in her life had she felt so scared and so desperate that the insane idea that she was going to be raped before she was eaten or worse, turned into what Amos was now, made her thrash like a caught fish. She used her nails to claw at Amos who only laughed even as she dug great furrows in his cheeks to accompany the bite marks. She used the pistol's grip and smacked it against Amos' head as well to try to throw him off and although he appeared dizzy, the pressure on her windpipe never ceased. All the while the ticking persisted somewhere in the resort.

Tiktik-ka-tiktik-ka-tiktik…

tik…

tik…

"She's coming!" Amos sang his eyes wide and mad and consuming. "She's coming!"

Victoria continued to gurgle in a way of screaming and continued to bludgeon the side of Amos' face. His cheek and temple split revealing the bloody flesh underneath and at one point it had split further revealing the dented bone underneath. Even as his blood began to speckle her face she did not stop hitting him, nor would she until she was freed of this man who until he had been turned into some sort of monster would never have harmed her like this. Black stars danced across her vision and little by little the ticking sound began to fade as she went in and out of consciousness.

The moment she felt Amos' grip slacken however, she only doubled her efforts, bucking and striking at him until at last, the hands came away from her throat and Amos upon getting smacked across the head once more, tottered and would have fallen over to his side on his own if not for Victoria bucking him off one more time. He collapsed and Victoria kicked at him to get herself as far away from him as possible all the while coughing and clinging to her throat. She watched him distrustingly as he laid there with labored breath and blood leaking from the side of his head. With a whimpered cry she began to crawl past him towards the door and she nearly screamed as she felt his hand grasp her ankle. She kicked out, her other foot connecting with his face and breaking his nose with a loud snapping sound. He let go immediately and she practically fell into the hallway. She scrambled to her feet using the wall for support and there she proceeded to run, run as far away from the women's restroom as possible and further still from Amos Mulderich who at his point was now bleeding out from his wounds next to his dead employee.

Breathing was difficult, her breath wheezing through her crushed windpipe as she ran. She nearly fell over several times but managed to push on until she reached the reception area. From there Victoria kept on running, right out the front doors and into the storm.

The wind made it difficult for her to run. Every strange noise caused by the wind caused her to cry out loud and turn her head to and fro like a frightened rabbit. Her clothes were soaked completely through and she was cold and miserable. She was heading in the direction of the bunks used by the employees who had once worked at this resort, but were now lying in heaps in the very resort she had fled. Screw them as well. Paul was right; it was time to just run and hide. If he had gotten out, if Victoria ever saw him again, then she would run and collapse to his feet and beg for his forgiveness. She would be a proper wife, and let go of her sins for the sake of him. She would treasure him, as she should have long ago, and would remain by his side as she should have when he suggested they should all leave.

She would do anything, as long as she could get out of here. As long as she could *live*.

Something struck Victoria in the side of her ribs, shoving her right off the path and into the underbrush. Wet leaves and sharp rocks ravished her until she came to a stop, and what had tackled her was now on top. A flash of lightning had arced across the sky, and Victoria caught the silhouette of the monster that had threatened to kill her in the resort. It banked around and as Victoria now sobbing tried to get up, she was immediately pinned to the ground like a rabbit caught in the talons of an owl.

She began to blubber incoherently, begging for the monster to let her go. To not hurt her and "Please, I don't wanna die! I don't wanna die!"

She felt herself turned over again, flipped right onto her back as if she weight nothing. The monster was now over her now, her claws pinning Victoria's wrists to the ground while the writhing entrails coiled around her legs like tentacles and pinned them likewise. The large bat-like wings stuck out on either side of them, assisting the Manananggal to keep her balance. Victoria's lips quivered, her voice completely gone in the face of pure evil.

"Please," she begged it, her eyes darting between those horrible shark-like teeth, and the just as bad if not worse crimson eyes. "Don't kill me… please…"

The monster regarded her for a long time. The rain dripping from it's mess of black hair and all the way down it's crooked chin. Lightning flashed over head and in the light Victoria could see her reflection in those terrible red eyes and see that her fear-stricken face appeared upside down. This detail while seeming so insignificant and lacking of importance, was all that helped Victoria cling to whatever hope of survival she had left, as well as whatever sanity she still had control of.

It seemed that the monster was indecisive for a moment. But then it grinned, a hideously amused smile at Victoria who could only pray now that it would be over soon. It opened it's mouth large and wide, and inside it's maw Victoria could see how many rows of triangular teeth was inside. The tongue writhed inside like an agitated worm, and Victoria

(Is that a bird?)

opened her mouth to scream but then something covered her mouth and went into her throat. The monster had pressed it's mouth against hers, it's teeth sawing through her lips and causing her to bleed. What had gone into her throat was no doubt that horrible tongue that touched her, and she squirmed and kicked until she finally just laid still and accepted it. Like she had let Paul just so he would stop nagging her, she just let go and let the Manananggal have it's way with her. She just let go, and slipped into a dark, but comforting void.

Forty-Three

The group was coming down the pathway from the grotto, keeping their eyes to the sky as best they could but they were all blinking away the stinging rain and resorted to just pushing forward. They would return to the resort and go from there.

The closer they got to the resort, more static came in through the radio. Kyra was trying to call them and so Derian tried to answer back, but all that was passed between them was more static. So, they all picked up their pace and pushed on to the best of their ability. All around them the tropical jungle of the island was in disarray and chaos from the storm, causing all of them to glance nervously about worse than they were on their way to the grotto. Cain Ashton in particular who had been drafted in Vietnam before he had come home and took up lessons under Amway to build his own business, felt like he was in hostile territory again. He often glanced from side to side, wondering if he would meet the eyes of some charlie before he got blown to smithereens. That of course never happened, he had been one of the lucky ones.

But there were many jungles in the world, and not all jungles could be traversed safely.

They suddenly all froze as they heard something they all recognized despite the thunder and the rain and the crashing of the waves a distance away. A horrible ticking sound, which made their blood run cold and created sweat despite how chilled the air was. Their hearts were all hammering in their chests and Cain in particular felt a pain in his left arm. He clutched at it without even realizing it was in pain, his expression grim with terror.

"We gotta hurry," he said to the others. It felt necessary to say something.

"No shit," said Elbi breathlessly, and they all hurried as the loathsome calling of the Mananangal proceeded to fade in and out as if someone were testing the volume on a broken stereo.

His wife appeared beside him and took up his hand. Winnifred knew the look on Cain's face all too well, having seen plenty of it on his return. He had been so young back then and so had she. He had come home an old man in a young one's body. He never spoke of the things he had seen nor what he had done, even when he had night terrors which left him crying helplessly like a baby into the wee hours of the morning. He looked at her and she smiled encouragingly. He smiled back, grateful for the comfort she was still willing to provide even in the midst of their danger.

He leaned forward and kissed her, his own way of telling her that he would be okay. He said nothing as he quickened his pace, causing her to do the same.

Every shift of the leaves of the palms or the rustle across the grounds nearby caused the group to lose their nerve, the winds making it absolutely impossible to accurately locate a sound or shift in movement. Flapping leaves sounded like flapping wings, the rattling of coconuts sounded like the ticking calling of the Mananangal. Everyone was on edge and despite their efforts to keep their eyes on the skies, they saw only darkness and got droplets of stinging rain striking down upon them. All felt helpless and lost in the dark, like rodents to a hunting owl. Every single one of these survivors feared they would be snatched up into the night never to be seen again, and face a horrific end.

Adam squeezed Cynthia's hand. She squeezed back. "It's gonna be all right," he said eyes darting to and fro.

"All right," Cynthia repeated fretfully.

"Shh," someone told them. It was Derian, whose wife clung to his arm like her life depended on it.

The resort came into view at last through the haze of the gloom. Lightning flashed and several seconds later a great boom sounded in the distance. The storm would be passing soon, and Winnifred wondered just how large the storm was and if such a storm was even possible. This had been going on literally since last night and never seemed to let up until now. Constant rain was one thing, but it felt like the storm just hovered over the island with no intention of moving on until now.

Maybe it's the monster, she thought tiredly. *Maybe it controls the weather.*

Still, there was no denying that the storm was slowly but surely subsiding. They were back on the path now, which was littered with debris from the storm. A palm tree had been knocked over and it's head rested on the path like a pillow. More of the front window that the monster had smashed through was missing now from the constant pommeling of the wind. Everyone picked up their pace, their terror and caution breaking just momentarily for the relief to settle in like a soothing ache.

"We made it," Cain Ashton was telling himself. His voice was hollow to the ears of many, but welcoming to say the least. "We-"

Something struck him with the force of a bullet train in the square of his back. He was then grabbed underneath his armpits and *yanked* into the air with a strangled cry as if the words were remaining on the ground while being dragged out of him. His grip had tightened around Winnifred's hand and he had nearly yanked her arm out of it's socket. At the last moment he let go, allowing her to drop crying out his name to the ground as he was lifted into the sky. Everyone turned with a collective and startled gasp and watched as a large shadow went higher and higher into the air as Cain's screams howled with the wind. At nearly fifty feet up, it was impossible to see what was happening up there. A shriller cry sounded from above at last Cain came flailing back down, his arms and legs flapping uselessly in the winds. Everyone stared in horror mouths covered as Cain came crashing into some nearby rocks head-first. His skull cracked and ruptured, his neck and spine collapsing like an accordion, sticking at odd angles as he crumpled to the ground dead. He was on his now mangled back, his head now leaking his brains and his eyes stared doll-like into the rain which pattered against them. Winnifred let loose a choked scream as she fell to her knees. She was sobbing hysterically as she attempted to crawl towards her husband dead husband.

Elbi Delgado had attempted to pull Winnifred to her feet but she fought him, shoving and kicking at him like a kid throwing a tantrum as she reached for her dead husband. He had gone through Napalm storms and gunfights in the midst of jungles ladened with traps- He did not survive all of that for *this* and why couldn't Elbi understand that and just-

"Let me go!" she wailed as she struck him across the side of the head with a balled fist.

This caused enough of a distraction for the Manananggal to move in close. The movement was so fast it was almost like a blur. Sharp talons drove into Elbi's right shoulder and with her probiscis-like tongue, drove it like a jackhammer into his right ear and deeper still into his brain matter. As the man twitched and convulsed like a puppet being controlled, the Manananggal turned her talons on Winnifred, grabbing her by the head and as the old woman screamed all the more, it twisted and wrenched the head free from it's shoulders, holding it in-between it's taloned hands with tatters of flesh and arteries spewing blood beneath. It turned to the horrified group who hadn't fled yet, frozen in terror by how quick and how brutal the attack had been. With Elbi still on her tongue it proceeded to make his body sway to and fro almost drunkenly beside her, and she gestured with Winnifred's head towards them as if to ask if they wanted it. That horrible smile of gleeful bloodlust shark-like and monstrous finally broke them free of their paralysis as they all turned and fled with all their might back to the resort.

"AH!" Cynthia screamed, her foot having been caught on the head of the palm. She crashed onto the wet pathway, scraping up her hands and wrists to the point of bleeding and Adam yanked her hard by the arms to her feet before she stumbled again. Steadying her he half-carried her right after the others who were already reaching the glass doors.

Derian Anderson purposefully waited near the entrance while the others ran inside. He waved for Adam and Cynthia to hurry because he saw the Manananggal coming for them fast, having left Elbi and Winnifred's body behind to catch up with them. As soon as the Whites passed through the doors he shut it behind them, securing the handles together with a nearby fallen sign reporting falling coconuts. When Carla realized her husband wasn't with them, she tried to go out but the doors held firm as Derian turned and aimed his weapon at the Manananggal coming in hot upon him. It ignored the flare of bullets he sent and as it crashed into him, he had whipped out the carving knife he had taken from the kitchens and plunged it into her right eye as her weight caused the glass behind him to crackle.

"Derian!" Carla screamed trying to get the door open. Her husband's back smashed against the glass again and above his head which whipped from side to side as the Manananggal thrashed him, black smoke belched from the wound he had planted in it's eye. The monster then roared and then took flight, shooting straight upwards and taking Derian with her. They passed the broken window above the doors and disappeared from sight. Carla who was still screaming was dragged away from the doors as her tears mixed with the rain still on her face.

They all got away from the doors, but the danger they were in was not over. Adam had been looking back and saw a shadow and then something came sailing through the broken window and over their heads, causing them to dug as some shards of caught glass sprinkled them.

Derian Anderson's body crashed into he reception desk, the furniture which was hard as a rock having snapped his back upon impact. But Derian didn't feel the pain of being thrown at the desk. In fact he didn't feel anything anymore. The front of his shirt was ruined and covered in blood, and the front of his face-

"NO!" Carla screamed as Adam tried to hold her back. "DERIAN!"

His face was gone. The entire front of his head was missing, even the lower jaw. The Manananggal while tossing Derian around in the sky outside, had managed to lock her jaws underneath his and on the top of his head. She had bitten down with enough force to slice cleanly through the bone and the front matter of his brain. Great torrents of blood waterfalled down Derian's ruined front, whatever brain he had left in his cleaved skull sliding out grotesquely with the front having been sliced clean through.

Someone cried. Someone was whimpering. Someone else screamed and they all turned and saw the monster there again, perched upon the broken window like a demonic crow, her entrails and black hair wavering as if she were underwater, her face a bloody mask as she grinned at them with those horrible, monstrous teeth.

The teeth came apart and chittered together like a bat's, and the horrible sound which had plagued the group for so long, came out so quietly that no one could hear it. Even if it was as loud as it should have been, no one would hear it over their thudding hearts and Carla's despairing wails.

Forty-Four

"Run," Adam said pulling on Carla with whatever strength he had left and he screamed louder to all the others, "FUCKING RUN!"

Like sheep fleeing a wolf the group fled. They rushed passed the destroyed desk and Derian Ashton. Adam was practically dragging Carla away but she thankfully did not rush for her dead husband. The Manananggal released a hellish screech and gave chase after them as they turned the corner and rushed down the hall.

Kyra was sticking out of the security room, waving them over with a nightstick she had taken to arm herself. She had been trying to warn them about what had happened to Amos and Victoria but upon seeing the Manananggal banking around using it's claws to make a sharp turn into the hallway, she waved her nightstick with greater desperation.

"Run!" she cried out with a terror-stricken face. If she could turn white with fright, she would have done so now.

Adam dared to look back and he stopped dead in his tracks when he saw they were missing one more person. Joshua had stopped running and now stood facing the incoming monster while drawing his bolos knife.

"Josh!" he cried out rushing for him. Cynthia made to grab at him to stop him but she just barely missed him.

With the knife out, Joshua squared up with the monster who was taking flight again and rushing straight towards him, her talons outstretched and tongue reaching past her monstrous maw. He shouted something incoherent and the Manananggal banked towards his left and came in fast and hard, striking at the boy with her talons and sending him crashing to the nearby wall. He was on the ground with four deep gashes across the side of his torso. She was upon him now, maw widening as her tongue writhed and that was when Adam charged in. She saw him coming and tried to buffet the air around her with her wing to slow him down. He threw his shoulder into the membranous wing and crash his full weight upon the monster. He stood up fast having knocked it to it's side and grasped at the writhing entrails. They slid in his grasp and made disgusting squishing sounds as he tightened his grip and then suddenly the Manananggal launched herself with a great flap of her wings. The force of which took Adam up with her as she smacked the ceiling with her back and immediately began to twist and swing her body around and him with it, causing him to smack against the opposite wall.

The air was knocked out of him as his head smacked against the wall. The monster was coming for him now but Joshua was already up again, his bolos clutched tightly in both hands and he made a rush for the space between the Manananggal's wings. She heard him coming, but it was too slow to react.

The bolos drove deep into the monster's back. Those who were rushing in to Adam and Joshua's aid were surprised to hear the Manananggal's horrible screech of pain, something that they had not believed possible given how many times she had been shot or stabbed with kitchenware. Her back arched and her wings stood straight out convulsively as she turned away from Adam, trying to reach for Joshua who was forced to dance around her, his legs becoming entangled in the writhing intestines who reached for them. Joshua twisted the knife, his face becoming spattered with a torrent of blood pissing from where the bolos had carved into the monster's back.

It was flapping it's wings feverishly, desperately, it's body suddenly turning away and rolling across the floor like a fish in order to get him off. When Joshua's grip finally failed him and he was knocked to the ground, the Manananggal lunged for him and snapped at him with her jaws as he scrambled to his feet. He was shouting verses of prayer in Tagalog, the different language echoing over the snarls and hisses of outrage only sounding more and more foreboding as Adam started to rise again. Cynthia had rushed for him, helped him to his feet. He spotted the bolos knife which had come free of the monster's back during the struggle and he started for it

"No!" Cynthia tried to hold him back but he slipped from her grasp and made a beeline for the weapon. He scooped it up and hurried for the two with the Manananggal's back facing him.

Joshua gave no indication that he saw Adam coming in from behind, and instead continued to back up as the Manananggal stalked him, hissing and wavering her loathsome tongue. All the while their gazes remained unbroken from each other, and the prayers coming forth from Joshua's chapped lips weighed heavily on the air as if he were an exorcist rebuking a demon.

"Iligtas mo ako, PANGINOON, mula sa masama; panatilihin mo ako mula sa marahas, mula sa mga nagpaplano ng kasamaan sa kanilang mga puso, na nagpupukaw ng mga salungatan araw-araw, na pinatalas ang kanilang dila tulad ng isang ahas, lason ng mga asps

The Manananggal roared in defiance against the one true God and all things holy, including the persistent boy who had chased her almost halfway across the world. The roar was so violent that Adam could feel it reverberating in his chest as he at last caught up to them. He looped his arms around the great wings, pinning them together and catching the monster by surprise. He felt the intestines reaching and grabbing at his pants but he pushed his weight down onto the creature all the while holding out the bolos to Joshua who noticed immediately rushed in. The Manananggal hissed like a snake and swiped at Joshua with it's claws. Adam pivoted his hips and proceeded to drag the monster to the ground while at the same time he dropped the knife. She thrashed and twisted and as she was reaching for him with her talons she managed to scratch at his face pretty good. At that moment Joshua had grabbed hold of the fallen knife and was rushing in towards them. Then with a final declaration in Tagalog, he brought the knife down upon the monster who let loose another shrill scream perhaps a message of mercy, before the bolos sank into her chest.

Joshua wrenched the knife free, the blood coming out with it being as black as night now and he brought it to her again and again, even as she went to grab at him he managed to stab her several times in the chest and those reaching arms lost their desire to grab and to tear little by little.

At last the Manananggal relaxed, groaning as it's mouth closed and it's writhing tongue laid limp on the hallway floor. It made one last attempt to dig her claws into the floor and pull herself away but it was no good. She had been struck at her weakest point other than the touch of burning sunlight, and she laid there dying in the Bonidada Resort with the boy who had chased her all the way here finally coming out on top. Adam had let go, crabwalking away from it and right into Cynthia who had stooped behind him and tackled him in a hug. Joshua stood over the creature, the blood dripping from his bolos steaming as if hot. His face was completely splattered with gore, and after a long pause, he spat upon the creature definitively.

For good measure, he had sprinkled some of the garlic and salt/sugar paste into the wounds he had inflicted, and the monster moaned and hissed in pain, and in pain she remained until she gave her last breath and died, the black smoke emitting from her wounds finally stopping like a candle whose flame had been snuffed out.

The monster was dead at last. With some help from the others he was helped to his feet. He placed a hand to his face and it came black bloody and his cheeks were now stinging. He wondered if he looked like a cougar had gotten to him and looking at Cynthia, who was worried about the wound be coming infected, could only smile in relief that her husband was okay.

They all joined Joshua then, all of them staring at the dead body of the monstrous woman whose wings were slowly shrinking, seeming to go into the woman's body as the talons retracted as well as the shark teeth in her mouth. The tongue came off completely and shriveled up like a worm in the sun until there was nothing left, and the monster looked more like a regular Filipino woman who had been cut in half and stabbed multiple times for good measure; appearing as if she had been dead for weeks rather than seconds. Her skin turned a sickly shade of gray, and the guts that had been as alive as tentacles, now laid in post mortem from the opened torso looking like dried and cracked worms after the rain ceased. Even Kyra who had suffered a minor stroke during the final attack emerged from the security room, clutching her arm and staring hatefully at the thing lying on the floor.

No one said anything. There was nothing to say.

It was over. They had killed the monster.

It was then that everyone becoming aware that Carla was no longer with them. They all hurried back to the receptionist area where Carla was huddled over the bloody body of Derian Anderson. She was holding him in her arms, sobbing bitterly. No one approached her, all stood around her tired and sore, not knowing that to say or do. Her entire front became smothered in what leaked from her husband, the skull which once held everything he once was seeming to stare back mockingly at her, the brain appearing like a perfectly cut sponge.

Finally, Kyra tried to step forward, her hands extended to the young woman. "Carla, honey, come on now... we can't-"

With a blood-soaked hand, Carla grabbed at Derian's gun and pointed it at Kyra, a savage look in her tearful eyes. The old woman stopped, her hands raised compliantly. Everyone tried to talk to Carla at the same time, but the woman only snapped at everyone to shut up and to leave her alone.

"GO AWAY!" she sobbed and begged. "Get away from me; *all* of you!"

Cynthia tried to approach her, but Adam held her back. The woman had snapped and was grieving, there was no getting through to her, not yet anyway. He suggested they all wait in the hallway for Carla to mourn, and then they would deal with Derian later. They returned to the hall, and were just discussing where to go and what to do now, one of which was to find Amos and the others.

BLAM!

All humans froze and realization dawned on every face. They all hurried to the reception area where only Joshua and Adam approached the desk. When they saw Carla hunched over Derian, the gun still in hand but a bleeding hole in her temple, only Adam remained for Joshua had to back away. He stared blankly at the wall beside the couple, the bloody bits of gray matter that clung to it with some dripping down still. Two more wonderful people he and Cynthia had the pleasure of meeting on this island were now gone.

Now it was just the two of them, Kyra the cook, and Joshua who had followed the Manananggal all the way here and ended up among the few survivors.

It was now 4:26AM, less than an hour until sunrise.

Forty-Five

They found Joshua's whip in the adjacent restroom having noticed the door being propped open by an extended hand covered in blood. With it, they found who owned that arm.

Seeing Amos' body, Kyra started to weep bitterly, having to be led away from the gruesome scene by Cynthia while Adam and Joshua took care of it lying him next to the body of the suicide victim and not taking notice of the bullet holes in the wall and door. Joshua had asked if they should move the bodies elsewhere, but Adam said no. He didn't want to risk moving either of the bodies considering the authorities who would no doubt need to see what happened here, but also didn't want to look at Amos' eviscerated belly anymore than he had already. The guts reminded him too much of the Manananggal.

Joshua nodded numbly, his expression appearing as that of a haunted old man rather than a spry child. The kid had been through a lot, Adam could tell, his whole worldview no doubt having been altered permanently.

I guess all of our worlds have changed, he thought to himself.

When they emerged from the bathroom they saw Kyra and Cynthia waiting for them. They all agreed to go somewhere else, anywhere else, until morning came around and perhaps they can figure out what to do from there. Kyra informed the group that while she had been watching the camera trying to tell everyone what was happening, she did at last manage to get a response from the S.O.S. transmission being sent out. Someone would be out here soon, and that they just needed to wait it out.

Though everyone was delighted by this news, no one was in any mood to celebrate. As they wandered down the hall away from the body of the Manananggal and the horrible scene in the restroom, the women had noticed Joshua's haunted expression as well, as well as the grief that was plain to see as they passed by the bathroom. Everyone knew that he was thinking about Amos, considering how close the two appeared to be prior to the monster attacking them.

"Did he and Amos get close?" Cynthia asked Kyra quietly, the two of them several steps behind Adam and Joshua who were silent in their own afterthoughts.

"Amos was concerned about the boy's health when he arrived," said Kyra. "We all were. I don't think it had anything to do with what Amos himself did. I think the kid just liked him and trusted him more. Given all that he has been through and then some, it's hard to blame him."

As they passed the ballroom whose doors were wide open, Kyra turned to look at the dead bodies still littering the floor. They were far enough away so that they weren't close to a body, but the stench was still lingering and the sight gruesome and sad; pointless even, like all shootings. All the death and for what? To prove some egotistic point or cause chaos. What was worse was that it had opened the door to another terrifying chaos that now only the four of them had survived.

Now it was 5:00AM, and sunrise was soon upon them.

They went out into the reception area to watch the storm slowly fade away. The skies were still gray and windy, but the rain had stopped. As the sun began to peek across the horizon it was easier to see the damage done to the island. More trees had toppled over as well as some power cables. One of the huts in the distance had a roof collapsed, and all across the beach seaweed and other oceanic garbage had washed up on the shore.

They all lingered near the front plot of the resort, Kyra by herself, Joshua standing near the doors hoping to watch the sun rise if he could, and the Whites sitting together with Cynthia's head on Adam's shoulder which had been hurt in the fight with the Manananggal. It had been dislocated, and so had to be put back with some help from the others. They had all suffered minor wounds compared to the rest of the souls on Isla Bonidada, but at last it was finished.

A surprise came to them up the pathway from the jungle in the direction of the grotto. A female figure who looked tattered and bloody. Cynthia recognized who it was immediately as Victoria and they all led her inside the reception area. The poor woman was freezing and had claw marks across her shoulders and back, revealing her close encounter with the demon and yet was otherwise unhurt.

"I passed out," she told them all. "And I... I don't know what happened. I don't know why it didn't kill me..."

Joshua was watching her with keen eyes, never taking them off the woman's face, specifically the eyes.

"Well, you're safe now," said Kyra stroking the young woman's hair. She trembled at the old cook's touch. "It's over, we killed it. Adam and Josh, they did it."

Victoria noticeably relaxed. "Good... I'm ready to go home. I'm so tired and hungry..."

"Want me to get you something to eat?" asked Kyra.

"I can do it," said Joshua standing up. "I got something I need to grab anyway."

"Want company?" asked Adam.

Joshua looked at Victoria, and said "No. Thank you." Then he strolled off without so much as a backwards glance.

"What's that about?" asked Cynthia.

"I don't know…"

Kyra stood and said, "I'm gonna check the HAM. Be right back." She hurried down the hall towards the security room to try her luck for the coast guard again. Outside the wind had died down some more, and in the ravaged palm trees they could see seagulls and parrots slowly daring to come back.

As if they knew it was safe at last, both because the storm had ended, and what had hunted in it was gone forever.

Joshua walked feeling numb aside from the cold fingers of terror creeping across his back as he made his way through the kitchens. The totes of food were right where they had left them, the very same that had tripped Amos and merely delayed his ultimate demise. He passed through entirely and turned up back in the ballroom where the lights had been kept on and the dead remained. He scanned the sea of bodies in search for one in particular. He felt sick and ashamed for what he was planning to do, but he had such a terrible feeling of what Victoria's arrival entailed. Plus the way she wouldn't meet him eye to eye only solidified his concern. What he thought was that if he happened to be wrong, then there would be nothing to be done and no one would be the wiser. The sense of calm

and relief would remain, and they would all wait for help
and at last return to the coast.

He had been thinking about going back to home
but that process had been halted by the arrival of Victoria
who the Manananggal spared. If there was one thing he
knew for certain about the beast, she never spared
anyone. She hadn't spared anyone in the village, and she
certainly wouldn't have here if she could help it. God bless,
she couldn't.

But perhaps she knew that, and took a drastic
measure? If Joshua was right...

He found who he was looking for. Frantz was right
where the monster had left him, his eyes glazed up at the
ceiling. One of the many who would have feed the
Manananggal, and would instead be charioted away back
to the States or wherever else he came from. The
Americans would make sure of that. Just as Joshua had to
make sure that only *humans* got off this island alive. He
stooped over the body, staring into the face of Frantz. He
apologized to the dead man, and then reaching for his
neck, he took the gold crucifix that still hung about it,
snapping the chain and holding it before him like a
hypnotist's watch. He felt no better than a graverobber for
this. He felt like a monster.

"Tao po," he told himself and he stood and
returned to the kitchen to look for something for Victoria
to eat.

She, meanwhile, was not feeling well. There was a
hot churning in her belly, and so she sat feeling miserable
and tired. Not only that, but despite the clouds the sun
that was just about to peek over the horizon felt all too
bright still and so she averted her eyes looking instead at

Cynthia and Adam who were together and whispering amongst themselves. Adam had his upper left arm in a makeshift bandage and blood had soaked through, turning the cloth red. The smell was strong in Victoria's nostrils, and she moaned as the pain in her stomach intensified.

Kyra took notice of this, and sat beside the young woman in order to comfort her. All the while wondering what in the world was taking Joshua so long.

By then, thankfully, Joshua had returned with some fresh fruit from the kitchens. She stood, about to take it from him when he said, "No, it's okay, let me."

She let him go. He stopped before Victoria and offered her the plate of fruit. She thanked him and took a grapefruit as bright as a miniature sun. Though she had thanked him, she had a dead look in her eyes and looking at the fruit, she appeared more sickly than ever.

Kyra was about to join them when Joshua said suddenly, quite harshly, "Kyra, stay back."

"Wait, what?" Kyra asked bewildered. The Whites were taking immediate notice, while Victoria turned those tired-looking, almost soulless eyes upon Joshua who stooped down to her level.

"I need to see something," he said. "Victoria, will you let me?"

"Let you what?" she asked nervously.

"Will you let me check something? You said the monster attacked you, and I want to make sure you are not... not... What is the word?"

Adam frowned. He had stood up, cradling his injured arm. "Infected? You didn't tell us that we could get infected."

"No, no, that isn't the right word," Joshua said thinking. "Nevertheless, I need to make sure of something. Will you let me?"

Victoria crossed her arms protectively over herself. "Depends on what it is…"

"It… It shouldn't hurt. I just want to touch your brow with this." He revealed the crucifix and Victoria stared at it puzzled despite the pain in her stomach intensifying at the very sight of it. She clutched at it as if she were about to vomit.

"Um, do you mean possessed?" asked Cynthia eyeing the cross with skeptic but at the same time uneasy distaste.

"You didn't mention anything like that either," said Adam distrustfully.

"There was no need at the time," said Joshua. "And yes, I have, actually, if you recall my story from my village."

Adam opened his mouth but then closed it almost immediately, the memory returning to him at last.

"All right," said Victoria still appearing dazed. "It cannot hurt…"

Joshua was glad of this. Her willingness meant there was a good chance that all was well, and he would only end up looking foolish for the time being. He thanked her, and then rose up the cross and brought it to her head as she closed her eyes.

But it *did* hurt Victoria. Evidently, it hurt her a lot. The moment the crucifix touched her brow, she screamed and shoved Joshua away, causing him to fall back. She clutched at her forehead and when she pulled her hands away, a blackened shape of a cross smoked on her brow, as if the crucifix had been hot enough to burn her skin.

"What the fuck…" Adam whispered in disbelief. Kyra and Cynthia were stunned into silence, their eyes wide on the smoking mark of Christ.

"Oh no…" said Joshua in despair still on the floor. "It gave you it's soul…"

"What does that mean?" asked Kyra staring at the burnt mark frightened.

"It means that in time, she will become a Manananggal."

"No…" Victoria whispered in terror, her eyes brimming with tears. "No… No!" She began to sob at once now.

Adam had helped Joshua to his feet, staring at Victoria with more distrust than ever. "What are we supposed to do now?" he asked. "Do we…"

He couldn't bear to say it and thankfully he did not need to. They all understood what he was going to ask. Victoria knew too, and she stared first at him for even insinuating the question and then to Joshua who wore a grim expression, and then looked to the women as if seeking support.

"There is a way to save her still," Joshua said at last. "We have time."

"Please!" Victoria pleaded desperately. "I don't want to become… I don't wanna die, I… I can't…"

"We won't let that happen," Adam assured her. Hearing Joshua sound confident filled him with confidence, and he looked to the young man still afraid but willing. "What do we do?"

Joshua looked at Adam squarely and said, "You guys might not like it…"

He told them, and after digesting his words everyone agreed, even Victoria who was willing to do anything to stay alive, and remain human. With that being said, they immediately set off to work.

It was easy to find some rope which was in the supply closet down the hall. With some effort the group finally decided on a beam from one of the gazebos out back, the storm having subsided to a soft groan rather than the violent rage it had expressed throughout the night. After looping the rope around a cloth that was wrapped around each of Victoria's ankles, Adam and Joshua both worked together haul the rope over the makeshift sling and together they managed to lift the young woman off the ground so that she hung upside down. Cynthia assisted by holding Victoria's shoulders so that she wouldn't fall on her head as she was hauled up. Once suspended upside down looking ready for slaughter, Victoria's face had already become red and a dizzy look in her eyes already, she stared at them all. To Cynthia, she looked like a woman about to be sacrificed to some pagan god.

"Now what?" Victoria demanded holding her ruined skirt up so it didn't flop over and expose her nether regions.

"Traditionally, you have boiling water under you," said Joshua. "This is dangerous and so we won't do it if we can help it. We will spin you around and hope you can cough up the spirit. Once we see the spirit, we will have to try to stop it from fleeing and kill it."

"This seems a little too easy..." said Adam.

Kyra laughed. "Easy? We have a girl hung upside down and are going to make her vomit some monster or whatever. This is crazy…"

"Not the craziest thing we've seen tonight though…" Cynthia put in but even she looked doubtful of Joshua's plan.

"Trust me," Joshua said. "There isn't any other way that can save her life." In his mind as well, if they could at least eject the spirit of the monster, even if it got away, at least they would be safe. He could figure out what to do with it later, his priority focused.

"I don't know if I get motion sickness though," said Victoria, which Adam thought was absolutely 'perfect' timing to disclose.

"Does not matter," Joshua assured. "The spirit will not be able to remain in a body that is unstable and in constant motion."

Kyra looked at Cynthia and asked if that made any sense. They both came to the conclusion that it didn't but that didn't matter considering all they've been through.

So, listening to Joshua's instructions, Adam took Victoria by the hips being careful not to grab her in the wrong areas, and began to spin her around. Slowly at first, but gradually Victoria picked up speed, the rope groaning as it twisted around and around with her weight on the other end. Already she was groaning with the rise of nausea. On one occasion Adam wondered if the rope would snap on them. He remembered being a kid and spinning his little sister around on a swing set and while rope was more flexible than chains, eventually, what got wound up would have to unwind, which means Victoria would be spinning in the other direction. When he inquired this thought to Joshua, the young man said it wouldn't matter. As long as they continued to spin her, the spirit would be ejected. The longer this process went on however, the constant spinning one way and then another once the rope needed to unwind, Victoria looked greener and greener, and she began to beg for the torture to stop.

"I'm gonna be sick…" she groaned, her words sounding lost in the constant motion as she spun. "Oh god, I'm…"

"Josh?" Adam asked nervously.

"Keep going," Joshua said almost feverishly. "Don't stop."

So he didn't. Victoria looked on the verge of passing out. By then she had forgotten to hold onto her skirt and it came up, revealing everything underneath but no one paid them any mind. They were all more concerned with what may or may not come out of her. At some point she did start to gag and cough and Kyra in particular had to turn away for she often became nauseous when it came to bodily fluids; if someone close by were to vomit, she would end up in the same boat. The coughing became more violent, and the retching began, spewing bile in every direction as she spun around and around freely, Adam having stepped back the moment it started to happen.

"Holy shit," Adam said sucking in a sharp breath, and they all watched as Victoria actually vomited the spirit of the Manananggal.

It started as a plume of feathers coming out of her mouth wet and tacky. They were as black as coal, and Cynthia stared mouth covered in stark horror as the more Victoria coughed, the more feathers sputtered out. It reminded Adam in particular of cartoons when cats successfully caught a bird and burped up feathers. This however was not in the least bit funny, and neither was when Victoria gagged and coughed out again, this time ejecting a whole bird which fell to the ground covered in saliva and bile. It landed upon the sand and the sand coated it's feathers, to which once it stood it shook them all off and tweeted like a normal bird. Even Kyra who had turned away had looked and was mortified to see what had come out of Victoria Jackson who was left hanging and coughing as if she still had stuff in her throat. The bird began to hop about as it tried to dry it's feathers and no doubt make it's escape.

Joshua stepped in, lifting up his foot above the blackbird and before it could fly away, it released a single defiant squawk as his foot came down hard, crushing the bird flat in a spray of feathers and black blood. He grounded it into the sand and when he lifted his foot away, the bird remained almost buried in the sand, it's brittle bones broken and it's body completely ruptured as a thin whisper of black smoke came out of it. It lingered for a moment, and then the last wind of the terrible storm that blew across the island sent it whisking away like candle smoke. They all stood there for a long time, staring at the dead bird until Victoria begged for someone to cut her down.

"Please…" she groaned spitting out more feathers. "Get me down…"

They turned away from the bizarre scene, eager to occupy themselves with anything. They got her back on the ground, and she joined them in looking down at the bird that had come out of her. She couldn't believe it herself, and forced herself to cough as if she still had a feather or two stuck along her esophagus.

"I don't believe it," Kyra said at last.

"Neither do I," said Adam.

"Is it over then?" asked Cynthia.

Joshua nodded, looking like he had aged ten or twenty years in the span of twenty-four hours. "Yes, I... I think so."

That was when they all became aware of sirens in the distance. The wailing of patrol boats slowly making their way across the wake in response to the SOS's sent out by the Bonidada Resort. They all looked at one another. This should have been a reason for celebration, relief, and yet they all just stared unsure of what they were going to say or how they were going to explain everything.

"How are we going to tell them about the monster?" asked Adam. "They're not going to believe us."

"They'll see the dead for themselves," said Joshua. "Whether they believe us or not, it doesn't matter I think."

"Because it's over..." Adam said as if to hear himself say it, because in his heart he needed to desperately believe that the worst was finally over. Whatever would happen next, was nothing compared to the trials he and Cynthia had managed to overcome, whether by luck or by their actions. He took her hand, and she thankfully took his.

"Well," she said in a soft voice, but a hesitant smile. "That's all right, isn't it?"

Those words filled Adam with so much relief that he threw his arms around his wife. After a momentary surprise, Cynthia embraced him back, both just glad to still be alive.

Kyra Lewis then cleared her throat and said, "I better do most of the talking. Come on, let's get it over with."

"Hey, Joshua," said Adam as he took up his wife's hand again.

"What?" asked the young man.

"When this is over, after the police and all, I owe you a beer."

"I don't drink..."

"I guess we'll see then," said Adam.

And so they all left together, and surrendered themselves to the care of the authorities, and allowed them to be questioned so they could tell their story. As for how their story would be accepted, there was circumstantial evidence given the bodies, as Joshua had said. There was also the cameras to consider, although James Crockett would pay a heavy price to ensure no one got the tapes and even bribe the Mexican Coast Guard to keep a lid on what had happened after the mass shooting. He could accept the shooting as a tragedy, and it would suffer in the business no doubt, but the idea of a monster loose on the island was something he could not tolerate.

In the time that passed since, Kyra Lewis was fired, and so she returned to Florida to live with her brother. Both the Whites and Victoria Jackson would return to their homes respectfully, under the guise that they would not speak of what had happened, and let the authorities figure everything out, including what had happened those who died on Isla Bonidada, and the closure the families may or may not receive.

As for Joshua Ramos, he kept in touch with the Whites as well as Victoria Jackson. He came with them to the United States, and would do everything in his power to move on, and to find his own closure, and leave the past behind and start anew. After all, he was the only one in his village who ever got to see a different country, let alone the United States. It would be a long time before he or any of the survivors would truly forget the horrors experienced on Isla Bonidada.

Because the thing about monsters, is that even when they are long gone and dead, they still linger, and they still haunt those who find sanctuary in the light.

10th Letter

This last letter was not necessary, but I had gotten into the habit of writing again, and I decided I should end this tale on a better note. I had included within an account of what happened on Isla Bonidada, along with these letters. My wife has read over them twice. The first time she had said nothing. The second time, she had spoken to me about them.

She had told me it explained many things, the constant calls from James Crockett every so often, the way I was reluctant to go anywhere outside the United States, specifically on some tropical island or even a cruise. It explained why I had nightmares, and woke up screaming from time to time. But she could not bring herself to believe I had ever seen such a thing. I can't blame her. I doubt I would have believed it either if I hadn't seen it with my own eyes. She tried to disclose it as a suppressed memory, and I suppose that might be true. But in the end, I did believe, and that belief as well as the pain I felt from the loss of my family and friends made me wish to end the suffering once and for all. I had, along with my good friends Victoria Jackson, Kyra Lewis (God bless her soul), and the Whites. I only hope Adam found peace when he finally passed on. I had received a call from his wife, letting me know about his unfortunate passing. My only true regret was that I never took him up on that beer he offered when we had finally gotten to the United States and out of Mexico.

As for my wife, she still doesn't believe it. She says she understands my fear, and what my cultural belief's were as a child, and I suppose that is for the best.

She doesn't have to believe me, she only has to love me, and be there for me when I am at my worst, just as it is my duty to be there for her when she is at her lowest point.

One thing I must confess however, is what I should have accepted long ago. Because in my heart, I know that if I had done something, or even said something, then perhaps all that had happened on Isla Bonidada would not have come to pass. Amos Mulderich would be alive and well. I don't know if things with Mathew Winklemann would have still happened or not, but I do know that if I had done something back at the village, then perhaps the Manananggal wouldn't have made it off the island and escaped my grasp.

I remember it being one of the many long nights that had passed since the passing of my mother as well as the shaman. We were all doing constant searches around the island, looking for any other hideouts the Manananggal might have used. We have used coconut oil to search houses, to see if the monster was hiding in plain sight and using the bodies of one of the victims to hide, but we had found nothing. Up the river from where the village was, me and one other had been searching along the cliffs, and we had found a couple of caves that housed the giant bats that often hunted in the area. We had looked all around, and we had found many human bones throughout all of them. Many, many bones, from years and years. We knew we had stumbled upon one of the hideouts, and what we had discovered in the rear of the final cave still burns into my memory and has filled me with so much dread I cannot even comprehend it as I write this.

We had found fresh bodies, fresh dead, children mostly, killed and partially devoured. It was close to night, and our torches casted ghostly shadows across the deceased. The smell was horrible, and I remember my friend vomiting nearby. I remember scanning all the dead, and out of all of them, seeing a pair of legs sitting cross-legged near the rear, the upper half of the body missing. I knew of what the Manananggal was capable of, knew what it did when it went out to hunt, but in my disgust and horror at the discovery of it's nest, my mind had failed to understand that the creature's lifeline was right there, and I had been unable to stop it. I could have said something, or did something myself, I had fire, and ashes from my dead family on my person; I could have killed the Manananggal right then and there.

But I hadn't. I wanted desperately to get out of the caves before it got too dark, to flee the sight of the mangled dead, and my friend was of similar opinion. We had fled, and had said nothing to the village. We did not go back, and considering all that had happened, no one else was lucky enough to stumble upon that place again. To this day I can never forgive myself for not taking action, and being too cowardly to end the nightmare then and there.

But the nightmare is truly over now, I have accepted it, and in a way, I am accepting that I cannot change what had happened and can only move forward. Because life is simply unfair, and the only way we can survive is to keep breathing. We get knocked down, we must get back up again. As a fish is prey to the hawk, we were the prey to the Manananggal, and yet we had evaded it, and are still here. We are still breathing. I am still breathing, and am blessed to have found a wife, and together have a child.

So, my son, I hope this letter tells you some of where I had come from, and what I had experienced. I do not tell you this in order to frighten you, but to inspire you to believe that any odds no matter how dire can be overcome. Along with everything I have upon my passing, these letters will go to you and your family. I only hope my story inspires you to never give up, and that you know that I pass without any regrets or guilt, not anymore.

Mahala ti ka, son.

Tao po, as we all are.

With love, Joshua Ramos

The End

Death is unstoppable,
So is birth,
Sometimes it comes unexpectedly,
Sometimes waiting,
Sometimes mandatory,
Similar to death.

-Pagpanaw

Afterword

Dear Constant Reader,

As Paraíso is a story that I sincerely hoped entertained you for at least a few nights, I also hope in a strange way that it encourages you to look into old legends. These legends shape the way the world around us has developed, and while we as humans have evolved beyond scary stories to warn us of the dangers lurking in the dark, we must still treasure them no matter how inconsistent or even dreary they may be. While the Manananggal and the Aswang are indeed monsters in Filipino folklore, there are many, many other legends that I implore you to look into yourself. You might just find a legend worth your time, and if you are an aspiring writer, you might find something you can tell a good story for. That being said while many aspects of the creature have been lifted from legend, I did take creative liberties here and there all with the intention of just as I said before: Tell a good story. Of course, that is up to you to decide whether or not it was good, and as said I sincerely hoped you were entertained.

As for the Manananggal itself, the idea came to me literally from a thumbnail. I was browsing YouTube looking for something and happened upon a picture of some winged creature with the lower half missing. I had watched it, got intrigued, and began looking more into it. As fate would have it, an idea was forming in my head. My curiosity spurred me forward and other than a few abstract stories left behind by the Filipinos who still tell stories of the monster, as well as a few movies from the seventies, there was really no other entertainment regarding this disturbing creature. My mission was clear: I wanted to tell a story about it for no other reason than to have my own. Most writers will often say they write their stories for someone or for some cause, and I myself write for the sake of my wife as you no doubt noticed, but at the end of the day I believe every writer wants to write the story for themselves first and foremost. After all, we are the first to experience the story.

When I first pitched the idea of Paraíso to a few family members, many were a bit skeptical. They were either intrigued by the idea of a horror story being on a tropical island, or simply by the Manananggal itself. But some had expressed concerns that this sort of creature would be too difficult to get done correctly, and perhaps too much for readers to handle. When I spoke to my wife at some time at this, she simply said, "If you think you can do it, do it. I think the idea of the Manananggal itself is a bit silly, but I know you can do it."

It's this sort of encouragement that keeps me wanting to write stories like this. I took up all the notes I have jotted down from my intrigue of the creature, and got to work on Paraíso, which turned out to be a total irony of a title. It took a lot of time and a lot of research, but it was always fun. I never mind when a story requires more work than fun, but this was a fun one and I hope you had a blast too.

In regards to Isla Bonidada and the resort that resides on it, it may sadden or gladden you to know that it does not exist. Obviously. There are a few islands off the Acapulco coast and obviously some tourist hotspots, but the place as well as the Crockett organization and those who are a part of it are all just as fictional as the Manananggal. Why does this terrifying story take place on an island? Who doesn't like a story taking place in an area of solitude? Besides, I certainly couldn't see the Manananggal appearing in some mountain range. The reason why I didn't tell a story in the Philippines is because I just wanted to bring the Manananggal to North America. I pictured it as any monster would possibly behave with the turn of the century. After all, a lot of people knew about the Manananggal in their home territory, why not seek out more closed-minded hunting grounds whom could be easy to influence or stir up into a panic? This of course is my excuse at any rate and so I'll leave it up to you whether or not it was a good idea. As someone who loves to travel as well, it gave me the opportunity to come up with my idea of an island resort somewhere in the pacific. As it is specifically a resort meant for couples in need of rekindling, I think the wife and I would go just for the food and drinks as well as to mess with the counselor. Gotta have some fun with it, right?

All right, it's time to go. Until we see each other again, go read some good books, find a new legend, be content, and of course, be kind.

Most sincerely,

-B.D. Weddell
January 31st, 2025

P.S.

Tao Po